grave duty

A Shelby Nichols Adventure

Colleen Helme

M̶B

MANETTO BOOKS

Grave Duty/ Colleen Helme. -- 1st ed.
ISBN: 9798860816459

Dedication

Thanks for the wonderful remodel of my home and all
the work you've done to make it amazing!
You guys are the Best!

Kirk Wahlen
Dave Hahn
Mike Chappell

ACKNOWLEDGEMENTS

This book has been a long time coming but that's because we've been doing a home re-model and I've been distracted. That said, I finished the book, even with all the hammering, tearing out of floors and walls, and everything else that's been going on. So if Shelby seems a little tense in this story... that's why!

Thanks to all of you who love Shelby as much as I do! Your support, encouragement, friendship, and great reviews keep me writing.

As always, I need to give a big shout-out and thanks to my daughter, Melissa who is a great sounding board and so encouraging of my writing career!. XOXO

I'd also like to give a huge thanks to Kristin Monson for editing this book and making it better. You're the best!

I am so grateful to the talented Wendy Tremont King for bringing Shelby and the gang to life on audio. Her voices for all the characters are amazing! Thanks for sticking with me through seventeen books! We make a great team! YOP Forever!

Last but not least, thanks to my wonderful husband, Tom, for believing in my dreams. Thanks to my awesome family for your continued encouragement and support.

I love you all!

~*Colleen*

Shelby Nichols Adventure Series

Carrots
Fast Money
Lie or Die
Secrets that Kill
Trapped by Revenge
Deep in Death
Crossing Danger
Devious Minds
Hidden Deception
Laced in Lies
Deadly Escape
Marked for Murder
Ghostly Serenade
Dying Wishes
High Stakes Crime
Ties That Bind
Grave Duty

Devil in a Black Suit ~ A Ramos Story
A Midsummer Night's Murder ~ A Shelby Nichols Novella
License to Steal ~ A Shelby Nichols Novella

Sand and Shadow Series
Angel Falls
Desert Devil

NEWSLETTER SIGNUP

For news, updates, and special offers, please sign up for my newsletter at www.colleenhelme.com.
To thank you for subscribing you will receive a **FREE** ebook: *Behind Blue Eyes: A Shelby Nichols Novella.*

Contents

Chapter 1

Representing a mob boss in a meeting with a challenging client was bound to get me into trouble. Still, if Uncle Joey thought I could handle it, how could I say no? He was in a bind because he and Ramos, his right-hand man, had to take care of an urgent matter at Uncle Joey's club. That left me with the task of meeting the client to tell him something he might not want to hear.

I arrived at the client's office and found the cute receptionist flirting with a handsome co-worker. Not wanting to stop in the middle of her story, she barely gave me a glance. I stepped closer so that she couldn't ignore me, and the young man glanced my way, effectively cutting off the conversation.

"Hi. I'm Shelby Nichols. I'm a private investigator, and I have an appointment with Howard Hoffman."

"Oh... of course. Just a moment." She gave the young man an apologetic shrug before picking up the phone to let Howard know I was there. At his terse reply, she twisted her lips, thinking that he'd been in a crappy mood all morning. Knowing that Howard was sure to be more offensive than normal, she glanced my way, hoping that I could hold my own against the conniving lout.

After hanging up the phone, she sent me a tepid smile. "He's ready for you. I'll show you to his office."

My trepidation about meeting him went right out the window, and I followed her down the hall, straightening my shoulders and holding my head high. If Howard thought he could intimidate me, then he was in for a surprise. She knocked before opening the door and poked her head in to announce my arrival. "Shelby Nichols is here to see you."

Without waiting for a response, she stepped aside, and I got my first look at the conniving lout. He sat in a big chair behind his massive wooden desk, wearing a dark suit that hugged his wide shoulders. The light reflected off his bald head, and his dark eyes flicked over me with a dismissive air.

His breath whistled out of his nostrils, like he was disgusted to see me, but I picked up that it was all for show. Deep down, he was thrilled that Uncle Joey had sent me. He pursed his lips tightly to hold back a grin and narrowed his eyes to give me a flinty glare, knowing his size alone was enough to intimidate a woman like me.

"Please sit down." He motioned to the chair in front of his desk.

Because it would be impolite to decline, I sat, realizing he had me at a disadvantage since I had to look up to meet his gaze. I didn't know it was possible for someone to loom over me while sitting in a chair behind a huge desk, but he seemed to puff up in size. Then I realized he'd raised his chair a couple of notches. I picked up that it was a tactic he'd used many times, and it always seemed to do the job, especially with women who thought they could tell him what to do.

With his elbows resting on his desk, he leaned forward and presented a toothy smile that didn't reach his eyes. "I have to admit I'm surprised Manetto sent you to do his job. Since he knows I'm not happy with him, he must have thought I'd go easy on you, but that's not going to happen unless you have the information he promised me."

"Mr. Hoffman—"

"Please... call me Howard."

I pursed my lips and continued without using his name. "You seem to be under the impression that I'm here to give you something, which is not the case. So let me spell it out for you. The deal you made with my uncle involves a payment for his services, and you seem to have forgotten that part."

His brows rose. If Manetto was my uncle that explained my involvement, but he didn't like my insinuation that he wasn't playing by the rules, even if it was true. "What do you mean... forgotten? I have every intention of paying, but not until I see what he has for me."

He was thinking that it might not be worth as much as he'd agreed upon, and he didn't want to overpay. His finances were stretched a little thin at the moment, so he had to play his cards right. If he could get away with it, maybe he could offer me something that sounded more valuable, and I'd take that deal for Manetto instead. Sizing me up, he thought it was worth a shot. Who knew? I might be gullible enough to fall for it.

I shook my head. "The agreement was that you pay up front... and frankly, I think Uncle Joey's cutting you more slack than you deserve."

Howard's brows rose, and he decided to change tactics. "I'm sorry you feel that way, but I'm not unreasonable. In fact, I'm willing to add a little extra to the pot to make up for it. I've been sitting on something that I'm sure your uncle will want to be in on. There's a sweet deal going down."

He lowered his voice and leaned forward. "He can triple his investment and make more than what I owe him. Believe me... this is something he'll want to know about." He thought that, with the market the way it was, the investment could go either way, but he doubted I knew that.

I shook my head. "Sorry... but there's no room for negotiation. I need the money now, or the deal's off."

Howard huffed out a breath. "But that would be a mistake. This is good information. He'll want to know."

I shook my head. "That's not what he sent me here to do."

"Sure... I get that. But you don't know Manetto like I do. Believe me, he'll want to get in on this. It will be worth it to him." He waited for me to give in, but, when I didn't, he continued. "I know you mean well, but honestly, you don't want to disappoint him."

"That's the only sincere thing you've said to me. And you're right, I'm not going to disappoint him, because you're going to pay up. Once I have the money, I'll happily hand over the information you bargained for. Understand?"

His lips flattened, and he glanced at my purse, correctly identifying the folder I had tucked inside as the information he wanted. A sudden impulse to take it came over him. He could overpower me easily enough and grab it. If I wasn't Manetto's niece, he'd do it in a heartbeat.

Licking his lips, he caught my gaze. "All right. I'll pay, but it's only fair to let me have a quick look to make sure everything I asked for is there."

"Nope." I put my hand protectively over the folder. "The only way you're getting your hands on this folder is if you pay first."

He didn't budge, so I stood. "I'd say it's been nice to meet you, but since that would be a lie, I'll just show myself out."

"Wait. You can't just take that and go."

"Watch me." I started toward the door.

"Wait. Come back here. I'm not done with you."

"Well I'm done with you."

"You're making a big mistake."

I pulled the door open and glanced over my shoulder, sending him a tight-lipped smile. "Funny you should say that, because now you're going to have to face Ramos, and he's not nearly as nice as I am."

I hurried out the door, shutting off the tirade of curses aimed my way. Of course, they were all in his mind, but I wasn't going to let that stop me from telling Uncle Joey all about it. Still, I felt bad that I hadn't done the job he'd sent me to do.

It wasn't my fault, but it was still a waste of time. Anger welled up in my chest. I'd thought that being Uncle Joey's niece carried some weight, but apparently I was wrong. I needed a reputation to go along with the name. Joey "The Knife" Manetto meant something, but Uncle Joey had earned that reputation for reasons I'd rather not know.

Shelby "The Psychic" Nichols didn't quite do it, and, since I was Uncle Joey's secret weapon, it wasn't something he'd want a lot of people to know. Plus, I had to remember that I'd worked hard to stay on the right side of things, so maybe it wasn't such a big deal to fail at intimidating a conniving lout.

"Shelby Nichols?" The young man I'd seen earlier waited at the elevator doors.

"Yes?"

"Hi. I'm Elliot Briggs, and I'd like to hire you."

My brows rose. "Oh." I pushed the elevator button to give me a moment to think. "What do you need?"

He glanced around the office and lowered his voice. "I just need you to watch someone and tell me where they go... that sort of thing."

The elevator doors opened, and I stepped inside. He quickly followed. Once the doors shut, his shoulders relaxed, and his lips twisted into a tentative smile. He was probably in his mid-twenties and wore khaki pants and a short-sleeved shirt. With short, sandy-colored hair and brown eyes, he had a sprinkle of freckles across his nose that made him seem trustworthy and innocent.

"I charge a hundred and fifty an hour. Does that change your mind?"

He inhaled sharply, surprised by the amount, but pursed his lips and made a decision. "No. As long as we limit it to five hours." He rounded up the cost, thinking he had eight hundred to spare.

Intrigued, I nodded. "Sure."

"Great." The elevator doors opened, and he stepped into the lobby with me. "Um... do you have time to grab a coffee? There's a coffee shop just around the corner, and I can give you the details."

I didn't think Uncle Joey and Ramos were back from their visit to the club yet, so I had plenty of time for a quick chat. "Okay."

"This is great. Thanks." Giving me a quick smile, he led the way to the shop, and we got in line. "It's on me. What would you like?"

I glanced at the menu board with all the flavors and went with my favorite. "How about a mocha latte?"

"Good choice."

We got through the line and found a small, round table by the window. Elliot waited to get his thoughts in order before he began. "The name of the guy I need you to follow is Paxton Savage."

He watched me closely for a sign that the name sounded familiar to me. When I didn't respond, relief swept over him. "I just need to know where he lives, and, if he has a job, who he's working for. And it would be good if you can see where he hangs out at night, too."

"Does he owe you money or something?"

"No." His brows drew together, and anger flooded his veins. "I just need to know what he's up to."

He was thinking that, once I gave him the information, he could take over from there and figure out his next moves. It might take him several weeks to figure out the best way to kill the bastard without getting caught, but there had to be a way to do it.

"Wait, what?"

His confused gaze met mine. "I just need the basics about him... you know... where he lives and his daily routine? Isn't that something private investigators do?"

"Uh... yes. Right. We do that."

"Great. Listen, I've got to get back to work. Do I need to pay you a retainer?"

I nodded. "Yeah. I usually ask for half up front, then the rest once the job is done."

"Okay. Just don't go over five hours. Do you have a Venmo account?"

Did I really want to help him kill someone? On the other hand, maybe I could figure out what was going on and stop him from ruining his life. He seemed like a good person, so something didn't add up. Nodding, I gave him my account name.

Using his phone, he quickly sent me four hundred dollars. Pulling a card from his wallet, he handed it over. "Here's my card. Call me when you're done."

"Sure."

"Thanks Shelby. This is just what I needed. I'm so glad I ran into you. Call me if you need anything from me, okay?" At my nod, he sent me a wave and hurried out of the shop.

I sat there in shock and questioned my sanity. What had I just gotten into? I should have told him I was too busy right now, but he'd seemed so nice and wholesome. Was he one of those people who passed for normal, but deep down was a psychopath?

Shaking my head, I threw my cup away and headed to my car. Ever since I got shot in the head and gained the ability to read minds, my life had changed drastically, and that was putting it mildly. Reading minds had gotten me into a lot of trouble, and now I had a permanent gig with a mob-boss, helped the police on a regular basis, and had opened my own consulting business.

I knew a lot of secrets, so it was a wonder that things could still surprise me, but someone as nice as Elliot, who wanted me to find someone so he could kill them, threw me for a loop.

I sighed. This was something I'd have to figure out later. Right now, I needed to let Uncle Joey know how my meeting went with Howard Hoffman.

Pulling into the underground parking lot, I headed to the elevators, taking a slight detour to check for Ramos's motorcycle. He was Uncle Joey's right hand man, bodyguard, and occasional hitman. He was the hunkiest, most drool-worthy man in the universe, which made riding behind him on a motorcycle even more enticing.

With the weather turning cold, my rides with Ramos were few and far between. Still, seeing the bike parked behind the pillar made my day. What can I say? Since riding behind him on a motorcycle was about as close as I'd ever get to holding him in my arms, I had to make the most of it. Right?

With a lighter step, I exited the elevator and passed through the double-doors into Thrasher Development. Uncle Joey's wife and secretary, Jackie, stood behind her desk, using a razor-tool to cut through the tape on a medium-sized box. She pulled the flaps open, and excitement came off her in waves. She reached inside and pulled out a book. As she admired it, I glanced over to see several more of the same books stacked up inside.

"What have you got there?"

Startled, she nearly dropped the book. "Oh... nothing." She quickly shoved it back in the box and stood in front of it to block my view.

"You know that's not going to work on me, right?"

"Oh... yeah... I guess not. So, you know what they are?"

"Of course. They're books. But why are you hiding them?"

She shrugged. "No reason." She was thinking that, if I didn't know more than that, she certainly wasn't going to tell me. Still, why did I have to come in right then and ruin her moment? "Joe and Ramos are in the conference room. Why don't you join them? I'm sure they'd be happy to see you."

Why was she trying to get rid of me? What moment did she mean? I couldn't see the books anymore, but I picked up her impatience to turn around and examine the cover up close. Although she'd used a pen name, it was still pretty exciting to see it in print.

I inhaled sharply and covered my mouth with my hand. "It's your book? You wrote a book? Oh my gosh! That's amazing. Let me see it."

She rolled her eyes, but it was mostly for show. "I should have known you'd figure it out." Stepping aside, she drew a book out of the box and handed it over.

The title read *Silent Justice,* with a subtitle of *A Mafia Romance.* A handsome man in a tux, with a sexy grin, and tugging at his tie, graced the cover, and the author's name was Jocelyn Drake.

"Wow... so your pen name is Jocelyn Drake? You wrote this? It looks amazing. I had no idea."

She shrugged. "I've been writing for a long time, but this is the first book that I've ever published."

"Congratulations! Who's your publisher?"

Jackie didn't answer right away, so I flipped the book open to the copyright page.

"Manetto Books." I glanced at Jackie. "That's... so you have your own publishing company?"

"Yeah. Joe bought a mid-list company and renamed it Manetto Books. I've been involved with getting it up and running for the last few months." She shook her head. "To be honest, he actually bought it for me, but I'm not the only author we represent. So far there are six of us. We all write different kinds of romance novels, and it's been really fun."

I nodded. "Wow... that's amazing."

She glanced at the book in my hand. "You can have that one if you want."

"Really? I'd love to read it. Thanks." Glancing at the cover, I couldn't resist teasing her. "A mafia romance, huh? I'll bet you know a lot about that."

She chuckled. "What can I say? You got me."

"Will I find characters based on Ramos and Uncle Joey in here?"

"Uh..." She chewed on her bottom lip. "You might see a resemblance to them, but I didn't include anything personal to set them apart." She was thinking that I wasn't in this book, and she hoped it didn't hurt my feelings. But... maybe in the next book she could put someone like me in the story. That could be fun.

"Nice. I can't wait to read it. But you have to sign it first." I held the book out for her to sign.

Her breath caught. This was the first book she'd ever signed for someone, and a little thrill went through her. Taking the book, she signed her pen name with a flourish before handing it back.

"Thanks Jackie... uh... Jocelyn."

She liked being called by her pen name and grinned. "Of course."

"Jocelyn? Who's that?"

We both turned as Ramos stepped into the office. He wore his usual outfit of black jeans, black leather jacket, and motorcycle boots. With his brow tilted up, and a curious smile on his face, he checked all the boxes for the sexiest-man-alive contest.

I glanced at Jackie. "You should totally use that look for your next book cover. It'll sell like hotcakes."

"You have a point," she conceded.

Ramos tilted his head for an explanation, so I pulled the book out of my purse and handed it over. "Jackie is Jocelyn Drake. She wrote the book. Isn't that awesome?"

"A mafia romance?" Ramos's brows drew together. His gaze landed on Jackie, and she blushed. "Uh... that's great." He handed it back to me.

"When I'm done, I'll let you borrow it."

He knew I was trying to tease him, and his eyes narrowed. "Sure." He turned to Jackie. "Am I in it?"

Her blush deepened. "No... well... not you exactly. But there is a hitman. I mean... how can you write about the mob without one? But nothing that you'd recognize... exactly."

She was lying through her teeth. He was totally in the book, but she'd never thought that he would actually read it. This was the worst.

He nodded my way. "Is Shelby in it, too?"

"No. Not this book... but I could always add a character like her in the next one."

"You should do that." He glanced at me, and mischief danced in his eyes. "I could tell you about an incident with a lizard that your readers would love. They'd laugh their heads off."

"A real lizard? Why, what happened?"

"He's just pulling your leg." I grabbed him by the arm and shoved him toward the conference room.

"No, I'm not." Even though he protested, he let me drag him away from Jackie's desk.

"It's okay," Jackie called. "You can tell me later."

"I will." Ramos sent her a nod and continued into the room by my side. I turned on him. "Don't do it. Promise me."

"Hey... nobody would know it was really you."

I huffed out a breath and stomped my foot. "That doesn't matter."

"Hmm..." His eyes narrowed, and he was thinking that this was something he could hold over me. What would I be willing to do for his silence?

"Ramos!"

He chuckled. "Fine... I won't tell her... for now."

I wanted to smack him, but since he was expecting that, I shook my head and closed my eyes. I realized I had nothing that I could threaten him with. Nothing. But now that I knew that, I would be on the lookout. Someday he'd mess up, and I'd be the one teasing him. There had to be a good story I could use, and then I'd have him.

"You've got that dazed look on your face. What are you up to?"

My grin widened. "Wouldn't you like to know?"

Before Ramos could respond, Uncle Joey walked in. "Shelby. You're back. How did your meeting go?" He was hoping Howard hadn't been his normal, obnoxious self.

Still grinning, I let out a huff. "No such luck. Even his secretary thinks he's a conniving lout, and he definitely lived up to the hype."

"That doesn't sound good. Let's all sit down, and you can tell me about it."

I explained the conversation, and Uncle Joey's eyes narrowed. After I got to the part where I told Howard that Ramos would be coming next, Ramos narrowed his eyes as well.

With both of them glaring at me, I smiled with satisfaction. "So I guess you get to talk to him next."

Ramos was thinking of doing more than talking, but he shuttered his thoughts before I could pick up how he would do that. "I'll make sure he regrets it."

"Good."

His brows lifted, and he glanced at Uncle Joey. "Bloodthirsty little thing, isn't she?"

Uncle Joey waited for me to deny it, but the words wouldn't come out of my mouth. How could I protest something that I thought the lout deserved? "Hey... I don't think a punch in the face would be so bad. He's a big guy. He can take it."

Ramos's lips quirked up, and he shook his head. Since I had no idea what he had planned, he wasn't going to tell me and ruin the moment. Hell, I'd probably feel bad enough for the guy that I'd ask Ramos to leave all his fingers attached, and he didn't want to do that.

"His fingers? Really?"

"No... probably just one of them."

I didn't know if he was serious or pulling my leg. Still... I couldn't take a chance. "No... leave the fingers."

Ramos shrugged. "A thumb then... got it."

"Hey, that's not—" I smacked his arm, and he chuckled. He loved teasing me because I was so easy to bait.

He was right, maybe I shouldn't respond... but what would be the fun in that?

Uncle Joey shook his head, wondering if we were through teasing each other. At my sheepish glance, he spoke. "I'm glad you're here, Shelby. David and Nick Berardini are coming in to talk. I don't know what it's about, but I'm afraid they might be hiding something, so I hope you can stay a little longer."

He knew they weren't happy about his arrangement with Forrest Slater, the hacker who'd helped him get his cryptocurrency back from a different conniving lout. But there was more going on, and he needed to get to the bottom of it.

That didn't sound so good. Given the amount of conniving louts Uncle Joey dealt with, it was a wonder he wasn't pulling his hair out. But I supposed it was just one more thing he took in stride as a mob boss.

Thank goodness he wasn't planning on leaving the business to me. With my recent change of heart, I'd probably tell Ramos to off them all, and I'd go to hell for sure.

"Yeah... I can stay."

"Good."

We spoke for a few minutes about Jackie and her new venture. Uncle Joey was pleased to have his own publishing company, but more pleased that Jackie was happy.

"So, have you read the book?" I asked.

"Of course. It's really good... I mean... I could do without all the sex, but it has a great plot, and I liked that not all the bad guys are bad. Some of them had good reason for what they did and actually made things better in the end."

He was thinking *like me,* and I couldn't help smiling. Before I could comment, a knock sounded at the door, and David Berardini stepped inside, followed closely by his son, Nick. David was one of Uncle Joey's closest business associates, who'd been with him from the beginning. We all stood to greet each other before getting down to business.

I picked up that David had some news to share, and he wished that Ramos and I weren't there. But maybe it didn't matter in the long run. At least Manetto couldn't put him off if we were there. Still, he didn't like the way things had turned out, and Manetto needed to know.

"Before we get started," David began. "I just want you to know that I'm retiring, and Nick is taking over the company. It's happening soon, and I'd like to make it as smooth a transition as possible."

His announcement was met with stunned silence. Uncle Joey frowned. "I'm sorry to hear that." He hated to lose David, but more than that, he hated to think about retiring. David was only a year or two older than him, hardly old enough to end his career. "But why now? I thought you were happy with the way things were going."

David sighed. "I am happy with the business. That's why it's the perfect time to let Nick take over." He glanced at Nick, glad that he was more than ready to head up the company. After David's close call, he was lucky that he'd only needed a couple of stents implanted into his heart to clear up his chest pains. But it had reminded him that there was more to life than work.

He gave Uncle Joey a pointed stare. "Although there is something that I'm not happy about, and I'm hoping we can clear it up." His eyes narrowed. "I understand you've hired someone else to take over your computer security, and I'd like to know why. I never thought you'd do that to me after all we've been through."

Uncle Joey actually flushed under David's scrutiny. "It's not what you think. Hiring Forrest Slater makes sense because he's a hacker... one of the best, and it has nothing to do with the accounting and market monitoring that you do for me. You've been great at keeping me up to date with current business standards, and I value your work."

"But not our security? All your financial records are guarded under several layers of firewalls." David pursed his lips. "And you trust this guy over us?"

"Not at all. But he knows the ins and outs of computer tech, and after my problems with the cryptocurrency debacle, I'm not about to let something like that happen again."

David nodded. "I understand that, but our security is top-notch. I pay our IT guy the big bucks to make sure of that. The system is secure."

Uncle Joey shook his head. "Not quite." Regret shone in his eyes, but he held David's gaze. "I happen to know you've been approached by someone for information that would be harmful to me. And it bothers me that you haven't said anything about it."

David's eyes widened before he glanced Nick's way. "Do you know what he's talking about?"

This time Nick flushed. "Not really. A salesman came in yesterday, but I handled it. He may have asked some questions about our clients, and Manetto specifically, but I didn't tell him anything."

"And you didn't think I needed to know?"

"Dad—you've been—" His gaze flitted to Uncle Joey and back. "—having some health concerns, and I wasn't sure it was good for you to know everything."

David swore under his breath. "What did he want?"

Nick scoffed. "He was selling a software program and wanted to know if his software was something we could use with our clients. He wanted to know the kind of clients we worked with, but I wasn't about to tell him anything. So, like I said, I handled it. If I thought it was serious, I would have told you."

Nick licked his lips and glanced at Uncle Joey. "Nothing happened... it was just a short exchange, so I don't understand why you're even bringing it up."

Uncle Joey sighed. "Let's just say that Forrest did a little hacking into your computer system... just to make sure you had adequate firewall protection... and set up a failsafe program."

"What the hell? You hacked us?" Incensed, Nick started to stand, but David held him back.

"Excuse my son," David said, somehow managing to look at the bigger picture despite Uncle Joey's revelation. "What are you getting at?"

Uncle Joey's lips thinned. "Someone tried to access your computer files using a remote software program late last night. The attempt triggered the failsafe that Forrest set up. The person didn't get far, but he managed to take a look at a couple of my files before he was locked out. Forrest got the alert and let me know... so, when you set up this meeting, I wasn't sure if it was connected."

"So someone, just like your hacker, hacked us last night?" David asked.

"That's right. But he wasn't as good as Forrest. He used a remote software system to get into your files, which means he had access to your computer during your little meeting and installed it. That's why I need to know who he is."

"Shit." Nick shook his head, realizing he'd been played when the guy had 'accidentally' knocked over his drink. It had spilled all over him, and he'd run out to get a towel, leaving the guy alone in his office. He'd only been gone a minute... but apparently, it was long enough.

"It wasn't Nick's fault," I said, giving Nick a nod. "Tell them what happened."

Nick shook his head, not liking how I knew things like that, but grateful that I could back him up. "When he asked questions about my clients and what we provided, I knew he was fishing, so I didn't tell him anything specific. That's when he *accidentally* knocked my drink onto me, and I had to leave to get cleaned up."

"Did he give you a business card?" Uncle Joey asked.

"Yeah, he left my office pretty quick after I got back, but he did give me a card. It's in my desk."

"Good. We'll start with that."

David huffed out a breath. "Joe... I'm sorry. I had no idea. If you blame anyone, blame me."

"I don't blame either of you. I'm just a little upset that it was so easy for someone to get into your computer. If not for Forrest's failsafe program, who knows what information he could have taken."

David slumped in his chair. "We knew the risks, and we've let you down. If you want to take your business elsewhere, I'll understand."

Uncle Joey huffed out a breath. "I'm not going to do that. It's a different world than it used to be when we first started out." He glanced at Nick. "And now it's your turn to run the business. I hope you'll learn something from this so it never happens again."

He turned to Ramos. "Why don't you go with Nick to his office for the card, and we'll see if we can track this guy down."

"I promise it won't happen again." Nick stood to leave, but hesitated. "I'd like to hire Forrest's services and have him take a look at all of our systems. Would that be possible?"

"Of course. I'll tell him to stop by."

David stood to leave as well, but his shoulders slumped, and he seemed to have aged a good ten years. He'd thought it would be hard to retire, but, after this, he was glad to let Nick figure things out. He just hoped it didn't make Nick a target.

After they left, Uncle Joey glanced my way. "What's going on with David?"

"It's his heart. He had to have stents inserted into some constricted veins, and it made him realize he needed to slow down and enjoy life a little more before he died."

"I had no idea. I wish he would have said something."

"Yeah."

"Did you pick up anything about Nick's visitor that will help us find him?"

I shook my head. "No. Nick barely remembered what he looked like. Nothing about him stood out, so it could be anyone."

Uncle Joey nodded. "Well, at least we have his card. Let's hope it's a real company, or we're screwed."

I nodded. "What files did he manage to look at? Anything illegal?"

"No, but they contained some information that I wouldn't want to get out. By itself, the information wouldn't mean anything, but paired with other information, it could have been bad."

"It's a good thing Forrest set up that failsafe then."

He huffed out a breath. "Yeah. No kidding." He was thinking that this attack was quite sophisticated, and he worried that it could be tied to the police.

"You mean like a sting operation?"

His lips flattened, but he shrugged. "I don't know. Maybe."

"I could go to the precinct and poke around if you want."

He almost objected, but then he remembered that, with my ability, I could just stand around and find out plenty. "Yeah... that's a good idea."

"Okay. I'll head over now."

We said our goodbyes, and I left the office. It was before noon, so I had plenty of time on my hands. Who knew? I might even solve a case or two. Still, I had to be sneaky about showing up without being asked by Detective Harris, aka Dimples. He was my partner whenever I worked with the police, and the only cop who knew that I could read minds. I told everyone else that I had premonitions, which was close enough to the truth to work.

Too bad I couldn't tell Dimples that I had a premonition that he needed me today. But, if it was like most days, he probably did. He'd be so glad to see me that he wouldn't question my real motive for showing up.

It hit me that I used to hate using my connection with the police to help a mob boss. Now I didn't give it a second thought. In fact, I volunteered. But things had changed since I'd first known Uncle Joey. Even though he wasn't my real uncle, he'd become as dear to me as if he were. Plus, he wasn't the horrible mob boss he'd been when we first met. Maybe he wasn't strictly law-abiding, but, for the most part, his business dealings were legitimate.

Still, it was a bone of contention between Dimples and me. Naturally, he hated that I worked for a mob boss. He used to hope that I'd turn on Uncle Joey so I could get out from under his thumb. I'd told him to quit asking, and he had, but he still worried that I could end up in jail.

So there was a definite possibility that the police were involved in breaking into Uncle Joey's computer files. Maybe they were setting him up, and I'd get caught in the snare? A shiver ran down my spine, but I pushed the worry away. So what if they were? With my ability, I'd find out long before they made a move. I'd be fine, and I'd make sure Uncle Joey was, too... because, even though he was a mob boss, he was still a good person.

I'd just have to make sure that siding with him didn't come back to haunt me. I pulled into the precinct parking lot and took a deep breath before getting out of the car. Sure it was a worry, but I'd played this balancing act before, and it had all worked out. I had nothing to worry about. Too bad that was easier said than done.

There was also the matter of my newest client, Elliot Briggs. There had to be a reason he wanted to kill Paxton Savage. Maybe I could look up both their names on my computer while I was there? It wasn't exactly right to use the police database for my personal cases, but if I needed to stop a killer, it wasn't wrong either, right?

Chapter 2

I sauntered into the precinct like I had every right to be there, and hoped Dimples would have something for me to do. Usually I tried to stay away until he called, so showing up like this might raise his suspicions. With that in mind, I took the scenic route to get to the detectives' offices, making a pit stop to say hello to Bob Spicer, the precinct therapist.

Noticing his open door, I knew there was a chance he would be there, and I hesitated. Did I really want to talk to him? Not necessarily, but, if it gave me a reason to be there, I might as well go for it.

I poked my head around the door frame and found him at his desk, tapping away on his keyboard. He glanced up to see me, and surprise flashed across his face. "Shelby. What a pleasant surprise. Come on in."

"Hi Bob... I just thought I'd stop by and say hello. It's been awhile."

"Yes... it has." He glanced at the clock on his wall, thinking he had plenty of time for a chat. "I have a few minutes before my next appointment. Why don't you have a seat, and we'll catch up."

"Oh... okay."

"And close the door behind you."

I stepped inside, closing the door as he'd asked, and took a seat in front of his desk.

"So... how are you doing?" He'd been wanting to visit with me for some time, and he was thrilled that I'd come to him all on my own. That meant I valued his opinion, and his smile widened.

I cleared my throat. "I'm doing pretty well, actually. I mean... I've been busy lately, but I'm still alive, so that's good."

He nodded, thinking that making light of being alive was a sure sign of distress. "Yeah... I heard about the case you solved with the stadium demolition. As I recall, you were inside the stadium when someone tried to blow it up. Is that right?"

My brows pinched together. "Uh... yeah." I tried not to think about that part of the experience, since it always gave me chills.

"Want to talk about it?"

"Not really." His brows rose, so I continued. "That's the reason I thought I'd better come see you." I smiled, hoping he couldn't tell that I was lying my head off.

His lips tilted up. "That's good. It shows you're committed to taking care of your mental and emotional health. So... how have you been coping with that? Had any nightmares or other kinds of reactions?"

"Um... yeah. A few. But they're not too bad. It's the ones where I'm drowning that are the worst. I've been around a few explosions, so I'm more used to them, but no one's ever tried to drown me before."

His mouth dropped open. "You mean... someone tried to drown you?"

Crap. That wasn't police business, so I should have kept my mouth shut. "Yeah, but I wasn't working for the police at the time. Anyways... the thing I wanted to talk to you about is a question I have. Do you think seeing so much of the bad side of things would make me more cynical? I'm normally a positive person, but lately I've found that it wouldn't bother me if some people happened to die... I mean... not all people. Just the bad ones. Is that normal?"

He took a moment to answer, hoping to say the right words that wouldn't alarm me, but would still get the point across. "I'm afraid there's no easy answer to that, but, on the whole, yes... it's a sign that you're under a certain amount of stress. Anger is a powerful motivator and can lead to extreme reactions. I'd like you to think about how you handle your anger and frustrations. You don't carry a gun, right?"

"No." I didn't mention that I always carried a stun flashlight, but that wasn't the same.

He nodded. "Okay. That's good. I only ask because it could be bad if you got upset enough that you actually shot someone." At my raised brows, he held both hands up in surrender. "I don't see that happening."

Whoa... he thought I'd do that? "No... I don't either. I mean... I get angry, but not that angry."

"Good. Then I would suggest doing some meditation exercises to help with your... frustrations. Do you still have the app I told you about on your phone?"

"Yeah."

"How many times have you used it?"

"Uh... two or maybe three times... I think." That was another lie, but I had to tell him something.

This time, his gaze narrowed. I hadn't fooled him. "I see. Well... I would suggest you try meditating at least once a day, probably before bed. It only takes a few minutes, and I really think it would help you with your anger issues."

"But I don't get that angry."

"Let's explore that." He thought that I fooling myself, and it wasn't healthy.

I opened my mouth to protest, but he raised his hands. "I just want you to pause for a moment, and connect with your emotions. Take your time and then tell me what you're feeling."

I sat back in my chair and let out a breath. The conniving lout had angered me this morning, and I was still angry, but there wasn't anything I could do about it. I was also upset that my new client wanted me to find someone so he could kill them. Then Uncle Joey was in trouble because someone had it in for him. It just never seemed to end.

"Okay... I admit I've been angrier than usual lately. Do you think that's why I'm more cynical about things?" At his nod, I continued. "But how am I supposed to get over it?"

"You can't change other people. You can only change yourself. That means you have to let go of your anger, or your fears, or whatever it is that's holding you back. Only then can you be the best version of yourself."

"Yeah... that makes sense, but sometimes I wonder if I'm a good person." That was as close as I could come to telling him that I was spying on the police for Uncle Joey.

His face lightened. "The fact that you question yourself means it's likely that you'll never go too far down that path. We all make mistakes, but it's what we do next that counts."

I'd heard that so many times before that it didn't instill a lot of hope in me. I dutifully nodded and tried to look pleasant. It didn't change the fact that I still planned to spy on the police for Uncle Joey, but I did feel better about doing it. It might be on the shady side of things, but it was for a good reason.

"Thanks. That really helped." I smiled and stood, ready to get out of there.

"Good. I'm glad you stopped by." He glanced at his computer and grabbed one of his cards. "I'd like to see you again next week. I have an opening on Wednesday. I'll put you down for that." He filled out the card and handed it over.

"Uh—" I took the card, knowing he wasn't about to take no for an answer. "Okay... I'll try and be here."

"Great. See you then. And be sure to try meditating before you go to bed. I think it will help with your nightmares."

"Oh... sure. It'll try it. See ya."

Letting out a breath, I hurried out the door and headed down to the detectives' offices. At least Bob hadn't asked about my premonitions this time, so that was progress. And maybe meeting with him again so soon wouldn't be all bad.

On the way, I remembered why I'd come in the first place and took a detour past the vice unit that focused on drugs, gangs, cybercrime, organized crime, and other criminal activities and threats.

As I meandered past them, I listened for any mention of Uncle Joey or a plot against him and his organization. I heard plenty about a gang bust they were working on, but nothing about organized crime. Maybe it wasn't them?

Continuing on, I found Dimples sitting at his desk, looking at his computer. His gaze lifted to meet mine, and his brows rose before his lips twisted into a happy smile, showing his deep, mesmerizing dimples.

"Hey Shelby. What brings you in today?"

"I had a quick session with Bob Spicer. After nearly getting blown up all those times, I thought I should talk to him."

"Did he say anything to help you?"

"Yeah. I'm going to try meditating before I go to sleep." I shrugged. "Who knows? It might help."

He nodded, thinking I probably had nightmares about all the crazy life-threatening experiences I'd had. Before he could think about all of them too hard, I changed the subject.

"So, what's going on here? You have any unsolved cases you'd like me to help with?"

His brows rose. He usually had to beg me for my help. What was going on?

I scoffed. "You don't have to beg me. I'm always willing to help."

He shook his head. "Uh... right... well, I actually do have a case you could help me with." He was thinking that it was uncanny how I always managed to show up just when he needed me. I told everyone I had premonitions in order to cover up my mind reading abilities, but there had to be some truth to it.

"The chief just gave me a cold case he wants me to solve." He sighed. "Apparently, his daughter is engaged to a man whose father was murdered about twenty years ago. The case was never solved, and now she's asked her dad to reopen it. I guess Chief Winder wants to make a good impression on the new in-laws, so he agreed and gave the case to me. I just got the files this morning."

He pointed to a box full of papers and manila folders. "Have a seat, and I'll explain."

As I sat down in the chair next to his desk, he opened the case folder.

"The victim's name is Rodney Shepard. He worked for an insurance company, so he traveled a lot. On his way home, late one night, he stopped at a gas station to fill up. When he went in to pay, he was shot and killed."

He shook his head. "The clerk, a young man named Kirk Wahlen, was also killed. If Rodney hadn't walked in right then, he'd probably still be alive."

"Oh wow. That's so sad."

"Yeah. Apparently, another motorist pulled in and noticed the empty car at the gas pump. He got out to fill up his car and heard shots coming from inside. It spooked him, so he took off and called the police from a safe distance. They got there pretty fast, but both men were dead, and the suspects had fled the scene."

"Did the motorist see anything?"

"Yes, he saw a car pull out from the back of the building with two people in it, but he wasn't close enough to see their faces. The description of the car wasn't much either, since it was too dark to get a make or model. Even worse, the building didn't have any type of surveillance cameras, inside or out, so there wasn't a lot to go on."

"What about fingerprints?"

"They got fingerprints, blood, and hair samples, so they did a good job of collecting evidence, but the evidence didn't lead anywhere, which is a little mystifying because one of their main suspects actually worked at the gas station."

"He worked there and didn't leave fingerprints? How does that happen?"

"Exactly. Unless he wiped everything down, you'd think he'd leave a fingerprint or two, right?"

"Yeah. So what happened?"

"They looked at him and a friend of his pretty close." Dimples shuffled a few files and found the one he wanted, opening to a photo of a young man with a scruffy beard and hair that hung down into his eyes. "This is the employee. His name is Erik Duffy. And his friend..." Dimples opened another file to a photo of a twenty-something man with cold, dark eyes and dark hair to his shoulders. "...is Lee Alvarez. It was rumored that they sold drugs behind the gas station. It made sense that if the clerk threatened to expose them, they would have had motive to kill him."

Dimples shook his head. "Not a single fingerprint at the scene matched either of the men. Of course the detectives questioned them, but without physical evidence to connect them to the murders, they couldn't make an arrest, and they both denied any involvement."

"Hmm... so maybe you and I should go pay them a visit? If one of them did it, I'll pick it up."

"That's what I was thinking." His gaze flashed to mine, and we shared a grin. "Let's see if I can find them." He tapped on his computer to bring up their names. "It looks like Lee Alvarez is in the state penitentiary. At least he won't be hard to find."

He brought up Erik Duffy's name from the database and shook his head. "It looks like Erik is dead. He died in a car crash a couple of years after the murders."

"Oh dang... that's too bad."

"Well... at least we've got one of them. Let me call the prison and tell them we're on our way." He met my gaze. "You can go with me now, right?"

"Sure. While you're setting that up, I'm going to see if there's anything on my desk I need to look at."

He nodded absently, and I hurried to the back of the room where my desk sat in the corner. It wasn't that long ago that the chief had given me my own desk and computer, and I felt a little guilty that I hadn't used them much lately.

Still, it wasn't enough to stop me from booting up my computer. I wasn't sure I'd have time to search both names, so I put in Paxton Savage's name first. His photo came up, along with an arrest record that spanned several pages.

Most of them had to do with drugs and petty theft. He'd spent some time in prison, but it looked like he'd been released recently.

"Shelby? You ready?"

"Yeah... coming." Paxton must be out on parole now, and that's why Elliot wanted to know where he was. But that didn't explain why Elliot wanted to kill him. I flicked off the computer and stood to leave, knowing I had my work cut out for me.

Dimples waited at the elevator, and we were soon headed to the prison. On the way, he told me about the suspect. "It looks like Alvarez is in prison for armed robbery and manslaughter. He won't be coming out for a long time, so I'm not sure he'll be willing to tell us anything useful. Luckily, I've got you."

"That's right... and who knows? The chief may even give you a commendation—or invite you to the wedding."

A big smile crossed Dimples's face, and his cheeks turned into little tornadoes, which always brightened my day. "I'd rather have the commendation, but it would be nice to do something for the chief." He was thinking it never hurt to be on the boss's good side.

"That's true." I knew exactly how he felt, even though we were talking about different bosses. "So how's Billy Jo doing? It's been a while since I talked to her." She was Dimples's wife and a journalist. He told me that she was getting all sorts of accolades from the article she wrote about the stadium demolition that Dimples and I stopped. I was happy that she'd uncovered all the dirt on the company, along with the part about the mayor going along with it.

"Do you think the mayor will resign?"

He shrugged. "Probably not. He's trying to blame it all on the company, but we'll see how it plays out."

We pulled into the reserved parking area at the prison and made our way inside. After getting through all the checkpoints, we waited in a room at a picnic-type table until Alvarez was brought in.

His hair was cut short, and he had a million tattoos all over his skin. He looked nothing like his younger self until I met his gaze. Those same dark, cold eyes sent a shiver down my spine.

Dimples made the introductions, and Alvarez's flat gaze scanned over me again. He was thinking that I had to be with the district attorney's office, since I looked too polished to be a cop.

"We're here to ask you a few questions about the murders of Rodney Shepard and Kirk Wahlen."

Alvarez narrowed his eyes. "Who are they? I don't know what you're talking about."

"Sure you do," Dimples continued. "You were friends with Erik Duffy, and he used to work at a gas station with Kirk Wahlen, remember? You and Erik used to sell drugs behind the building. Sound familiar?"

He shrugged. "I remember Erik, but we never sold drugs."

I picked up that he remembered everything, but he wasn't about to admit to it, so I decided it was my turn. "Why did you kill them? Did Kirk find out about the drugs and threaten to go to the police?"

His dark gaze turned to me. "I didn't kill anyone."

"So Erik killed him? As you know, Erik's dead, so you might as well tell us what happened that night."

He scoffed and leaned across the table toward me. "And if I do, will you get them to reduce my sentence?"

Not liking how close he was, I pulled back against my chair. "Uh... maybe."

Dimples cut in. "It depends on what you have to say. Either way, it would be nice to give the family some closure. And it would look good at your next parole hearing."

Alvarez snorted. "I doubt that. Look... I already told the cops everything I know. I have nothing to add." He began to stand, but Dimples put out a hand.

"Wait. I still have a couple more questions."

At that, Alvarez huffed out a long-suffering breath and sat down.

"Were you at the gas station that night?"

He leaned back in his chair and first studied Dimples and then me, thinking he didn't owe us a thing, and he hated helping us for any reason. Sure, he remembered spending time with Erik and selling drugs at the gas station.

Kirk Wahlen was a pain in the ass. As far as he was concerned, he got what he deserved. Even after that, it had felt good to ransack his room and bust up all his stupid trophies.

My eyes widened. "You knew Kirk Wahlen?"

His lips flattened. "Sure. After his murder, everyone knew who he was." He shook his head and stood, menace dripping from his cold eyes. "I have nothing more to say." With a sneer, he stalked to the guard standing by the door.

"Wait!" I called. "Did you kill Kirk?"

He glanced my way and smirked, thinking *wouldn't you like to know*. The guard opened the door, and Alvarez disappeared inside the prison.

"Damn!"

Dimples glanced at me. "Please tell me you got something useful."

I huffed out a breath. "Not exactly. I picked up that he knew Kirk Wahlen and hated him, but not that he actually killed the guy."

"So he didn't think it?"

I shook my head. "No... when I asked him, he was thinking, *wouldn't you like to know.* That's all I got before he left."

Dimples cursed a blue streak in his mind. "So we have nothing?"

"Not exactly. I picked up that he may have broken into Kirk's house. Is there anything about that in the files?"

"Not that I know of, but we can take a look." Dimples wasn't sure how that would help. "Either way, I guess we're done here." I followed him out of the room, and we gathered our things before heading to the car.

Inside the car, Dimples grabbed the files from the backseat and handed them to me. "Why don't you look through those and see if we missed anything on Alvarez?"

"Sure."

While Dimples began the drive back, I opened the file on the murders. The first thing I saw was a photo of the crime scene. Rodney was lying in front of the cash register on his stomach in a pool of blood. The next photo showed Kirk's bloody body in the aisle closer to the back. His battered face showed signs of a beating, and the back of his head was caved in.

I closed my eyes and tried to stem the sudden nausea that burned my throat. "I thought you said they were shot? It looks like Kirk got beat up."

"Oh... yeah. I was talking about Rodney. He was shot, but Kirk died from blunt force trauma to the head. There's a photo of the fire extinguisher that was used to deal the final blow."

"Oh yeah... I see it." The photo showed the extinguisher lying beside Kirk. "So are you sure the same person killed Rodney?"

He shrugged. "Maybe not. But we know two people were there. The detectives thought one of them probably beat up

Kirk, and the other one shot Rodney when he walked in. At least... that's the theory."

"Right. So if we find Kirk's killer, we'll find Rodney's?"

"Yes. That's the idea."

I let out a breath and skimmed through the other pictures. There were photos of bloody dollar bills and coins on the floor of the gas station along with a bullet casing and other evidence. The gas station itself looked familiar, but I didn't think I'd ever filled up my car there.

I turned to the written files and skimmed over them, stopping at an entry that caught my eye. "Here it is. It says that, after Kirk's death, someone broke into his parents' house. They made a mess, but the worst of it was in Kirk's old room. Several items were either broken or stolen.

"It says that Kirk's mother told the police it was probably a neighbor boy who had always hated Kirk. The neighbor was Lee Alvarez. The police got a search warrant and found all the stolen items under Lee's bed."

I glanced at Dimples. "I wonder why he hated Kirk so much?"

"His mom might know. But it sure looks like he killed Kirk."

"I agree, but even if he did, how would we ever prove it? With no fingerprints, what else is there?"

Dimples's eyes widened. "I know. They collected hair samples from the crime scene. Back then they didn't have the type of testing we do now. Maybe we could match his hair to the sample?"

"That's a great idea."

"I'll put in a request when we get back."

I nodded. "Good deal. Is there anything else you want to do?"

"If Erik wasn't dead... I'd want to talk to him. He might have been the one who shot Rodney. Unless..." His eyes narrowed. "Should we swing by the cemetery? Maybe visit Kirk's grave? And Erik's?" He was thinking that I sometimes picked things up from dead people, especially if they'd been murdered.

"Uh... I don't know. It's been a long time since Kirk died. I'm sure he's moved on by now."

Dimples pursed his lips. "Maybe, but what have we got to lose? If that doesn't work, we could always swing by the gas station. Since he was murdered there, it might be a better place for you to pick something up. What's the address? Maybe it's on the way?"

I huffed out a breath. "Let me look." I found the address and read it to Dimples.

He grinned. "That's not too far out of the way. Let's do it."

"Sure. But don't get your hopes up."

Dimples just shrugged. He'd seen my abilities up close and personal, so it was easy to hope I'd pick something up. In fact, the last time we'd investigated a murder, the ghost of the murdered person had caused a small earthquake and scared his killer half to death... along with the rest of us.

I didn't have the heart to tell Dimples I thought that was a once-in-a-lifetime circumstance, but what did I know? Still, twenty years after the murders, I doubted that I'd pick up anything.

We rounded a street corner, and the gas station came into view. I'd half expected it to be torn down, but just seeing it sent shivers down my spine. From the photos, I could see that little had changed in the last twenty years, and I tried not to let the black cloud of death overcome my perception. It was still a bright, sunny day, so I focused on that.

Dimples parked in front of the doors, and we got out. Stepping inside, we found the layout exactly the same as it had been twenty years ago. I couldn't help glancing at the spot on the floor where Rodney had died.

Of course there wasn't any blood, but it seemed a dark, circular shadow stained the tan linoleum floor, making it look dirty. I glanced down the aisle to the spot where Kirk had died and found a similar shadow. Shaking my head, I scanned the rest of the area, but nothing else seemed out of the ordinary.

A couple of people came to the register to pay and were soon joined by a third, forming a line. As they waited, I noticed that they stood to the right of the spot where Rodney had fallen.

As each of them continued to the register, they automatically moved around it, avoiding the area. Of course, the register was closer to that end of the counter, so that could explain it, but it was still strange how they moved to the precise edge of the shadow without consciously knowing it.

Maybe a remnant Rodney's ghost was still here? I found Dimples standing at the sunglasses stand and trying on a pair. While he was occupied, I went to the soda fountain, and filled a large cup with diet soda. They had pumps of flavoring, so I added a couple of shots of cherry.

On my way to pay for it, I deliberately stepped on the shadowed spot. A cold chill ran over me, almost like I'd stepped inside a freezer. The unpleasant feeling left as soon as I moved to the right.

Dimples joined me, holding a pair of sunglasses. "What do you think?" He put them on his face and waited expectantly.

"Not bad. You look like a secret service agent."

His brows tugged together. "Oh." Turning around, he headed back to the glasses. I followed him, knowing that wasn't the reaction he'd hoped for.

I found a pair of aviator glasses and handed them over. With his lips in a flat line, he tried them on, but that wasn't the look he was going for.

"So you want something more sporty?"

"Yeah."

"Okay... here. Try these." I handed him a black pair that were more like the kind Neo wore in *The Matrix*.

He slipped them on and grinned. "Yeah."

They looked so good that I wanted a pair just like them. I found a smaller version that was more gray than black and put them on.

"Nice." Dimples nodded, thinking that, if I pulled my hair back, or slicked it down on top, I'd totally fit the bad-ass biker look, especially with my black leather jacket.

"I know, right?" Instead of pulling my hair back, I flipped it to the side of my head and let the curls splash down the side of my face. After posing for a few seconds, I shook my hair back in place and laughed. "I guess I'm getting these."

"Yup. It would be a shame if you didn't."

As we moved to the counter to pay, I jostled Dimples toward the shadowed place on the floor. His foot landed in the cold spot, and he immediately moved to stand on my other side.

"Why did you move over here?"

"So I can pay?" His eyes narrowed. What was I getting at? This was the line.

I shook my head. "Just come stand over here on this side of me."

"Why?"

"I want to try something."

Heaving out a breath, he stepped to that side of me, right onto the shadow. He immediately hunched his shoulders and pressed his lips together. After a couple of seconds, he moved behind me.

"Why did you do that?"

"Because I'm behind you in line."

I frowned. "That's the only reason?"

"Sure." He met my gaze, and sudden understanding widened his eyes. Stepping around me, he glanced at the floor, thinking about the photo of Rodney's body lying in that exact same spot. Taking a quick step back, he let out a breath. "That's the spot, isn't it?"

"Yeah. Everyone's been subconsciously avoiding it. Even you. What made you step away?"

"I don't know. It just felt... wrong to stand there."

"Yeah. Shall we see if it's the same over there?" I motioned toward the spot where Kirk had died. Dimples nodded and followed me in that direction. The shadowed area was larger here, but the same coldness came through.

Dimples shook his head. "This is so weird." He quickly moved out of the spot. "Usually you're the only one who senses stuff like this."

I nodded toward the other spot. "Yeah, and it's not just us, everyone keeps going around it."

He leaned closer. "Are you getting anything else? Any voices in your head?"

I snorted. If anyone had been close enough to hear his question, they'd think we were nuts. "No. Nothing so far."

"Should we stay a little longer?"

I glanced around the small area. Besides the shadows, there wasn't anything else going on here. "I don't think it will matter, so we might as well go, although I think it would be nice to stop at Kirk's house and talk to his mom. There must be a reason for Alvarez's animosity toward Kirk. I'd like to know what it is."

"That's a good idea."

"From the file, I noticed that she's still in the same house, so it's not far."

"Even better. And we can find out which cemetery he's buried in."

Finding his grave seemed like overkill to me, but, if it wasn't too far away, we might as well visit. Who knew? Maybe I'd get something.

We paid for our purchases and drove the short distance to Kirk's house wearing our new sunglasses. His mom came to the door with a smile, which immediately fell when we she spotted us. She thought we looked like secret agents of some sort.

Dimples told her who we were, and that we were re-opening Kirk's case. She nodded, hope filling her heart that maybe she'd finally get some answers, and ushered us into the living room. We sat down on the couch, taking in the pictures of her family above the fireplace.

In one photo, Kirk smiled from his place between his brother and sister. Next to that photo came one with his parents, and between them both was a large picture of Kirk, smiling and handsome in a suit coat and tie.

After the horrific crime scene photos, it was nice to see him alive and vibrant. But it reminded me that he'd had his whole life ahead of him, and it had been snuffed out for no good reason. Sorrow lanced through my heart and I took a deep breath to steady myself.

"Why are you re-opening the case?" Kirk's mother asked. "Did you find something new?" Her lined face carried the scars of grief, and she seemed older than her seventy-plus years.

I kept my mouth shut and let Dimples explain. "We go through cold cases every now and then and thought we'd take another look at this one. What can you tell us about Lee Alvarez? How did he know Kirk?"

She sighed. "He grew up in the neighborhood, so they knew each other. I think Lee's a year or two older than Kirk.

But... yeah... they were friends of a sort back in high school. It all changed when Lee started selling drugs in the school parking lot. I think Kirk was the one who told the school principal, and Lee got expelled.

"He never forgave Kirk for doing that. Even in the years after high school, he took every chance he got to make Kirk's life a living hell." She shook her head. "I've always thought Lee was the one who killed Kirk, but the police could never prove it."

Dimples nodded. "Well... we're going to see if we can prove it now. Is there anything else you remember about that time?"

She shook her head. "Kirk was a good son. He never did anything wrong in his life. He always tried to help people. Did you know he was working an extra shift that night to save up for a wedding ring?" Tears filled her eyes. "He'd found the girl of his dreams, and he never got to propose... or get married... or have a family."

She sniffed and wiped her eyes before meeting my gaze. "Over the years, I've tried to put this behind me, but it would sure mean a lot if you could find the person who killed my son."

I nodded. "We'll do our best." Her sorrow made my heart hurt. I couldn't imagine how painful losing her son had been. If anything like this happened to my son, Josh, I didn't think I could bear it.

"Thank you." She blinked away her tears and shook her head. "There is one thing I don't understand."

"What's that?" Dimples asked.

"I don't understand why Lee broke into our house after Kirk's death. He destroyed Kirk's room and stole some of Kirk's trophies and other personal items. If he'd killed Kirk why would he do that? Wasn't it enough that he'd brutally beaten my son to death? What kind of a sick person does that?"

What kind indeed? She was right. It didn't make a lot of sense... unless he didn't kill Kirk in the first place. But if he didn't do it, who did?

Chapter 3

Dimples offered Mrs. Wahlen some comforting platitudes that I missed, but his next words sent alarm down my spine. "Do you have anything of Kirk's that Shelby could touch?" I gasped and widened my eyes at him. He went on as if not noticing. "Shelby sometimes gets little flashes of insight when she touches things. I know it sounds strange, but she has a psychic ability that could help us with the case. It's part of the reason I wanted her along."

Mrs. Wahlen glanced my way with raised brows, and I tried not to grimace. "Um... sure. I kept a few of his things. I'll go get them."

After she left the room, I turned on Dimples. "What are you doing? I can't do that."

"Yes, you can. You've done it before."

"No, I haven't."

He shook his head. "Didn't you pick up something after we went to that one guy's apartment? It was the guy who died at the mortuary... I can't think of his name, but don't you remember how he lived in the basement?"

"Yes, of course I do. He had that cat that ran up your leg." Just picturing the cat racing up his leg sent a snort of laughter out of me. Dimples frowned, so I continued. "Um... but it wasn't from touching anything, it was because I smelled something."

"Okay... but what about the girl with amnesia? It was her husband who caused that earthquake, remember? Didn't you touch something then?"

"Nope." I shook my head. "I'm pretty sure I smelled his cologne then too... and I did kind of sense him in the room, but that was different from this. He'd just been killed. This case is so old, I doubt anything like that could happen now."

"Oh... okay. But..." He was thinking that I'd sensed both of the victims' auras in the gas station, so what was different? Wasn't it worth trying everything just to make sure?

I sighed. "Yeah... I guess you have a point. I'll see if I can pick up a scent from his stuff."

A sudden snort came from Dimples. He was thinking I was just like my dog, Coco, only on the metaphysical plane, and it tickled his funny bone.

I shook my head. "Whatever."

Mrs. Wahlen came back into the room with a big box, and Dimples managed to smooth his features. "Thanks." He took the proffered box and tried to hand it off to me. I just scooted closer to him so it stayed on his lap, and we could look at the contents together.

There were several items inside, most of them photos and ribbons from his days in school. I dutifully ran my fingers over the ribbons and picked up one of the soccer trophies to study it. Of course, nothing came to me, and I felt like a hypocrite, especially since Mrs. Wahlen watched me with hopeful eyes.

After rummaging through most of the contents, I found a CD with a play-list on it. The first song listed was "Kiss From A Rose," by Seal.

"Oh wow... I loved this "Kiss From A Rose" song. Did Kirk make this CD?"

She nodded. "Yeah. Those were some of his favorites."

"Cool." Another one I recognized was "I'll Be Your Angel" by Celine Dion. Then there were a few others like "Ordinary World" by Duran Duran. "This looks like a great CD."

"If you want it, you can have it," Mrs. Wahlen said. "I don't know any of that music."

"Are you sure?" I didn't want to take it, but I'd been known to hear music that had meaning from dead people before. Maybe it would help? At her nod, I slipped it into my purse. "Thanks."

Dimples kept rummaging in the box and found a bottle of cologne. "Look at this." He handed it to me. The label said it was Dolce & Gabbana, and the square bottle had a copper-colored rectangular lid. The bottle was nearly full.

"Did he wear this much?" I asked Kirk's mom.

She nodded. "Yes. It was his favorite, but that's because his girlfriend gave it to him. He'd do anything to impress her."

"You should smell it." Dimples nudged my arm, excitement coming off him.

I glanced at Mrs. Wahlen. "Is it okay?"

"Sure."

Taking off the cap, I sprayed it into the air. A second later, the smell hit me, and I knew I'd smelled it before. It had the woody scent of sandalwood and a hint of vanilla spice, making it warm and spicy at the same time. Just like Uncle Joey.

"That smells pretty good," Dimples said. "Even after twenty years."

"Sure does." I nodded and quickly put the cologne back into the box. "Thanks for bringing this out. I'm not sure it will help, but it was worth a try."

"So you didn't get anything?" she asked.

"Not specifically." I shrugged. "But you never know. It might help in the future."

Frowning, she swallowed, realizing that she hadn't smelled that scent since Kirk had died. Smelling it again brought him back, almost like he was here in the room. She'd missed that... missed him. Maybe when she got lonely for him, she could spray a bit of the cologne and bring him back, even if it was just for a few minutes.

That just about broke my heart, and I quickly stood, ready to leave. "Uh... sorry, but we need to go."

Catching my mood, Dimples put the lid on the box and set it on the coffee table. "She's right. Thanks for your time. We'll be sure to keep you updated."

Mrs. Wahlen showed us to the door, and we started down the porch steps. Dimples stopped and turned back. "Oh... there is one more thing. Could you tell us where Kirk's buried?"

Her brows rose. "Uh... sure." She gave us the name of the cemetery, along with the spot where Kirk was buried. Dimples thanked her again, and we hurried to his car.

Inside, I turned to face Dimples. "I don't think going to the cemetery will help."

He shrugged. "Well... maybe not, but now that you know his scent, you might pick it up there. Wouldn't that be something?"

I shook my head. "How in the world would that help us find his killer?"

His excitement waned. "Oh... I don't know, but it would still be cool to see if it worked."

I sighed. "Yeah... sure, but stopping at the cemetery won't help."

"I guess you have a point. We'll head back to the station then. I need a court order to get a hair sample from Alvarez, so I'll do that next. If it's a match, we'll have our killer, and the case will be solved."

I smiled back at him, but I doubted it would be that easy. At least I had the scent of Kirk's cologne, along with his play-list of music. Between the two of them, something might turn up. I shook my head. Dimples was right. I was like a dog on the trail of a killer. It made me cringe just a little.

Not that there was anything wrong with dogs, but being compared to one hurt my feelings. But maybe it wasn't so bad. My dog was great, so there was nothing to feel bad about, right?

After we got back to the precinct, I jumped out of Dimples's car, ready to head home. Before I'd taken more than two steps, someone called my name. I turned to find Chief Winder entering the building. "Shelby... it's nice to see you. Are you helping Harris with a case?"

"Yeah. I'm helping with the cold case you gave him."

"That's great. Did you find anything?"

"Yeah... we might have a lead."

"Good. Come to my office, and fill me in."

I opened my mouth to tell him I needed to go home, but he'd already headed into the building, with Dimples right on his heel.

Sighing, I followed them inside. It wouldn't hurt to stay on the chief's good side, since I needed to use the police database for my own research. If I had time, I could look up Paxton Savage again.

We headed straight to Chief Winder's office. After sitting down in front of his desk, Dimples gave him the run-down about what we'd picked up.

"Good thinking about the hair sample," the Chief said. "That might do the trick." He glanced my way. "And I'm glad you're helping Harris with the case. You've got that special touch with... well... your premonitions, and I know it can make all the difference."

He was wishing that he could get me to work for the police full time. I was an asset to the department, and it would certainly help them solve cases. "Have you ever thought of joining us full time? We could sure use you. Just think of all the good you could do."

"Oh... right... but actually I'm pretty busy, and I already help a lot of people."

"Would you consider it?" He was thinking that it would certainly please the mayor. After the stadium debacle, the mayor hoped getting more arrests and solving more crimes would help his image.

The mayor had even mentioned putting Manetto behind bars. That would certainly turn the tide, but Manetto had proven way too smart and savvy to get caught. But what if I helped them? Didn't I have ties to the mob boss? What were they?

Yikes. I needed to stop that train of thought right now. "Thanks for the offer, Chief... but working for you full time is not going to happen. I've got too many other commitments, and I spend a lot of my time helping you already, you know? In fact..." I glanced at my watch and stood. "I need to get going."

"Oh... of course." He stood as well, realizing he'd scared me off somehow. "We appreciate every minute that you help... right Harris?" He knew Dimples and I shared a special bond, and he wasn't above using it.

"Uh... right." Dimples got to his feet, wondering what had me spooked. "Thanks for helping me today. I'll keep you updated. Maybe you can come back tomorrow?"

I shrugged. "Yeah... that might work. Give me a call. See ya."

I hurried out of the office and headed straight to the elevators. Now I remembered why I didn't like coming here. Working for the police and a mob boss just didn't mesh... at all.

On the other hand, at least I knew who might be targeting Uncle Joey. But did the mayor have the resources to hack into Uncle Joey's computer files? That didn't quite fit, but I wouldn't put it past the mayor to try something underhanded.

In my time working for the police and Uncle Joey, I'd found that they both operated above the law at some point or another. From a crooked attorney general to the mayor making underhanded deals... it was worse than anything Uncle Joey did. Well, maybe not quite, but taking into account that they were supposed to be on the 'good' side of the law, it was totally true.

I let out a breath and slid into my car. I was ready to call it a day. I'd tell Uncle Joey about the mayor tomorrow. Right now, my kids would be on their way home from school, and I wanted to be there when they arrived.

I made it home with time to spare, and opened the door to be greeted by Coco, our search-and-rescue dog. I shared a special bond with him because I could understand what his woofs meant... like they were words in my mind. He'd also saved my life a couple of times, so he deserved all the love and hugs I could give him.

I felt bad that he'd been home alone all day, so, after changing my clothes, I spent some quality time playing catch with him in the backyard. Josh came home before Savannah and took over throwing Coco's disc for him.

We spoke about his day, but I picked up that there was something else he'd rather talk about. With his sixteenth birthday in a couple of days, he'd been dreaming of getting a car. Chris and I hadn't told him he could have one.

He thought we might be waiting to surprise him for his birthday, but that was kind of sucky, since he'd been saving up, and he knew just what he wanted. Plus, if he was paying for half of it, shouldn't he get a say in what kind of car he got?

I thought he made a good point, especially if he paid some of the cost. But Chris wanted to buy it and tell Josh to save his money for college. I liked that idea too, and, if we bought the car, it would be the car Josh used, but not exactly his car.

We'd mostly figured it out, but I was still struggling about the decision. Still, now that Josh had his driver's license, it would be nice to have another car instead of letting him borrow mine, mostly because I needed a car for my own job, and it wasn't available often.

"So what do you think?"

My gaze jerked to Josh's. Oops. "Oh... sorry. What did you say?"

He huffed out a breath, thinking I zoned out a lot lately. Was I getting old? "I was talking about my birthday. I need a car, Mom. I found one that I'd like to take a look at. Will you ask Dad if we can check it out?"

How could I say no to that? "Sure. We can both talk to him when he gets home."

"Sweet." He was thinking, *Yay! She's on my side. Now she can convince Dad! Finally.*

I wanted to tell him I wasn't siding with him over Chris, but I couldn't do that or he'd know I'd read his mind.

Just then, Savannah came outside and demanded my attention. We talked about her day, which she said was okay, but she couldn't wait to jet off to New York and Maggie's wedding a week from tomorrow. "I wish it was next week already. Are you sure we can only stay for a couple of days? I mean... if we're going that far, why not stay one or two days more?"

I'd gone over this with her several times already. "You're already missing one day of school. You'll be behind if you miss more than that."

"No I won't. Everyone misses school. It's not that big of a deal. Ashley missed a whole week when school started and she's fine."

I shook my head. "I'm sorry, but we're at the mercy of Uncle Joey. We go when he goes, and we leave when he leaves. That's the way it works."

"I know. But leaving home on Friday and coming back on Sunday is hardly worth it. Please ask him if we can stay another day or two."

It was tempting to tell her I wouldn't mind an extra day or two myself, but Uncle Joey had other things he needed to do, and staying wasn't one of them. "I can't do that. But you never know... he might surprise us with another night."

Her face lit up. "You think so?"

Oops. "No, I don't."

"Then what did you say that for?"

I wanted to say it was to get her off my back, and that she and Josh were so demanding that it was driving me crazy. "I just thought it was a possibility, even if I don't think it will happen."

She huffed out a breath, thinking I should just say what I mean. She wasn't a kid anymore, and she wasn't interested in possibilities. Adults were so stupid sometimes, especially me. "I'm going to my room."

She stalked into the house, leaving me feeling like a failure.

"Hey Mom?" Josh thought now was the right time to be the good child. I turned to face him. "Lance told me that Coco and I are ready for the next call. He put us on the search-and-rescue list. Isn't that great?"

"He did?" He nodded, and I slumped.

His disappointment that I wasn't more excited came through loud and clear. This was what he'd been working for. I should be proud.

"I'm so proud of you Josh. Way to go."

His face cleared, and he sent me a smile. "Thanks. It's a good thing we're getting another car, since I'll probably need it."

I just nodded and hoped that was enough to appease him. "I'm going inside to get dinner started."

"Okay." He was thinking, *Yes! I'm starving!* but held back for my sake.

Hmm... that was progress. It showed that he thought of my feelings once in a while, right? I hurried into the house and grabbed a diet soda from the fridge. After taking a few swallows, I opened the cupboard, then the freezer, and then the fridge, to see what I could make.

The only thing that I had all the ingredients for was white chicken chili, so I got to work on that. Luckily I found a box of corn bread mix, and I quickly put it in the oven while the chili finished cooking.

Chris made it home right before dinner was ready, and I wondered if he'd planned it that way just so he wouldn't have to help me make it. Since that wasn't very charitable, I reminded myself that I liked to make nutritious meals for my family. It was what good mothers and wives did all over the world, and I was one of them.

"Hi honey." Chris set down his briefcase and pulled me into his arms. "It's good to be home."

My heart melted a little, and I squeezed him back.

"Dinner smells amazing. What is it?"

Since dinner was only part of the reason he was happy to be home, I didn't let it bother me and pulled away. "White chicken chili."

"Awesome. I'll go change and be right back."

I pulled the bread from the oven, and the food was ready. The only thing left was setting the table. Wanting Savannah to help out a little, I stepped to the bottom of the staircase and shouted for her to come down and help out. She didn't answer, so I hurried up the stairs and opened her door. "Did you hear me?"

"Mom! You can't just barge in." Lounging on her bed, she slammed the book she was reading shut, and tried to hide it under her pillow. But I couldn't miss the sexy mob boss on the front cover.

"Where did you get that? Did you take it from my purse?"

Her eyes got big. "No. You left it on the table." She sniffed. "I thought I'd see if it was any good... jeez... it's just a book... don't have a cow."

Naturally, she was lying. She'd grabbed it from my purse after getting an eyeful of the cover. She'd only meant to read a little before putting it back, but she'd gotten caught up in all the kissing and... whoa... is that what sex was like?

Oh my hell! Had I just ruined my thirteen-year-old daughter? "Give it to me. Right now." I held out my hand and wiggled my fingers.

She handed it over while letting out a huge sigh. "Whatever. It's just a book."

"We'll talk about this later. Now get downstairs and set the table."

I took the book and hurried down the hall to my room. Chris was just coming out, so I tugged him back inside, and shut the door.

"What's going on?"

I huffed out a breath. "Savannah took this out of my purse and was reading it." I held it up for him to see, and his brows rose.

He took it from my hand. "Is this one of those sexy romance novels?" He already knew it was, and his lips turned down. A real man could never measure up to the fictional men in these kinds of novels. It was one of the reasons he didn't like that I read them. "*Silent Justice: A Mafia Romance?*" He met my gaze. "Why would you want to read a book about the mafia?"

I sighed, and my shoulders fell. "That's not what this is about. Look at the copyright page." As he opened it, I leaned against him and pointed to the publisher. "See that? Manetto Books."

"Oh... so you got it from Uncle Joey? He's a book publisher now?"

"Yes, but that's not all. I have the book because of the author. You'll never believe this, but Jocelyn Drake is Jackie's pen name. She wrote the book and gave me a copy."

"Holy hell. Now it makes sense."

"Yeah, and Savannah was reading it. I think she may have been reading a sex scene."

"They have sex right at the beginning of the book?"

I huffed out a breath. "I don't know... but that's not the point."

He raised his hands. "I know, I know. Just giving you a hard time. I don't think you need to worry. I mean... sure, talk to her, but it's nothing she doesn't know about."

"I know that... but there's more to sex than having sex."

His brows rose. "Of course... so talk to her about it."

I sighed and grumbled under my breath. "Besides that, she took it out of my purse without asking."

"Yeah... that wasn't right." He was wondering if dinner was going to burn if I didn't get back to the kitchen soon.

"It's not going to burn." I put the book on my dresser and hurried down the stairs. Savannah already had the plates and silverware on the table, and finished up by setting the glasses next to the plates. She eyed me warily, and I picked up that she was trying to be the good daughter so I wouldn't be mad at her.

I wanted to tell her I wasn't mad... I was disappointed. But I didn't want to make too big of a deal out of it. Sex was part of life, and I wanted to be able to talk about it. But she'd taken my book without asking, and that was not a good way to start the conversation.

I met her gaze and raised my brow. "After dinner, you and I are going to have a talk."

She chewed on her bottom lip. "Fine. Whatever." She thought she probably shouldn't have taken the book out of my purse, but she'd sure enjoyed reading it. Now she wanted to know what happened next. Maybe she'd have to sneak it out again later when I wasn't home.

Ugh! I shook my head. Were all teenagers this challenging? Savannah used to be so sweet. Now she was pushing my buttons and trying to grow up way too fast. After the day I'd had, I just wanted to enjoy my dinner. With that in mind, I put up my shields and called everyone to the table.

It didn't last.

While we were eating, Josh told Chris that I'd agreed to let him pick out a car. I opened my mouth to object, but he continued before I could do more than stammer. "Mom thought it was a good idea, and I found something I like."

"She did?" Chris glanced my way, thinking we'd already discussed this, and now I'd changed my mind?

I pursed my lips. "Josh likes what he likes. So... I guess the surprise we had in mind for his birthday is... well... I guess we can take it back." We'd been trying so hard to keep it a secret, but I didn't see another way around it now.

Josh's eyes got big. "What surprise?"

"If I told you, it wouldn't be a surprise anymore."

He shook his head. "Are you talking about a car?"

"Josh." Savannah chided. "Don't be such an idiot. Of course she is. You've only been talking about it for months!"

"Oh." He could hardly believe we'd decided to give him a car for his birthday. His very own car. But what if he didn't like it?

I glanced at Chris and smiled. He took my hand, thinking Josh's birthday couldn't come soon enough. Maybe we shouldn't have been so secretive about the car we'd arranged for him. But Josh would love it, so we just needed to hold out until Monday.

"Three more days." I nodded and glanced at Josh. "Think you can wait that long?"

"Uh... yeah... I guess."

"Good. Now let's finish our dinner."

That night, I found it hard to sleep. Not because of Josh's birthday, or my talk with Savannah, which had proven to be much easier than I'd anticipated, especially since she'd apologized for taking my book in the first place. It wasn't even because of all the planning I needed to do for our trip to New York and Maggie's wedding next week.

Nope. None of that held a candle to the "Kissed by a Rose" song that kept playing over and over in my head. It wouldn't stop, and I knew it had something to do with the cold case. Maybe it would be a good idea to visit the grave.

Then there was Elliot Briggs and my newest job to track down Paxton Savage and follow him around for a few days. I hadn't had time to do a deep-dive search on him at the precinct, but since it was probably wrong to use their database, I could go to Thrasher instead. Ramos had showed me the websites he'd used to get information a few weeks ago, so I could use them for my search.

And what about Uncle Joey's mysterious hacker? Would Ramos and Nick figure out who'd come to Nick's office and managed to get into his computer? It didn't sound like it was the police to me, so who else would be interested?

That was kind of a no brainer, since it included just about everyone Uncle Joey did business with. At least Ramos was working on it, and maybe I'd see if I could help him with that. As long as he didn't mention lizards again.

Sighing, I finally turned on my lamp and pulled out Jackie's book. I called it 'reading therapy,' since it was always a good way to take my mind off my troubles. Two hours later, I was still at it. I totally recognized several incidents in the story, and if Uncle Joey didn't realize he was the model for the mob boss, he was kidding himself.

Then there was Ramos. I sure hoped he read the book so I could give him a hard time about the hitman's "smoldering eyes and sexy lips." Sighing, I flipped off the light and turned on my side, content to let thoughts of smoldering eyes and sexy lips lull me to sleep.

Chapter 4

Morning came too early, and I crawled out of bed with my eyes half shut. I moved at a snail's pace and barely managed to get everyone out the door on time. Ready to head back to bed, Coco pressed his nose against my hand. He woofed, and I heard *walk, you take.*

I glanced out the window to see the beginnings of a beautiful, sunny, autumn day. Unable to say no to Coco's bright-eyed enthusiasm, I threw on my walking clothes, and we started out.

The fresh air and brisk pace got my blood pumping, flushing the cobwebs from my sleep-deprived brain. We took our regular route at a brisk pace. By the time we got back home, I'd figured out a plan of action for the day, beginning with a visit to Thrasher Development to search the Internet for Paxton Savage.

After a quick shower, I threw on my black jeans, a warm top, my ankle boots, and my leather motorcycle jacket. The day was shaping up to be one of those amazing, beautiful, autumn days with bright blue skies and white, puffy clouds.

A little thrill rushed over me that I might get to go on a motorcycle ride. With that in mind, I looked forward to wearing my new motorcycle helmet and the gloves Ramos had given me, grateful that he kept them in the trunk of his car.

After parking, I took the elevator to Thrasher and hurried through the doors to the office. Jackie sat at her desk, and I rushed to her side. "Your book is amazing! I could hardly put it down last night. I stayed up way too late."

Her face brightened. "So you're enjoying it?"

"It's awesome. I can't wait to find out what happens next."

She beamed and clapped her hands together. "I'm so happy you like it."

"Yeah... it's great. I especially like the hitman, Stone. His smoldering eyes and sexy lips somehow remind me of someone."

She chuckled. "Yeah... well, I thought you'd get a kick out of that part."

"A kick out of what?"

I twisted around to find Ramos stepping through the door. It relieved me to see him, since I'd been disappointed that his motorcycle wasn't in the parking garage. "Jackie's book. You totally have to read it."

"I guess I'd better." His gaze flicked over me, and his left brow rose. He thought that I looked ready for a ride. Is that why I'd come in so early today? Maybe if I played my cards right, we could head back to that barn and look for lizards.

I shook my head. "You are so—" Ramos's warning gaze flicked to Jackie, and I scrambled to change my words. "—right. It's a lot of fun. I think you'll like it."

Jackie popped up from behind her desk with a book in her hand. "Great. Here's a copy for you. It's signed and everything."

Ramos knew what was good for him and took the book. He hadn't actually intended to read it, but now he had no choice. "Great. Thanks." He studied the cover, realizing it was a romance novel, something he'd never read before. He hoped there was more to it than a sappy love story. He hated sentimental love stories. "I look forward to it."

Since there was more than a fair amount of sappiness and sentiment, I sent him a sly grin but held back a snicker and hurried down the hall. "I'll be in my office if you need anything."

"Wait." Ramos caught up with me. "Did you happen to find out anything at the police station yesterday?"

"About what?"

He shook his head. "About the crime unit targeting Manetto? Didn't you go there yesterday?"

"Oh, yeah. I forgot. As far as I know, the crime unit's not after him, but someone else might be. The chief asked me to work for them full-time. He was thinking that the mayor would like to get Uncle Joey, but, without my help, it would be next to impossible because Uncle Joey was practically untouchable."

Ramos's brows rose. "So what did you tell him?"

I shrugged. "I turned him down."

"Okay. I'll let Manetto know."

"Sounds good."

As I pulled my door open, I heard Ramos wondering what I needed to do in my office. I glanced over my shoulder. "I have a client who wants me to find someone."

"Oh." He lifted a brow, and I sent him a smile before closing the door.

The abstract painting that Uncle Joey had bought for me hung on the wall, bringing a smile to my lips. I loved the burst of colors and the design that made me feel light and free. Just looking at it pushed the darkness of my worries away and put me in a better mood.

I got settled and booted up my computer to begin my search. It wasn't that long ago that Ramos had shown me how to search the Internet for this type of information, and I quickly typed Paxton Savage's name into the public records site we'd used.

It still surprised me that I could find his criminal records online, but there wasn't a lot of information that I didn't already know. He'd been sentenced to five years in prison for petty theft and dealing drugs, but with a chance for parole after two years, he'd been released early for good behavior.

The date of his release was just last week, and, luckily for me, there was an address listed for his residence. As I wrote it down, Ramos opened my office door and poked his head inside. "Manetto needs us in his office."

"Okay." I picked up from Ramos that something bad was going on, and I hurried after him.

We stepped inside, and Uncle Joey stood from behind his desk. "I just got a call from Jimmy at the restaurant. He said the health inspector just closed him down for bogus reasons. The inspector's still there, so I need you and Shelby to head over and find out what's really going on."

"Sure." Ramos glanced my way and cocked his brow. "Ready to ride?"

I grinned. "You bet."

Uncle Joey shook his head, thinking that, if nothing else, at least his misfortune had made my day.

I sent him a tiny shrug and eagerly followed Ramos out of the office and down the hall to the elevators. In the parking garage, Ramos opened the trunk to his car and pulled out my new helmet and gloves.

He handed them over, and I slipped on the helmet before pulling on the gloves. Ramos glanced my way and admired how I looked in my black motorcycle jacket, black helmet with the pink rose on the side, and black gloves. I looked pretty bad-ass.

The only thing that would make me look better would be replacing my jacket for one that wasn't so shabby. All those places where the leather had been worn off didn't look so good.

He was probably right, but I'd grown attached to this jacket and all its scrapes and shabby edges. Besides, it had saved my skin from abrasions and injury after the recent explosions I'd barely escaped.

Of course, replacing it with a new one wouldn't be so bad. I could keep this one and still have a new one that matched Ramos's image of me.

"You're right. I need a new one."

He nodded, thinking how nice it was to convince me of something without even opening his mouth.

I sent him a sly smile. "Are you going to pick it out?"

"Would you like me to?" His low tone and intimate gaze sent a thrill through my heart. He really did have smoldering eyes and sexy lips—at least when they were directed at me.

"I... uh... well... you sure did a great job with this one."

His lips twisted into a wry smile. He knew the reason I liked it so much was because he'd given it to me.

I shrugged. "That's true. So if you picked out a new one, I wouldn't feel so bad about retiring this one."

"I see your point, but now I'm wondering if you're just saying that so I'll buy it for you."

He was teasing me, but I couldn't stop myself from taking the bait. "Of course not. I just want you to pick it out because... you know... it'll be something you like, and that means I'll like it, too."

His brows rose. "Well... in that case, I'll see what I can find." He knew the jacket symbolized a lot more than either of us wanted to admit out loud, so he was happy to go along with it.

He was right about that. "Thanks."

Straddling the bike, he started it up, then held out a hand. I took it and slung my leg over the seat to settle down behind him, just like a pro. After pulling the visor down over my face, I tightly wrapped my arms around him, and we took off up the ramp. As I settled in, I couldn't keep the grin from my face.

The restaurant wasn't far, so it didn't take nearly as long as I would have liked before we pulled around back. One of Jimmy's workers was waiting for us, and he held the door open. "Jimmy said to go straight to his office."

Since Ramos knew where that was, I followed him down a hall to an office door that stood ajar. Inside, Jimmy was standing beside the health inspector, who held a clipboard and spoke as he pointed at the paper.

Relieved that we were there, Jimmy let out a deep sigh and glanced at the inspector. "Mr. Hansen, these are my business associates. Would you mind showing them the results? I'm still not convinced that we deserve to be shut down. If you would explain it again for all of us, I'd appreciate it."

Hansen's lips pressed into a flat line, and his nostrils flared. He didn't like being blindsided by us. "There's really nothing to tell you. As I've explained, it's all here in the report."

Ramos folded his arms across his chest and raised a brow. Hansen wasn't much taller than me, and he got the message pretty quick. He'd already been flustered by Jimmy, and now, with Ramos looming over him, sweat popped out on his forehead. Swallowing, he turned the report toward us so we could see it.

"This is the list of requirements, and this is where Lugano's fell short. Anything less than a perfect score is grounds for being shut down until these issues can be addressed. It usually only takes a day or two. Then I'll be happy to come back and pass you off."

I glanced at the requirements, finding several checks in the 'below standard' category. "I can see that," I began. "But I'd like to see the area in the kitchen that you gave these marks to."

Hansen huffed out a breath and wanted to argue, but, with Ramos standing beside me, he didn't have a choice. "Fine. Come with me."

We followed him into the kitchen, and he hurried straight to the sink. "There were a few hairs right there."

The sink looked spotless to me.

Ramos frowned. "I don't see any hairs." He glanced at Jimmy. "Do you see any hair?"

"No."

Hansen licked his lips, thinking this was going to be harder than he thought. "Well, they may not be there now, but they were there earlier."

Before Ramos could grab him around the neck, I stepped in. "Maybe so, but now that there's no hair like you thought, you can change your evaluation."

Hansen's gaze jerked from mine to Ramos's. Taking in his menacing glare, Hansen swallowed. "Sure... sure. It's only fair that I change it." After erasing the mark, he checked the passing box. Pursing his lips, he knew that if we checked on each of his low evaluations, we'd find out that he'd done it deliberately. Damn it!

"Mr. Hansen, did someone pay you off?" I asked.

His face drained of color. "I have no idea what you're talking about."

I shook my head. "I think you know exactly what I'm talking about, but believe me when I tell you that the money you were paid isn't worth it. We know you lowered the marks on your inspection for some extra cash. But you know what? We're willing to let it go if you tell us who paid you to do it."

"I... uh..."

Narrowing his eyes, Ramos took a deep breath and began to roll his neck, like he was getting ready for a fight. Hansen stiffened before grabbing his pencil and erasing each of the failing marks. "I'm changing them all. See? There. You've passed. There's no need for this to go any further."

Signing his name to the bottom of the page, he handed it to Jimmy. "There. We're done here. I'll see myself out."

He tried to scoot past me, but Ramos blocked his way. "The name?"

Hansen shook his head. "I don't have a name." Ramos stepped closer to him, and he cringed. "Look. I got into my car after work yesterday and found an envelope full of cash on my seat. The note inside said that I'd get double what was in the envelope if I failed the inspection for Lugano's. That's it."

"How much was in the envelope?"

He let out a breath. "Two grand."

Ramos glanced at me and raised a brow. I nodded to let him know Hansen was telling the truth. "Okay... you can go. But if anything like this ever happens again, you won't be walking out."

Hansen's breath caught. "It won't. I assure you."

Ramos stepped away and motioned to the door. "Good. Now get out of here before I change my mind."

Hansen didn't waste any time. He rushed out of the office and down the hall to the back exit and disappeared.

Jimmy shook his head. "Thanks you guys. I wish I knew what this was all about, but I have no idea."

"Yeah." Ramos glanced at me. "Whoever did this is going to great lengths to remain anonymous. Did you get any premonitions about it?"

Since there wasn't anything I'd picked up from Hansen, I shook my head. "Nope. But it has to be someone who wants to hurt the business." I turned to Jimmy. "You have any enemies or disgruntled employees who'd want to shut you down?"

He shook his head. "Nah. Whoever did this has a lot of money to throw away, so I'd say that it's gotta be tied to Manetto."

Ramos nodded. "I agree." His lips twisted. "Well... keep a watch out, and let me know if you notice anything suspicious happening in the next few days."

"Sure thing."

We said our goodbyes and headed back to Ramos's bike. Before putting on my helmet, I quirked a brow. "You have any ideas about who would do that to Uncle Joey?"

"Not right off the bat, but most of Manetto's associates know he uses the restaurant for... certain business dealings."

"You mean like..." Before I said money-laundering, I shut my mouth. "You know what? Never mind."

Ramos grinned. "Good call."

"Hey... if it's not too much trouble, do you think we could ride past the South City Cemetery? It's kind of on the way back, and there's a grave I'd like to visit."

He cocked a brow. "Anyone I know?"

"No. It's for a cold case I'm working on with Dimples. I just thought that, since it was a beautiful day and we were out on the bike, you wouldn't mind the detour."

"That's true. Let's do it."

I smiled. "Great."

It didn't take long before we turned into the cemetery. Ramos pulled over and took off his helmet before asking me if I knew where the grave was. Taking my helmet off, I gave him the general directions, and we continued slowly down the road until reaching the area where Kirk's mom had said he was buried.

"This is it. I think it will be over there somewhere." We got off the bike and meandered in that direction, checking each grave stone for Kirk Wahlen's name.

A woman knelt in front of a headstone about fifty yards away, brushing some of the dirt from the headstone. Curious, I stepped a little closer, ducking behind a tree so she wouldn't see me.

She spoke softly, but I was able to pick up her words. "... I promised you I'd always remember your birthday, so here I am. I'm sorry that Fern couldn't come, but she had a class she couldn't miss at the university. She finally chose her major, and you'll never believe it... but she's going into landscape architecture. I never told her that was your dream, so I guess it's in the genes or something. Or maybe her name has something to do with it? Anyway... happy birthday... I still miss you... but I want you to know that I'm happy."

She placed a red rose on top of the headstone and straightened. As she walked away, I stepped close enough to read the name. Kirk Wahlen. Without thinking too hard, I hurried after the woman. "Um... excuse me?!"

Startled, she glanced over her shoulder. "Are you talking to me?"

"Yes. I'm sorry to impose, but I'm Shelby Nichols. I'm a private investigator, and I work with the police. I noticed you at Kirk Wahlen's grave, and it's kind of a crazy coincidence, but I'm helping the police solve his murder."

Her brows rose. "Oh." Surprise and confusion washed over her. "I thought they gave up a long time ago."

I nodded. "They did, but the detective I'm working with was assigned to re-open the case. With all the new tests they can do, they're hoping to figure out what happened." The spicy vanilla and sandalwood scent of Dolce & Gabbana hit my nose, and I froze. What the freak? He was still here?

"Are you okay?" The woman asked, thinking I looked a little spooked.

"Oh... yeah. Sorry. I forgot to mention that I'm a psychic, and I sometimes pick things up from... you know... the deceased."

Her eyes rounded, and she took a step back. "Like what?"

I shook my head. "I just got a whiff of cologne. I'm sure it was Dolce & Gabbana. Did Kirk wear that brand?"

She swallowed. "Yeah. He did. I gave it to him."

"So you're the fiancée?"

"We spoke about getting married..."

"Yeah... his mom told us he was going to propose to someone. We visited her yesterday. She had a box of some of his things. In fact—" I rummaged through my purse and pulled out the music CD. "She said this was his favorite playlist. You can have it if you'd like."

She reached for it, holding it gently while reading the names of the songs on the list. "Oh... these are great. I haven't heard some of them for a while." She met my gaze. "Thanks. Uh... I'm Heather Benson. I guess you heard me talking to him."

I nodded. "Yes. Is there anything you can tell me about that time that might help us find his killer?"

She shook her head. "Not really. It was just so... unexpected, you know? One day he was there, and the next, he wasn't. I'd just found out that I was pregnant, and after his death... I dropped out of school and stayed with my aunt until Fern was born.

"I brought her home, but I never told his family. I probably should have, but they were so strict about sex before marriage that I didn't want to include them in her life. Besides that, I'd found a wonderful man who raised Fern as his own, and I didn't want to muddy the waters.

"Anyway, I always come to visit Kirk's grave on his birthday." She shrugged. "What a coincidence that you're here at the same time."

"I know... I was just thinking that. Well... thanks for talking to me. Hey... if we figure out what happened to him, would you like to know?"

She nodded. "Yes... I would, very much." She pulled a business card from her purse and handed it to me. "Here's my number."

I took it and handed her one of mine. "And here's mine, in case you remember anything."

"Thanks." She slipped it inside her purse. "I hope you figure it out. It would be nice to have some closure. And... if you talk to his mother again, please don't tell her about me or Fern, okay?"

"Sure. No problem."

"Thanks." She sent me a nod and turned away to head toward her car.

I turned in the opposite direction, finding Ramos back at his bike, leaning against the seat. "You'll never guess who that was." He raised a brow, so I continued. "Kirk's intended fiancée. He was killed before he could ask her to marry him. It's quite a coincidence that she was here. What are the odds?"

Ramos shrugged. "With you, anything's possible. So what happened to him?"

"He was murdered while he was working at a gas station. They never found his killer." I let out a disgruntled breath. "But he's not the reason the police re-opened the case. There was another man who walked in on it, who was killed as well. The chief's daughter is marrying that man's son, so the chief said he'd look into his father's death."

"Ah... I see. And you think this guy will lead you to the killer?"

"That's the idea."

Ramos was thinking it would be a hard task, since the killer was probably just some random dude passing through.

"We have some evidence, so if we can match the DNA to someone who may have been there, we might nail the guy."

"I take it you have a suspect?"

I nodded. "Yup. I guess we'll see what happens."

"Well... good luck. Ready to ride?"

"You know it." I raised my brows. "Any more detours we need to take?"

"I'm afraid not."

I sighed. "That's okay. We can take a spin through the cemetery on the way out, right?"

He chuckled. "Sure."

We made it back to Thrasher and filled Uncle Joey in on our dealings with the health inspector. He frowned, thinking that was pretty bold of whoever paid him off. He could only think of two people who might do something like that. He turned to Ramos. "Why don't you pay a visit to Chatwin and Branigan and let them know that whoever's messing with me needs to stop. See what they have to say for themselves."

Uncle Joey glanced my way, thinking I could be useful in ferreting out lies, but he didn't want me too involved unless it was necessary. "Anything you'd like to add, Shelby?"

"No. I think Ramos is really good at intimidating people, so he's got it covered."

Ramos snorted. "Thanks. I'll see you later."

He left, and I turned to Uncle Joey. "Did you find out anything more about the guy who got into Nick's computer?"

"No." His lips turned down. "But we're still working on it."

"Good. Well, I guess I'll go. I've got to track down a bad guy, so call me if you need me."

Uncle Joey's brows drew together. "For the police?"

"No... it's for a client. I don't have to talk to him or anything, I'm just supposed to follow him for a few days and then tell my client where he goes. No big deal." I didn't add that it was because my client wanted to kill him, but I wasn't sure Elliot would really go through with it, so there was no need to panic yet.

"Oh... sure." Uncle Joey wondered why I was taking on jobs like that. Didn't I have enough going on in my life? He thought, after nearly getting blown up and drowned, I'd try to simplify things a little.

"Following some guy isn't like getting blown up or drowned. It's simple enough."

He huffed. "I suppose. So how are the plans for Josh's birthday coming?

I sighed and told him all about Josh's idea to pick out his own car. "I think he's finally resigned to letting it be a surprise. Are you sure we're doing the right thing?"

"Of course. He's a responsible young man. He'll be fine."

"Okay. I'll see you later." I sent him a quick wave and left the office. Since I had an hour or so before I needed to go home, I drove to the address I'd found for Paxton Savage.

He probably wasn't home at this time of day, but it was still worth checking out. The apartment complex had seen better days, but the rent was probably cheaper than a lot of other places, so it made sense that a newly released convict would live here.

I pulled into the lot, parked in one of the visitor spaces with a clear view of the exit, and settled in to watch. After an hour, I'd counted only three people coming or going. It was tempting to head up to his apartment and knock, but, if he was there, I didn't want to give myself away quite yet.

Maybe I'd have better luck later. I started my car to leave, when a man matching the photos I'd seen came out of the complex. I froze, watching him walk to a beat-up sedan. The excitement of the hunt washed over me, and I eagerly followed as he drove out of the parking lot.

A few minutes later, we came to a familiar part of the city, and my jaw dropped as he pulled into the parking lot of Uncle Joey's club. What the heck? It was too early for The Comet Club to be open, so what was he doing here?

Pulling to a stop along the street, I watched him walk to the back entrance and go inside. He had to be working here. Maybe he was a waiter or a bartender? Or even a cook?

Since I'd met the manager, I decided it wouldn't hurt to see if Russ could tell me more about Savage. After pulling into the parking lot, I headed inside to the office and knocked at the manager's door.

"Come in."

Opening the door, I slipped inside with a smile on my face. "Hey Russ. How's it going?" A man in his forties, with his long, dark hair pulled back into a ponytail, and wearing casual clothes, glanced up from his work at the desk.

He scrunched his brows together, knowing he'd met me before, but he couldn't quite place me.

"I'm Shelby. Uncle Joey's niece?"

"Oh... of course, I remember now. Did he need something?"

"Uh... not exactly. I'm just here to check on one of your employees... at least I think that's what he is. Paxton Savage? I just saw him come in. He works here, right?"

"Oh... yeah." His enthusiasm waned, and he twisted his lips. "I haven't had any more complaints about him, if that's what you're wondering."

"Complaints?"

"Isn't that why you're here?" He'd just worked all this out with Manetto and Ramos yesterday morning, so what was I doing here? Did Manetto have second thoughts? He could have just called instead of sending me.

"Oh... right... yes. Actually, I just needed a little more information about Savage. Can we go over everything you know about him?"

"You mean besides what I told Manetto?"

"Uh... why don't you pretend like I don't know anything? That way you won't have to worry about leaving anything out."

His brows dipped, and he wondered why I was questioning him. Did Manetto think he'd left something out? "Sure." He sighed and pulled his thoughts together. "When I hired Savage, I knew he'd been recently released from prison, but we have a policy about giving convicts a second chance around here."

He shrugged. "Savage had been released early for good behavior, which was in his favor, so I hired him. Normally, we give new hires like him a few weeks to prove themselves, so we didn't expect any trouble. After the incident, I called Ramos, and he brought Manetto with him. I think it freaked Savage out."

"What happened?"

He raised a brow. Why didn't I know this already? "Savage stayed late the other night to help restock our supplies. He caught one of the other workers helping himself to a case of the special brew we sell.

"They argued, and it turned into a fight. Savage beat Cal badly enough that he ended up in the hospital. The police came to investigate, and Savage would have been sent back to prison if not for Manetto.

"He cleared things up for Savage and gave him a second chance on the condition that if he ever did anything stupid like that again, he'd be fired."

The manager shook his head. "It was nice that Manetto gave him another chance, but I'm not sure he should have."

"Why?"

"Savage lost control. I've seen people like him before. He's like a piece of dynamite waiting to explode. Once he gets started, he can't stop."

"Did you tell Uncle Joey that?"

"Not in so many words, but now that I've told you, you could tell him."

I nodded reluctantly. "Right. Okay. But what do we do in the meantime?"

He sighed. "Not much I can do. As long as no one gets on his bad side, I guess it will be all right."

"Right." I didn't like the way that sounded. This guy had anger issues. Maybe it was tied to his last name, I mean... Savage didn't exactly sound warm or friendly. "I'll let Uncle Joey know."

"Good."

"So what's his job today?"

"Right now, he's prepping the bar for opening. It's nothing that should set him off, so I don't expect any trouble."

"That's good. Is it okay if I take a look around? I don't want to talk to him, but I'd like to watch him for a bit. Maybe I could take some peanuts or pretzels to the bar? Would that work?"

Peanuts or pretzels? He didn't serve peanuts or pretzels in the club. This was a high-class, respectable place. Peanuts? What was I thinking?

"But I guess you don't serve peanuts in a classy place like this. Is there something else I could do?"

He heaved a sigh. "Sure. You can help clean up the bar if you want. He's the only one working at it, so he could probably use the help."

"Oh... okay."

"Come with me." He was thinking he could get me to clean out the ice machines. That would take a few minutes and put me close to where Savage was working.

Since I thought that was a good idea, I followed Russ down the hall and into the club. As we got closer to the bar, he called Savage over. "Savage... this is Shelby. She's making sure the ice machines are clean and working. Show her where they are and what to do."

Savage nodded, but wondered why the boss thought he needed help with the ice machines. He'd already checked them over, and they were working just fine. So what was really going on?

As the manager left, Savage looked me over, taking in my black jeans, boots, and worn-out motorcycle jacket. I didn't look like an employee, and his distrust rose.

"The ice machines are behind the bar. There's one at each end. Go ahead and take a look, but, just so you know, I've already cleaned them up."

"Okay... thanks." I hurried to the end of the bar and opened the lid to look at the ice. It was plenty full and the machine didn't look dirty. Still, I found a washcloth beside the sink and began to wipe it down.

Savage watched me for a few seconds before shaking his head and getting back to stocking the shelves. He'd volunteered to come in early and stay late, hoping to make up for his colossal mistake the other night.

His plans hinged on making a good impression on Manetto, and he'd practically ruined everything. If he didn't get his shit together, he could kiss it all goodbye. He glanced my way again, thinking that I didn't fit in with the regular workers.

Had I been sent here to clean up as penance for a mistake? If so, did that mean I knew Manetto? Maybe he should be a little more friendly to me and find out?

"I haven't seen you here before, but I'm new, so that may be why. Still, you don't look like one of the regulars. Are you a new hire?"

Since I knew just what he wanted, I played along. "No, but every once in a while, I end up here *helping out*. It's usually after I've made a stupid mistake. I think it gives Uncle Joey some pleasure to know I'm paying my dues, you know?"

"Uncle? Manetto's your uncle?"

"Yeah."

"Oh." He wondered if this was his lucky day. Maybe I could put in a good word for him. He stepped closer to me, and I smelled a familiar floral scent, like juniper and sage. Was he wearing women's perfume? Why would he do that?

"Uh... Shelby?"

"Huh?"

He blinked. "I just asked you how well you knew your uncle. Are you close?"

I shrugged. "Oh... yeah, I guess. I mean... I know him as well as most people I'm related to. But he's been pretty good to me, so I'm not going to complain."

His eyes lit up. "That's great. I'd really like to move up in the organization. Could you put in a good word for me? My name's Paxton Savage. If Manetto ever needs some muscle, I'd be great at the job. I'm really good in a fight."

I looked him over, taking in the signs of his recent brawl. It was easy to see that he worked out, even if he did wear perfume. "From your split lip and bruised jaw, it looks like you've already been in one."

He shrugged. "This is nothing. You should see the other guy."

I chuckled. "Right." I caught his gaze. "Is there any particular reason you want to work for a mob boss?"

"Well... maybe. I mean... I have talents I think he'd appreciate."

"Like beating people up?"

His mouth dropped open. "That's just what I was thinking... but... yeah. A mob boss needs people who do that for him, so why not?"

"Why not, indeed?" I pushed the ice machine closed and set the rag to hang on the sink. "Okay... I'll mention it to him, but I can't guarantee anything."

"Oh... sure... and hey... I appreciate anything you can do." He thought working for a mob boss was perfect. Manetto would help keep him out of jail, and he'd get all the benefits. If his past came back to haunt him, he'd have the might of a mob boss behind him. It could be enough that no one in their right mind would ever come after him.

I wasn't so sure of that. Uncle Joey would just as easily throw him to the wolves as save his sorry hide. But I wasn't about to crush his dreams. Our conversation still hadn't told me what I needed to know about his past, and why my client, Elliot, wanted him dead, so I dug a little deeper.

"What did you do before this job?" I asked.

His brows rose, and his eyes narrowed. "Why?"

"Just wondering if references would help, that's all."

"I was a... um... a machinist." He'd learned how to do some machine work in prison and was pretty good at it. The work he'd done that put him in prison wasn't worth mentioning at this point. But it might come in handy in the future. It made sense that Manetto would value his organizational skills. "Not much call for it here, but I was ready for a change anyway."

"Okay... sure. I'll see what I can do."

"Thanks."

I nodded and turned to leave. On an impulse, I glanced back. "What was the name of the gang you were in?"

His brows drew together, and he shook his head. "I never said I was in a gang."

"Oh... right. I'm sorry. I thought for sure you said something about that. Never mind, I'm sure Uncle Joey could use another good hitman."

His jaw dropped. How did I know that was his goal all along?

My jaw dropped. I could hardly believe I'd nailed his intentions. Then I picked up his thoughts about the name of the gang he'd been part of, and dread tightened my stomach.

He'd been part of The Punishers, a gang I'd tangled with before. In fact, I'd nearly been killed by Redman, their notorious leader. During a police op, we'd caught him and his gang at a warehouse with a shipment of guns they were going to sell, and I'd gone along to wait in the car.

Unfortunately, I'd seen Redman sneak out of the building during the shoot-out, and I'd followed him. He was dead now, thanks to Dante, the police firearms instructor, who'd killed him to save me. The gang members who hadn't been killed were now in prison, so Savage must have already been in jail when that went down.

No wonder he couldn't go back to the gang. They probably didn't exist anymore. Now he'd set his sights on joining Uncle Joey. Damn!

As I left the bar, I picked up Savage's thoughts about all the money he could make by doing hits for a mob boss. In the last few days since he'd been released, he'd felt haunted by his past, like a dark shadow was following him around. But this could give him a second chance. It could change everything.

My stomach soured. That guy was bad news, and I didn't want him anywhere near Uncle Joey. At least I could tell Uncle Joey to steer clear of him. But would he? I sure hoped so. And what did that mean about my client, Elliot? He wanted to kill Savage. I didn't know why, but I could certainly come up with a few reasons, now that I knew he'd been part of The Punishers.

Knowing the kind of person Savage was, should I even try to stop Elliot?

Ugh! Why did these things always happen to me?

I got home about an hour after my kids. Josh was out throwing the Frisbee for Coco, so I said a quick hello and went upstairs to say hi to Savannah. Her door was shut, so I knocked before turning the handle and poked my head inside. "Hey there. How was your day?"

She glanced up from her phone and raised a brow. "Fine." She turned her attention back to her phone, ignoring me.

That's when I remembered something I'd learned from a parenting podcast. They'd said that when talking to your teenager, you were supposed to ask more detailed questions, like, "how did your math test go?" Or, "what did you find out about the assignment you were worried about?"

They'd also said *fine* was never a good answer... it was just a thing we all said when we didn't want to talk. I had to agree that it was probably true. I said it—

"Mom! Did you hear me?"

"Uh... sorry. What did you say?"

She rolled her eyes. "I need the money for the field trip if I'm doing the extra activity. You said I could, remember?"

"Oh... right. When is that again?"

She filled me in on all the details and told me how much my 'donation' to the school would be. "You can pay on the school website, but you have to do it today or it'll be too late."

"Okay. I'll go take care of it." As I turned to leave, Savannah had already turned her focus back to her phone. I picked up that she was reading a book, and the character's name she thought of sounded familiar. Where had I heard that? Wait! It was the name of the protagonist in Jackie's book.

"Are you reading my book?"

"What are you talking about? This is a phone, not a book. Duh." She quickly swiped the ebook app away and opened a new one. "I'm playing a game. See?" She held the phone up, and I saw a couple of animated figures moving across the screen.

I huffed out a breath and shook my head. Confronting her about the book was not worth the trouble. Instead of making a big deal out of it, I shrugged. "Okay. But you need to come down and help me with dinner in a few minutes."

"Sure."

I knew she had no intention of doing that, and I tried not to get angry. Sometimes reading minds was a curse. At least it came in handy most of the time, but this? Argh. What had happened to the sweet girl I'd known only a few months ago? She'd been replaced by this hormonal maniac who was starting to drive me crazy.

Josh came inside with a tired dog, and he was happy to help me with dinner. He could barely contain the excitement about his birthday in a couple of days, and the car he was going to get. He couldn't wait to drive it to school and show it off.

"Uh... Josh... we'll probably wait until after school to open your presents."

"Oh... sure." Disappointment crept over him, but he tried not to show it.

"It'll be worth the wait... you'll see." His smile warmed my heart, and I gave him a big hug. "But if I'm going to be honest, I can't wait either. It's going to be awesome!"

Later that night, I snuggled in bed with Chris, and we figured out all the logistics for bringing the car home. We decided that Chris would get off work early, and I'd have the car sitting in the driveway when Josh got home from school.

Warmth bubbled up inside of me. "I'm so excited. I can't wait to see his face."

Chris nodded. "Yeah. It's hard to believe he'll be sixteen and driving. These years have gone by so fast. Before you know it, he'll be off to college."

That put a damper on things. "Yeah... well let's not think about that, okay?"

"Sure." He pulled me close. "So, how was your day?"

"A little weird." I told Chris all about it, from meeting the cold case's fiancée at his gravesite, to learning that Paxton Savage was working for Uncle Joey.

He agreed that I needed to tell Uncle Joey to leave Savage alone. "You can't let your client kill him, either."

"Are you sure?"

"Shelby..."

"I know. I sent Elliot a text that I had some information for him, so I'll talk to him on Monday. Hopefully, I'll be able to find out why he wants Savage dead, and I can talk him out of it."

Chris told me about his day, and it was really nice to think that my day was a lot more interesting than his. A couple of years ago, I never would have guessed where I'd be today, and it pleased me that I'd come so far.

Who knew going grocery shopping for carrots would completely change my life? Now I had a career of my own, I helped solve cases for the police, and I'd even managed to influence a mob boss for good. It made the times when I'd barely escaped with my life totally worth it.

And Monday was Josh's birthday. A little shadow fell over me that something might go wrong, but I quickly pushed that awful thought away and replaced it with all the positive vibes I could manage.

It was going to be great, and nothing would happen to change that.

Chapter 5

Monday morning finally arrived, and I got up early to make Josh waffles for his special day. He came into the kitchen, and I swore he'd grown another inch overnight.

"Happy Birthday!" I gave him a big hug and enjoyed holding him for just a minute longer than normal. "Okay... you know the drill."

"Ma... do we have to?"

"Yes." I motioned him toward the pantry door where I'd marked his height on every birthday. As he stood up straight and tall, I had to reach up to hold the ruler at the top of his head.

He ducked away and turned to see where the new mark was. I gasped. "Holy smokes! You've grown four inches! You're just over six feet tall!"

"Cool." He shrugged like it was no big deal, but inside he was completely thrilled.

"No wonder you're so hungry all the time."

"That's true."

"Come on... your birthday waffles are waiting."

As he began to eat, Savannah came in, and I served her some waffles too. She told Josh happy birthday, but she didn't want to seem too excited for him. Still, she could hardly wait to see what kind of car we got him.

She had all sorts of plans for that car and hoped Josh would agree to drive her and her friends where they needed to go, since that was a lot cooler than having me drive them.

She was probably right about that, so I tried not to roll my eyes.

After I got them off to school, I took Coco on a nice walk, happy that it was another beautiful, fall day. Not only would it be great for Josh's birthday, but it might hold another motorcycle ride for me. What's not to love?

I had an appointment with Elliot at nine in the coffee shop by his office, so I hurried to get ready in time to meet him. As I walked in, he sent me a wave, and I hurried to his table in the corner.

"Hey Shelby. I'm excited to hear what you found." That was true, but only because he was determined to kill Savage. But how was he going to do it? He really wanted to shoot him, or stab him a hundred times, but he wasn't sure he could get away with that. Still, no matter what it took, he knew it was his duty to put the dirty bastard in his grave.

"Yeah... well... about that. Did you know he just got out of prison?"

Elliot's brows tightened. "Yeah, so?"

"Do you know why he was in there?"

His lips drew down, and he shrugged. "What does that have to do with anything?"

"Well... I think he might be dangerous, and I'd hate to see anything happen to you."

"Oh... you don't need to worry about me. I can take care of myself."

"Okay... good." This was going to be harder than I thought... unless... maybe Elliot wasn't as squeaky clean as I'd thought. Had he been part of The Punishers as well? They were assassins for hire, and, since he wanted to kill Savage, maybe I shouldn't be so worried about him.

"Uh... Shelby? You going to tell me what you found out? If you're worried about the money, I can send it to you first."

"Oh... no that's not necessary. I have his address for you, and I know where he works, I just have a question I'd like you to answer first."

"Yeah?"

I took a deep breath. "Savage isn't a good person. He belonged to a gang called The Punishers. I don't know if you've heard of them, but they're like mercenaries... you know... like assassins for hire?"

His left brow rose, but he didn't react, so I pressed my point. "The Punishers' leader was killed by the police not that long ago, and most of the gang is either dead or in jail." He wasn't fazed by my information, so I pushed harder. "Have you ever heard of them?"

"Uh... I'm not sure." I picked up that he definitely knew them, but he didn't want me to know that. "So, can I get his address?"

Now what? Was he one of them or not? I sighed. How was I supposed to stop him now? With nothing left to do, I pulled up my notes on my phone and gave him the address. "He just started working at The Comet Club, so he's there most nights. You ever been there?"

"No... too high class for me. This is great. Thanks Shelby."

"Do you need anything else?"

"Nope. How much do I owe you?" He took out his phone to pay me, so I gave him the dollar amount and my account information. He transferred the money, and we were done. "Thanks Shelby. I'll let you know if I need anything else."

He stood to leave, but I grabbed his arm. "I don't think it's a good idea."

"Huh?"

"I don't think you should kill him."

His eyes widened, and he jerked his arm out of my grasp. "What the hell?"

I wasn't sure what to say to explain that, so I sent him a motherly smile and listened real hard to his thoughts. Besides feeling shock, a sliver of guilt slipped over him. I'd sounded just like his sister. How was that possible?

Taking a chance, I barreled on. "Your sister wouldn't like it."

His face drained of color, and he sank down into his seat so hard that I knew his legs had given out. "Who are you? How did you know? I haven't told anyone. What the hell is going on? Are you..." He shook his head, knowing the only thing that made sense was divine intervention, but he didn't believe in angels or stuff like that. So what else could it be? "Did you know my sister?"

"No... but I do have some special psychic abilities. That's how I know she's the reason you want Savage dead, but, before I explain, I'd like to know more about your sister."

"But you just said—"

I held up my hands. "Right... I know how it sounds, but what I've picked up about her with my psychic ability is a little muddled, so anything you can tell me would help."

Still in shock, he rubbed his face with his hands and took a few deep breaths. "It's hard for me to talk about." He swallowed and closed his eyes. "I guess you know she was murdered."

He met my gaze, so I nodded, even though I had no idea. "Yes... I got that. And... it was Savage who killed her? That's why you want him dead?"

He clenched his fists, and hot rage washed over him. "Of course I do. The bastard got away with cold-blooded murder. Sure, he went to prison, but it wasn't for her death. They got him on something else because they didn't have enough evidence to pin her murder on him."

Shaking his head, he ran his fingers through his hair. "Somehow, I'm supposed to be okay with that, but how could I be? The detectives knew he did it. Hell, everyone who worked on the case knew it. But they couldn't prove it, so they settled for lesser charges."

"I'm sorry." I placed my hand over his clenched fist. "I know this is hard, but I can help you."

He pulled his hand away and shook his head. Zoe deserved justice, and the only justice that he could give her was to kill the man responsible. Nothing else was good enough. "What... so you'll help me kill him?" He was being sarcastic, but I wouldn't let that deter me.

I shook my head, grateful I'd picked up her name. "No. That's not what I meant, and you know it." I let out a breath and went for it. "Besides, you have to know that Zoe doesn't want you to kill him."

Elliot sucked in a breath. "How did you know her name? Wait... did you look into my background? Is that it?"

"Actually... no, I didn't. Like I said... I have psychic abilities. But I'm limited in what I can pick up. That's why I need you to tell me more about her. That way, I can... um... get a better feel for her and what she wants... I mean... besides that she doesn't want you to kill Savage."

I was totally making this up as I went, but I was pretty sure his sister wouldn't want Elliot to kill Savage. But what if she did? Then I was in real trouble.

Since he wasn't talking, I gave him an encouraging nod. "Was she older or younger than you?"

"She was older... she liked bossing me around when we were growing up, but she always looked out for me, like I should have looked out for her."

"So what happened? How did she know Savage?"

"It all started at the gym. She belonged to a twenty-four-hour fitness center, and, because of her work, she usually ended up going there late at night. I guess that's when she met some guy there, and they became friends. For her safety, he started walking her out to her car.

"One night as they walked out, she realized she'd left her water bottle inside, so she went back. When she came out, she saw her friend arguing with another man."

He shook his head. "She didn't want to get involved, so she hung back. Then this guy starts yelling, and the next thing she knows, her friend is on the ground. The guy ran off, and she hurried to her friend's side to find him holding his stomach, with blood all over him. The last words he spoke were the guy's name, Paxton Savage."

"The police and the ambulance came, but not before he died right there in her arms. It was traumatizing as hell. She told the police what happened, and they brought Savage in for questioning. She identified him in the lineup, and they arrested him for murder."

Elliot closed his eyes and sat back in his chair. "As you can imagine, it took several months to put the case together, and somehow, Savage managed to get out on bail. Just before the case went to trial, Zoe was killed in a hit-and-run accident."

"Oh no."

"Without her testimony, the prosecution didn't have enough evidence to convict him for murder. They did manage to press charges for an unrelated offense, and he took a plea deal to spend the next five years in prison, with a chance for parole after two years. As you can guess, the two years just ended."

"What about the hit-and-run? Did the police trace it back to him?"

"No... they never could, even though everyone knew it was him. He covered his tracks too well."

I sighed. "That sucks. He got away with it."

Elliot caught my gaze. "Exactly. So, if you're offering to help me kill him, I'll take it. Otherwise, get out of my way."

My lips thinned. "I'm sorry. As much as he deserves it, you're on your own."

He shrugged, acting like he didn't care. "Whatever. Just don't tell anyone."

"I won't, but what about Zoe? What do you think she'd want?"

He shook his head. "I can't think about that."

I nodded. "That's because you know she wouldn't want that for you." I cocked my head and closed my eyes, picking up a scent of floral perfume. "She'd say something like, *What the hell Elliot... don't be such an idiot. Life is short... live yours and stop beating yourself up about what happened to me. It's not worth it.*"

I swallowed. Where had that come from? Then I recognized the scent of juniper and sage and nearly choked. Savage had worn that perfume... or maybe it wasn't him at all? A cold chill ran down my spine.

Elliot's eyes widened, and he swallowed. "That was... you sounded just like her."

"I did? Wow... that was weird."

"I... my break's up. I've got to go." He jumped up and started toward the door.

Once again, I grabbed his arm. "Elliot—wait!"

Stopping, he shook my hand off his arm. "Look. I'll think about it. That's all I can do."

I watched him hurry away with a sense of dread. That was... I shook my head. I had no words for that. Had Zoe spoken through me, or did I just channel her, or what? The scent definitely tied her to Savage. Would Elliot go after Savage anyway? Could I stop him if he did?

The scent of juniper and sage wafted past my nose, and I heard, *you'd better.*

Gah! I jerked back in my chair. The scent lingered a second longer before dissipating. My heart racing, I shook my head. What the freak? I did not want to become some dead person's pawn. I muttered a few curses of my own and put my shields up. No way was she getting into my head again. Too bad I couldn't shield my nose.

Feeling a little spooked, I got to my feet and left the shop. Outside in the sunshine, the chill left me, and I calmed down. It was still early in the day, but since I had to stop at Thrasher anyway, I might as well head over there. Besides, after what had just happened, I needed some motorcycle therapy.

After fastening my seat belt, I started up the car just in time to hear my phone ring. The ringtone was set to *Scooby Doo,* so I knew who it was. "Hey Dimples. What's up?"

"The results from the hair sample just came back. Can you stop by for a few minutes?"

It took me a second to remember what he was talking about. "Oh... right... the hair sample. I just finished an appointment, so yeah... I can stop by." That meant putting off my therapy a little longer, but I could hold it together until then.

"Great. See you soon."

He hung up before I could ask him if it was good news, but, since he wanted me to come in, I figured it wasn't, or he would have just told me, right? The hair sample at the crime scene must not have matched the guy in prison. What was his name? Oh yeah... Lee Alvarez. We'd spoken to him last week, and I hadn't had any luck picking up if he'd killed Kirk Wahlen and Rodney Shepard.

Was it just Friday that I'd met Kirk's fiancée at his grave? Keeping everything straight might be a problem. I couldn't remember the last time I'd had this much on my plate. Could my life get any more complicated?

I strode into the precinct with my lanyard around my neck and found Dimples sitting at his desk. "Hey... I made it. Is it good news?"

He sighed. "Not exactly. Sit down so we can talk."

I sat in the chair beside his desk and picked up that the news was bad, even though it didn't make sense. "The hair didn't match, so I guess that means we have to rule out Lee Alvarez." He shook his head. "I thought for sure he was the one... but now..." He shrugged. "I don't know what to do."

"Bummer."

"You have any ideas? Or pick up anything from the dead guys?"

I closed my eyes. Getting things from the dead was starting to sound like a theme at the moment. One dead person talking to me was enough. "Nope... although something strange happened when I visited Kirk's grave on Friday." I told him about meeting Heather and smelling the cologne.

"I told you it would come in handy. So, did you get anything else?"

"No. But I really want to find the person responsible. It would be nice to give his loved ones some closure." I rubbed my jaw. "Maybe we should go through all the evidence again. You still have the list?"

"Yeah." He opened the file and pulled out the list of all the evidence that had been gathered. Starting at the top, we ran down the list, looking for anything that might seem worth checking into. The victim's bloody clothes were still in storage along with a few other items at the scene.

"What's this?" I pointed to a line that listed a dollar bill with blood stains on it, but nothing about a DNA test.

"Let me see what the report says about it." Dimples flipped a few pages until coming to the information. "It looks like the blood on the bill was never tested because it was found by Rodney's body, and they figured the blood was his."

"That makes sense to me."

"Sure. But what if the blood belongs to the killer? What if he was giving the money back to Rodney as change, and he bled on it because his hands were cut up from beating Kirk?"

"Wait. What? I thought Rodney walked in on it and got shot."

"Well yeah... but I was studying the report and found out that one of the detectives came up with a theory. He thought that Rodney filled up his car with gas and the killer came out to take his money like he was the attendant.

"Rodney gave him a ten dollar bill, so the killer went back in to get change. Rodney waited for his change, but when the killer didn't come back with it, he went in to get it. That's when he was shot because he saw Kirk's body."

"What made the detective think that?"

"Because the money on the ground came to one dollar and some change. The detective thought the killer had it in his hands to take back out to Rodney, but dropped it to shoot Rodney when he came inside. They also found a ten dollar bill next to the cash register, so it made sense."

"Okay. Yeah, I can see that. But what makes you think the blood on the dollar bill could belong to the killer and not the victims?"

"Because Kirk was badly beaten. From the medical examiner's report, the killer used his fists before tying Kirk up. Kirk fought back and had defensive wounds on his hands. It only makes sense that the killer's hands would look the same, if not worse. He may have even had a bloody nose from being punched in the face."

"Okay... I get it, but why didn't they test the money back then?"

He shrugged. "From the notes, the lead detective didn't buy the theory, mostly because the bill was found on the floor next to the body and the blood. It's been preserved in the freezer of the state crime lab all these years, so we might as well get it tested. I mean... what have we got to lose? I'll call and tell them the chief wants it ASAP, so we can get the DNA results back quicker. You have any other ideas?"

I shook my head. "Not really."

"Okay. We'll try it and see what happens."

"Sure." I stood to leave, and Dimples cocked his head to the side.

"You know what's weird about this? Somehow Alvarez found out about the subpoena for the hair sample, because when they brought him out to collect the sample, he'd shaved all the hair off his body."

"Eww... really? That just makes him look guilty, right?"

"Yeah."

"So what did they do?"

He shrugged. "Oh they found one on him, and you can guess where, but I won't tell you."

"Ugh! Stop!" I closed my eyes and threw up my shields, but it was too late.

He snickered. "That's why it was such a shock that the hairs didn't match."

"Well... maybe the blood will match him instead, and we'll have our killer."

"That would be nice."

"For sure." I checked the time, knowing that if I hurried, I could still get in a motorcycle ride with Ramos. "I've got to go. Call me when you get the results."

"I will. See you later."

I hurried out before anyone could stop me and made it back to the safety of my car. Relieved, I drove the short distance to Thrasher. After parking, I stepped toward the elevators, glancing behind the pillar to find the motorcycle sitting there in all its glory. The sight of it put a smile on my face and a spring in my step.

On the twenty-sixth floor, I walked through the doors into Thrasher and found Jackie sitting at her desk. "Hey Jackie. How's it going? I'm almost done with the book. It's fantastic."

"Oh thanks. Let me know when you're finished!" She really wanted to ask me to write a review, but she thought that, if I liked the book, I'd write one anyway. But if I didn't write a review, did that mean I didn't like the book and had just been trying to be nice all this time?

Were all authors this insecure? Of course, this was her first book, so maybe that had something to do with it. "I'll be sure and write a five-star review when I'm done. You deserve it."

"Oh really? That would be great! Thanks!"

"You bet. Is Ramos around? I have a question for him."

"Sure... I think he's with Joe."

"Thanks." I stepped down the hall to Uncle Joey's office and knocked before sticking my head inside. Uncle Joey sat behind his desk, and Ramos stood beside him. "Hey there."

Uncle Joey glanced up. "Shelby. You're just the person I wanted to see."

"Really?"

"Yes. I have the car ready to go. When were you picking it up?"

"That's why I'm here. I don't really need it yet, but I have to have it home before two-thirty when Josh gets out of school."

"Okay. That will work." His phone began to ring, and he picked it up. "Hello?"

While he spoke, Ramos came to my side. "What's going on?"

I smiled. "Well... you know how Uncle Joey bought that black Jeep Wrangler for our prospecting trip?"

"Sure."

"Well... he's not really using it anymore, and he was willing to sell it to us so we could give it to Josh for his birthday. Isn't that great? You know it's a hybrid and fully loaded. Even better, it's great for off-roading, which I think is perfect for Josh since he's been training with Coco for the search-and-rescue team."

Ramos's eyes lit up. "That's great. So how much is Manetto giving it to you for?"

My lips turned down. "Giving it? I wouldn't say that. We put a hefty amount down on it. But... we probably got a pretty good deal since it's basically brand new." I shrugged. "I guess you could say that I'll be working for Uncle Joey for the rest of my life. But, since I'd be doing that anyway, it all works out."

Ramos nodded, and his lips twisted. He liked hearing that I'd be working for Manetto for the rest of my life.

"Why's that?"

His grin widened. "Because I will be too. And you know what that means?"

My eyes got big. "Motorcycle rides forever?"

Ramos snickered, and he imagined both of us with white hair, a little stooped, but still rocking the black leather jackets and taking the corners with ease.

I laughed, loving that image. Who knew? It could happen.

"Dammit!" Uncle Joey hung up his phone. "That was Ricky. He's at the construction site of the housing project we're managing."

He heaved out an exasperated breath and shook his head. "Someone's been threatening the workers, and they're walking off the job. Ramos, I need you to get over there and find out what the hell's going on."

"You got it."

I stepped closer. "Do you need me to go, too?"

Uncle Joey raised his brow. "That would be great, but do you have time?"

"Oh sure... I've got a good two hours before I need to get home."

"Good. Then go."

I tried to contain my happiness about going for a ride, since I didn't want Uncle Joey to get a complex. Ramos just lifted a brow and followed me out of the office. As we rode down in the elevator, he was thinking that this incident felt a little off. After yesterday, another disturbance seemed almost more than a coincidence. And it added up to three if he counted the hacker who'd compromised Nick's computer. Was something else going on?

"Oh... I didn't even think of that." I stepped closer to knock shoulders with him. "Good thing I'm coming, right?"

He slanted his eyes my way and was thinking *don't get cocky*, but his lips twisted into that lopsided grin that I loved, and it didn't bother me at all. The doors opened, and we hurried to the Harley.

The only thing that would make the ride more perfect would be a new leather jacket. Still, knowing I looked bad-ass behind Ramos boosted my confidence. Once I'd settled in behind him, with my arms holding him tight, I enjoyed each second of the ride to the construction site.

After we parked, I managed to climb off the bike with fluid grace. I even pulled my helmet off and shook my hair out like those models on TV. I didn't think anyone was watching, but I was with Ramos, and that always shot my coolness factor way up. So why not act the part?

A soft chuckle brought me up short, and I turned to find Ramos shaking his head. With his eyes twinkling, he held out his hand for my helmet. I stuffed my gloves inside and handed it over. He attached our helmets to his bike, thinking that I'd better be careful or he might have to fight off the construction workers who were ogling me from the building.

Instead of being mortified, I thought that was one of the nicest complements he could ever give me. "Why, thank you." Since women always ogled him wherever we went, it was nice to have the tables turned for a change.

His lips twisted, and he almost rolled his eyes, but the sound of raised voices inside the construction zone caught his attention. He stepped toward the entrance, and the two men standing near the doorway moved to block his way.

It surprised me until I realized that they were both as big and intimidating as Ramos. One of them held up his hand. "Private property. No one's allowed inside without a hard hat and a security badge."

Ramos studied them with narrowed eyes, not recognizing them as part of the construction security detail. I focused on them and picked up that they were only there to stop the project and had nothing to do with the job.

One of them was hoping that Ramos wouldn't challenge him because, judging by Ramos's appearance, it was bound to be a painful experience. He'd been paid a couple of grand, but that wasn't enough to make it worth a trip to the hospital.

"Who hired you?" I asked, stepping beside Ramos. I didn't pick up a name, so I asked a different question. "Why does someone want to stop the project?"

"How did you—" The man glanced at his companion, wondering what was going on.

"I know you were paid two grand each to stop the project, but I don't know who hired you. If you don't want to end up in a body-bag, I suggest you start talking."

Ramos glanced at me, thinking *Look at you. You're certainly getting the hang of this. Manetto would be so proud.*

I sent him a wide-eyed stare and held back the urge to smack him. A cry sounded from inside the building, spurring Ramos into action. He sucker punched the man closest to him, then butted the other man aside and rushed through the entrance.

Inside, we found Ricky pushing against another burly man who held a knife inches away from Ricky's throat. Ramos quickly punched the attacker in his side. The man cringed, dropping his hold on Ricky, and turned to face Ramos.

He lunged, but Ramos stepped aside and grabbed the attacker's arm, using the man's momentum to spin him around. Pulling the man's arm back and up, he twisted his wrist until the knife fell from his fingers. Ramos continued pushing him to the floor, holding his arm in a painful grip against his back in a classic Aikido move.

By now, the two men guarding the door had recovered and charged inside. I ducked the swing of the first man and jabbed my trusty stun flashlight into his stomach, hitting the button. One million volts of attack-stopping power slammed into him, and he fell like a rock.

The other guy stepped into the fray, but after seeing his friend go down, and finding Ramos holding the other attacker, he lost interest in the fight and rushed back out the way he'd come.

With the threat gone, Ricky helped Ramos immobilize the attacker's hands and ankles with duct tape. The guy I'd stunned was just coming around, so I used more of the tape on his wrists and ankles. Since he was in no shape to talk, we focused our attention on the knife guy for answers. Ramos pushed him into a sitting position against a wall and held the knife up to examine it.

I knew he did it to intimidate the attacker, especially when he crouched beside the man and held it next to his throat. "You've made an enemy of a powerful man by coming here today. Frankly, I don't know if you'll survive, at least not without losing something important, like a few fingers or an eye."

The man blinked, but otherwise held his emotions in check. What powerful man? He had no idea who Ramos was talking about. He'd been told this was an easy assignment with no repercussions. So who did Ramos represent?

I stepped closer to the man and folded my arms. "Who hired you?"

The man lowered his eyes, knowing it wouldn't do him any good to keep his mouth shut. "I never got a name. I was contacted through an account I use on the dark web. After I agreed, the first half of the payment was delivered to my account. The rest was to be delivered on condition that I complete the assignment. Guess that's not going to happen now."

Picking up the amount he'd been paid, I shook my head. "So you got twenty grand to stop the project, which means ten up front, minus the four grand you used to pay your two goons." I motioned toward the guy I'd stunned. "Which leaves you with six." I shook my head. "It doesn't seem like it's worth it to me."

He rocked back as if I'd struck him. "How the hell did you know how much I was getting paid? I never told anyone."

I shrugged. "I've got friends in low places." I wanted to start singing the rest of the song, but I refrained and met Ramos's gaze. "That's all I got unless there's something else you want to ask him."

"No. I think you've covered just about everything."

I nodded and prodded the man further. "I'm just curious. Besides threats, how were you going to shut the project down?"

He shrugged. "Just by using some good, old-fashioned sabotage techniques. You know... things like ruining the equipment and the port-a-potties. Maybe making the supplies disappear or get damaged... stuff like that."

He was thinking that he'd already ruined a couple of the compressors, but he hoped he'd be long gone before we figured that out.

"Hey, Ricky... you might want to check the air compressors before they're used again. It looks like our friend here has already done some damage."

Ricky shook his head, thinking this job was more trouble than it was worth. "Thanks Shelby. Why don't you ask him which ones? That will save me the trouble."

"Sure." I glanced at the attacker. "Want to tell us now, or do you need to lose a finger or two?"

This time Ramos rolled his eyes, but he smiled while he did it, and I was happy to provide him with a lighthearted moment.

Letting out a long sigh, the guy told Ricky which compressors he'd damaged before glancing at Ramos. "That's everything. Will you cut me loose now?"

Ramos didn't want to do that quite yet. Besides the monetary damage to the equipment, this guy had caused Manetto grief, and nobody did that without consequences. He glanced my way. "Shelby... you might want to wait outside for this."

"Really?"

He shrugged. "I know how you feel about blood, so I think it would be best."

I glanced at the guy, worry tightening my mouth. "Um... okay." If Ramos wanted to scare the guy, he was doing a pretty good job. The man's face had gone pale, and he swallowed several times.

As I turned to the door, he shouted. "Wait! I might have something else, but you have to promise not to hurt me." He was thinking that the name of the group he'd contacted on the dark web might be enough to save his neck.

"What's that?" Ramos asked, glad he'd followed his instincts.

"She stays until you cut me loose, and I'll tell you."

Ramos caught my gaze, wondering if I'd already picked the name up. I shook my head, so he turned to the man. "All right. She'll stay. What is it?"

He swallowed. "The group who hired me... they go by the name of Vigilant Crows. They're pretty active on the dark web, so you might be able to get a lead from them." He was thinking *if the price was right.*

"You mean for the right price?" I asked.

"Uh... yeah... exactly."

Ramos shook his head. "Groups like that pride themselves on discretion, so I doubt that they'll tell us anything." He caught my gaze and motioned his head toward the door. "You might as well go."

The guy straightened. "Wait... you're right... I have a name, but it can't be traced back to me, okay? They can't know I told you."

Ramos put on a show of considering it before he answered. "Sure. I'll even let Shelby untie you if it's legit."

The man closed his eyes and sighed. "It is. The name is Dagger."

"That's not a real name," I said.

He shrugged. "That's how it works. Like I said, I was contacted through the Vigilant Crows network. He was the one who did the hiring and paid for this job. That's it. I swear I don't know anything else. Now let me go." He was telling the truth, so I glanced at Ramos and sent him a nod.

Ramos nodded back and jerked his head toward the door, thinking I needed to play along with him and leave, even though he'd said I would stay. I hesitated for a few seconds before walking out of the construction zone, and all the way to the bike on the street.

It didn't seem like Ramos was going to go through with his threats, but he still needed to put the fear of the mob into both men. At least he wasn't thinking that he needed to spare me from seeing blood, so that was a good sign.

A few minutes later, the men came out with Ramos following behind. Once through the entrance, they took off pretty fast, and I picked up their relief of narrowly escaping the wrath of Manetto's hitman.

Ramos stepped to my side, oozing with self-satisfaction. He'd scared the shit out of them, and he'd enjoyed it immensely. "Ready to ride?"

I chuckled and sent him a smile. "You know it."

Chapter 6

We made it back to Thrasher and spent the next few minutes filling Uncle Joey in on what had happened. When we got to the part about the dark web, he stopped us and asked Forrest Slater to come into his office.

Forrest worked for Uncle Joey as an independent contractor, so he didn't spend a lot of time in the office, and we were lucky he was there. We explained the incident again, mentioning that the job had been posted on the dark web.

"He said the job came through a group known as The Vigilant Crows," I said. "And the contact name was Dagger."

He nodded. "Okay. I can work with that. At least the Vigilant Crows should be traceable, but Dagger is obviously made up."

"But you can check out the Vigilant Crows?" Uncle Joey asked.

"Yeah... but if they're a front group, I'm not sure finding them will help. It sounds like they're comparable to a broker group who helps people find each other for the jobs they want filled."

Forrest was thinking it was kind of ingenious, and probably something Uncle Joey could take advantage of. "For example... let's say you're in Los Angeles, and you have a job in New York City. Instead of sending one of your guys, you go through The Vigilant Crows.

"They post the job on the dark web to those individuals living in New York City who work for them. Someone takes the contract, and you arrange payment through an untraceable account. People who take the jobs get rated by the contractors, so it behooves them to fulfill their contracts. That way, they'll have the credibility they need to be hired again."

My brows rose. "And this is a real thing?"

He shrugged. "It's fairly new... but yeah."

Ramos unfolded his arms. "So the people who use this service most likely don't live in the same city. Is that what you're saying?"

"I think the probability is high that this is true. It's becoming a more popular way to get your dirty work done these days, mostly because it's anonymous for all parties involved."

Uncle Joey nodded. "I see what you mean." He could see the advantages for someone like him. Still, in light of what had happened today, it clearly wasn't as dependable as doing it within his own organization.

I thought he made a good point against it, but what the freak? "That's nuts. It's like ordering a hit through an Internet service. What's this world coming to?"

Everyone silently agreed with me.

Uncle Joey turned to Forrest. "I'm interested in this group. See what you can find out about The Vigilant Crows, and let me know what you come up with."

"Will do."

After he left, Ramos shook his head. "I think we can all agree that someone is targeting us. This is the third incident in as many days. It makes me wonder what could happen tomorrow."

Uncle Joey stiffened. "You think they're related?"

"It sure looks that way to me."

"What can we do about it?"

I huffed, and they both glanced my way. I held up my hands. "Uh... it seems kind of obvious. We need to figure out which one of your enemies would benefit from your demise, right? I mean... not literally, but if your business took a hit, who would benefit from that?"

Uncle Joey nodded, already thinking of a few people who held grudges against him. "I might need you to help me out with that." He thought it shouldn't take long to find the person responsible if I was involved.

"You make a good point," I agreed. "But can we do that tomorrow? I've got a birthday present I need to deliver."

He nodded. "That's right." He opened his drawer and pulled out a key fob. "I just had it detailed, so it's as good as new."

"Oh wow... that's great!"

He thought it would be fun to see Josh's face in person, but he didn't want to imply that the car was from him. "Take lots of pictures so you can show them to us tomorrow."

"I will. Thanks."

"What about your car?" Ramos asked. "You leaving it here?"

"Yeah. But it's okay. Chris can give me a ride tomorrow."

Ramos nodded. "Well, if it doesn't work out, I'll pick you up."

"Sweet. Thanks... I'll let you know if I need it, but I should be fine." As I turned to leave, I waved. "See you."

Making my way to the Jeep Wrangler, I tried not to feel too guilty that I'd rather have Ramos bring me to work than Chris... but it was only because of the motorcycle. That wasn't so bad, right?

I got inside the Jeep and realized I didn't know how to turn it on. It was keyless, and I spotted the button to the right of the steering wheel and pushed. Nothing happened. Now what? I was pretty sure that was the right button.

Maybe I needed to adjust the seat and put on my seat belt? Once that was done, I tried it again, but got the same result. Now I felt like an idiot. Maybe I needed to push on the brake pedal? Holding the brake down, I pushed the button again, and it started right up.

Now I just needed to find reverse. I glanced at the center console and the two sticks. One had a manual gear-shift diagram on the top, and the other one was a standard with park, drive, and reverse. Did that mean I had to push another button to indicate the type I wanted to use?

I couldn't see any kind of button for that, so maybe it was okay to just use the standard shifter? Still, I didn't want to break the car before I even got it home, so I swallowed my pride and called Uncle Joey.

"Shelby?"

"Yeah, it's me. Sorry to bother you, but it's about the car. I figured out how to turn it on, but I don't know which shifter to use. I'd rather use the standard gear shift instead of the stick one, but I don't want to do it wrong. Is there a button I need to push for that?"

"Uh... hang on." He covered the phone with his hand before coming back on. "Ramos is on his way. He'll show you what to do."

"Really? You can't just tell me?"

He hesitated. "I always say it's better to be safe than sorry, and Ramos doesn't mind."

"But—"

"You don't want to ruin your son's birthday surprise, right?"

"No, of course not."

"Good. He'll be there in a minute."

We disconnected, and I hoped that this wasn't one of those things that Ramos would tease me about. It wasn't like I was incompetent. I just needed a little instruction, that's all.

Ramos gave me a head nod as he walked up to my side of the Jeep. I rolled the window down and opened the door, ready to climb out, but he stopped me. "Don't get out. I just need to show you how it works."

"Okay."

He leaned in to check the console, reaching over me with his arm. The side of his face just inches from mine, and I pulled my head back to give him room. Barely a second passed before I leaned closer to his neck and breathed in his heavenly scent.

I may have sniffed louder than normal, because his lips curved up, and he turned his head slightly toward me. "It looks like you've figured out how to start it. Do you want to use the stick shift, or the standard shift?"

His closeness, along with his low voice, sent a pulse of awareness through me, and I swallowed. "The manual..." Realizing my mistake I shook my head. "I mean... the standard one... where you don't have to use the shifting pedal."

He chewed on his cheek to keep from smiling, happy that I got so flustered at his close proximity. Drawing out the moment, his gaze flicked to my lips before returning to the console. "In that case, you just use this one to put the Jeep into reverse. But if you were using the stick, all you'd need to do is push in the clutch with your foot, and start out in first gear with this one."

He spoke slowly, and his voice was barely above a low growl, sending shivers down my spine. I'd tried to keep focused on his hands, but he quit talking, so I glanced at his face, and my gaze settled on his lips.

"It's pretty straightforward. Got it?"

He pulled back slightly, and I could finally breathe again. I swallowed. "Yes. I've got it. Thanks."

Nodding, he pulled his head out of the car. "Do you need to take a turn around the parking lot? Just to get comfortable?"

"No, no. I'm sure I'll be fine. Thanks for your help."

"Okay." He moved to shut the door, but hesitated. "One more thing."

"What's that?"

"I think I deserve something for helping you."

My brows rose. "Like what?"

He touched his cheek with his forefinger. "Just a kiss, right there." He leaned in close, just like he had before, making it easy to peck his cheek.

"Fine." My voice sounded a little breathless, and I may have given in too quickly, but it was getting late, and I needed to get home before Josh did. Closing the gap to his face, I puckered my lips to kiss the spot on his cheek. Before I made contact, he turned his face in a classic move, and I ended up kissing the side of his mouth.

Before I could pull back, he turned so that his lips captured mine. He tugged on them slightly, drawing me closer, with a teasing invitation for something more. Before I could give in, he pulled away, tugging on my lower lip and leaving me breathless.

Anger tightened my chest. "Hey!"

Still standing between me and the door, he raised a brow, thinking that was way easier than it should have been. Even better, I'd enjoyed it, and... was I angry because he'd stopped?

I gasped. "Of course not. You shouldn't have done that. It was wrong."

His mouth twisted into that lopsided grin of his, and he stepped back, thinking I'd forgotten that he was a bad guy. "You're right. I'll apologize later if it will make you feel better." Moving to close the door, he hesitated. "Tell Josh happy birthday." After shutting the door, he retraced his steps back to the elevator.

Fuming, I took a deep breath and tried to calm my racing heart. He'd better apologize. That was not my fault. He couldn't do stuff like that. Jeez. I huffed out a breath and shook my head, doing my best not to listen to the part of me that had enjoyed it immensely... and wanted more... a lot more. Gah! I was going to hell for sure.

I barely made it home in time to park in the driveway and run inside to get the huge bow I'd bought. Chris drove in right after me and pulled into the garage so Josh's car was the only one in the driveway.

With five minutes to spare, we looked over the Jeep to make sure it was ready. I picked up that Chris wanted to take it for a spin. Then he was thinking that maybe he should get the Jeep, and give Josh his car. I could definitely relate to that. What did it say that your kid had a nicer car than you?

"We'll share with him... right?" I asked Chris.

"I hope we're doing the right thing."

"Yeah. Me too. You know Savannah will want her own car when she turns sixteen, right?"

"Oh hell... that's right. I'm not sure she'll be ready. I mean... Josh is ready because he's more responsible, but I don't know about Savannah."

I shook my head. "I guess we'll cross that bridge when we come to it."

Just then Josh's carpool drove up. I could hear a few excited yells before the car stopped, and kids erupted out the doors. They rushed to the Jeep, hardly giving Josh a chance to see it himself.

But the big grin on his face warmed my heart. Chris took several photos, and I was grateful he'd remembered to do that, because I'd totally spaced it. Then Josh came over and pulled us both into a hug. "Wow! This is the best! It's amazing!"

He opened the Jeep door and got inside. The rest of his friends crowded around, most of them jumping in as well. Of course, he wanted to take it for a spin with all his friends. I wanted to say *hell no*, but refrained and told him he could do that another time, after we went over the ground rules.

He protested, but it was mostly for show, and I let out a breath. I already had about five rules in mind, with most of them only allowing him to drive with me or Chris. That was probably not going to work, but for now, that was the best I could do.

After his friends left, he begged to drive it, and Chris went with him. They got back fifteen minutes later and had to go again because Savannah got home while they were gone. This time we all jumped in, and it relieved me to see how carefully Josh drove. He was thinking that the last thing he wanted to do was wreck this beautiful car.

Later, right before dinner, Josh cornered Chris and me in the kitchen and asked the question he'd been thinking all along. "So... did you get the Jeep from Uncle Joey?" He knew we had, because he'd recognized it from our time prospecting in the mountains. "Did he give it to you?" He was concerned about 'owing' Uncle Joey.

"It was his, but we bought it from him," I answered. "He hasn't driven it since that trip, and when I mentioned getting an extra car for you to drive, he suggested the Jeep. He gave us a pretty good price, so we bought it. I'll have to work for him forever now... but it's worth it, right?" I was mostly teasing, but it was good for Josh to know.

His eyes widened. "Mom... I have some money saved up. I can help."

"Good," Chris said. "Because we'd like you to chip in on the insurance." He shook his head. "Not the whole amount, but insuring a teenager these days is almost as much as a car payment."

Josh's mouth dropped open. He hadn't even thought about that. "Um... okay. I'll help out with that." He hoped he had enough money to cover it.

Chris nodded. "We'll figure it out so it doesn't drain your savings."

"Oh... okay." Josh nodded, relieved and a little shocked. Was this what it was like to be an adult? But he'd wanted a car, and he'd offered to help out, he just hadn't realized what it all meant. Still... it was worth it.

I hadn't wanted to spoil his birthday with a hefty dose of reality, but, on the other hand, it was good for him to know that nothing was ever free. "But you're okay with the Jeep?"

"I'm more than okay... I never thought a car like that was even possible, so yeah... it's amazing. And now I can use it when I go on search-and-rescue missions with Coco."

"That's what we were thinking," Chris said. "Although I'd feel better if your mom or I went with you the first time or two. I think it's in the rules or something... you know... because you're a minor."

He was just making that up, but since he hadn't looked into the rules, it could be true.

"Yeah." Josh nodded. "I think Lance Hobbs mentioned something like that. But I don't think it has to be you or mom... he could probably fill in, but I don't know for sure."

"We'll have to check with him." Lance was in charge of the local search-and-rescue and had trained Josh and Coco. As Chris thought about all the legalities involved, he figured he could come up with something, even if it wasn't already on the books.

Sometimes, having a lawyer for a husband really came in handy.

Dinner with the grandparents, followed by opening presents and giving rides in the Jeep, took up the rest of the evening. We had a great time, and it was a relief that everything had worked out.

Moving forward, I knew it wouldn't be smooth sailing, but we'd done our best to prepare, so I tried not to worry about Josh's newfound freedom. But damn... it was still hard to see him grow up.

The next day, Josh drove the Jeep to school. I held my breath as I watched him back out of the driveway and drive off. My shoulders sagged with a sense of loss. I'd thought having my kids grow up would be easier than chasing after them when they were toddlers, but now I wasn't so sure.

As the garage door shut, I realized it was empty, and my car was still at Thrasher. I'd totally forgotten that part. Chris had gone into work early since he'd taken time off yesterday, and I doubted that he'd be able to come home and give me a ride to Thrasher.

That left asking Ramos to come get me. Normally, I would have jumped at the chance, but after he'd tricked me into that kiss, I felt a little guilty about asking him. Besides, what would the neighbors think?

Before I could figure out an alternative, Coco nudged my hand and woofed *walk, you take*. Since it was another gorgeous fall day, I quickly agreed, and we started out on our usual route. Almost home, my phone rang with the ring tone of "Devil Rider," and I quickly answered. "Hey Ramos, what's up?"

"Where are you?"

"I'm just bringing Coco home from a walk. Why? What's going on?"

He huffed. "More trouble. Can you meet me at the strip mall where the jewelry store is?"

"Um... sure, but... Chris left early, and Josh took the Jeep to school, so I'm stuck."

"I'll come get you."

He hung up before I could ask him if he was on the bike, but maybe that was okay since I didn't want him to think that was all I cared about. Ha ha. Only now I had to jog home and hope I could get ready before he showed up.

It took me only a record-breaking fifteen minutes to pull myself together, which was a good thing, since Ramos pulled in front of my house a couple of minutes after that. He was on his bike, and dressed all in black, with his leather jacket and black helmet visor covering his face. It made him look dangerous and sexy at the same time, and was enough to make any woman swoon, so I tried not to feel guilty about getting a ride from him.

With my heart all a-flutter, I hurried out and met him at the curb. He handed me my helmet and gloves, thinking he'd explain the situation on the way, and I climbed on behind him. As we took off, I held on tight, feeling a bit like a spy who led a double-life. How cool was that?

Ramos enjoyed my tight hold around him before his thoughts turned to the problem at hand, and I picked up that it looked like someone had tried to rob the jewelry store early this morning. It was the same store that Hodges had owned before his death and was now under new management.

Naturally, the alarm had sounded, and the police had been called. They'd spent the morning working on the crime scene, but now that they were gone, Ramos wanted me to see what I could get out of the witness who'd seen the incident.

We pulled into the strip mall and parked in front of the jewelry store. The large display window had been boarded up, and glass still littered the walkway. Yellow crime-scene tape fluttered across the door, but the police were nowhere in sight.

I took off my helmet and shook my hair out so it wouldn't be plastered to my head. Ramos raised a brow, thinking I was like a different person when I rode the bike. It was almost like I was playing a part. The wife and mom part of me was long gone, replaced by a kick-ass vigilante.

I couldn't help smiling at that, but shook my head. "How much did they get away with?"

He motioned me toward the door. "Not much. After the glass broke, they grabbed a couple of things and took off. We figure it amounted to less than five grand in merchandise."

"Well... at least that's not so bad, right?"

Ramos's lips twisted up, and he thought it was typical that I always tried to look on the bright side of things. "Sure. But Manetto's not happy. At least we have security footage, so we know what they look like. But the quality isn't the best."

"Then it's a good thing you have a witness. Let's go talk to him."

Ramos nodded, but he held back a smile, and I picked up that something was off with our eyewitness. I tried to pick up more, but Ramos shuttered his thoughts, and I couldn't understand why.

He pulled the door open and ushered me inside, where we found the owner cataloging several pieces of jewelry that were spread across the counter. He glanced up, and Ramos introduced me. "Shelby, this is Dale Brinkman. He and his son, Don, own the store. Dale, this is Shelby Nichols, Manetto's niece."

Dale shook my hand, thinking that I looked familiar. "Have we met before?"

I didn't want to tell him that I'd been there the day he and his son had tried to push a stolen ring onto Dimples, instead of the engagement ring he'd already bought. "I think I've been in your store before, but it's been a while."

"Is that right? I hope we gave you a good deal."

"Oh... I didn't buy anything. I was just looking."

"Well... if you ever decide you want something, please come to me first. I'm sure I can get you a great deal. Better than anyone around." He was thinking that staying on Manetto's good side was more important than making a profit.

I nodded. "Thanks. I'll do that."

Wanting to get back to business, Ramos caught Dale's eye. "So, did you find anything else that was missing?"

"No... just those few pieces. I had to give the security tape to the police. But there wasn't much to see. There were two of them, and they wore hoodies, so their faces were in the shadows." He shook his head. "If I were to guess, it was more like harassment than a robbery."

"That's what it looks like to me, too." Ramos turned to me. "The only things they touched were the pieces they took, but the police found a set of partial prints. I guess we'll have to see if they're a match to anyone in the system."

A black and white cat jumped up on the counter, surprising me. It arched its back, and Dale reached over to rub its head. As the cat began to purr, Dale glanced my way. "This is Tux. See how his black and white coloring makes him look like he's wearing a tuxedo over a white shirt?"

"Oh yeah. He's so cute."

Dale nodded. "He sleeps here at night, so he saw the whole thing. I think he's a little traumatized though, because he wants a lot of attention. He usually isn't so affectionate." He rubbed the cat's head. "Aren't you a good kitty? Who's a good kitty?"

Tux meowed, and I almost made out a couple of words, but they sounded like *rat-face*, so I wasn't sure I'd heard right. I was just about to ask Dale about the witness, but Ramos tapped my shoulder and nodded toward the cat. He wondered if I could pick up anything from the animal, and it hit me that the cat was the witness he'd been talking about all along.

"Are you kidding me?"

Ramos's lips twisted, but he managed to hold back his smile. "Why not?"

I huffed out a breath and threw up my hands. "I don't think so."

"It wouldn't hurt to try." His challenging gaze met mine, and he raised a brow. "What have you got to lose?"

What could I say to that? My dignity? How was I supposed to talk to a cat, anyway?

"Did I miss something?" Dale asked, glancing between us.

Ramos clamped his mouth shut, leaving me to answer. "Not really, I was just—" I sighed, knowing Ramos wouldn't leave it alone unless I tried. "I haven't ever had a cat before. Is it okay if I pet him?"

"Oh... sure, I guess." He knew Tux didn't like strangers, but maybe he'd be okay with me since he was feeling affectionate this morning.

I swallowed and smiled at the cat, offering my hand for him to sniff, like I did with dogs. The cat pulled back and let out a weird *mrrowerr* noise. Before I could move, he batted my hand away with a swipe of his claws.

As I recoiled, he arched his back and opened his mouth, showing all his pointy teeth, and hissed at me. I jerked back, somehow knowing that he was getting ready to launch himself at my face. Knocking into Ramos, I grabbed his arm and pulled him in front of me.

Still hissing, the cat launched itself from the counter and landed mere inches from Ramos's feet. It barely touched down before it took off like a bolt of lightning and disappeared into the back of the store.

Holy hell! I'd barely escaped with my face intact. A few choice swear words came from Ramos's mind as well. He could hardly believe that a cat could be so dangerous. "Are you okay?" He peeled my fingers off his arm to examine my hand, finding a line of blood just below my knuckles.

"Yeah... it's just a scratch."

His eyes widened, and his gaze caught mine. "I'm so sorry. I had no idea—"

"Did he get you?" Dale rushed over to see my wound. "I don't know what's gotten into that cat, but like I said, I think he was traumatized by the burglary. Wait here and I'll get some ointment and a bandage."

As he disappeared into the back room, I shook my head. "That was... unexpected." I turned to face Ramos. "I don't think cats think the same way as dogs."

"Why's that?"

"When he first hissed at me, there was nothing but self-preservation in his mind. But before that, he called me rat-face. Can you believe it? Of course he called Dale that too... and I think he used it again as he ran off. In fact, that's probably the only thing he said at all."

Ramos held back a chuckle. "Okay. Rat-face, huh? That's kind of funny."

Dale rushed out of the back room with his hands full of first aid supplies. He set them all on the counter and opened a bottle of rubbing alcohol. After saturating a cotton ball, he held out his hand.

"Okay... let's see that hand of yours. I'll get it fixed up in a jiffy."

I held back, not wanting him to do something I could do for myself. But I picked up his desperation to bandage my hand to make up for his cat. Sighing, I gave him my hand and braced for the pain.

The alcohol burned, and I hissed just like the cat. For all I knew, I might have even said *rat-face*. He blew it dry before dabbing the antiseptic over the wound and placing two Band-Aids over the top.

"There," he said. "That should do it. Make sure to keep it dry, and re-bandage it with ointment every day for at least a week."

I raised my brow. "You sound like you've done this before."

His lips twisted. "Yeah... unfortunately Tux has a mind of his own."

"Is there a chance he might have gotten one of the burglars? Maybe that's why they left so fast?"

His brow puckered. "Hmm... I didn't see anything like that on the security tape, but there might be something. Let's take a look at it and see."

"I thought you gave it to the police?"

"Yeah, but I always have a backup on my computer." He took out his laptop and turned it on. A few seconds later, he'd found the surveillance footage and pulled up the one from this morning.

The quality wasn't the best, and, with the low lighting, it was mostly shadows and movement. The camera angle was centered on the cash register, but panned out to the windows.

With no sound, it was still a shock to see two people smash the window open. One of them began shoveling jewelry into a bag, but abruptly jerked away. After a slight hesitation, they both took off.

Dale kept the video rolling and, a few seconds later, a cat-like shadow jumped down from the display case and disappeared from view. "It was Tux! The cat got him. That's why they left so fast."

I shrugged. "Well... at least if someone turns up with scratches on their hands, we'll know it's them, right?"

"Yeah." Ramos was thinking it was a long-shot, but crazier things had happened. "Let's head back to Thrasher. Manetto will want an update." He turned to Dale. "Let us know if you find anything else."

He nodded, and we left the store. I took my helmet from him and grinned. "I've heard of attack dogs, but never attack cats."

He chuckled. "No kidding. That cat was ferocious. So it really said rat-face?"

"You think I'd make that up?"

"Probably not."

I shook my head. "It was totally rat-face." I shivered. "I don't mind cats, but I sure hope I never run into that one again."

Chapter 7

The ride to Thrasher was much more relaxing than the ride to the jewelry store. I wasn't sure if we'd solved anything by going there, but at least I knew more about what cats thought, so it wasn't totally wasted.

We hurried to Uncle Joey's office and explained what we'd found.

"Someone's targeting me." Uncle Joey rubbed his chin. "We need to find out who it is and retaliate. This can't go on."

I nodded, even though I wasn't sure about the retaliating part. "We'll figure it out." I assured him. "I'll check the police report and see if they turn up anything on the prints. Maybe we'll get a hit."

"Good thinking." Uncle Joey nodded. "In the meantime, we found a lead with the guy who got into Nick's computer. We think he works for a new start-up tech company that sells anti-virus software. The way Forrest explained it, they first break into your system, and then they offer to fix it. If you don't take them up on it, your whole system fails. At that point, they're the only ones with the right anti-virus program to fix it, so you end up working with them anyway for double the cost."

"Oh wow. So they weren't specifically targeting your accounts?"

He nodded. "Yes they were, but we think it was to get the virus into our system as well as Nick's. You know... kill two birds with one stone?" He shook his head. "It's ruthless, but it works."

"So you want us to go talk to them?" I asked.

"That's the thing. Forrest hasn't been able to find an office." He shook his head. "They have an on-line presence, but not much more."

"Maybe we could lure him in with a bogus company?"

Uncle Joey's brows rose. "That might work. Let me see if Forrest can put something together. You could be the point of contact, and we could set it up in one of the offices in the building."

I nodded. "Yeah. That could do it."

"Before you get all excited about that," Ramos said. "There's something else you should consider."

We both turned to him.

"There's a concerted effort here to attack us, and it's not just Nick's place. There was the restaurant, the construction project, and now the jewelry store. I think it's all tied together. They may only respond if you lure them in directly. Not with a bogus company... but you, personally."

He glanced at me. "There's a risk involved, but it might be the only way we get the person who's behind it all."

Uncle Joey nodded. "So we set a trap?"

"Yeah. So far, the people who've targeted our businesses have been paid by someone else, and they don't even know who it is."

"So how do we get to the person behind it?" I asked.

He pursed his lips. "Like I said, we set a trap for them. It's got to be good enough that it lures the mastermind out. But I have a feeling that the guy who went to Nick's office might know who the mastermind is, or it could even be him. I think he's the one we need to start with."

"Okay," Uncle Joey agreed. "I think you might be right. We'll have to spend some time to figure out a trap, but I'm sure we can come up with something."

Ramos was thinking it could involve The Comet Club, since it was known that Uncle Joey owned the business. The club would be a great place for a trap.

That reminded me about my visit with Paxton Savage, and that Elliot wanted to kill him. "Oh... speaking about The Comet Club. You have an employee there. Paxton Savage? You remember him?"

Uncle Joey raised his brows. They hadn't said a word about The Comet Club.

"Oh... sorry. Ramos was thinking about the club... that it might be a good place for a trap, and it reminded me of Paxton Savage."

Ramos narrowed his eyes, thinking that it usually didn't bother him when I read his mind, but this seemed like an invasion of privacy.

Oops. "Uh... sorry Ramos. I didn't mean to invade your privacy." Oops, now I'd just done it again. "So... anyway... you remember the guy? I mean... with a name like that, how can you forget, right?" I smiled brightly, hoping to smooth things over.

"I remember," Ramos said, his voice low and menacing. "What about him?"

"Um... he's interested in moving up in the organization, but I'm not sure you should let him because... well... he wants to be a hitman."

That surprised Ramos, but he could understand the allure.

Uncle Joey was thinking that he could understand why I'd have qualms about that, but good hitmen were hard to find. His brows drew together. "You don't think he'd be loyal to me?"

"What? You don't need another hitman... you've got Ramos. Besides, you're more on the law-abiding side these days, right?"

Uncle Joey grinned and let out a huff. "I'm just joking with you. Of course I don't need someone else. So is that why you brought him up?"

"Not exactly. I have a client who wants to kill him."

Now both of them glanced at me with widened eyes. "I know... right? It sure took me by surprise. But seriously... Savage is a bad guy. He's responsible for the death of my client's sister. Now my client wants him dead because the charges were dropped, and Savage got away with murder."

Ramos and Uncle Joey stared at me, and I realized who I was talking to. Especially after I picked up that Ramos wondered if I'd forgotten *he* was a bad guy. "Yeah... but you're different... both of you. You don't go around killing people in cold blood."

"That's right," Uncle Joey was quick to agree. "We've both changed. So you don't have to worry... I'll leave Savage alone."

"Good. Thank you."

Ramos twisted his lips. "How are you going to stop your client from killing him?"

I shrugged. "I have no idea, but I'll come up with something."

Ramos was thinking that maybe I should just stay out of it. What my client did wasn't my responsibility. And if Savage had killed his sister, he probably deserved it.

"But he'll probably get caught. Good guys don't know how to kill people and get away with it."

Uncle Joey raised a brow. "You might be surprised. I remember a time when—"

My phone began to ring with the tone from *Scooby Doo*, and they both froze. "Oh... that's Dimples, I'd better answer. You guys go ahead... I'll take it in my office."

As I hurried out the door, I picked up that they wondered what my ringtones were for them. I threw a little smile over my shoulder and stepped into the hall.

"Hey, what's up?"

"Hey Shelby. You busy? I've got some information on the case you'll want to see."

"Oh... sure." I hesitated, but figured that going over there right now was probably a good idea, since I didn't want any advice from a mob boss about how to help my client get away with murder. "I'll be there in a few minutes."

"Great. See you soon."

I poked my head back into Uncle Joey's office. "Is it okay if I take off? I can come back if you need me."

"Come in and close the door," Uncle Joey said, his voice like steel.

Before I could ask him what was going on, my phone began to ring with the tune from *The Godfather*. My eyes widened, and I glanced at him. His lips twisted, then he shook his head and grinned. "Okay... you can go now."

"Not yet," Ramos said. "My turn."

Since Uncle Joey had already disconnected, Ramos's call came right through, playing "Devil Rider" by Jodie McAllister. His eyes warmed and his sexy half-smile tilted his lips. "I like it."

Ugh! I rolled my eyes. "Okay... I'm going now." I hurried out the door, hearing their chuckles, and catching their mirth about *Scooby Doo* and Dimples. Well... at least I'd made them laugh. Still, it was a good thing they liked their ringtones or I might be in trouble.

Ten minutes later, I walked into the detectives' offices and hurried over to Dimples's desk. "I'm here."

"Hey Shelby. Thanks for coming."

"Of course. So what's going on?"

"I got the blood results from the lab."

It took me a second to process what he was talking about. "Oh... right. The blood on the money. We were going to see if any of it belonged to someone besides the victim."

"Right." Dimples's brows drew together. "How many other things are you working on right now?"

"Oh." I waved my hand. "Just a couple. Plus it was Josh's birthday yesterday. He turned sixteen, and he's got his driver's license and everything. He's six feet tall."

"Wow. That's nuts. So what did you give him?"

"A Jeep."

Dimples froze. Did I just say we'd given Josh a Jeep? What the hell? He'd barely turned sixteen. Didn't I know kids his age were way too stupid to be trusted with that much freedom? He'd seen too many accidents and broken bodies to ever make that okay. What was I thinking?

"You think Josh is gonna die? That I made a huge mistake?"

Realizing what he'd done, he waved his hands. "No, no, I didn't say that. It was just a gut reaction. I'm sure he'll be fine. Josh isn't stupid. He's probably the exception to the rule. Not all kids get... in accidents."

He was going to say *killed*, but changed to accidents at the last second.

I sank down in the chair beside him, all my energy gone. It was a mistake. I'd worried about that all along, but Dimples was right. Josh was still a kid. A really tall, good-looking, responsible kid, but still a kid. What was I thinking? "I was worried about this, but a car was all he wanted, you know?"

I caught his gaze. "It's so hard to say no to your kids when they really want something. I mean... he was even saving up his money to buy it himself."

"Shelby... I'm sure it'll be fine. Tell me about the Jeep. If it's a newer model, it's probably rated high for safety, so you shouldn't worry, even if he gets in an accident."

"It's a Rubicon... a 4ve or xv... something like that."

His brows rose. "Seriously? That's a really nice Jeep. It's a hybrid, right?"

"Yeah. I think it's nicer than my car. But the deal was too good to pass up."

"Oh yeah? That's great. How did you manage that?" He was thinking that it probably had something to do with my mad mind-reading skills.

"Actually... we bought it from Uncle Joey. He bought it when we went prospecting to find the gold mine and hasn't used it since. When I told him we were thinking about a car for Josh, he brought up the Jeep. He agreed to sell it to us..." I stopped before adding *at a deep discount* because Dimples's face had gone slack, and his brow had started to twitch. Oops.

I took a deep breath. "Anyways... you think he'll be okay driving a car like that?"

He took a second before answering, thinking that I just had to keep making deals with the devil. At this rate—he shuttered his thoughts. "Uh... yeah. It should be safe enough."

"Good... that makes me feel better. So... how about those lab results? What did you want to tell me?"

He let out a long sigh, knowing my relationship with my 'uncle' would always be a wedge between us. He hated that part, but it was only because he worried about me.

My heart softened, and I wanted to give him a hug, but I held back, knowing this was not the place or the time.

"Yeah... take a look at this." He pulled the results up on the computer. "The lab work is a lot better now than it was twenty years ago, and they actually got a hit."

"Really? That's great. Who is it?"

"A guy named Wade Keller." With a few taps on the keyboard, a mugshot of the man came up on the screen. He had shaggy, sandy-red hair and a beard, and his dark eyes looked flat and defiant "He's been in and out of prison for most of his adult life. Right now he's there for a bank robbery."

"Oh wow. But that kind of fits, right?"

"Yeah. And right here..." He pulled up the arrest record with all the information and scrolled to the last page. "It says he's getting out on parole at the end of next week."

"Oh no. If it's him, we've got to move fast."

"Yeah. But just so you know, the DNA match isn't enough to press charges. We need more evidence than that. So it would help if you could pick up something, like what he did with the gun or anything related to the murder. Want to go talk to him?"

I nodded. "You know it."

"Good, because I've already made an appointment for today."

"Ah... you had great faith in me."

He grinned, showing off his dimples and making me smile. "Of course. You're my partner. We show up for each other."

"You bet we do." I raised my hand for a high-five, and he slapped it. With good feelings restored, and our partnership intact, we left the office.

The drive to the prison, along with checking in, was becoming routine by now. Had it only been a few days ago that I'd been here? We waited in an interview room for Wade Keller, and I had a sudden case of nerves. What if he wasn't the one? But what if he was and I couldn't pick up anything that would prove it?

Knowing the fate of the case rested on my shoulders was a little daunting, but I straightened my spine. I could do this. My superpower would come through and, if he was guilty, he was going down.

The door opened and a prison guard led in a man wearing handcuffs and an orange jumpsuit. His dark-reddish hair was about the same length as in his picture, but had a few strands of grey in it. He still wore a beard, but it was even grayer than his hair.

He glanced at both of us, and I picked up his wariness. He had no idea why we were there, but with his release coming up, he wasn't about to do anything to jeopardize that. Whatever we wanted, he planned to say as little as possible.

Sliding into the seat across from us, he held his hands apart so the guard could attach his cuffs to the table. Then he met my gaze, and his dead eyes sent a shiver down my spine.

This guy was bad news. Instead of feelings, all he had was a deep, black hole that seemed to go on forever. No remorse, no love, no regret, nothing. I'd never sat across from someone so devoid of feelings before, and it was unnerving.

Dimples nodded toward me. "Keller, I'm Detective Harris, and this is Special Agent Nichols. We'd like to ask you a few questions."

I kept a straight face and picked up that Dimples had used that title so Keller would think I was trained for anything and wouldn't take any guff. I wanted to tell him it wasn't necessary, since being a mom to teenagers was about the same thing. Still, it helped to calm my nerves, so I appreciated it.

Keller shrugged and kept his mouth shut. He couldn't care less about us and what we wanted. Still, he was curious about why a special agent would want to talk to him. His crimes were too low-level to merit that, so we must want his help with something else. Another inmate perhaps?

"About twenty years ago, a gas station was robbed, and the attendant was killed, along with an innocent bystander. We're here because we think you might know something about it."

Keller huffed. "Twenty years is a long time ago. Why do you think I would know anything?"

"We found your blood at the scene. Does the name Kirk Wahlen ring a bell? He was the attendant at the gas station."

"I have no idea what you're talking about."

Dimples had expected that answer. "Then let me jog your memory. Your blood was found on a dollar bill at a gas station where the attendant and an innocent bystander were murdered. We know you were involved, so why don't you just tell us what happened."

Keller shook his head. "So you're saying that because my blood was on a dollar bill you found at some gas station, that now I'm a murderer?" He thought that even if it was his, it didn't prove he'd killed anyone.

"You lived in the area at the time, and you'd been arrested before this incident took place, so you had a record. Given your penchant for assault with a deadly weapon, it was easy to connect the dots."

Keller shook his head. We were searching for a needle in a haystack. We had nothing on him. "I had nothing to do with it. What gas station are you even talking about?"

"The one that goes along the highway near the old ballpark in Portersville. You remember that one, right?"

His lips twisted. After all this time, we were asking about that? Maybe he'd play along for a bit, just for the hell of it. It would be interesting to get our hopes up and then dash them into little pieces. "I may have gone there a time or two, but I don't know about any murder."

Dimples went on to describe the scene, how Kirk had been beaten to death. First, by someone's fists, and then, after being bound with duct tape, by being hit repeatedly with a fire extinguisher. Sometime during the beating, Rodney Shepard had interrupted. When he'd walked in to get his change, he'd been shot.

Not only was it gruesome to hear, but I caught flashes of it happening in Keller's mind. All the anger and rage came through, and my stomach began to churn. Before Dimples had finished, I threw up my shields to keep from throwing up my food.

This was way worse than I'd imagined, and this horrible person sitting in front of me with a sneer on his face had enjoyed it. Ugh! I didn't know how much longer I could sit there without puking my guts out.

"Excuse me." I jumped up and rushed to the door, pulling it open and stepping down the hall. Taking big gulps of air, I leaned over with my hands on my thighs and my head down.

"Are you okay?" The guard who'd been standing in the room had followed me out. He took in my pale face and shaking hands and wondered if he needed to call the medical team.

I shook my head. "I just need a minute. I'm a little sensitive, and talking to that guy was making me sick."

He silently agreed, thinking Keller was a piece of shit. "Would you like some water?" I nodded and picked up that he wasn't supposed to leave his station, so he signaled to another guard through a window on the other side of the hallway door and asked him to grab a bottle of water.

While he did that, I slid down the wall into a sitting position on the floor, letting the wall prop me up. I took some deep, calming breaths and started to feel better.

Dimples poked his head out the door. "Shelby? Are you okay?"

"Yeah... just give me a minute."

"Do you want to stop?"

"No... I have a question I need to ask. Then we can go."

The guard handed me the bottle, and I fumbled with the cap. He took it from me, twisted it open, and handed it back.

"Thanks." I knew I looked pathetic, but right now, I didn't care. After drinking about half the water, I leaned my head back against the wall and closed my eyes.

My equilibrium returned, and the panic subsided, replaced by a burning desire to nail that monster to the wall. I glanced up to find that Dimples had replaced the guard, and he offered me his hand.

"Ready?" From my reaction, he knew we had the right guy.

"Yeah." He helped me up, and we walked back into the room. I braced myself against the revulsion to look at him and sat down in my chair.

I could feel Keller's gaze on me. He couldn't figure out why a special agent would get queasy listening to a description of a crime, unless... was I related to Kirk? Is that why the case had been reopened? Now he wanted to play the part even more... just to see the bleak desperation in my eyes when I lost.

I managed to raise my gaze to his and even got my lips to curve into a tiny smile. "Sorry... morning sickness... it can strike at the worst of times."

His brows rose. He thought it made sense, but something about my cheerfulness felt a little off, so I could be lying.

I felt utter shock from Dimples. Why hadn't I told him? We were partners, and now, if anything happened to my unborn child, it would be his fault.

I sent him a little shrug, but that was the best I could do until later.

Taking a breath, I met Keller's gaze and raised a brow. "Wasn't there someone else with you that night? A friend? What was his name?" I paused, listening real close. "Oh right... Tommy... no... Freddie? No... Danny... that's right. Danny. Where is Danny these days? I don't suppose you've kept in touch?"

His face turned to stone, but his eyes darkened with rage. He didn't know how I knew about Danny. No one knew about Danny. If I hadn't gotten the name right, he'd think I was messing with him. "I'm done here."

He didn't care if leaving made him look guilty. He motioned to the guard, who came to his side and released him. He ignored us as he left, but, at the door, he hesitated. Glancing back at me, his lips flattened.

He knew he'd be out soon, and all he had to do was keep his mouth shut. I couldn't touch him. Then he'd be able to punish me for bringing up Danny. He hadn't thought of his friend for years, but if Danny ever spoke a word about that night, he'd track him down and punish him too. The tension left his shoulders, and his lips twisted into a tight smile of anticipation. He could hardly wait to put me in my place.

The door shut, and Dimples caught my gaze. Taking in my pale face and widened eyes, his brows dipped, and he cursed under his breath. "I'm so sorry. If I would have known you were pregnant—"

"I'm not. Pregnant. Sorry... I definitely would have told you if I was."

"Then why did you say that?"

Ready to get the hell out of there, I pushed my chair back and slowly rose to my feet, careful to make sure I wouldn't faint. "Let's get out of here, and I'll explain."

With a grim set to his lips, Dimples nodded, knowing it was most likely my reaction to the murders that had made me sick. He hovered by my side until we successfully made it outside.

Walking to the car, I took several big gulps of air and finally started to feel better. As we buckled our seatbelts, Dimples started the car, and we began the trip back to the precinct.

Dimples glanced my way. "So I take it he's the one?"

I nodded. "Yup. Keller's the killer."

"So what happened back there?"

I closed my eyes. "Your description was bad enough, but seeing it in his mind was what made me sick. That's why I had to get out of there. Keller thought my reaction was a little overboard, especially for a special agent, so he figured I had a connection to Kirk, like he was a relative or something. That's why I made up the part about being pregnant, since it seemed like a good excuse for my nausea."

"Oh... sure. I guess that makes sense." But it didn't make sense to him at all. Did it matter if Keller thought I was related to Kirk? It wouldn't change anything, would it?

"Probably not," I answered. "Since he's planning on coming after me once he's released anyway."

"What?"

I shook my head. "Yeah. Bringing up Danny really shook him up, so he wants to punish me. He wants to punish Danny as well, so I guess we'd better find Danny before Keller does."

"No kidding. So tell me what you picked up about Danny that will help me know how to find him."

"I picked up that Danny was with Keller at the gas station, so he's an eye witness." I wrinkled my nose. "Keller didn't think of him as a friend, necessarily, but as someone he could boss around. He never worried that Danny would tell anyone what had happened that night, because he told Danny he'd kill him if he did, and Danny knew he'd do it."

Dimples glanced at me sideways. "With friends like that, who needs enemies?"

"I know, right? But even if we found him, I'm not sure Danny would help us."

Dimples shrugged. "It wouldn't hurt to track him down. Since the blood match isn't enough to convict Keller, Danny's testimony might be the only thing to keep him in jail."

"That's true. So where do we find him?"

"It shouldn't be too hard. First, we need to see if Keller has any relatives or even anyone in his old neighborhood who would remember him. They'd probably know enough about Danny that we could track him down. Once we find Danny, we could tell him that his testimony would keep Keller in jail for the rest of his life. It might be enough to get him to testify."

I nodded. "Let's hope he will, because it gives me the creeps just thinking about that monster getting out of jail next week."

That put both of us in a somber mood. It was even worse, knowing that Keller would come after me if he got out of jail. In spite of the warmth in the car, a cold chill ran down my spine.

How did I get into these messes? I almost wished it was Keller that Elliot wanted to kill instead of Savage. But how was Savage any better? Where did these people come from? I shook my head. I needed my faith in humanity restored, or I might have to quit all my jobs for the rest of my life.

Back at the precinct, Dimples put me to work at my computer, looking for Keller's relatives while he concentrated on the old files for anything we might have missed. Knowing it was Keller made a big difference in how he looked at the information, and if there was just one other piece of evidence that could tie him to the crime, we wouldn't need to track down Danny at all.

My job was easy. I looked up the address where Keller grew up and found that a woman named Susan Keller still lived there. She had to be Wade's mother. After writing down the address, I showed it to Dimples. "I found his mother. She still lives in the house where he grew up."

"That's great. So far, I haven't found more information to use against Keller, so let's hope she knows who Danny is so we can track him down."

"You want to pay her a visit now?"

"Yup."

I sighed. "Okay. Let's go."

Another jaunt in the car took us to an older sub-division of Portersville where the small, brick houses all had shrubbery growing on both sides of the porch. We rang the bell and Mrs. Keller answered. After getting a good look at us, her eyes narrowed.

Dimples introduced us and she hesitated, knowing we were there because of Wade. She sighed, wishing things had been different. Why couldn't her son have made better choices? He'd wasted his life, and everything he'd ever done hadn't just hurt him—it had hurt her too, and he didn't seem to care. "You might as well come in."

"Thanks," Dimples said. "We just have a few questions about your son, so it won't take long."

After we sat down on her living room couch, Dimples asked her to tell us about Wade. She told us that he'd been in trouble all his life. Not only had he acted out as a child, but as he got older, it had just gotten worse, and sorrow lanced into her heart.

Finally, Dimples asked her if Wade had been living in the house twenty years ago. Her brows rose. "Uh... let me think. That would have put him a year or two out of high school, so yeah, he was living here. But he had a nasty habit of taking off for days, and I wouldn't see him for a while. Eventually, he quit coming back."

"Did he hang out with a friend named Danny?" I asked.

She hadn't heard that name in a long time. "Danny Fowler... yes. Wade hung out with Danny quite a bit back then, but Wade wasn't much of a friend. He bullied Danny and threatened him all the time, but Danny followed him anyway and did whatever Wade told him to do. Then something happened and they lost touch. I think Danny might have joined the service, but I'm not sure."

"Did you know Wade is getting released from prison soon?" I asked.

Her lips turned down. "Yes... but he knows he's not welcome here." She shook her head. "That boy has caused me nothing but grief, and I won't be part of his life again. So if you want to talk to him, you'd better do it while he's in jail, because once he's out, it's anyone's guess as to where he'll go."

She thought he'd probably end up back in jail after a few months, and she almost hoped it would happen. Thoughts of a confrontation with him made her stomach hurt.

A knock sounded at the door. "Just a minute." Frowning, she got up and opened the door. "What do you want?"

"Hi Mrs. Keller. I promised Wade I'd stop by for some of his old things. He told me you kept them in the closet of his room, and he asked me to get them before he gets out."

"Now's not a good time."

"That's okay... it won't take long." The woman shoved her way inside, but stopped short to see us sitting on the couch. Her hair was dyed bright red, and she wore baggy jeans and a crop top under a military style jacket. "Oh... I didn't know you had company." She glanced at both of us before rushing into the hallway. A door slammed shut, and Mrs. Keller shook her head.

"Sorry about that." She rubbed her nose. "That's Wade's girlfriend." She raised both hands in the air. "Don't ask me how they met, I have no idea."

I caught her general dislike of the woman. "I take it she's been here a few times?"

"Just once before. I told her Wade was no good, but she didn't want to listen to me."

"Yeah... I get that."

"Wade knows he can't stay here when he gets out, so I guess he sent her to get his stuff." She thought that Chelsea was really looking for the money Wade had hidden under the floorboards, but she'd taken it years ago, and it was long gone.

Once Wade got out, she figured he'd come looking for it. But it wasn't her fault she'd spent it, since it was the least he could do after putting her through hell. She didn't regret spending one dime of it, and if he didn't like it, too bad.

Yikes. I wanted to tell her to get out of town before he got released, but I kept my mouth shut for now. Besides, it wasn't any of my business, right? Still, if she turned up dead, I'd feel bad.

The bedroom door opened, and Chelsea soon came through the living room holding an old box. Her face was tight, and frustration vibrated through her body. She was thinking that the money wasn't where he'd said, and he was going to be so pissed. At least she knew that wasn't the only place he'd stashed his take, so she'd have to keep humoring him until he told her where the rest of it was if she wanted to get her hands on it.

Yikes. She was using Wade too? I didn't see how that could end well for her either, but it wasn't my problem.

"Thanks, Mrs. Keller." She hurried out the door, shutting it tightly behind her.

Mrs. Keller turned to us. "Sorry about that. Is there anything else? I've got things to do."

Dimples scratched his chin. "Uh... I just have a couple more questions. Do you happen to remember anything about a murder at a gas station along the highway near the old ballpark? It happened about twenty years ago?"

"Twenty years?" Her brows rose, and she shook her head. "I'm not sure. Why? What happened?"

Dimples explained the incident and told her that two men had been murdered there.

"Oh... yeah. I remember hearing about that. It was big news at the time."

"Was Wade around then?"

She inhaled, thinking. "Yes... he was. But, like I said, he was in and out a lot." She cocked her head to the side and her eyes narrowed. "Do you think he had something to do with it?"

I shrugged. "Maybe. Do you remember a time when his hands were all busted up, like his knuckles were bleeding... or anything like that?"

She grimaced. "Not anything specific." Her heart began to race as a memory took shape. There was one morning back then when he'd hid his hands from her. She remembered because he wouldn't look her in the eye after she'd offered to bandage them. It had worried her because his excuse didn't make sense, and she knew he was lying. It was around the same time as those killings, but she hadn't put it together.

Had her son killed those people? She shook her head and pushed the thought away. It couldn't be true. He wasn't a monster. "I'm sorry, but you have to leave now."

"Are you okay?"

She straightened. "Of course. I just remembered something I have to do." She surged to her feet and opened the door.

"Sure." Dimples stood, wondering what had happened to change her mind. "Thanks for your time. We appreciate it."

I followed him out, hearing the door click behind me. Whoa, that was rough. Deep down, she knew it was him, but she couldn't bring herself to face it. If it were me, I didn't think I could either.

We got into Dimples's car and began the trip back. "What was that all about?"

I told him all about the missing money, along with the reason for Mrs. Keller's abrupt change of heart. "I guess she spent what she found, but it looks like there might be more money hidden somewhere else."

"Well, I sure hope he doesn't kill her over it."

"I know... should we warn her?"

He shook his head. "We're not even supposed to know about it. So how can we? Besides, she should know her son by now. She'll leave before he gets out if she needs to. That's the best I can come up with."

"Yeah. I think you're right."

"At least we got Danny's full name. Now we can find him."

I nodded, but a swirl of dread tightened my stomach. If we couldn't find Danny... or if he was dead, keeping Keller behind bars would be next to impossible. That meant he'd come after me, and I wasn't sure my stun flashlight was enough to stop a killer like him.

Chapter 8

Back at the precinct, I sat beside Dimples's desk while he put Danny Fowler's name into the system. He found out that Danny had moved to New York City after receiving a dishonorable discharge from the Army. He had a few arrests on his record for smaller crimes, but nothing that he'd done time for.

Luckily for us, I knew a detective in New York City who could help us find Danny, so I put the call through to Detective Nate Hawkins, or Hawk, as he liked to be called. He answered right away. "This is Hawk."

"Hey there. It's Shelby Nichols. How are you doing?"

"Shelby? This is a surprise. After what happened last time, I never thought I'd hear from you again."

I chuckled. "Well... I thought so too, but something has come up, and I was hoping you could help me out."

"Sure... anything I can do."

"Awesome. I need to track down a guy who may have been involved in a murder here about twenty years ago. It looks like he's in your neck of the woods, and I wondered if you could look him up for me?"

"Okay. What's his name?"

I gave Hawk Danny's name and the other pertinent information he needed. After putting me on hold for a couple of minutes, he came right back on. "I found him. Funny coincidence, but he's a witness in another investigation we're working on."

"He is? That's nuts."

"Yeah. What charges would you be bringing against him?"

"He could be an accessory to murder, but we're hoping we can get him to testify against the actual murderer, and offer him immunity in exchange."

"Hmm... well, good luck with that. He's only helping us to save his own skin and stay out of jail, but I guess it wouldn't hurt for you to talk to him."

"Great. I'm actually headed to New York on Friday, so I was hoping I could talk to him that afternoon."

"You are? What for?"

"A wedding for my aunt. She was a nun for a while, but now she's found the love of her life, so she's getting married." I left out the part where she was Uncle Joey's sister, since he might not like that.

"Does she happen to be related to your Uncle Joey?"

"Oh... yeah. How did you know?"

"Hey... I'm a good detective. It's easy to put two and two together."

"You're right about that." Since I didn't want to talk about my connection to the mob, I quickly continued. "So... about Danny?"

"Well, how about this? Why don't I tell him to come in under the pretense of talking about the investigation he's involved in, and you can be here to talk to him about your case? That way, he won't be able to avoid you."

"That's a great idea. I can text you when I land at the airport, and we can set it up then. Will that work?"

"Sounds good."

I told him the time I would be arriving, and he said he'd make all the arrangements.

After disconnecting, I picked up from Dimples that he felt left out. He should be coming with me... it was his investigation after all.

"Oh... yeah, it is. Um... you want to meet me there? We're going in Uncle Joey's private jet, but you could still come on your own. Do you think the chief will approve the expense?"

He groaned. "Probably not, especially if you'll already be there, and it won't cost us a dime. But I'll see what I can do. Even if he won't pay, I might want to come anyway."

"I totally get that. Why don't you get Billie to come with you? It could be a mini-vacation for you guys."

"She'd love that, but I don't know if she can get off work."

"True... but it doesn't hurt to ask. Maybe if you promised her an exclusive interview about the case after we solve it, she could talk her boss into it."

"Sure. I'll see if that will work." He thought it would be nice if she could come, but he'd still plan on coming without her. "There's just one problem. I'm not sure we can get Danny's cooperation in time to keep Keller in prison."

"Yeah... we'd be cutting it close. But if Danny agrees to testify, couldn't you keep Keller in jail? There should be a prosecuting attorney and a judge who'd be happy to help you out."

"That's a good idea. I'll talk to someone today and get things started. But if Danny doesn't agree to testify, I'd better see what else I can find to keep Keller behind bars. Under no circumstances do we want him to get out."

"I couldn't agree more."

"Okay. I think I'll go update the chief and ask about getting a plane ticket to New York City. Let's keep our fingers crossed that he'll agree."

"I think he will. Just don't tell him I'm going." Since Dimples was already thinking that, I didn't feel bad about suggesting it.

He caught my gaze and shook his head before heading into the chief's office. As I left, I heard the "Kissed by a Rose" song, and couldn't shake the feeling that I was walking on thin ice with Keller. I tried not to worry that we were cutting it too close. What if he got out? Maybe I should go to New York earlier, instead of waiting?

This case suddenly reminded me about Elliot and his determination to kill Savage because he'd gotten away with murder. If Keller got out of prison and disappeared, it would be the exact same scenario. How was any of this right?

It was nearly four in the afternoon and time to head home. I hoped Uncle Joey and Ramos could figure out a trap without me, because I was ready to call it a day. I pulled into my driveway and found that Josh had taken my spot in the garage.

Letting out a breath, I pulled into Chris's spot in the garage. He wouldn't like that anymore than I did, but at least it meant he'd have to come up with a better solution. Who knew adding another car could be so much trouble?

Inside, I spotted Josh and Savannah, along with Chloe, Josh's almost girlfriend, in the backyard with Coco, so I grabbed a diet soda and joined them. It felt good to sit down on the swing and forget about the day I'd had. It would have worked out better if my hand didn't hurt from getting scratched by the attack cat.

That reminded me that I'd completely forgotten to look into the jewelry store break-in at the precinct. Oh well... it was just one more thing I'd have to do tomorrow.

"Hey Mom," Savannah called, coming over to sit beside me. "Josh has to take Chloe home, and said he could take me over to Ashley's house on the way. Is that okay?" She was thinking that she'd loaned Ashley her Kindle so she could read Jackie's book, but now she wanted it back so she could finish the story.

Crap. I hoped Ashley's mom didn't find out, or she might be upset with me. "Uh... yeah, that's fine."

"Okay. We'll be back in a few." She stood up and waved her arms. "Josh, Chloe. Let's go."

"Just a minute." Josh and Chloe were throwing the Frisbee for Coco, and Josh didn't want Savannah to think he was at her beck and call, so they threw the disc a few more times before putting it away.

"Hey Shelby," Chloe said. "Josh gave me a ride in his new Jeep. I love it."

"Yeah... it's perfect for him."

Josh smiled, still on cloud nine about the Jeep. "I guess we'll head out, but I'll bring Savannah home in time for dinner." Josh thought that, with the extra time, he and Chloe could stop for some French fries or a shake and hang out at her house for a bit. He sure loved having the freedom to do what he wanted with his own car.

I nodded. "Okay. See you in a bit."

After they left, I had to admit that it was nice to have another driver in the house, and now Chris could park in the garage, so it all worked out. Coco came over to greet me and sniffed my hand. He woofed, and I heard *you hurt, I lick.*

"Thanks Coco, but it's okay. Come sit down by me." He sprawled out on the deck with his tongue lolling, and I ran my hand over his soft fur. Pretty soon, the tightness in my shoulders began to relax. I let out a sigh. Dog therapy wasn't quite motorcycle therapy, but it was a close second.

The patio door opened, and Chris stepped out. He'd already changed into more comfortable clothes, and came to sit beside me. "I thought I'd find you out here. Where are the kids?"

I explained where they'd gone, and Chris raised a brow. "So we're all alone?" He was thinking there were some nice benefits of having another driver in the house.

"That's true." I snuggled into his chest, and he put his arms around me. Sighing with contentment, I closed my eyes. "Oh man... that feels so good. It's been a rough day."

"What happened?"

I told him the worst part, beginning with tracking down Wade Keller and interviewing him at the prison. "Hearing about the murder was pretty bad, but seeing it in his mind made me sick. I nearly threw up and had to leave the room."

He held me a little closer, and I dropped my head into the crook of his neck. "Then we found the address for Keller's mom and visited her." I told him how our conversation went. "Deep down, I think she knew he'd killed them, but she couldn't face it. Then there's the money." I told him she'd found it and had already spent nearly all of it. "Do you think she'll be okay? Should I warn her?"

"That's a tough one. I mean... would he kill his own mother?"

"He killed Kirk over small change. So... yeah... I think it's a possibility."

Chris stroked my back and kissed the top of my head. "I think she'll figure it out. I'm just sorry you had to see all that. It's hard for me to imagine picking up so many feelings from people. And seeing the bad things in their minds..." He shook his head. "It must be a real burden to carry."

I heaved out a sigh. "I never thought of it like that... but you're right... it's really hard... this case especially."

He kissed my head again, thinking that I probably needed a break, so it was a good thing we were headed to New York in a couple of days.

"About that..."

He groaned and closed his eyes. "What now?"

"It's not too bad."

He raised a brow. "Uh-huh."

I pursed my lips. "We found out that Wade had an accomplice, and he's in New York. I talked to Hawk and found out that this accomplice... Danny... is an informant for the police on another case, so Hawk's going to have him come in, and Dimples and I can question him. If we can get him to testify against Wade, it'll solve everything."

"So Dimples is going?"

"Yeah... if he can get the chief to spring for the airfare."

Chris sighed. "But what if the informant won't testify?"

"Dimples is working on an alternative solution."

His brow dipped. "And when does Keller get out of prison?"

"The end of next week."

Chris shook his head, thinking that Dimples needed to get a prosecuting attorney on it right away. "He'll have to work fast then."

"Yeah... Dimples thought of that too."

"Good."

Chris's stomach growled, and I glanced up at him. "Somebody's hungry."

"Yeah... I missed lunch today." He leaned down and captured my lips in a sweet kiss. "If we get take-out, that will give us more time for something else." He was thinking of sexy times, but he could start with a foot massage and work his way up if that helped me forget my troubles.

"Hell yeah."

The rest of the night went by without any major problems. We spent a good amount of time planning for our trip with the kids, and it seemed crazy that we'd be leaving for New York the day after tomorrow. Savannah's whining to stay a little longer didn't sway anyone, mostly because we all had to get back to school and work.

Later, after those promised sexy times, I snuggled in bed with Chris, happy and content to be loved by such an amazing man. As I drifted off to sleep, I realized I hadn't told Chris a thing about what was happening with Uncle Joey. I hadn't mentioned Elliot or his sister, Zoe, either.

Hopefully Uncle Joey had figured out a plan to stop his antagonist, but I had no idea what to do about Elliot. Since I didn't want Zoe to haunt me for the rest of my life, I knew I'd better talk to Elliot soon, before he did something we'd both regret.

The next morning dawned with cooler temperatures and gray skies. I braved the north wind and took Coco on a brisk walk. The wind grabbed what remained of the leaves, plucking them from bare branches, pushing them into fences, and scattering them down the sidewalks.

My cheeks and nose were red by the time I got home, but at least the walk had warmed me up. After a shower, I got ready for the day. Knowing it was too chilly for a motorcycle ride, I wore my blue jeans and a light sweater that would keep me warm under my leather jacket.

With luck, maybe I could get a new jacket today. I'd have to corner Ramos and see what he thought. It would be nice to take it to New York with me. I could tell Ramos I needed it to help cheer me up, and he wouldn't be able to resist.

My phone rang with my fallback ringtone, which usually meant it was a spam call. I checked it just to make sure, and Bob Spicer's name came up on the display. I hesitated only a moment before answering. "Hello?"

"Shelby, it's Bob Spicer. I'm just calling to remind you of your appointment this morning."

Hmm... he really didn't want me to get out of it, did he? "Sure. I'll be there. It's at nine, right?"

"Yeah... in fifteen minutes."

"Oh, crap. I might be a little late, but I'll get there as soon as I can."

"No worries... I'll see you soon."

I slipped on my boots and hurried out the door, making it to the police station only a few minutes late. I skipped the detectives' offices and went straight to Bob's door, finding it open with Bob sitting behind his desk. "Hey there. I made it."

"Shelby! It's good to see you. Come on in." He was thinking that it was a good thing he'd called, or I would have missed it.

"Thanks for the reminder. I've had a lot on my plate lately and totally spaced it."

"No problem. So, how are you doing? I heard you were helping Detective Harris with a rather grisly cold case. How's that going?"

"It's going all right. We found the killer, who happens to be in prison for something else, but proving it will be a challenge."

"How do you know he did it?"

I shrugged. "I picked it up from his... I mean... I got it with my premonitions."

Bob nodded, but he knew something was off. What had I been about to say? "So your premonitions told you he was guilty?"

"No... there was more to it than that."

"Like what? I don't understand."

It irked me that he thought I'd base the killer's guilt on premonitions alone, but how could I explain it otherwise? "I know when someone's lying, and he lied about everything."

"So that's how you knew he was guilty?"

I let out a huff. "No. Normally I get them to confess."

"So this guy confessed?"

"No. But I know he did it. Anyway, we have information about an accomplice, so if the accomplice confirms it and agrees to testify, we'll have enough to put him away."

"I see... that's amazing that you could pick all of that up just from talking to him." If he didn't know better, he'd say there was a lot more to my premonitions than I let on. What if I could hear thoughts? That would explain a lot. But how could that be possible? Maybe he'd try something and see what happened.

"Last time we spoke, you worried that all of your experiences were making you callous and unfeeling. Do you still feel that way?"

I shrugged. "Not so much anymore, but now I'm worried that it's affecting my positivity. It's easier for me to think the worst of people, and I don't like doing that." I glanced down at my purse and rummaged through it to find my lip gloss.

It was just the moment he needed to test his theory. Covering his mouth, he thought *maybe you need a break,* hoping that I'd answer his thoughts and confirm his suspicions.

I glanced up at him. "I am headed to New York on Friday, so that will give me a break from all this."

His eyes widened. "That's just what I was thinking."

"Really? That I was going to New York?"

"No... that you might need a break. Maybe you picked up on that with your premonitions... that's amazing."

"Yeah... maybe." I hoped I didn't sound too sarcastic, but I was ready to quit playing this little game of his. "Well, I've got to go, but this has been a good talk. I'll stop by sometime next week."

Since he was thinking that exact same thing, I hoped it appeased him enough that he'd quit trying to trap me.

"That's... sure... sounds good." As I headed out the door, he raised his hand. "And don't forget to keep up with your meditation exercises before you go to sleep."

"I won't. Thanks. See ya." I sent him a smile and stepped into the hallway. As I hurried through the building toward the detectives' offices, I let out a sigh, a little shocked that he'd tried to trap me. Then I started to chuckle. He totally gave himself away by thinking about tricking me. How ironic was that?

"What's so funny?" Dimples asked.

Somehow, I'd made it all the way to his desk without noticing. Shaking my head, I sat down in the chair beside him. "I just had an appointment with Bob Spicer. He thought about tricking me into answering his thoughts, but since he thought about it first, it didn't work."

"Oh yeah... that is kind of funny."

"Yup. So... are you coming to New York?"

He grinned, making his dimples swirl. "I sure am."

"Saweet!"

"Yeah. I'm catching an early flight Friday morning. Billie couldn't come, so I'll be coming back the next day. You have any good ideas on where I can stay?"

"Of course. You have to stay at the Hotel Perona. I'll call them right now and get you a reservation. It's the best."

He nodded, but he was thinking he only had three hundred dollars for the hotel, so it was probably out of his budget.

"I'm sure I can get you a room for that price."

His eyes brightened. "Really? Okay. Thanks." Then he thought it might be awkward staying in Uncle Joey's hotel, and his shoulders slumped.

"Don't worry... he owns it, but his cousin runs it. The cousins aren't in the business, so it's no big deal. Besides... you're not going to be there long enough to run into him."

He let out a sigh. "Are you sure?"

"Yup." I put the call through and was surprised to hear Frank's voice on the other end.

"Hotel Perona. This is Frank Manetto. Would you like to book a reservation?"

"Hi Frank. This is Shelby. How are you doing?"

"Shelby! What a nice surprise. You're still coming on Friday aren't you?"

"Yes. We're all looking forward to seeing you. I just wondered if you might have an extra room on Friday night for a friend of mine."

"Certainly. Would you like them on the same floor as you guys?"

"Oh... that's not necessary... in fact... it might be better if he wasn't anywhere near the rest of us."

Silence met me, so I rushed to explain. "He's a police detective here, so there's a bit of a conflict. I mean... he and

Uncle Joey know each other, but it would be best if they didn't run into each other."

"So what's he coming here for?"

"We need to interview a suspect in a murder case we're working on. The guy lives in New York City, so we thought Friday afternoon would be a good time to do it. The detective will be flying out on Saturday. So it's just a one night stay, but I was hoping he'd be close so we could go to the precinct together. Do you have anything for about three hundred dollars?"

"Uh... I'm sure I can find something."

"Great. I really appreciate it."

"For you, it's no problem. But if Joey finds out, you have to answer for it, capiche?"

"Sure. I take full responsibility."

"Good. Give me his name, and I'll set it up."

We got all the arrangements made and said our goodbyes.

Dimples was still a little skeptical, so I punched him in the arm. "Hey... fuggetaboudid."

"Really?" Dimples raised a brow, thinking *don't ever do that again.*

"Oh come on... it was kind of funny."

"Maybe if it wasn't true it would be funny."

I shrugged. "I guess. But I promise you'll be glad you're staying there. It's the best, and it smells amazing."

"How does a hotel smell good?" He thought that most old buildings had a musty, stale smell. Did I like that?

"No... of course I don't." I shook my head. "I guess you'll just have to take my word for it."

He nodded, thinking he liked teasing me. His phone began to ring, so I left him to answer it and stepped to my desk. Since I'd wanted to look into the robbery at the Brinkman Jewelry Store, this was a perfect time to do it.

After booting up my ancient computer, I finally managed to log in. Searching through the robbery case numbers, I finally found the right one and opened it up. So far, not much had been done, which didn't surprise me, since there wasn't a lot to go on.

At least they had the surveillance video on file, and I got a perverse pleasure watching the cat attack the perpetrator. Nothing about the two criminals looked vaguely familiar, so I turned it off and decided to head to Thrasher. By now, Uncle Joey and Ramos probably had something figured out to catch whoever was doing this.

As I walked out, Dimples was still on his phone, so I sent him a smile and a wave. He waved back, and I walked out feeling lighter than I had coming in. It didn't take long before I was back at Thrasher. Seeing Jackie at her desk reminded me that I'd finished the book and had left a five-star review.

She caught sight of me and smiled. "Hey Shelby. Thanks for the review. It was great."

"Oh, you read it? Good deal. I really liked the twist at the end. Are you writing another one?"

"Sure am."

"Great! So how's it going? Have you sold many books?"

"Yeah... actually it's going pretty well." She didn't want to brag, but the book was climbing up the charts in the mafia-romance category.

"Nice! I'm so happy for you."

"Thanks. It's pretty exciting."

"I'll bet."

"Joe and Ramos are in his office planning something. Why don't you go on down?"

"Okay. Thanks." Once again, I hurried down the hall to Uncle Joey's office and knocked before poking my head inside. "Hey there."

"Shelby... come on in." Uncle Joey motioned me in, and I took a chair next to Ramos in front of his desk.

"Did you come up with a trap?"

"No but there was an incident the other day that now seems like it might be connected." Uncle Joey narrowed his gaze. "It could be the lead we need."

"What happened?"

"Remember the morning you spoke to Howard Hoffman for me, and Ramos and I went to the club to settle a problem?"

"Yeah."

"Apparently, the guy Paxton Savage beat up may have had ulterior motives. The club manager, Russ, spoke to him about it earlier. At first, Cal let it slip that Savage messed up all his plans, and Russ needed to fire Savage. Russ asked a few leading questions, but Cal wouldn't give him a straight answer. Because of that, Russ is convinced that Cal is hiding something." He shrugged. "It could be the lead we need to find out who's targeting me."

"I like it."

Uncle Joey grinned. "Good. Then you and Ramos can pay Cal a visit and find out if he's involved. He got released from the hospital, but he's still recovering at home. You up for that?"

"I guess so."

Uncle Joey frowned. "You guess so?"

I glanced between him and Ramos and my eyes widened. "That's not... I mean... hell yeah... I just said that because I'm sad that it's too cold to take the bike." I shrugged and glanced at Ramos. "Sorry. It'll still be nice to be with you, I just won't... well... you know."

He nodded sagely. "Get to put your arms around me?" He was thinking of how I liked to sniff him too, but he didn't want to say that out loud.

I caught my breath. "No. That's not it."

He raised his left brow and folded his arms across his firm chest, giving me an eyeful of his bulging muscles.

I sighed. "Okay... maybe it is, but you don't have to be so cocky about it."

"Come on." He took hold of my arm and steered me toward the door. "Let's get going."

I didn't try to jerk my arm out of his grasp. I probably should have, but it went against my principles of enjoying every touch he gave me, even this kind. I was going to hell for sure.

He let go of my arm on the way down the hall, and I tried not to sigh.

"What's got you down?"

I shrugged. "I was hoping for some motorcycle therapy. Without it, I'm not sure I can handle everything."

"Like what?"

"Oh... mostly the murder I'm investigating. I had to talk to the murderer in prison, and what he did—" I shook my head. "It was pretty gruesome to see it all play out in his mind, you know?"

"I can imagine. Maybe you should take a break from helping the police. Have you ever considered that?"

"All the time."

"So why not do it?" He pushed the elevator call button, and we stepped inside.

I pursed my lips. "Because... well, someone's got to stop the bad guys, and I have this... talent... so I need to use it."

He shook his head. "Not if it gets you down."

"Well... about that. I know something that would help me feel better."

The elevator doors opened, and we stepped toward the corner where Ramos kept his bike and his car. He glanced my way with narrowed eyes. "You mean besides a bike ride? What are you up to?"

I shook my head. "It's nothing bad, I promise."

"Uh-huh." If he didn't know me so well, he'd feel bad about that, because he could think of several amazing ways to take my mind off my troubles. "What then?"

I tried not to react to those amazing ways he was thinking about, and shrugged like it wasn't a big deal. "How about a new motorcycle jacket?"

His face relaxed, and his lips quirked up. "I should have known that's what you were after." He motioned toward his car. "Get in."

I sighed, but picked up enough to know that he'd already found a jacket and was just waiting for the right time to give it to me.

A big grin spread over my face. "Really?"

He rolled his eyes and opened his door. I slid inside and fastened my seatbelt. Sitting inside the black, sleek, sporty car, I inhaled the new-car scent and my brows rose. "Wait. Is this a new car?"

Surprised I'd noticed, he nodded. "Yeah."

"Hmm... I like it. I mean... it's not the motorcycle, but it's a good second."

"I'm glad you approve."

"Well, when it comes to cars, you know how picky I am."

He huffed. "And what is your criteria?"

I wanted to say *anything you drive*, but I managed to hold that in, grateful he couldn't read my mind. I didn't know cars well, so I shrugged. "I guess this one, or Uncle Joey's Tesla. They're both pretty awesome."

Ramos nodded, knowing I had no idea.

Since that was true, I sat back in the seat and closed my eyes, enjoying the smooth ride. "I guess it really boils down to who I'm with. I'm happy in just about any car, as long as I have good company. But it doesn't hurt if the car is hot."

Ramos grunted, thinking I might not be as honest with myself as I thought.

"What do you mean by that?"

His lips twisted. "Would you be as excited to be with me if I was driving a clunker car? Or if I didn't have a motorcycle?"

"But... you wouldn't be driving that kind of a car. Just like you'd always have a motorcycle."

"How do you know that?"

"Because I know you." He opened his mouth to argue, but I shook my head. "Don't even think about arguing with me. I'm right, and you know it."

He huffed out a breath and shook his head, a little surprised that I was so adamant. Still, he had to admit that it felt pretty good that I knew him so well—which meant I was probably right.

That cheered me up, and a big grin spread across my face. Still, I wasn't about to tell him that I'd be happy to be with him no matter what he drove, even though I knew he'd still have a motorcycle. It had to be in his DNA, right?

We pulled up in front of an apartment complex that was in a rundown part of town. Graffiti decorated the walls, and several windows were patched with cardboard. This place was even worse than the apartment complex where Savage lived.

Ramos parked the car on the street, and I had a sudden worry that his car might get hijacked. "Are you sure it's safe to leave your car here?"

"I think so. We won't be long, and I have a loud alarm."

"Oh... okay." I got out and waited while Ramos came around so we could enter the building together. Cal's apartment was on the second floor, so we took the elevator and stepped to room two-eleven.

Ramos knocked before moving to the side, and tugged me to stand in front of the door. "He'll probably open the door if he sees you first."

A few seconds later, the door opened, and a thirty-something man wearing a cast on his wrist, and sporting a swollen cheek and black eye, stood before me. His brows drew together, and he looked me over, trying to remember if we'd met before.

"Hey Cal." I gave him a bright smile. "Do you have a minute to talk?"

His gaze slipped behind me, and panic flooded his chest. Before he could slam the door in my face, Ramos stopped it with his hand and hustled me inside.

"Cal... that's no way to treat your boss's niece."

His gaze flicked to me before centering on Ramos. "No... of course not. Uh... come on in." Cal backed away from the door, and Ramos closed it behind us.

"Good." Ramos motioned to me. "The boss sent Shelby and me to ask a few questions about what happened to you the other night. Want to fill us in?"

He swallowed. "Uh... sure. It all happened pretty fast. That guy... Savage... didn't like how I handled things. But I swear, I did nothing wrong. If anyone should be questioned, it's him."

"Oh, we already spoke with him. Now we need to hear your side of it."

Cal sighed and slowly lowered himself into an easy chair, wincing with pain and holding his ribs. He motioned toward the couch, and we both sat down. "Fine. I don't know what he told you, but Savage is a liar who just got out of prison. He probably told you I'd taken a few bottles that didn't belong to me, but he was the one who took them. I was just trying to stop him."

Ramos sat forward, resting his elbows on his knees and staring Cal down. "I don't really care about that. I want to know what else was going on that night."

Cal's eyes widened, and he thought about the cash he had stashed away in his underwear drawer. "Nothing. That was it. Savage jumped to the wrong conclusion and lost his mind. He has anger issues. He shouldn't be allowed to work for Manetto." Cal absently rubbed the skin above his cast, thinking about the rest of the money he'd get once the job was done. "He'll do something stupid, and you'll be sorry."

"He does have a record." I agreed. "But we know someone paid you to make trouble for Uncle Joey. That's why we're here. Uncle Joey sent us to find out who paid you and what they wanted."

Cal knew that being on the bad side of a mob boss was never a good idea, especially with Ramos staring daggers at him. Instead of denying it, he decided to tell us enough to keep him alive. "Fine. I don't know a lot, but I know what he had planned."

"What's that?" Ramos asked.

"He wants to burn down the club."

I took a breath and narrowed my eyes. "There's a lot more to it than that." I turned to Ramos. "He plans to do it with you and Uncle Joey trapped inside."

Chapter 9

Ramos turned to face Cal, his whole body radiating danger and death. If I was Cal, I'd be scared out of my mind. "When?"

Fear tightened Cal's face, and his heart began to race. "Uh... to..tomorrow night."

Ramos glanced at me, asking if Cal was telling the truth. I nodded, and Ramos turned back to Cal, his voice low and menacing. "So, who is this guy? And why would you ever agree to go against Manetto?"

Cal closed his eyes, knowing he was in big trouble, but he needed to fess up or he was a goner. "I have some debts, and somehow, the guy found out."

"Debts to who?"

"Titus... he's the bookie for the fights. I owe him close to fifty grand." Cal lowered his head in shame. "A few weeks ago, I got a call from a guy who tells me he'll clear my debt to Titus if I do a few things for him. They weren't too big a deal, so I agreed."

He glanced at Ramos, his brow crinkled and his eyes pleading. "The first thing I had to do was easy, and I got away free and clear. He paid me five grand for it."

Picking up what it was, my brows dipped. "You broke into Uncle Joey's storage unit? What did you take?"

"How did you—" He swallowed, shocked that Uncle Joey knew his storage unit had been broken into. He'd been so careful. "It was nothing... just a shoebox that had yellow tape on it. It was marked fragile, but I don't know what was in it, and I didn't want to know."

Ramos pursed his lips. "Does this guy have a name?"

"He told me to call him Dagger." Cal shrugged. "That's the only time we spoke. After that, he just sent me messages."

"But you met up with Dagger and gave him the box?"

"No... I've never met him. He messaged me with instructions to put the box in a garbage can in the park. Once I did that, he sent another message with the place where he'd left the five grand. I found it where he said, and the money was all there, so I knew it was legit."

"So what happened the second time?" I asked.

"That was at the club." Cal chewed on his bottom lip, thinking that taking the booze wasn't part of the deal, but since the place was going to burn down, he'd slipped a few cases out, not realizing that Savage had seen him do it.

My brows rose. "What were you supposed to do at the club?"

"Just take a few cases of beer, but Savage caught me, and I ended up in the hospital." He hoped I bought it, because, if Ramos found out how involved he really was, he wouldn't stand a chance in hell. Ramos would probably skin him alive. Maybe it was better to keep quiet about the rest of the plan, because, if Manetto and Ramos were both dead, he wouldn't have to worry about being killed by them.

I shook my head. "You're lying. We know stealing the cases of beer had nothing to do with the plan. You'd better come clean and tell us everything, because, if you don't,

Ramos won't hesitate to put you in an early grave." I didn't want to say that Ramos was so mad that he'd probably do it anyway, and, since I didn't feel like stopping him, it could happen.

Cal froze. It finally sank in that he wasn't fooling anyone. How did I know so much? Had we already figured out the plan and we were just toying with him? But how could we know? He hadn't said a word to anyone, and Dagger was just a voice on the line. It made no sense.

Ramos shoved the easy chair into a reclining position and wrapped his hand around Cal's throat. "Start talking."

Cal raised his hands to his throat and tried to peel Ramos's fingers from their iron grip. Ramos held him so tightly that he couldn't take a breath or say a word. A gurgling noise came from Cal's throat, and Ramos finally loosened his hold, but kept his hand in place.

After a few gasps of air, Cal spoke. "Okay... okay... just ease up. I'll tell you everything."

Ramos released him before shoving the chair back into a sitting position. Cal held in a whimper, but he didn't dare complain, even though the rough treatment hurt his broken ribs.

"The plan..." His voice rasped, and he had to swallow a time or two before he could speak. "...after I got hurt... it got changed to tomorrow night. That's when I'm supposed to pour a few bottles out along the wall in the back of the storage room. Someone else will do the same in the kitchen and another person is supposed to spill some on the curtains and tablecloths in the main room. I don't know who else he got to help do it. I just know my part."

I shook my head. "How was Dagger planning to keep Ramos and Uncle Joey in the building?"

"I'm not sure."

He was telling the truth, so I knew we wouldn't get more from him. I glanced at Ramos. "That's all he knows."

Ramos nodded. "I'd like to kill him now, but he might still be useful."

"How?"

He glanced at Cal. "Can you get in touch with Dagger?"

Cal's eyes widened, but he'd tell us anything if it kept him alive. "Uh... yeah, I think so." He swallowed and took out his phone. "I can instant message him. What do you want me to say?"

Ramos narrowed his eyes. "Maybe you could tell him you're having second thoughts."

"Uh... but won't that make him suspicious?"

"No. Smart people do it all the time. You can use it as a way to ask for more money in advance. You know... tell him it's something to keep you motivated to stay in the game."

"Oh... right." Cal nodded, just now realizing that he had some power of his own.

Ramos continued. "Tell him that once you have the money, you'll be happy to go through with the plan; otherwise, you'll tell Manetto everything."

Cal shook his head. "He's not gonna like that."

Ramos's lips turned down. "Then remind him how dangerous it is to cross a mob boss."

Cal swallowed. "Sure, sure. Then what?"

"Then you'll tell him when and where you want him to leave the money, and we'll be there to take him out."

"And... if I'm still alive, you'll let me go?"

"I'll let you live, but only because you owe a debt to Manetto. It may take you the rest of your life to repay, but it's better than being dead, don't you think?"

"Right... sure."

"Good. Now let's work out the details and get that message sent."

After discussing things, we decided to set the time for tonight at eleven, and the place at a used car dealership with ties to Uncle Joey. Dagger would put the envelope under the windshield wiper of the last car in the southeast corner of the lot. We'd be watching from the diner across the street. After Dagger left the money, we'd nab him and find out who he was working for.

It sounded like a good plan to me, but what if Dagger didn't go for it? "Are you sure Dagger will play along? I mean... he's risking a lot for not much in return."

"Cal's silence is worth it." Ramos turned to Cal. "Okay... we're good. Send the message."

Cal took a deep breath and brought up the app. After typing in the message, he sent it off. We waited for a minute or two before Cal's phone dinged with a notification. He quickly opened the app and read the message.

I picked up the colorful reply and tried not to flinch.

"Whoa... he's mad," Cal said. "But it looks like he'll do it."

"Good." Ramos glanced my way and motioned toward the door. "Let's go."

"Wait." Cal's eyes widened. "What about me? How do I know he won't kill me when I get there?"

"We'll be watching."

"But what if something happens and—"

"You know what? Just be there... because if you don't show up, I'll track you down and kill you myself."

Yikes. We left the apartment, and I felt a little sorry for Cal. Ramos was furious with him and wanted to punch him for double-crossing Uncle Joey. He had a point, but at least now we had a plan.

As we exited the elevator into the lobby, an ear-piercing alarm started up. Ramos took off out the door, running straight to his car. Two men dressed in hoodies were backing away from it, and Ramos charged toward them.

They yelped and turned to run. The closest man stumbled over his own feet but managed to catch his balance and took off down the street. The other guy ran in the opposite direction, leaving Ramos in the middle of the street.

Swearing, Ramos pulled out his key fob and turned off the alarm.

"Whoa... that was close." I stepped beside him, looking down each side of the road, but both men had disappeared.

He shook his head. "Not really. They wouldn't have managed to steal the car, but it would have been nice to catch one of them." He thought how satisfying it would have been to punch someone in the face right about now.

I nodded. "Yeah... I get that. Talking to Cal was a little frustrating."

He huffed out a breath. "Yeah, but at least we got the truth out of him. Let's hope he shows up tonight."

"Yeah."

We got into the car and began the drive back to Thrasher. The plan seemed a little too easy to me, and I doubted that Dagger would show up, but it didn't hurt to try.

I glanced at Ramos. "Do you think it will work?"

He shook his head. "It'll take a miracle."

I froze for a second and then burst out laughing. "You just quoted *The Princess Bride*. That was awesome. I didn't even know you watched shows like that."

He wanted to deny it, but knew I'd pick it up anyway. "As long as it doesn't spoil my badass image."

I huffed. "After what happened back there, nothing could ever spoil it. Cal was so scared, I'm surprised he didn't... you know... have an accident."

Ramos snorted. "You sure he didn't?"

"Actually... no."

Ramos glanced sideways at me. "You're certainly taking this well. I thought for some reason you'd be begging me to spare his life, but you just played along. Why is that?"

"Well... I'm still on the fence about him." I sighed. "I mean... it pains me to say that if Dagger killed him, I wouldn't feel too bad." I shook my head. "That's not a good sign."

"A good sign for what?"

"That I'm a good person."

He burst out laughing. "Shelby... you crack me up."

I grinned back at him, realizing that he had no idea if I was serious or not. He didn't know the guilt I suffered. But, since most of it was because of him, that was probably a good thing. If he knew, he'd just try and make it worse. Then where would I be?

We pulled into the underground parking garage at Thrasher and got out of the car. I sent a look of longing toward the motorcycle and ran my fingers across the handlebars before we headed to the elevator.

"Humph." Ramos grunted.

"What?"

"If I didn't know you better, I'd say you were trying to give me a complex... you know... that you only like being with me because of the bike. But since you think the motorcycle and I are all wrapped up in one nice package, it really means that when you're caressing the bike, you're actually caressing me."

My eyes bulged. Was he right? "What? No way."

He smirked. "Deny it all you want, but you know I'm right."

I waved my hand dismissively. "Yeah... yeah... whatever."

His lips quirked into that sexy half-smile of his that always sent my pulse racing. He got me, and he knew it. His self-satisfied smirk stayed on his face all the way up to the twenty-sixth floor.

We stepped into Thrasher and found Jackie staring at her computer with a frown on her face, totally the opposite from earlier. I picked up that she'd just received her first one-star review, and she was devastated.

Glancing up at us, she tried to smile, but the reviewer's words had struck a nerve, especially the part that said "a real mafia boss would never act the way she portrayed him in the book." I also picked up the sentence that said her amateur writing skills needed work, and a real writer would 'show' not 'tell' the story.

Yikes. I glanced at Ramos. "Why don't you go on down to Uncle Joey's office? I'll be there in a minute." He gave me a nod, and I turned to Jackie.

"What's wrong? Is it about your book?"

"Yeah... a couple of the reviews haven't been the best, but this one is down-right mean."

"Let me see." I walked around the desk to her side and read the review. "Wow... you're right. They obviously have a chip on their shoulders." I shook my head. "I'm sorry, but—" I chuckled. "You have to admit that the part about how a *real* mafia boss would act is kind of funny. If only they knew. Right?"

"Yeah, I guess."

"You know what this means, don't you?"

She nodded, thinking that, if Joe saw the review, he'd find out who wrote it and kill them. She'd have to make sure he never saw it, although she kind of wanted him to kill the person for ruining her rating. One star brought everything down. This was terrible.

"Uh... you might think this is terrible, but you have to remember that sometimes one-star reviews are actually good."

"What? How do you know that?"

"Well... just think about it." I took a big breath and tried to sound optimistic. "I'm sure all of the best authors get one-star reviews. It's like a right-of-passage, you know? It means a lot of people are reading your book, even those who may not be into the whole mafia-romance thing. You should be glad you're reaching such a large audience."

"Really?"

"Of course." I glanced at the page. "Scroll up. I want to see how many reviews you have."

She scrolled to the spot with the rank and number of reviews. "Wow. Look at that! You're number seven in mafia-romance. And your review average is four-point-five out of five, even counting that one-star review. Plus, you have over three hundred reviews! That's incredible."

Jackie let out a breath and nodded. "You're right. That is good. I shouldn't be so worried about the bad ones."

"Exactly. In fact, I think you should be working on your next book instead. I really want to read it."

Her face broke into a big smile. "Thanks Shelby. That means a lot."

I shrugged. "Of course. Just be careful that Uncle Joey doesn't see that review. I'm a little worried about what he'd do, you know?"

She chuckled. "For sure."

"Well... I'd better get to his office. I don't want them to plan anything without me."

"That's true. You keep them in line."

I sent her a smile and hurried down the hall. Did I keep them in line, or were their cut-throat ways changing me? Slipping into the office, I caught the last of Ramos's explanation about our plan to ambush Dagger at the auto dealership tonight.

Uncle Joey nodded. "That's good, but in case he doesn't show up, we'd better see what we can come up with for tomorrow at the club." Uncle Joey glanced my way. "Shelby would be the best one for that, because she'll know who's thinking about starting a fire."

"That's right. I can be on club duty. But let's hope we get to the bottom of it tonight."

"That would be best." He wondered if Cal would survive until then. If Dagger was smart, he'd make sure Cal was dead long before that happened.

"You're right." Worried, I glanced at Ramos. "We should have brought Cal with us or found a safe place for him. Maybe we'd better go back and make sure he's okay."

"Why?" Ramos rubbed his chin. "You think Dagger will kill him?"

"Well... not me... Uncle Joey was thinking that."

I motioned toward Uncle Joey, and he shrugged. "It's what I'd do."

Ramos grunted. Why was I worried about Cal's death when, just an hour ago, I'd been okay with it?

"It's not the same thing. We need him alive for our plan to work."

"I understand that part." He glanced at Uncle Joey with a raised brow, and Uncle Joey nodded. Letting out a breath, he turned my way. "Okay... let's go back. We might have to bring him here, but I guess he can stay in the apartment."

"That works," I agreed.

We took the elevator back to the garage and passed the motorcycle on the way. "You know this would be so much better on the bike."

"Let's take it then."

My mouth dropped open. "But it's too chilly."

He shrugged. "You can wear a warmer coat."

"But I don't have one."

He popped open the trunk of his car and pulled a bag from under my helmet. "I've been saving this for the right time."

My heart skipped a beat, and I watched him pull a different kind of motorcycle jacket from the bag. It was black and gray, but had a touch of yellow at the waist. The tag said it was a Lady Gore Tex Jacket that was waterproof, breathable, and provided excellent comfort and protection all year long in a unique racing fit and design.

It was also abrasion-resistant, including armor protection in the shoulders, back, and on the elbows. With a removable thermal lining and collar, it also sported a surprising number of inner and outer pockets.

"Whoa. This is so cool."

"Try it on."

I pulled my cross-body purse over my head and took off my leather jacket, throwing them into Ramos's trunk. Ramos held the coat as I slipped my arms inside the sleeves. It fit like it was made for me, and the immediate warmth was heavenly. After zipping and snapping it up, there was only one thing left to do.

"Ready to ride?"

I grinned. "You know it."

Ramos handed me my helmet and gloves, and I put them on while he took out his gear. He'd traded in his regular jacket for one similar to mine, but in black, and closed the trunk to his car.

After tugging on his gloves and helmet, he got on the bike and started it up. He held out his hand, and I took it and climbed on behind him. Feeling just a tad wicked, and grinning like a crazy person, I wrapped my arms around his waist, and we took off.

The ride to Cal's apartment went by too fast, and it amazed me that I wasn't freezing my butt off. This jacket was the best.

After parking in front of the building, I pulled off my helmet and realized I'd left my purse in Ramos's trunk. Hopefully I wouldn't need my stun flashlight, but it also meant I didn't have my phone.

I glanced around, suddenly worried about Ramos's bike getting stolen. "After what happened earlier with the car, are you sure it's safe to leave the bike? Maybe you should wait here, and I'll go get Cal."

Glancing up and down the street, he frowned, realizing that I had a point. He spotted a couple of men standing in the doorway of the other apartment complex down the street. They didn't look like the same guys from earlier, and they were eyeing him with interest.

He thought about making me stay, but that might encourage them to come over. "Damn. I guess I'd better stay. But get him out to his car as fast as you can."

"I will." Taking my helmet with me, I hurried inside the building and took the stairs to the second floor. Stopping at number two-eleven, I raised my hand to knock, but the door wasn't latched shut.

A shiver of dread ran down my spine. What now? A shout came from inside, and I shoved the door open. "Cal? Are you okay?"

I caught sight of a man pointing a gun toward Cal's easy chair. "Hey! I'm calling the police!"

He spared me a glance before turning back and pulling the trigger. I blinked before stumbling back into the hall. With my heart racing, I took off down the hall to the staircase. As I shoved the door open, the crack of a bullet hitting wood shattered the silence. I ducked into the stairwell while splinters of wood flew from the door.

Holding onto the railing, I tried to take the stairs two at a time and nearly fell on my face. The door I'd come through crashed open, and I rounded the corner to the next level down, ducking low to avoid two more bullets.

Still running as fast as I could, I made it to the final bank of stairs and rushed down. Another shot rang out right above me, and I jerked toward the wall for protection.

The door on the ground floor crashed open, and Ramos rushed in, pointing his gun up the stairwell. Spotting the shooter, he took a couple of shots, giving me the cover I needed to rush down the remaining stairs. Ramos tugged me behind him and took a cautious step up the staircase.

Footsteps echoed above us, but instead of coming closer, they went up. Ramos immediately followed, taking the stairs two at a time. I followed behind, but he was already too far away to catch.

I continued upward, hearing another staircase door close above me. I wasn't sure how far up they'd gone, but I knew it was further than Cal's floor, so I decided to check on him. Worried that he'd been shot, I glanced into the hallway. Finding it empty, I continued to Cal's room.

The door was still ajar, so I pushed it open. "Cal? Are you all right?"

Not sure what I'd find, I hesitated before stepping inside. The living room and kitchen area were the same as before, but with one exception. Cal sat still on the easy chair. His eyes were open and glassy, and his chest was covered in blood.

The door squeaked behind me, and I whipped around to find Ramos.

"Is he dead?"

I swallowed and nodded. "Looks like it."

"Let's get out of here."

"But—"

"No. We need to go."

I followed Ramos out of the apartment to the stairwell, noting that both of us still had on our riding gloves. At least we hadn't left fingerprints, so that was good. I'd dropped my helmet along the way, and Ramos picked it up and handed it to me.

"The shooter?"

Ramos shook his head. "I lost him."

Before leaving the building, Ramos stopped me. "Put your helmet on."

I slipped it on, and we rushed to the bike. Ramos had left his helmet behind, but it sat on the seat. He tugged it on and mounted the bike. I climbed on behind, and we sped away.

I checked both sides of the street for witnesses to our escape, but there wasn't a soul around. Or, if there was anyone, they'd all gone to ground. Maybe shootings like that happened a lot around here, and people didn't get involved?

Either way, it unnerved me, and I held onto Ramos extra-tight, grateful that we'd made it out alive.

Back at Thrasher, Ramos parked the bike in his usual spot and helped me off. The adrenaline rush had worn off, and my legs were a little shaky. I managed to take off my helmet and gloves and slipped them into the trunk of Ramos's car.

Taking off my new jacket was harder, and it took me several tries to pull the snaps apart. Ramos had been quicker removing his gear, and he stepped to my side. His nimble fingers moved over the remaining snaps and tugged down the zipper.

While he worked, he was thinking that he never should have sent me in there alone. He could always get another bike, but I was irreplaceable. It was a stupid mistake that could have cost me my life.

"Don't be so hard on yourself. We couldn't have known that Slicer... or whatever his name is... would come for Cal so quickly."

"Slicer?" He shook his head. "It's Dagger, and I should have gone with you. Together we might have caught him. Now he's long gone."

Ramos helped me out of my jacket and placed it back in his trunk. Next, he handed me my purse, along with my old leather jacket. Still a little shaky, I slipped it on, grateful for the warmth.

"Well... at least we're both okay, and my new jacket worked like a dream... so thanks again."

As we stepped toward the elevator, his lips twisted. "Too bad it's not bulletproof, then maybe I'd feel better."

I chuckled. "Hey... I don't get shot at that much. In fact... this is the first time in a long while."

His eyes narrowed. "Yeah... right. What's it been? Two weeks? Three?"

"No... I think it's at least four."

He huffed out a breath and then pulled me into a hug. My eyes widened, but the shock only lasted a split-second before I melted against his firm chest. I took a deep breath, content to breathe in his earthy, spiced scent. "You know... this totally makes it worth getting shot at."

A low growl rumbled deep in his chest. "Yeah? Well I'm more than willing to do this more often... although I can't guarantee I'd want it to stop there."

I swallowed, knowing I wouldn't want it to stop either, and pulled away. "Thanks for the hug. I feel better now."

He hated to admit it, but he felt better, too. Shaking his head, he pushed the call button, and we took the elevator to the twenty-sixth floor. I didn't think Uncle Joey was going to be happy that Cal was dead. I also worried that we'd left the scene of a murder without calling the police.

How was I going to make that right? What if someone came forward with our descriptions, and the police figured out that we'd been there? Wasn't leaving the scene of a crime a felony or something?

"Do you think someone will turn us in?" I met Ramos's gaze, panic seizing my chest. "Maybe we should have stayed to talk to the police. I've never run off like that before. What if we get arrested? We shouldn't have left."

Ramos shook his head. "No one's going to turn us in."

"How do you know?"

His eyes narrowed. "Because of the neighborhood. Most of them know better than to get involved."

"Oh. Okay." That helped calm me down, but it also reminded me of the slippery slope I was on. I suddenly realized that Dimples's concern that I could get in trouble with the law because of Uncle Joey was a real possibility. Too bad there was nothing I could do to change that.

Chapter 10

We hurried straight to Uncle Joey's office and told him everything that had happened. His lips twisted, and he shook his head. "So Dagger killed him?"

"Yeah." I let out a breath. "We got there too late."

"Damn." Uncle Joey thought our timing was awful. He glanced at Ramos. "And he got away?"

"Yes. I tried to catch him, but he disappeared on one of the upper floors, and I wasn't sure which one. Since I'd left Shelby behind unprotected, I decided to go back. I found her in Cal's apartment. By then, Cal was dead."

Uncle Joey glanced my way. "How about you? You see anything else?"

"Uh... well, if you count Dagger, I got a pretty good look at him. Maybe that's why he came after me. So what happens next?"

Uncle Joey let out a breath. "We need to stop him from burning down the club. Cal said it was tomorrow night?"

"Yes. But do you think he'll go through with it now that he knows we know?"

"But does he know we know?" Uncle Joey asked. "Dagger may not have seen you there the first time."

"Oh, that's right."

"Either way," Ramos said. "We should head to the club and talk to Russ. He can help us come up with a plan for tomorrow night."

Uncle Joey checked the time. "We can go now. There won't be as many workers there yet, so we can talk freely and take a look around."

The *Scooby Doo* ringtone sounded from my phone, and I froze. Was it about Cal's murder, and somehow Dimples knew I was involved? Was he calling to tell me to turn myself in?

Ramos motioned toward my purse. "Don't look so guilty. Just answer the phone."

I nodded, taking a deep breath to calm down. "Hey Dimples. What's up?"

"Hey, I just wanted you to know that I got a prosecuting attorney to help with the case. When I told him that Wade Keller is our prime murder suspect, he was more than happy to get the paperwork ready to keep him in jail. There's only one problem."

"What's that?"

"We don't have much of a window. Keller's supposed to be released at the end of next week, but it's been moved up a few days, so we only have until he's released Wednesday afternoon. But it should still work out, as long as Danny agrees to testify."

"Oh crap. Let's hope he does."

"No kidding. Hey... I'm here at a homicide in an apartment building and wondered if you could help me out. No one we've questioned is willing to talk to us. It's like they're afraid of something. There's a lot of gang activity in this neighborhood, and especially this building, so that's probably it, but if you were here, you'd know what they're keeping quiet about. Could you come by?"

I swallowed. "Uh... I'm right in the middle of a meeting with a client, but maybe after that?"

"Okay... sure. We'll be here for a while. Text me when you're done."

"Will do. Bye." I disconnected and slumped in my chair.

"Everything okay?" Ramos asked.

"No. Dimples just asked me to help with a homicide he got called to." I shook my head. "I'm pretty sure it's Cal."

"How do you know?"

"Because he said it's in an apartment building and no one's talking. That's why he needs me to read their minds. Dang! Why do these things always happen to me?"

"Don't worry, Shelby," Uncle Joey patted my arm. "You handled it perfectly. By the time you're done with your client, it will be too late to help him, so no worries."

"Yeah... right."

"But don't forget that you have options when you help the police." He continued. "Take this case. Even if you helped him interview the people, you wouldn't have to tell him what they're really thinking. In fact, you could misdirect him, which might be even better. Then he'd never suspect you or Ramos had anything to do with it."

Holy hell. He was offering me a way out, but I couldn't lie about what happened. I'd never be able to keep it straight. On the other hand, I could help the police, and they might even catch Dagger for us.

I met Uncle Joey's gaze. "I could tell Dimples that I picked up what the killer looks like. That might actually work, and since we left the scene of the crime, it would ease my conscience. And don't forget that if the police are looking for Dagger, it will help us too, right? What do you think? Should I go help him?"

Ramos shook his head, knowing my propensity to say too much would get me into trouble. "No. I don't think you should be involved. Just come with us to the club, and forget the detective."

Uncle Joey rubbed his chin. "I'm not so sure. Maybe you should help Harris. That way you'll know if anyone saw you or Ramos leaving the building. You'd also know if anyone saw Dagger. They could even point us in the right direction to find him. Any information on him would be valuable to us."

I nodded, but my mouth twisted since I wasn't sure I liked the idea of being a double-agent. But, if we got a tip on Dagger, it would be worth it, right? Plus, I'd know if anyone saw Ramos and me there. I might sleep better tonight if I knew I was in the clear.

"Okay. I'll text him that I can help and head straight over there."

Ramos huffed out a breath, exasperated that I'd take such a big chance. "Fine, but make sure he gives you the address before you show up."

I pursed my lips. "I was going to do that." Ha! That was a big fat lie.

"Uh-huh."

I sent the text, and Dimples responded with the address and a thumbs-up emoji. "Okay. I'm all set."

"Good," Uncle Joey said. "If you find out anything important, let us know, otherwise, we'll regroup here tomorrow and come up with a plan."

"All right. I'll be in touch." I hurried out of the office and headed to the parking lot and my car. On the way back to the apartment, I went over the sequence of events so I wouldn't get confused.

The first time I'd been there, I'd been in a car, and the second time, I'd been on a motorcycle with a different jacket and a helmet. No one would put it together that it was me both times, so I was pretty confident I'd be okay. Even if they did, they wouldn't tell the police, right?

Dimples waited for me outside the apartment building. At least with the police presence, I didn't worry about anyone trying to steal my car. As I joined him, he gave me his biggest smile, hoping his dimples would do their magic, and I'd be glad I'd come.

"Hey Shelby. Thanks for coming."

I smiled back, hoping to fool him. "Of course. So what's going on?"

He explained that someone in the building had called in because they'd heard gunfire. The police arrived and found a man, dead in his easy chair, with a bullet wound to his chest. While they waited for a search warrant, they were canvassing the building for witnesses.

"Like I said, so far, no one's saying anything, but I've narrowed the list down to a couple of people who, I think, might have more on their minds." He tapped his forehead and sent me a grin.

Unable to resist his charm, I returned his smile. "Great. Let's go talk to them."

The staircase was blocked off with crime scene tape, so he led me to the elevator. "Why is the staircase blocked?"

"We found bullet holes in the walls, so we're checking it out." He thought the killer might have been after someone else who saw something... maybe even the killer's face. That's why he thought someone knew more than they'd said.

The elevator took us to the second floor, and I followed Dimples to Cal's apartment. He was still in there, and I tried not to gag at the smell of blood. Dimples knocked at the apartment across the hall and waited.

The door opened a few inches, and a silver-haired woman dressed in a purple sweat suit narrowed her eyes at us.

Dimples smiled. "Hi again. I know we spoke earlier, but would you mind sharing what you heard with my colleague?" He motioned to me, and I gave her a little wave.

"Hi."

Her brow dipped, and she studied me more closely. Wasn't I the same person who'd been there to see Cal earlier? Before he was shot? "Are you a cop or something?"

"Yes, I work with the police." Not wanting her to blurt that she'd seen me earlier, I hurried to my next question. "So you heard something? Was it a gunshot?"

She nodded, and her lips twisted. "Yeah... but I didn't see anyone. I know better than to stick my head out the door when I hear anything crazy." But that didn't stop her from looking out her larger-than-normal-sized peephole.

She'd had it installed so she could see what was going on in the hallway without opening her door. She didn't always see everything, but she'd caught sight of me and that guy I was with. She wished she could have seen more of him. He was one handsome man, and his backside wasn't bad either.

"What about when you heard the gunfire? Did you see anything then?"

Her lips turned down. "No. I already told you I know better." But she had seen a man rushing out of the room, and she knew he was chasing someone, but she'd missed seeing who it was.

The man had a full head of brown hair and a bushy beard, so it was hard to make out his features. Still, his dark eyes were on fire with rage. Plus, he was holding a gun. It had scared her to death, and she wasn't about to admit that she'd seen him. He'd probably kill her too.

"Did... um... your neighbor have a lot of visitors?" I almost said Cal, but luckily caught it in time.

Her gaze met mine, and her brows drew together. "You mean like—"

Before she could say *you*, I cut her off. "Like someone you've seen here more than once... maybe a girlfriend, or another friend who spent time with him? Anyone familiar?"

She shook her head. "Not that I could say. He wasn't friendly to me, and I've only seen him a few times." From his habits of being out late and coming home drunk, she'd intentionally stayed out of his way.

"Sure. Well, thanks so much for your time. If you remember anything else, please let us know." I glanced at Dimples. "Did you give her your card?"

"Yes."

She started closing her door, so I backed out of the way. "Thanks again."

She sniffed, thinking that, next time, she wouldn't open the door. If I'd been there earlier, I probably knew more about it than she did, and it was a—

The door shut, cutting off her thoughts, and I couldn't believe how close I'd come to getting busted. She'd seen Ramos and me. Crap. At least she thought we were with the police. On the plus side, I'd gotten enough to give Dimples a description of Dagger, so maybe it wasn't so bad.

The elevator doors opened, and a forensics team pulling a gurney filed out. Detective Bates followed behind them, holding a paper. He caught sight of Dimples and me and waved it in the air. "Search warrant. We can search inside now and find out who this poor bastard is."

Wearing his booties and gloves, the medical investigator entered first. He began taking photos of the body while the rest of the team slipped on their gloves and booties.

I stayed put, unsure that I wanted to go in there. But what if I had left a hair or something from my time talking to Cal? They were sure to vacuum everything up. That meant I had to go in, so I followed Dimples's example and slipped on my own booties and gloves.

He glanced at me and frowned, knowing how much I hated the sight of blood. But he shrugged it off, grateful that I was taking this seriously. He also thought I might pick up something from the dead man's ghost, so a little blood was probably worth it.

Yikes. I did not want that to happen. Cal would probably haunt me forever. Stepping inside, I hurried into the kitchen area before heading into the bedroom. I doubted that Dagger had gotten this far, but at least it kept me away from the body.

Still, coming inside the apartment brought it all back, and I remembered that Dagger had been standing in front of Cal with his gun pointed at him. I'd yelled to stop him, but it hadn't worked. He'd glanced my way before pulling the trigger and killing Cal in cold blood. I remembered it clearly now.

My knees got a little wobbly, and I sat down on the side of the bed. Studying the room, I noticed how nice and tidy the place was. It was small, but clean. I shook my head, sad that Cal was dead. Why had I thought his death wouldn't bother me?

My gaze landed on a notebook resting on the dresser. I picked it up and found an address at the top of the page. My heart skipped a beat to realize it was The Comet Club.

I contemplated slipping the notebook into my purse, but set it back down. The cops were sure to find out that Cal had made deliveries to the club, so this wasn't anything new. There might be something else in the notebook that would link Cal to Dagger, so I had to leave it alone. What about the money in his underwear drawer?

If I gave Dagger's description to Dimples, that would point them in the right direction. Then, if they somehow managed to find Dagger and bring him in, I could tell Dimples about Dagger's deal with Cal, and use the money angle to prove it. That might actually work.

I stepped into the hallway to find Dimples, but found the medical people lifting the body into a body bag. The smell of blood and all those bodily fluids hit me like a ton of bricks, and I gagged.

Rushing into the bathroom, I barely made it to the toilet before I threw up. Finished, I stepped to the sink, pulled off my gloves and rinsed my mouth out with water. After taking a few gulps, I splashed a little water on my face and patted it dry with a tissue.

"Shelby? You're not supposed to touch anything." I jerked a little, finding Detective Bates frowning at me and thinking I looked sickly and pale. "Did you throw up?"

"Yes." Straightening, I shook my head. "Is the body gone yet?"

"Yeah... they just left."

I sighed. "Good. I need to go, too. Is Dimples out there somewhere? I need to talk to him first."

"Sure." Instead of moving out of my way, he hesitated. "Did you pick up anything?" He hoped I'd tell him instead of Harris. He was on this case too, so why not?

I nodded, mostly because I wanted to stay on his good side. "Yeah... a few impressions. I think the victim was deep in debt, and that was part of why he was killed. You might want to check into his finances. Oh... and while you're at it..." I motioned to his dresser. "Check his dresser drawers. I have a feeling that he's hiding something in there."

His eyes lit up. "Okay. Thanks for the tip."

"Of course."

While Bates began his search of the dresser, I finally spotted Dimples and hurried to his side. "I've got something."

He took in my pale face, and his brows dipped. "Are you okay?"

"Yeah, but let's go somewhere else to talk... like outside?"

"Sure." In the elevator, I had to take a few deep breaths to keep it together. We finally stepped into the lobby and crossed to the doors. Outside, the chill breeze hit me in the face, instantly reviving me.

"That's better." I turned to face him. "The woman across the hall got a good look at the killer."

"That's awesome. Had she seen him before, or did she know who he was?"

"Not that I could tell." I explained what she saw in as much detail as I could. "She heard the gunfire right before he left, so he's definitely the killer."

"Great... thanks Shelby. Do you think she'll help us out? Maybe even be a witness?"

"I wouldn't count on it, but you never know." I closed my eyes and shook my head, still feeling a little queasy. "Listen... I've got to go, but maybe I can help with interviews tomorrow. Is that okay?"

He nodded, studying my pale face more closely. "Did you throw up?"

I nodded, hating to admit it. "Yeah."

"Damn. That's too bad." He elbowed me and smiled. "At least you're not pregnant though... right?"

I huffed out a breath. "Yeah... thank goodness for that."

He grinned and shook his head. "Get out of here. I'll talk to you tomorrow."

"Thanks." I sent him a grateful smile and headed to my car. Opening my car door, the back of my neck prickled, and

I glanced around. Was someone watching me? I opened my mind, but couldn't pick up any thoughts directed my way.

Still, I quickly slid inside my car and shut the door. On a whim, I checked the back seat. Finding it empty, I let out a breath. Was I getting paranoid, or was something else going on?

Starting the car, I pulled onto the street and began the drive home. I hadn't found out anything for Uncle Joey that couldn't wait until tomorrow, and I needed a diet soda and some crackers something fierce.

As I pulled into my driveway, it was nice to see the Jeep parked in the garage. That meant Josh was home, and I decided that I liked seeing his Jeep in my spot. Naturally, I parked in Chris's spot and hurried inside.

Coco rushed to greet me, and I heard *you home, you home.* It sent the stress of the day right out the window. "Hey buddy. It's good to see you, too." After giving me all kinds of doggy kisses, he rushed to the patio door, raised his paw to the glass, and woofed *play, outside.*

"Didn't anyone play with you yet? I mean... I'd like to, but it's kind of cold out there, and, to be honest, I've had a rough day. Let me get a diet soda first, and I'll see what I can do. I might want a cookie, too. Do you want a cookie?"

"Hey, Mom." Savannah came into the kitchen. "Who are you talking to?"

"Coco wants me to play with him. Didn't Josh throw the Frisbee with him when he got home?"

She shrugged. "I don't know. Maybe."

I glanced at Coco. "Didn't Josh already play with you?"

Him no play, Josh sad, no like.

"What happened to Josh?"

Him sad.

"That's not good. I'd better go talk to him."

"Mom? What's going on?" Savannah glanced between me and Coco. "Are you... is Coco talking to you?"

Oops. "Uh... not exactly, but I'm picking up something about Josh. Did he seem upset to you?"

Savannah's brows dipped. He hadn't been very nice to her today, but that wasn't anything new. "I don't know. What are you getting from Coco?"

"He says Josh is sad. I'm going to go talk to him."

Her brows rose. "Wow. That's nuts. You got all that from Coco?"

"Yeah. But don't forget how smart Coco is."

Coco woofed *Play, now.*

"See? He still wants to play." I twisted my lips and glanced at Savannah. "Hey... do you mind throwing the Frisbee for a minute? I mean... look at him. Isn't he adorable? How can you resist that face?"

Savannah rolled her eyes. "Okay, fine." She stepped to the patio door and opened it. Coco bounded out, full of excitement, and Savannah followed. She tried to act like she was doing me a favor, but deep down, she enjoyed playing with Coco. He was the best dog ever.

I nodded, glad to know that she really did care, and took a swig of soda. I grabbed a couple of cookies before heading down to the basement. I paused to knock on his door and waited. "Josh? You in there?"

"Yeah. What do you want?"

"I brought you a cookie."

A few seconds later, the door opened, and I handed him the cookie. "Thanks." He glanced at me, knowing I was up to something. "What?"

"I just found out that you didn't throw the Frisbee for Coco and he's sad."

"Coco's sad?" Josh shook his head. Sometimes I said the weirdest things. "So?"

"So, is something wrong?"

Josh frowned. "Like what?"

I shrugged. "I don't know. But something's got you down. What is it?"

Knowing I wasn't going to leave him alone until I got an answer, he sighed. "It's nothing. I'm just frustrated with soccer practice. One of the players won't ever pass me the ball when I'm open. It's stupid. It's like he's got something against me, but I can't think of anything I've ever done to him."

"Oh... that's too bad."

He shook his head. "It's okay. I think the coach is getting frustrated with him too, so I think he'll talk to him." He huffed out a breath. "It's just stupid to play a team sport if you're not willing to be a team player. You know?"

I nodded. "Of course, I'm sure that's frustrating."

"Yeah... I was really mad." He quirked a brow. "So... Coco was sad? Because of me? You got that from your premonitions?"

"Yup."

Guilt crept up his neck. "Maybe I'll go play with him." He hurried past me and up the stairs to the backyard. I didn't have the heart to tell him that he'd been replaced by Savannah, but it wouldn't hurt to have them both out there at the same time. Who knew? Maybe they'd even have fun?

Later that night, I filled Chris in on my day. I sort of left out the part where I got shot at, and concentrated on the part where Dimples called to ask for my help in solving

Cal's murder. "So I went back to the apartment and helped him. Isn't that nuts?"

Chris stared at me, his mind swirling with incredulity. How in the hell did these things happen to me? "Wait... so Cal made a deal with someone named Dagger to burn down The Comet Club?"

"Yup."

"And you went to Cal's apartment and saw Dagger kill him?"

"Uh... I didn't exactly see it, because I took off running... but I heard the gunshot... so yeah, I saw Dagger."

Chris shook his head, his blood pressure soaring to new heights. "And you told Dimples?"

"Not that I saw him, but that the neighbor across the hall saw him... which she totally did."

"So she's a witness?"

"Maybe." I didn't want to tell him that she didn't want to be involved, or that she'd seen me and Ramos there earlier. I mean... I was in enough trouble already. "But it's okay because now the police are looking for Dagger. Don't you think it would be best if the police found him before Uncle Joey did?"

"I don't know." Chris was thinking that if Manetto found Dagger, he'd probably kill him, which might be better for me. Because if Dagger was dead, he couldn't tell the police that I'd been there, or worse, come after me himself.

I frowned. "I don't think Uncle Joey should kill Dagger... at least not before we find out why he's targeting us."

Chris closed his eyes and shook his head. Did I even recognize how I sounded? Of course, if he wanted Dagger dead, he wasn't much better. "So what's the plan for the club?"

"With the fire planned for tomorrow, we need to find the other people involved before they burn the place down. But it shouldn't be too hard to get to the bottom of it since I'm a world-class psychic. And just think, if Dagger shows up, we could catch him at the same time."

Chris rolled his eyes, unimpressed with my positive attitude. It was still hard to believe that Dimples had asked for my help and I hadn't told him the truth. That might come back to haunt me.

And now the killer knew I could identify him. Even worse, I'd left the scene of a murder. "I still can't believe you left the scene. I mean... I get it because of Manetto, but you could go to jail for that. At least no one saw you." He sighed. "It's a good thing we're going to New York on Friday. This is getting too close for comfort."

"Yeah... but who knows? Maybe by the time we get back, the police will have Dagger behind bars."

Chris wondered what kind of fantasy land I was living in, because that was the least likely thing to happen. How did I always get caught in the middle of everything? Someday it was bound to catch up with me, and he hated to think that I'd either be killed or end up in jail.

"Chris... stop. Everything's fine. It will all work out. You'll see."

He sighed and pulled me close. "I hope so, but you can't blame me for worrying."

"Hey... when we get to New York, let's be sure to get some of that chocolate cake at the hotel. Wasn't it amazing?"

He huffed. "I don't know. You ate it all and didn't leave any for me."

"I did? Well, you'll have to get your own then."

"I'll do that. Is there anything we need to do tomorrow besides pack?"

"No. Josh is taking Coco to Lance Hobbs's place after school. That way, we can just get up on Friday morning and go. Uncle Joey wanted to get an early start, so we need to be to the airport at seven-thirty."

"Okay. That will give us most of the day Friday to do something fun."

"Yeah... about that. I'm meeting with Hawk for an hour or so in the afternoon. It's about the cold case I'm helping Dimples with. Dimples is actually coming too. I even managed to get him a room at the hotel for Friday night."

Chris froze. "Are you kidding me? Does Manetto know?"

"Don't worry. They won't run into each other. It'll be fine."

"Oh Shelby... what am I going to do with you?"

Chapter 11

The next morning came with less wind and warmer temperatures. It was still cooler than I liked, but now that I had an all-weather motorcycle jacket, it wouldn't stop me from going on a ride.

After taking Coco for a walk, I took a quick shower and got ready for the day. As I ate a piece of toast, the *Scooby Doo* ringtone sounded from my phone. A pulse of worry tightened my stomach, but I pushed it aside and answered. "Hey there. What's up?"

"Hey Shelby. We got a lead on a person of interest in that murder case yesterday. I'm interviewing him in about an hour. Want to come?"

"Yeah. That should work."

"Great. See you then."

I hung up, grateful the case was moving in the right direction. Even better, I wasn't a suspect. Maybe the police would have Dagger in custody before anything happened at the club tonight. Wouldn't that be something?

I arrived at the precinct an hour later and found Dimples at his desk waiting for me. "Did I make it in time?"

"Yup, the suspect just got here. Let's head into the interrogation room."

I followed Dimples into the room and froze. Paxton Savage sat on the other side of the desk. He took one look at me, and his eyes widened. Confusion clouded his mind, but he decided to keep his mouth shut until he knew what the hell was going on.

Dimples sent him a friendly smile. "Hi, Mr. Savage. Thanks for coming in today. This is my partner, Shelby Nichols. She'll be helping with the interview."

"Hi." I sent him a little wave and gave him a tight smile. "I actually work as a consultant for the police. It's so nice to meet you."

"You too." He narrowed his eyes, thinking that I must be Manetto's eyes and ears in the police department. That meant I had a hard job keeping my connection with Manetto a secret. He'd have to make sure he didn't give me away.

I sent him a nod before catching myself. Still, what the hell was he doing here?

Dimples glanced down at the file in his hand. "We asked you here because Cal Schaefer was killed yesterday afternoon. Do you know anything about that?"

Savage glanced at me, wondering what was going on. "No. I had no idea he was dead."

"We understand that you had an altercation with him a few nights ago at your place of employment. Could you tell us what that was about?"

Savage glanced at me again, wondering how he should answer. If I was Manetto's niece, my allegiance had to be to Manetto, right? So that meant I was on his side.

I nodded at him. "Yes. Just tell us what happened."

The tightness in his shoulders relaxed. "Sure. Cal delivers the booze to the club where I work. It's my responsibility to accept the delivery and make sure the shipment is all there. The last time he made a delivery there were a couple of boxes missing. I confronted him about the missing boxes, and he confessed to keeping them for himself."

Savage took a deep breath and spoke quietly. "It took a little persuading on my part, but he eventually "found" the rest of the delivery and handed it over."

Dimples raised a brow. "Did you know he ended up in the hospital with several broken bones?"

"I didn't know that." Savage glanced my way, wondering if I was going to throw him under the bus or help him out.

"Is that why you killed him yesterday?" Dimples asked, pressing his point.

Savage narrowed his eyes, pinning Dimples with an angry stare. "I had nothing to do with that."

"Where were you between two and four yesterday afternoon?"

"I was at home until three-thirty when I left for work."

"Were you alone?"

"Yes... but I took my garbage down to the dumpster around two-thirty. There was another renter there, and we spoke for a few minutes. His name is David Hahn. I'm sure he'll vouch for me."

Dimples glanced my way, wanting to know if Savage was telling the truth. I nodded, and Dimples's shoulders fell. He glanced back at Savage. "Do you know anyone who might have wanted Cal dead?"

Savage shook his head. "No. I hardly knew the guy."

Dimples sighed and turned to me. "Shelby, do you have any questions for him?"

"No. I'm good." I sent Savage an appreciative smile. "Thanks for coming in, we really appreciate it."

"Sure." Relieved he was being dismissed, Savage rushed out the door without a backward glance.

"Dang." Dimples huffed out a breath. "I thought for sure he was the one. I mean... he just got out of prison, and he has a rap sheet a mile long."

"Yeah, I get that, but... you realize that he doesn't fit the description, right?"

"I know, but people can alter their appearances." He shrugged. "I'd hoped that's what he'd done. Guess I was wrong."

"Yeah. So what now?"

"We've been going through Cal's acquaintances for anyone matching the description you gave us, but we haven't had any luck. Since there aren't any security cameras in the building or the surrounding area, we've had to look at nearby street cams, which is like finding a needle in a haystack."

His lips flattened. "Bates found a couple of thousand in Cal's underwear drawer, so we're thinking his death might have something to do with the money. Bates thought he might be in some kind of financial trouble, so we're getting a warrant for his bank statements. He's also following up with Cal's co-workers, so we'll see if they have any idea about what he was involved with. Are you getting anything?"

"Uh... no, not really. I'm as clueless as you are." That was a big fat lie, but what could I say? At least Bates had followed up on my suggestion and found the money.

Dimples wrinkled his brow, thinking that I was usually more helpful. At least I'd picked up a description from the neighbor.

"Yeah... that was a nice break." Wanting to change the subject, I asked about his flight. "So what time does your plane leave tomorrow morning?"

"Six-fifteen. That's too early, if you ask me."

"Wow. No kidding. So you'll get there about an hour earlier than us. That might be good, since you're less likely to run into Uncle Joey at that time."

"True. I guess I'll take a cab to the hotel and meet you there?"

"Yeah. I'll call you after we check in, and we can head to the precinct together. Bring a copy of the cold case file with you. That way we can show Hawk what we're up against."

"Sounds good. I'll let you know if we need your help with anything else on this case. Otherwise, I'll see you tomorrow."

"Okay. See you then." I hurried out of the building and headed to my car. It was nice that Dimples trusted me so much, but I also felt a twinge of guilt that I wasn't being entirely honest with him. Still... that could change. Maybe I could give Dimples more information about Cal's murder after I talked with Uncle Joey and found out what he knew.

Uncle Joey should welcome help from the police if it put Dagger behind bars, right? If I played my cards right, I could appease both sides of the law at the same time. Ha! Who was I kidding? Something like that would take a miracle.

Nearly to my car, I caught a whiff of juniper and sage. I froze and glanced around, unsure if that meant Savage was stalking me, or if it was Zoe. Of course, Savage should be long gone if he knew what was good for him.

Unease ran along my spine, and I continued toward my car, unlocking it with my fob so I could jump inside and get out of there. As I reached for the handle, Savage stepped out from behind the SUV next to my car. My heart jerked in my chest, and I took a step back. "Gah!"

"Sorry!" Savage raised both his hands. "I didn't mean to startle you." He glanced behind me to make sure we were alone and spoke in a hushed tone. "I just wanted to know if the cops are coming after me. I didn't kill Cal. I'm sure they're looking at me because of my record, but I swear I had nothing to do with it."

"I know it wasn't you, but you shouldn't be talking to me right now. If anyone sees us, it's going to look bad. You need to go."

Savage ducked a little lower. "Right, right. I'll go."

He slid back behind the parked cars and continued down the row until coming to his own car. I pulled on my door handle and heard *Elliot, no!*

Jerking around, I caught sight of Elliot sneaking up behind Savage. He held a knife in his hand and paused for a split second before raising it to stab Savage in the back.

"Elliot! Stop!"

Savage had his car door open, and glanced over his shoulder to find Elliot looming over him. In a quick move, he lashed out, knocking the knife from Elliot's hand. Drawing his fist back, he threw a punch at Elliot's face.

Luckily, Elliot managed to move his head enough that the blow caught him in the jaw. Still, it knocked him backwards, and he fell against the car parked beside him.

Savage stepped closer, ready to beat the crap out of Elliot, but I got there first and held up my hands. "Stop it, Savage! You need to get out of here. Go! Now!"

My words finally penetrated Savage's rage-filled mind. With a shake of his head, he stepped to his car and slipped inside.

As he drove away, I bent over Elliot, who managed to sit up and touch his throbbing jaw. "Are you okay?"

"What the hell? I almost had him. Why did you do that?"

"Are you crazy? How could you even think about killing Savage in the precinct parking lot? That's insane!"

His eyes narrowed. I'd ruined everything. He could have killed the guy, and it would have been over. His pride kicked in, and he went on the defense. "Hey... it could have worked. No one was here."

I pointed at the surveillance cameras at the top of the tall light poles. "And what about those? It would all be recorded, and you'd never get away with it."

His brows dipped, and he shook his head. "I didn't... I didn't even notice them." He dropped his head into his hands and closed his eyes, thinking he'd been a stupid idiot. Needing to get out of there, he rose unsteadily to his feet. He swayed, and I grabbed his arm to steady him.

"Come on. I'll help you get to your car. Where is it?"

"It's down the street."

"Okay. My car's close. I'll drive you there."

He let me lead him to my car, but he wasn't happy about it. After he slid into the passenger seat, I got behind the wheel and pulled out of the lot. "Where am I going?"

"My car's down that way. About a block. The white sedan."

"Got it." A few seconds later, I pulled up behind it. As he opened the door, I grabbed his arm. "Wait. We need to talk about this."

His nostrils flared, but he let out a resigned breath and closed the door. "Fine." He didn't think he'd like what I had to say, but he knew the path he was on was bound to get him killed, or land him in jail for the rest of his life. Maybe I could talk him out of it. What he really needed was coffee, then maybe he could think straight.

"I think you need some coffee so you can think straight." I motioned down the road. "There's a coffee shop not far from here. Let's hang out there for a bit. Sound good?"

His eyes widened. How did I know? He shook his head before swallowing. Maybe he'd better do whatever I said. "Sure."

I managed to keep from rolling my eyes and sent him a tight smile. He hardly noticed, still in a daze about what had happened. I pulled into the coffee shop parking lot and found a place in the back. Walking to the shop, he only wobbled a little, so I didn't offer my help to keep him steady.

Inside the shop, we placed our orders and found a corner booth. After taking a moment to settle in, I crossed my arms on the table and leaned forward. "Well... that was a surprise. Have you been tracking Savage for long?"

His lips turned down, and he grimaced at the pain in his jaw. "Why were you there? When he came out of the building, he ducked behind that SUV like he was waiting for someone.

"Then you came out, and I watched him sneak up on you. I was afraid he might try something, so I headed in your direction. Next thing I know, you're talking to him like you know him." He held his thumb and forefinger up. "I was this close. Why did you have to stop me? How do you know him, anyway?"

The worker called our order, and I held up a finger. "I'll be right back." After setting our order on the table, I went back for a glass of ice and handed it to Elliot. "Here... hold that on your jaw."

With a nod of thanks, he placed it on his jawline and sank back against the chair, closing his eyes.

Taking a long sip of my soda, I gave him a minute to relax. "I do consulting work for the police, so I'm there a lot. We just got this homicide case, and Savage was a person of interest, so I was there to help the detectives question him."

"But Savage waited for you. It was like he knew you."

"Of course he knows me! He knows me because I spoke to him while I was working for you. You can imagine my surprise when he came into the precinct for the interview. It surprised him too, but he played along with it. That's why he waited for me... he wanted to know what was going on."

"Fine... I get that, but... I heard you talk to him. You didn't explain anything. You just told him to leave, and he did. That doesn't make any sense. Why would he do that?"

I huffed out a breath and reined in my irritation, knowing I had to explain as much as I could without giving anything away. "You know I'm a PI, right?" At his nod, I continued. "So I do consulting work for the police as well as some highly influential people. Savage knows my reputation, so he's willing to go along with me." I shook my head. "But that's beside the point. You're the one who needs to stay away from him."

His brows rose. "Hey... I almost had him, but you gave me away."

"Please." I rolled my eyes. "You know how that would have turned out. Besides, it wasn't just me. Your sister's the one who warned me, or I never would have stopped you in time."

His lips pressed into a thin line, and anger reared up inside him. "Are you kidding me? You really expect me to believe that you're not just making that up?"

I let out a long sigh. "Do I have to explain my psychic abilities again?"

He slumped in his chair. "No... you don't. But it's all so damn frustrating."

"Elliot... Zoe does *not* want you to kill Savage for her. She wants you to let it go and get on with your life."

His lips twisted, and he was thinking that I'd say anything to stop him. Zoe wasn't part of this. She was...

gone... dead... and I was just using her so I could say whatever I wanted, and he'd fall for it.

I huffed out a breath. I needed to find a way to get through to him. "What will it take for you to believe me?"

Skepticism clouded his thoughts. "I don't know."

I listened closely and picked up his anger... and his fear. He was afraid that if he didn't kill Savage, then Zoe's death was for nothing. He wanted it to mean something, but it wouldn't if Savage was still alive.

You need to tell him to quit focusing on my death. I jerked in my seat. What the hell? Zoe was in my head, and I didn't like it one bit.

Just listen to me. It's the life I lived that matters, not how I died. Sure... what happened to me wasn't fair, but he's just making it worse. He's wasting his time and energy on something he can't change. Ask him what he'll do once Savage is dead. Go on... ask him.

Ugh! She was right, but I didn't like sharing head-space with her. *Please... just ask him.* I took a deep breath. "Fine." I met Elliot's gaze. "Listen... let's say you did it. You killed Savage. Now what? Are you happy? Does it fill that hole in your heart?"

Elliot's shoulders sagged, and he sank into his chair, knowing deep down that it wouldn't change a thing. Zoe would still be dead. But... so would Savage. So... yeah. He'd feel better.

He straightened, resolve tightening his chest. "Nothing can replace what I lost, but I'm sure I'd feel better if Savage were dead." He shrugged. "And look at it this way... at least he wouldn't be around to kill anyone else, so I'd be doing the world a favor."

I sighed. In a way, I could relate to that. Hadn't I thought that if Cal was dead, it wouldn't bother me too much? Of course, when it happened, it did bother me, so that was a relief.

But what about Savage? If he hadn't roughed up Cal, would Ramos and Uncle Joey be dead right now? So killing him wasn't that great of an idea.

"It's still wrong."

Elliot stood so abruptly that his chair nearly fell over. He leaned over the table and snarled. "Yeah? Well so was killing my sister."

"Elliot... I'm sorry. I know it was. Please sit down, and let's talk. There are other options. Let me help you."

He pulled away. "I have to go."

I stood, taking a step closer to him. "Wait... at least let me help you figure out a plan. Like I said... there might be a better option that would still give you the closure you need."

He hesitated, thinking that putting Savage behind bars might satisfy him, but how would we do that? He shook his head. "I don't know."

"Just give me a couple of days to figure something out. Okay?"

He huffed out a breath. "I'll think about it."

"Good. I'll call you."

His lips twisted, but he gave me a nod before stalking off.

I sighed and sank into my chair. That was close, and Zoe's reasoning hadn't helped me at all. A blast of frustration hit me before I heard her. *Ugh! He can be so dense sometimes.* Her anger swelled before flying away, almost like she was going after Elliot.

It scared me that Zoe's presence was so strong, and I blew out a breath, ready to get out of there. At least she only seemed close when I was around Elliot, so that was good. Now I just had to hope that Elliot would talk to me before he did anything stupid again.

—◦►─◄█████►─◄◦—

I pulled into the parking garage at Thrasher and strolled to the elevator. On the way, I took a small detour toward the pillar in the corner and found the Harley parked in its usual spot.

Elation filled my heart. So far, the day had been rough, and just seeing it brought me comfort. In fact, right now, I could use a little motorcycle therapy. At least I didn't have to worry about Elliot killing Savage right away, so that was a win, right?

But what about Savage? He'd want some answers about Elliot, and why Elliot wanted him dead. How could I explain that to Savage? Since I had no idea, I hoped I could come up with a plausible story before I ran into him again.

The elevator doors opened, and I stepped into Thrasher. Jackie wasn't at her desk, but I could hear talking in the conference room. I followed the voices and found the doors open. Inside, Uncle Joey, Ramos, David and Nick Berardini, along with Forrest Slater, were all talking at the same time.

I picked up that it had something to do with the Berardini's computer security, and that there had been another hack. Only this time, it had been successful. No wonder everyone looked so glum.

"I think Forrest is right," Uncle Joey said, silencing them all. "We can't risk it. I need all the files you have on my businesses in your system deleted. This second breach shows that your system isn't up to the standards I need."

Forrest thought Uncle Joey was right. "It's the only way to protect Mr. Manetto's information. Once we take care of the threat, we can figure something else out." He shook his head. "This hacker is good... one of the best I've seen. With anyone else, he'd have been in and out in a flash, but your security was good enough to send an alert."

"Yeah, but he still got in." Nick shook his head. "But thanks to my father, it wasn't as bad as it could have been." Nick and David exchanged glances. David nodded, thinking *go ahead and tell them.*

"What do you mean?" Uncle Joey asked.

I gasped. "You tricked them!"

All eyes turned to me, and I sent them a little wave. "Hey everyone. I didn't mean to interrupt. Go ahead Nick... tell them what you did."

I'd stolen his thunder, and his lips thinned, but since I was so excited about it, he took it in stride. "The files he got into were fake. After the first hack, I downloaded all the Thrasher files onto a thumb-drive and deleted them from our system. Next, I created several new files similar to the old ones, but with fake names and invoices. The files that were breached last night were those."

He pulled out a thumb-drive. "This is what you want. All your clients and lists are here."

He handed it to Uncle Joey, who took it with a glint in his eyes. "My boy, that was brilliant."

Everyone was pleased except Forrest. He smiled and said all the right things, but deep down he was a little angry. Besides the fact that he wished he'd thought of it, he regretted that Nick hadn't told them ahead of time.

It would have given him the opportunity to plant a code that would have helped identify the hacker once he'd opened the file. Using it, he could have pinpointed the hacker's location, which would have given him an idea of their identity.

But maybe he could still do something. "Hey Nick. Do you mind if I take a look at your server? Maybe I can see how they got in, and if they left anything behind."

"Like what?" Uncle Joey asked.

Forrest shrugged. "I don't know... a line of code or an IP address would be helpful, but I doubt they were that careless. Still... you never know."

"Sure," Nick said. "Maybe you'll find something." He was feeling generous since he'd outsmarted the hacker this time. "We should work together."

As they discussed the logistics, Ramos came to my side. "Where have you been?"

"At the police station. You'll never guess who I ran into." I told him all about interviewing Savage with Dimples. "At least Savage went along with the interview and didn't give me away. After he left, I told Dimples that Savage didn't have anything to do with the murder, so he's off the hook. But as I was leaving, Savage nearly scared me to death in the parking lot. He jumped out of nowhere to ask me what was going on, and I had to put him off. He'll probably tell Uncle Joey to keep an eye on me since I might be feeding the police information."

I wasn't sure that I should tell Ramos about Elliot. Now that he'd decided not to kill Savage, it didn't matter so much.

"I guess it's good to know that Savage isn't a suspect, but what about Dagger? Did you tell the police anything about him?"

"Oh... yeah. When I went over to the scene yesterday, I spoke with a woman who actually saw Dagger leaving Cal's apartment. She didn't have the best view because she was looking through her peep-hole, but it was him. Naturally, she didn't admit to seeing him, but I used her as a reason to give Dimples a description of Dagger."

His brows drew together. "But if she saw Dagger, then what about us?"

"Oh... that's right. She remembered seeing me earlier in the day, but when I told her I worked with the police, she quit thinking about it. She might have seen you too, but mostly because she admired your—" I glanced around him and took my time to examine the object of her admiration "—backside." I shrugged. "I guess it's all right." Twisting my lips into a sassy grin, I met his gaze.

He raised a brow, thinking that I was walking on thin ice, but he'd get me back. "So she saw us, but didn't tell the police?"

"That's right... because I am the police... at least to her."

"Right."

"But I made sure Dimples got Dagger's description, and now the cops are looking for him, which should help us out, right?"

"I guess." Ramos wasn't sure it would help, especially if he turned up dead.

My brows dipped. "I must be missing something. Do you have a plan?"

"We were just discussing that when the Berardini's showed up. Now that they're leaving, we can get back to our discussion."

"Okay." I turned my attention back to the room. Nick and Forrest had already left, and David spoke in low tones to Uncle Joey, telling him that he and his wife were headed to Hawaii for a couple of weeks. Uncle Joey wished him a safe trip and he left, smiling broadly and saying goodbye to Ramos and me.

Thinking things were working out, Uncle Joey came to my side, hoping I had some good news. "I take it you have some information for me?"

"Sure do."

"Good. Let's head to my office where we can get more comfortable and discuss it."

It didn't take me long to fill Uncle Joey in on the police investigation. He kept his attention focused on me, and it pleased him that I hadn't told Dimples the truth. It meant I was getting the hang of putting him first. After I finished my explanation, his brows drew together. "I didn't realize that Dagger knows you can identify him. It might put you in danger."

"I don't think he'll come after me. I mean..." I glanced at Ramos. "You saw him too, right?"

Ramos's lips twisted. "Yeah. I caught a brief glimpse of him, so you're not the only one. But at this point, I think he'll focus on getting rid of all of us tonight."

I twisted my lips. "But what if he has a good idea that we already know about it?"

Uncle Joey huffed. "That won't stop him. In fact, it could be exactly what he wanted. I mean... aren't we planning to be there in order to stop it? We're playing right into his hands."

"Oh." I sat back in my chair. "I hadn't thought of it that way. So what do we do?"

"We kill the son of a bitch first."

Chapter 12

I hadn't expected such drastic measures from Uncle Joey. "But... we don't even know where to find him."

"Maybe not. But we know where he's going to be. We'll all show up at the club tonight, but we'll sneak out right after we put in an appearance. When Dagger comes to finish the job, Savage will kill him."

"Savage?"

"Yes. I was at the club last night, and Russ mentioned that Savage wanted to speak with me. I know you don't approve, but when he offered his services, I thought he was the perfect person for the job. Dagger has no idea who he is, so he won't be expecting it."

Uncle Joey's logic made perfect sense, but I wasn't sure I wanted to be included in *this part* of the business. "Yeah, I see that. But, as your niece, I'd like to offer you a different solution that doesn't involve... uh... killing someone."

Uncle Joey bristled. "It's self-defense. He tried to kill you, yesterday, or did you forget that part?"

"Oh, no... I understand that, in fact Chris was thinking the same thing, but... could we at least try to come up with an alternative? I'm working with the police on Cal's murder, and if we could get Dagger for that, he'd go to prison for the rest of his life."

Uncle Joey wasn't sold on the idea, so I went for the big guns. "Besides, we need to talk to him first. We need to know why he's targeting you. As far as we know, he might not even be the person behind all the attacks. What if he's working for someone else? It would be nice to know who that is, right?"

"I suppose so. But that means we'll have to stick around and wait for him to make his move. That would put us all in danger."

Ramos raised a brow, bristling under Uncle Joey's lack of confidence in him to protect us.

I patted his arm. "It's not that... he just likes to be in control." I smiled at Uncle Joey and continued. "We know it's a risk, but you've got Ramos, who is amazing at his job, and you've got me. I'll know everything he's thinking before he does it. Between the two of us, he doesn't stand a chance."

Uncle Joey's eyes narrowed. "I suppose you're right. This is just bad timing with the wedding, and I don't want anything to keep us from making it."

I nodded, knowing exactly how he felt.

Later that night, I stood at my front door waiting for Uncle Joey to pull up in his limo. He'd insisted that he pick me up and we go to his club together. That way he didn't have to worry about anything happening to me... like getting waylaid by Dagger.

Since that was a possibility, I was happy to agree, especially because following his orders made it easier to leave my family behind. The car pulled up, and I yelled over my shoulder. "He's here. I'll be back soon."

Chris came in from the kitchen and gave me a quick kiss. "Be safe, honey."

"I will."

"I love you."

"I love you, too."

As I shut the door behind me, I swallowed the lump in my throat. Chris hated the risks that I took, but he also knew better than to try to stop me. He was thinking that, if the worst happened, at least I'd know he loved me no matter what. I probably didn't deserve him, but it also made me more determined than ever not to let him down.

I climbed into the limo, finding Uncle Joey and Ramos waiting for me with Ricky in the driver's seat. Ramos wore his usual black hitman attire, only with a black blazer instead of his leather jacket. Uncle Joey had changed into a dark dress-shirt-and-blazer-combo that made him look distinguished and commanding.

I'd contemplated wearing pants, but had changed my mind at the last minute and thrown on my little red dress with the key-hole back. Combined with my black boots and black lace jacket, I felt confident and sexy at the same time. It also didn't hurt that I wore a cute, cross-body purse holding my stun flashlight.

As I settled in beside them, both Ramos and Uncle Joey nodded with appreciation. Uncle Joey was proud to call me his niece, since I fit the part so well. Ramos appreciated that I'd adopted a confident, no-nonsense attitude. He briefly wondered if I'd been that way before I'd gotten my mind-reading abilities.

I wanted to tell him that I'd always been confident and straight-forward, but that wasn't entirely true. Knowing people's thoughts had definitely changed me. I might be more confident, but it came with a price.

Knowing what people thought about me wasn't easy. My feelings had been hurt more times than I liked, but it had also made me realize that a lot of people were more insecure than they ever let on. So, in the end... it all evened out.

I glanced at Uncle Joey. "Was the manager on board with our plans?"

"Yes. Russ is ready to roll once we get there. When we get there, you and Ramos will go straight to his office, while I head to the game room. Tonight's poker match should be in full swing, and I'll join them like usual. Let me know the minute you have the double-crossers."

Ramos nodded. "Will do."

A few minutes later, we pulled in front of the club and exited the limo. Ramos got out first, then Uncle Joey, who held out a hand for me. After tucking my arm in his, we walked straight to the entrance, and the doorman quickly ushered us through the door, holding back anyone who stood in our way.

Inside, Uncle Joey headed for the back room, where he and his high-rolling friends played poker on Thursday nights. I followed Ramos to the bar and ducked down the hall behind the bar toward the offices.

The sounds of the club grew distant as we traversed the back of the building. Stopping in front of the manager's door, Ramos knocked before stepping inside.

Russ sat behind his desk and glanced up, giving Ramos a nod. "We're ready." He motioned us to follow him into a large break room, where five people sat waiting around a table.

As soon as we entered, they all froze, and I picked up a sliver of fear from each one of them. This impromptu meeting with Ramos, who only showed up when there was trouble, set their nerves jangling, and they all wondered who'd done something wrong.

Ramos took charge, looming larger than life with his dangerous vibe. He glanced at each one in turn, his eyes narrowing with suspicion. "We have learned that a few members of our wait staff have been paid to burn down the club tonight. Naturally, Manetto doesn't want that to happen. Each of you is here to tell us if you know anything about it. And I would advise against lying, if you know what's good for you. Anyone like to go first?"

They all shook their heads, several of them blurting that they didn't know anything. I listened to each of them, picking up enough to know that they weren't involved. Stepping close to Ramos, I stood on tiptoe to whisper in his ear. "They're good."

With a nod, he straightened. "All right. You may go, but don't breathe a word of this to anyone. We're bringing all the staff members in tonight, and I don't want them warned. Do I make myself clear?"

After they all agreed, Ramos dismissed them, and Russ opened the door to let them out. He disappeared for a few minutes before returning with five more waiters, along with Ricky for backup. Ramos did his spiel again, and I used my ability to scour their minds.

Finding nothing, we repeated the process two more times. With only one more group to question, I worried that we'd find the double-crossers.

As the last five employees took their seats, I knew it had to be one of them. During Ramos's talk, I caught a wave of panic from two people sitting at the end of the row.

Relieved, I zeroed in on them, and picked up that they'd both been approached and had agreed to the scheme.

Ramos finished speaking and glanced my way.

"Thanks Ramos. Everyone can go except for you two." I pointed at the two of them and they both paled. As the others skittered out, the two men shrank in their seats. Russ and Ricky joined us, both eager to hear what they had to say.

"You have one chance to tell us what you know." I began. "After that... well... I guess you know what happens to double-crossers." Narrowing my eyes, I pulled my finger across my throat.

It was mostly for show, since I knew Ramos wasn't going to kill them, but it still surprised me how much I enjoyed witnessing their panic. Did that mean I'd totally turned to the dark side?

They both started talking at once, and Ramos raised his hands to stop them. "You go first." He nodded toward the guy on the left. "And don't leave anything out."

The man swallowed before he began. "I didn't think it was anything big... I mean, all this guy wanted me to do was spill a few drinks on the carpet... and maybe the drapes if I could manage it. I had no idea he wanted to burn down the club, or I wouldn't have agreed."

Ramos shook his head. "How much did he pay you?"

"He offered me a couple grand. He gave me half, and I'm supposed to get the rest after the job's done." He shook his head. "But I haven't done what he asked. I swear I wasn't going to do it."

I frowned. All this lying was getting on my nerves. "Who put you up to this? We need a name."

He swallowed. "He goes by Dagger. That's all I know."

I glanced at the other guy. "What about you?"

"About the same, only I'm supposed to empty a few bottles in the storage closet by the kitchen. But he never said anything about burning down the place, I swear."

They were both lying through their teeth. Of course they knew someone was going to start a fire, even if it wasn't either of them. "Cut the crap. You both knew the reason was to start a fire. So who was supposed to light the match?"

Glancing at each other, they thought about the same person. The bartender. She was the one who got them involved with Dagger in the first place.

"What's in it for Stella?"

Their eyes widened, but it was Ramos who flinched. He knew she'd been angry about things, but he thought they'd worked it out. It stung a little that she'd be vindictive enough to even consider burning down the club.

I turned to him. "What do you want to do?"

He sighed. "These two need to be taught a lesson."

"You mean like losing a finger?"

A brief smile flitted across his lips. "Yeah... something like that."

Both men jumped to their feet, but Ramos and Ricky shoved them back into their chairs. Ramos turned to Russ. "I'll let you and Ricky decide what to do with them. Shelby and I are going to pay Stella a visit."

I glanced at Russ, who was seriously considering taking off a finger. "Uh... I was kidding about the finger. Maybe you could just fire them without their back pay?"

In a show of anger, Russ cursed and shook his head. "But they crossed a mob boss."

"True. But it's kind of hard to find work without a couple of fingers."

Russ pursed his lips, acting like he was disappointed, even though he planned to fire them without chopping off a finger. "Fine. As long as Manetto knows it was your idea."

"I'll make sure Uncle Joey knows." I glanced at the men. "You're lucky I'm feeling generous. You can thank me later."

I hurried after Ramos, who waited by the door with a smirk on his face. He was thinking that I was enjoying my role a lot more than I ever had. What had gotten into me?

"That's a good question. It must be a coping mechanism for all the stress." He just grunted, so I barreled on, talking as we walked to the bar. "So what's going on with Stella? Did you date her and then drop her or something?"

Ramos huffed. "Hell no. I don't date employees."

"Oh... okay. So what happened?"

"A few weeks ago, Stella had a big fight with Russ. He'd cut her hours back because she kept missing her shifts. Since we were on friendly terms, she begged me to intervene. She even promised that she'd change her ways and be more dependable."

He shook his head. "I don't usually interfere, but she's kind of had it rough, and I felt sorry for her." Now he wondered if any of it was true. "Anyway, I spoke to Russ about it, and he refused to give her shifts back. So I got them together to work out a compromise. In the end, Russ told her that, as long as she didn't miss any of her current shifts, he'd give her more work next month. She agreed, but she wasn't too happy about it. I didn't think much of it until now."

I nodded. "I guess Dagger found out about her fight with Russ and used it to get to her."

"Yeah. This Dagger person has done his homework. If not for Savage beating the shit out of Cal, this place might have burned down that night."

A chill ran down my spine. He was right, but it pained me to admit that someone like Savage had done something good, even though what he did was bad. Sometimes life didn't make any sense.

Ramos spotted Stella at the bar and stopped. "I want to talk to her in private. Wait here."

As he stepped to the bar, I caught sight of Savage sitting at the opposite end of the room, close to the door where Uncle Joey played poker. He gave me a nod, thinking that he liked being in on the action and part of the Manetto team. He hoped this Dagger person showed up so he could do his job and kill the bastard.

I shook my head. How many killers were here to kill people? It's like they were coming out of the woodwork. That... or I was in the wrong business.

Stepping to the bar, Ramos caught the attention of the other bartender. After a brief conversation, he moved to Stella's end of the bar and motioned to her. He said something about wanting to talk in private, and she nodded and left the bar to follow him.

Ramos caught my gaze and thought that I should head to Russ's office and meet them there. He didn't want Stella to know I was involved, or she might not be as interested in talking to him.

I nodded, picking up that, deep down, he knew she liked him and had wanted more, so seeing me might put a damper on her willingness to talk to him. I quickly turned back the way we'd come and half-jogged down the hall before she saw me. After ducking into Russ's office, I slid into his chair behind the desk.

Seconds later, Ramos opened the door and ushered Stella inside. Seeing me, she hesitated, but, with Ramos at her back, she didn't have a choice but to come in. Ramos closed the door, his lips twisting to find me in Russ's chair.

His brows rose, but he thought *you're getting pretty good at this. Why don't you go ahead and ask the questions.*

I nodded and caught Stella's gaze. "Hi Stella, I'm Shelby. Thanks for coming."

"Who are you?"

"I work for Mr. Manetto. In fact, he's my Uncle."

Glancing between me and Ramos, her brows drew together. "What's this about?"

"I think you already know."

She shook her head. "No I don't. I don't know anything." Little shards of fear ran down her spine, and she tried to figure a way out of this. No one knew... he swore no one would know, so what was going on? She glanced behind her and found Ramos with his back against the door, barricading her in.

He motioned for me to continue, so I shook my head like Uncle Joey did when someone had disappointed him. "We know about the plan to burn down the club. And we know that you're the one who's supposed to light the match."

Her breath caught, and panic seized her chest.

"You have two choices. You can tell me everything you know, or you can wait here while I go get my Uncle."

Sudden worry tightened my stomach, and I glanced at Ramos. "Uh... didn't he tell us to get him as soon as we found the double-crossers? I should probably get him. I don't want him to be mad that he missed this." I got to my feet, ready to leave.

"You have a point." Ramos knew I was serious instead of playing a part, but he thought my tactics were perfect.

"Wait!" Stella raised a hand, fear tightening her throat. "I'll tell you everything I know."

"Um..." I hesitated, glancing at Ramos. He thought we should go ahead since I was channeling Uncle Joey so well. My lips quirked up and I sat back down. I faced Stella and narrowed my eyes. "Fine. But if I catch you lying, I'm getting him, no matter what."

She swallowed. "Sure... just hear me out. First of all... it's not what it looks like. A guy started coming in during my shifts a few weeks ago and... we hit it off." She was thinking that he was a poor substitute for Ramos, but at least he seemed to like her.

"Anyway... I complained that Russ had cut my hours and I had some bills coming due. He told me I could make some easy money if I dropped a match in the storage closet by the kitchen. He said it was just a distraction, and no one would get hurt."

She chewed on her lower lip, realizing he hadn't told her what the distraction was for, and she hadn't asked. She'd also left out the two servers who were helping her, but if we knew she'd recruited them, it would just make it worse.

She glanced at Ramos, and anger tightened her eyes. If he hadn't humiliated her, she wouldn't have agreed to the scheme. She'd thought they had something between them, especially after he'd spoken to Russ for her. But when she'd asked him if he wanted to hook up, he'd practically laughed in her face. If anything, it was his fault that she'd agreed to Dagger's plan... of course, the twenty grand didn't hurt either, but still...

"He's paying you twenty grand to do it?"

Her face paled. How did I know?

I pursed my lips. "When is this supposed to happen?"

She let out a deep breath and lowered her gaze. "At eleven tonight." She glanced at Ramos. The cold disregard in his eyes sent a chill down her spine. She suddenly realized that Ramos wasn't someone to mess with, and getting sympathy from him at this point was next to impossible. "But I won't do it, Ramos. I swear. I'll even help you catch him... then you can tell Manetto that I helped you... and forget about the agreement I made, okay?"

If anything, Ramos's face turned harder, and she began to panic. "Please. I'll do whatever you need, even if it puts me in danger. I promise... I'll come through for you." He still hesitated, and the realization of how much trouble she was in sent fear into her heart. "Ramos... you have to let me do this... if our friendship meant anything at all, you have to give me that much."

Ramos narrowed his eyes, trying to decide if it was worth letting her help. She wasn't trustworthy, so what was the point? He caught my gaze and raised a brow.

I shrugged. "Um... it all depends." I glanced at Stella. "I'm not sure Ramos needs your help, but I'll bite. What did you have in mind? Are you supposed to meet up with Dagger?"

Her breath caught. I knew his name? No wonder Ramos was so mad. "Uh... yeah. He's supposed to come in and give me the go ahead."

"How?"

"He'll just sit at the bar and tell me." She'd insisted that he give her the other half of the money before she set the fire. With the way things were going, it was good she'd thought ahead. Once she had the money, she could disappear and start over someplace else.

"So, instead of starting the fire, you'll just run off with the money?"

Her brow crinkled. "No... I'll do my part."

"Which is?"

"I'll leave to start the fire while he waits. When I return, I'll let him know I did the job. Then he can go ahead with his plans."

"And you're sure you don't know what his plans are?"

She shook her head. "No... I promise... I don't know more than that."

I couldn't pick up any deception, but once she had all that money, she might change her mind. I glanced at Ramos. "I don't exactly trust her. What do you think we should do?"

Ramos took his time answering. He stepped away from the door and faced her, his eyes narrowing dangerously. "Okay... I'll agree to this. But Stella... you make one wrong move... or decide to run..." He stepped closer, invading her space. "I will find you, and it will be the last thing you ever do."

Her throat moved, but none of her words came out, so she jerked her head up and down instead. Taking his time, Ramos opened the door, and she bolted down the hall.

"Wow... I'd forgotten how scary you can be."

He pursed his lips, thinking that he was a bad guy, so what did I expect? Besides, she was ready to burn down the club, she didn't deserve his sympathy. He also wasn't happy that she'd used him in the first place.

I nodded. "Yeah... I get that. I picked up that she was disappointed you turned her down, so she was blaming you for taking the job... but... not to knock you or anything... it was really the twenty grand that did it."

He snorted. "Right."

"So what do we do now?"

"Besides keeping an eye on Stella, we tell Manetto." He shook his head. "I'm finding it hard to believe that Dagger would show up here. I mean... we've both seen him, so why would he risk being caught?"

I shrugged. "Maybe he's wearing a disguise? Come to think of it, Dimples thought he might have been disguised when I saw him before. I guess it's possible he had on a wig and a fake beard at Cal's apartment. I mean... I only got a glimpse of him, but if you're planning to murder someone, a disguise might be the way to go."

"Maybe." Ramos checked his watch. "It's just after ten, so we have time to figure it out. Let's tell Manetto what's going on."

We entered the main floor of the club from the hallway behind the bar, and Ramos led the way to the game room at the other side. On the way, he spotted Ricky and stopped to ask him to keep an eye on Stella.

That done, we continued to the game room where Uncle Joey and his guests played their friendly game of poker. Spotting us, Uncle Joey excused himself and led us to a private office he kept in the club.

Shutting the door, he motioned for us to sit down in front of his desk. "Did you find the traitors? When can I talk to them?"

Grateful that Ramos had to explain that we'd left him out, I kept my mouth shut and only added a few things here and there. As I'd expected, Uncle Joey wasn't happy we'd done the questioning without him, but his eyes brightened to hear our plans to catch Dagger and find out what was going on.

Unknown to most patrons, Uncle Joey had a state-of-the-art security camera system installed, which had views of the bar and surrounding tables, along with other angles of the band and dance floor.

Since Ramos and I were the only ones who'd seen Dagger, we decided that Ramos would watch from the security room with all the video feeds, while I took a booth closer to the bar where I could pick up his thoughts if he came inside without his beard and long hair. Ramos sent Ricky to watch the club entrance, and alerted Russ to move his trusted men to guard the storage room and keep an eye on Stella.

At ten-thirty, I took a seat in the booth with my back to the bar where it would be harder for Dagger to see my face.

I wished I had my black wig, but it was too late for that. As I nursed a diet soda with lime, I kept my senses open for anyone thinking about treachery, murder, or burning the place down.

I wasn't sure Dagger would turn up, since he knew we'd spoken with Cal, but it was still our best chance to catch him. By eleven-twenty, my head started to pound. Listening to hundreds of thoughts, and trying to pinpoint specifics, had taken a toll.

From what I could see, Dagger hadn't shown up, and now I wasn't sure he would. At eleven-thirty, with no sign of him, I finished off the last of my soda and took out my phone to call Uncle Joey and see what he wanted me to do.

"Shelby?" A clean-cut younger man in a green dress shirt and black slacks slid into my booth. He wore glasses and seemed familiar, but I couldn't place him.

"Hi. Do I know you?" I listened to his thoughts, but he was mostly just thinking about me.

"Yeah, but you might not remember me. It's been a while. We met at a poker tournament in Las Vegas."

"Oh... did I play against you?"

"No. I didn't make it that far, but I watched you play. You were amazing." He was thinking that we hadn't met at the tournament, but it was a good reference point, since he didn't want me to remember where I'd seen him.

My brows puckered. "I think I would remember you from the tournament. I must have met you somewhere else."

He ducked his head. "Oh... it's okay, I'm not someone who's very memorable. But what you did at the tournament was... spectacular. I guess you could say I'm a huge fan." He smiled, hoping to win me over with his charm.

"Well... thanks." I smiled back, still trying to place where I'd seen him before. "You do look familiar... just not from the tournament. Are you sure we didn't meet somewhere else?"

Shaking his head, he glanced at the bar, thinking that he had to keep me talking for a little longer. Concerned that there wasn't any smoke coming from that area, he rubbed his hands together. It should have begun by now.

I started to scoot out of the booth, but he grabbed my wrist and jerked me back. He leaned over, all of his friendliness gone, and snarled in my face. "If you leave, your uncle is a dead man."

Shocked by the hatred pouring from him, I froze. "What do you want?" Taking a chance, I glanced toward the bar, hoping to spot Ricky or Ramos.

Stella was gone, and a man with long dark hair and a beard was rushing toward the exit. Ricky moved to intercept him, but Dagger had other ideas and plunged a knife into Ricky's stomach. As Ricky fell, Dagger waved his bloody knife if the air, threatening anyone who stood in his way.

"Ricky!" I tried to jerk my arm away, but the man's hold tightened.

"You don't want to do that."

"Let go of me."

"Do you want your uncle to die?"

"Of course not."

"Then do exactly what I say."

A woman screamed, and several people shouted. Word spread that someone had a knife and was stabbing people. The crowd scattered in panic, heading for the exits, and shoving people out of the way.

In a matter of seconds, the club was in utter chaos. I strained to see if anyone was helping Ricky, but the crowd blocked my view. With my heart racing, I turned back to the man in front of me. "Did you do this?"

Before he could answer, I picked it up. Even without the fire, his plan was working, and now he could get his revenge.

"Who the hell are you?"

He gritted his teeth. At that moment, I recognized his face. His hair was darker than I remembered, and he wore glasses without the scruff on his face, but it was him. "You're Max's partner with the Crypto-Knights. Gavin. You were in the meeting with Rathmore."

My heart sank. Dammit. Why hadn't I recognized him earlier? I could have stopped this from happening. Was Ricky going to die? Was he already dead? "What do you want?"

"I want you to come with me."

Chapter 13

Dropping my wrist, he slid to his feet and motioned for me to do the same. As I scooted out, I felt inside my cross-body purse for my stun flashlight and palmed it. Sliding out of the booth, I held it slightly behind me and flipped it on, ready to push the stun button at the first opportunity.

Before he turned his back on me, his eyes narrowed, and he was thinking that I looked like I had something up my sleeve. "Whatever you're planning to do, I suggest you think twice about it. If anything happens to me, your uncle dies."

I shook my head. "How do I know you're not just making that up?"

He huffed, thinking I wasn't as good at reading people as he'd been led to believe. Wasn't I supposed to be psychic or something? What a load of crap.

"So where is my uncle?"

"You'll find out soon enough. Come along." He grabbed my upper arm and led me toward the back exit behind the band. I followed willingly enough, picking up that he needed to get me out of there before anyone figured out that I was gone.

As we got closer to the exit, I picked up his sudden nerves. He was thinking that the whole success of his plan hinged on this one moment, and he stepped up the pace, tugging on my arm to hurry me along.

I slowed my step, realizing it was all a bluff. He didn't have Uncle Joey.

Using my Aikido training, I jerked my arm out of his grasp and lunged toward him with my stun flashlight. Just before connecting, he hopped back, and I barely missed him. He used my momentum to grab my wrist and twisted. With a yelp, I lost my grip on the flashlight.

As it clattered to the floor, he grabbed me around the waist and dragged me toward the door. Bending my arm, I flung my elbow into his head, connecting with his face. His head snapped back and he cried out.

His hold loosened enough for me to elbow him hard in the stomach. This time, he let me go, and I fell to my knees. Scrambling to my feet, I twisted to face him, but he'd already shoved through the crowd and was running to the exit.

Wanting to stop him, I started to follow, but there were too many people in my way. My chest heaving, I leaned over to catch my breath. As the crowd thinned around me, I spotted my stun flashlight and hurried to retrieve it.

With it safely back in my purse, I rushed toward the entrance to find Ricky. A crowd surrounded him, and I shoved my way through. Ramos held a towel to Ricky's stomach, muttering to him to hang on. I knelt beside Ricky, taking in his pale, sweaty face, and brushed his hair back from his forehead.

"Hang on Ricky. You're going to be fine. Help is on the way." His breathing was shallow, and he groaned in pain, but at least he wasn't dead.

A team of paramedics swarmed in and took over, pushing me and Ramos aside. I watched them check Ricky's vitals and pull an oxygen mask over his nose and mouth. After slipping a pad under him, they lifted him onto a gurney and wheeled him out of the club to a waiting ambulance.

As the ambulance took off, I turned to Ramos. "Do you think he'll make it?"

He heaved out a breath. "I don't know."

I swallowed. "This is terrible. I feel like it's my fault."

"Why?"

"Because I didn't figure it out in time. I was... wait... is Uncle Joey okay?"

Ramos's brows rose. "Last time I checked."

"Where is he?"

"In the game room or his office... come on."

I followed him away from the crowd and around the bar to the room where Uncle Joey and his friends had been playing poker. Inside, all the tables had been cleared, and the players were gone. We stepped across the room to Uncle Joey's office, but he wasn't there either.

"I'm down here." Uncle Joey stood outside the security office. "I've been watching the surveillance videos. How does it look for Ricky?"

Ramos shook his head. "Not good, but he should pull through."

Uncle Joey swore under his breath. "I need to get to the hospital. But first, I need to know what happened. That was Dagger, right?"

"Yes. He left faster than we expected, and Ricky—" Ramos shook his head. "Ricky paid the price."

Uncle Joey turned to me. "So who were you talking to?"

Ramos's brows rose. "Someone got to you?"

"Yeah. It's why I missed Dagger."

Ramos heaved out a breath. "Who was it?"

I swallowed. "It was Gavin... Max's partner." I glanced at Uncle Joey. "Gavin was at the meeting Ramos and I went to in Las Vegas. When we took Max down and got all your cryptocurrency back, Gavin lost everything. I think he's the one who's been behind all of the trouble we've had."

"What did he want with you?" Uncle Joey asked.

"I don't know exactly, but he wanted revenge to start with. He told me if I didn't go with him, you'd die. By the time I realized he was bluffing, Ricky had been stabbed, and we were halfway to the exit. I think when the fire didn't start, Dagger stabbed Ricky so Gavin could get me away."

"He had you?" Ramos growled. "How did you escape?"

Uncle Joey snorted. "You can see it all on the surveillance tape." He backed up the surveillance feed that covered the back exit, and hit play. Gavin came into view, dragging me behind him. After I elbowed him in the face, the rest of it took less than a few seconds, but it was disconcerting to see myself fighting him off. At least I kicked his butt.

I sighed. "He still got away."

"The police detectives are here." Uncle Joey pointed to the surveillance feed showing the front entrance. Russ had stepped up to talk to them, but I recognized Detectives Bates and Clue. "Russ knows they can't do a search without a warrant, so he'll keep them at bay until they get one. But that means they'll want the surveillance feed."

He glanced at Ramos. "Make sure they only get the one with Dagger and the attack on Ricky. Do what you have to with the rest. I'm taking Shelby home. I don't want either of us involved."

Ramos nodded. "I'll take care of it."

"Thanks. I'll be in touch."

As I followed Uncle Joey out of the VIP exit, I glanced over my shoulder to give Ramos an appreciative nod. He'd been thinking that he was glad I was all right, and that it was extremely satisfying to watch me elbow Gavin in the face and stomach.

One of the club's security men waited for us at the outside door, ready to take us home. He ushered us to the limo, and I climbed into the backseat, relaxing for the first time all night. Uncle Joey got in beside me and took out his phone to call Jackie for an update on Ricky.

Apparently, he'd already asked her to take Aubree, Ricky's wife, to the hospital, and they'd met the ambulance there. Jackie filled Uncle Joey in, and I picked up enough to know that Ricky was headed to surgery, and they'd know more once he got out.

He ended the call, and worry overwhelmed me. "I hope he'll be okay."

Uncle Joey patted my hand. "It's not your fault. Even if Gavin hadn't interfered, you never would have made it to Ricky in time. He'll pull through... you'll see."

"What should we do now? You still want to go to New York in the morning?"

"Yes. In fact, it's probably a good thing to get out of town with Gavin after us. It will give us time to figure out a way to end... uh... catch him. In fact, I'm going to get my best people to work on finding him while we're gone."

"Good idea." We pulled up in front of my house, and I opened the door. "Thanks Uncle Joey."

"Of course. I'll send the limo to pick all of you up at six-thirty sharp."

"Okay. We'll see you then."

Closing the car door, I rushed into the house, locking the door behind me. Chris had left a light on, and I hurried up the stairs to our room. He was still awake, propped up in bed and reading a book. He took one look at me and got out of bed. "What's wrong?"

I stepped into his arms, still trembling. Holding him tightly, I let out a breath, finally feeling safe. He was worried that someone had died, so I rushed to explain. "Everyone's okay but Ricky. He tried to stop Dagger, but Dagger had a knife and stabbed him. Right now he's in surgery."

"Oh man... that's rough. But you're okay?" He pulled away to study my face, pushing a few wisps of hair from my cheek.

"Yeah."

"What happened?"

I heaved out a breath and shook my head. "We had a plan, but it didn't quite work out." I kicked off my heels, and Chris helped me unzip my dress. By the time I'd changed out of my clothes and thrown on a large t-shirt, I'd told him everything.

Climbing into bed, he tucked me into the crook of his arm and held me close. "That's nuts. I'd forgotten all about Gavin. I hope Ricky pulls through."

"Me too." Tears gathered in my eyes. I'd held them back until now, but thinking about Ricky dying... it was too much.

"He'll be okay, honey. It's not your fault. Shhh... try and get some rest. I've got you."

I slept fitfully until five-thirty in the morning and finally got up to take a shower and get ready. It was strange not having Coco at home, but at least I knew he was in good hands. When six-thirty arrived, we were all packed and ready to go.

The limo pulled up, and we all piled in. The kids were excited, but they knew something was bothering me. I finally had a minute to send a text to Uncle Joey about Ricky. His text came back, and I held my breath in case it was bad news.

Luckily, it said that Ricky had made it through the night and was expected to make a full recovery. Relief swept over me, and I closed my eyes, resting my head on the back of the seat.

"Good news?" Chris asked.

"Yes. He made it."

Josh's brows drew together. "What's going on?"

"One of Uncle Joey's men was... hurt at the club last night, but he's going to be okay."

"Ramos?"

"No. Ramos is fine. It was Ricky. You haven't met him, but he's been with Uncle Joey for a while."

"What happened?"

I hated to tell them the truth, but I didn't want to lie either. "Last night, a man was planning to set the club on fire. It didn't work, but as he ran out, Ricky tried to stop him. The man put up a fight and stabbed Ricky to get away. It was bad, but it sounds like he's going to make a full recovery."

"Whoa... that's intense. Did you see it happen?"

I nodded. "Yeah. I had a hard time sleeping last night. But now that I know he's going to pull through, I feel a lot better."

"Did they catch the guy?"

"No, but I'm sure the police are looking for him. Hopefully by the time we get back, he'll be behind bars."

Josh was a little surprised that the police were involved. "So Uncle Joey's not looking for him too?"

"Oh... yeah... I'm sure he is."

Josh's brow wrinkled. Before he could ask what Uncle Joey would do with him, Savannah spoke up.

"But what about the wedding? Is Uncle Joey still coming?"

"Yes... he wouldn't miss it... especially now that we know Ricky's okay. We'll see him and Jackie at the airport in a few minutes."

"Oh... that's good."

We pulled into the private air strip and hustled out of the limo. Dragging our bags, we walked across the tarmac to Uncle Joey's waiting jet. Uncle Joey stood at the top of the staircase and hurried down the stairs to greet us, giving everyone a hearty welcome.

With the help of the crew, we soon had all our bags stowed away, and we settled in for the flight. I actually fell asleep during the last two hours, waking up to hear that we were landing in twenty minutes.

"Feel better?" Chris asked.

"Yes. Much. Did you get any sleep?"

"A little."

After landing, my heart fluttered to see the van with *Hotel Perona* across the side waiting for us. While everyone got off the plane, I remembered to send a quick text to Hawk that we'd arrived.

Quickly joining the others, I found Syd stepping out of the van with a welcoming smile. We surrounded him, happily greeting the soon-to-be groom.

During the car ride, Uncle Joey couldn't resist ribbing him. "I can't believe you talked my sister into giving up her vows and marrying you. I never thought I'd see the day she'd do something that drastic."

"Yeah, yeah... you forget that she just needed the right man."

"I guess... but it kind of blows my mind that it's you."

"Shut up already. So how's business going?"

Uncle Joey shrugged. "It could be worse." They traded stories, and the rest of us made small talk until we reached the hotel.

Uncle Joey's cousin, Frank, and his wife Sylvie, greeted us in the lobby. After giving us our room keys, Frank pulled me aside and lowered his voice. "Your detective friend got here just before you. He's in his room, but that was cutting it close." He thought that, if Joey found out, he hoped I didn't expect him to vouch for me, since it wasn't his idea.

"Oh... good. I'm glad he made it. And... don't worry... if the worst happens, I'll take full responsibility."

He nodded thinking that he hoped I could handle it, because, if he'd learned anything... the truth was bound to come out sooner or later. It reminded him of the lies I'd told him for weeks, and how that had ended. Maybe I should just tell Joey the truth and get it over with?

I opened my mouth to tell him he might have a point, but caught myself. "Uh... thanks Frank... for everything." He shrugged, thinking it was my funeral, and took our bags to the luggage cart to be brought up to our rooms.

He'd given us the same suite we'd had before, and we stepped inside to find a sitting room with chairs, a couch, a coffee table and a flat-screen TV mounted on the wall. The master bedroom had a separate bath for Chris and me, and there was a connecting bedroom and bath, along with a pull-out bed in the couch for one of our kids.

"I get the connecting bedroom!" Savannah yelled, rushing inside. That left Josh to use the couch with the pull-out bed. Luckily, he didn't seem to mind and made himself at home.

Chris and I headed into the large bedroom with a king-size bed, a flat-screen TV on the wall over a chest of drawers, an easy-chair in the corner, and our own private bathroom. I stepped to the window, loving the view which overlooked the street, and sighed.

Grateful to be here, I sank onto the bed, breathing in the wonderful scent I'd remembered. Just being in this hotel lifted my spirits. No more worries about Gavin or Savage, or even Elliot. I could finally relax and get away from it all.

My phone rang with the *Scooby Doo* ringtone and I quickly answered. "Hey Dimples. How was your flight?"

"It was okay. Too early, but at least I made it to the hotel. Did you talk to Hawk?"

"I sent him a text." Just then my phone chimed with a notification. "Oh... he just answered... just a sec." I pulled up my texts to find the message from Hawk that said we could come now. "Okay... it looks like we're good to head over there. Give me a few minutes, and I'll meet you in the lobby."

"Sure."

We disconnected, and I hurried into the bathroom to freshen up. Chris had heard my side of the conversation and stood in the bathroom doorway with his arms crossed. "You should have told Harris to wait for you out on the street. Manetto might see him in the lobby."

"Uncle Joey's not going to see him. I'm sure he's gone to his room by now. It'll be fine." Finished, I hurried past him, stopping for a second to give him a quick kiss. "I'll be back in a couple of hours. If you go anywhere, let me know where you are, and I'll meet up with you there."

"Okay. Good luck."

As I continued through the sitting area to the door, Savannah's brows rose. "Where are you going?"

"Police business, but I'll be back soon."

She twisted her lips, knowing that police business was code for trouble. Was I going to mess up our time here? If it was anything like last time, this could be a disaster, and her meager moments with Miguel would be ruined forever. Shaking her head, she hoped I'd stay home next time.

Whoa... that was harsh. Managing a smile, I gave her a kiss on the top of her head and hurried out the door. Exiting the elevator, I stepped into the lobby and found Uncle Joey talking to Frank. Crap. Couldn't they talk in Frank's office? Uncle Joey glanced my way and frowned. "Going somewhere?"

"Uh... yeah. I have an errand to run, but I'll be back in about an hour."

His brows rose. What wasn't I telling him? I edged toward the doors, hoping Dimples had somehow managed to sneak out and was already waiting on the sidewalk.

Just then, the elevator doors opened, and Dimples strode out. He saw me and smiled, but his smile vanished as his gaze landed on Uncle Joey. All kinds of swear words flooded his mind, and his face paled.

Noticing that my attention was behind him, Uncle Joey turned. Surprise, followed by anger, jolted through him. "What the hell are you doing here?" He glanced at me, catching my guilt-stricken face, and his lips turned down.

I rushed to Dimples's side. "We're working on a case together and there's an informant here in New York we needed to talk to, so I suggested that Dimples stay here... you know... because we're working together. I hope you don't mind."

A low growl came from Uncle Joey's throat, and he leveled me with a flinty gaze. "And you didn't think I needed to know?"

"I was sort of hoping to avoid that."

He shook his head and turned to Frank. "And you knew?"

Frank shook his head and lied. "I had no idea."

Uncle Joey pursed his lips and sent a baleful gaze at Dimples. "How long are you staying?"

"My flight leaves first thing in the morning."

"Good. Well... go on then." He motioned toward the door. His gaze landed on me, and he was thinking that I should have told him, but since I didn't, I owed him big time.

Accepting defeat, I nodded. "Okay. See ya."

Outside, the doorman hailed a taxi for us, and we got into the back seat. Dimples glanced at me, wondering how much trouble I was in.

I shrugged. "I don't think it's too bad... I mean, I owe him for it... but I owe him for a lot of things, so it's nothing new."

Dimples rubbed his face and swore under his breath. "I should have listened to my gut. I knew we were taking a chance, but you made it sound like he wasn't around the hotel much, so it would be fine."

"Oh come on... it's not that bad."

"Yeah... until he wants something from me."

I shook my head. "He knows that won't work." But I knew just as well as he did that it was a possibility. "Uh... I'd better text Hawk and tell him we're on our way."

Ignoring Dimples's inner swearing, I sent the text. Hawk replied that the suspect, Danny Fowler, was already there, so it was perfect timing. "Hey... look at that. Danny's already there. See... it's all working out."

Dimples gave me a tight nod, thinking *there she goes again... always looking on the bright side.* Then he wondered if that was a coping mechanism or just a way to change the subject?

Since it was a little of both, I just shrugged and smiled, amazed at how well he knew me. As we drove along, I pointed out some of the sights to get his mind off his troubles.

We arrived at the precinct and found Hawk waiting for us in the precinct lobby. He looked exactly the same, with his piercing, green eyes, clean-shaven face, and the deep cleft in his chin. I automatically compared it to Dimples's cheeks and blinked. Yup... they were both mesmerizing.

I gave Hawk a quick hug and introduced the two detectives. "Hawk, this is my partner, Drew Harris."

"Nice to meet you," Dimples said, shaking Hawk's hand. "Shelby told me all about the case you worked on together when she was here last. It sounded like it was lucky you both survived. On the other hand, it's kind of what happens when Shelby's involved."

They both glanced at me, and I rolled my eyes. "Oh come on, give me a break."

Hawk grinned at me and glanced at Dimples with a raised brow. "I'll bet you've got some stories you could tell."

Dimples huffed out a breath and shook his head. "Oh man... you wouldn't believe half of them."

Hawk chuckled. "Actually... I think I would. How long are you going to be here? Maybe we could trade stories later?"

Dimples's smile widened. "That would be great." He glanced my way. "Shelby's got family stuff with her uncle, so I'm on my own."

"Oh yeah? So you've met him?"

Dimples huffed out a breath. "Yeah... for some reason he doesn't like me much."

They shared a laugh, both of them feeling at ease with the other. "Then why don't you stick around after the interview, and I'll show you how we do things here in New York."

Dimples nodded, relief loosening his tight shoulders. "That sounds great." He slanted his head my way. "Her uncle isn't too happy I'm staying at his hotel."

Hawk's eyes widened. "What? Whose crazy idea was that?"

They both looked at me, and I held up my hands. "Okay... okay... maybe it wasn't the best idea, but I didn't think Uncle Joey would find out."

Hawk's eyes widened. "I take it he did?" At my sigh, he shook his head. "O..kay... I bet that was fun."

"You don't know the half of it," Dimples said.

Tired of them talking around me, I changed the subject. "Uh... what about that interview? We don't want to keep Danny waiting too long, or he might change his mind."

Hawk's lips twisted. He knew a diversion when he saw one. "Right. It's just this way." He led the way through the precinct to the interrogation rooms. "He's in there. I'll introduce you and watch through the observation window."

"Great," Dimples said. "Make sure you record it, too."

"Will do." Hawk opened the door and ushered us inside.

Dressed in worn-out jeans, a denim jacket that had seen better days, and a grease-stained shirt, Danny glanced our way, and his boredom changed to suspicion. With his long nose and thinning hair pulled back into a ponytail, he looked a little weasel-ish... just like the informant he was.

"Hey Danny," Hawk said. "Thanks for waiting. I'd like to introduce you to Detective Harris and Shelby Nichols. They have a couple of questions for you about a cold case they're working on."

Danny's dull eyes turned wary, but he nodded, knowing his cooperation was the only thing keeping him out of jail.

"I'll be back to work out the details of our arrangement." Hawk sent us each a nod and backed out of the room, closing the door behind him.

"Hey Danny," Dimples began. "This may seem out of the blue, but we have information that links you to a cold case from about twenty years ago. Do you remember your old friend, Wade Keller?"

Danny's face paled, and he swallowed, but he kept a straight face. "I'm not sure."

"We think Wade killed a couple of people at a gas station." Dimples pulled the file from his briefcase, opening it up to show Danny the gruesome crime scene photos. He tapped his finger on the photo of Kirk's broken and battered face.

Danny jerked away from the table and swore in his mind. He vividly remembered what had happened twenty years ago, but, after all this time, he never thought it would catch up with him.

"This is Kirk Wahlen," Dimples continued. "He was only twenty-two. He had his whole life ahead of him. He was even engaged to be married, but none of that happened. His life was stolen from him twenty years ago, and we think you know it was Wade Keller who did it."

Danny shook his head and covered his face. He'd tried to banish the vision of Kirk's broken body from his mind, but seeing the photos brought it all back. He broke out in a cold sweat, but thought he could save his own skin if he cooperated. We were targeting Wade, not him.

He rubbed his forehead before glancing at Dimples. "Yeah... I remember Wade. But I didn't do anything. He was the one who did it, not me."

"What happened that night? Can you walk us through it?"

He shook his head and glanced away. "Yeah. We went to the gas station for cigarettes. Wade bought them, and the kid... Kirk... gave Wade back his change, but Wade thought it wasn't the right amount, and they argued. It got pretty heated, and Kirk finally told Wade to leave."

Danny closed his eyes and shook his head. "The kid shouldn't have done that. It set Wade off, and he went ballistic. He started pounding on the kid. Hitting him again and again. It was like he couldn't stop."

I closed my eyes and put up my shields. I'd already seen this in Wade's mind, but seeing it from Danny's point of view was almost worse. I swallowed, concentrating on blocking my mind until the scene vanished and I could breathe again.

"Do you remember the motorist who came inside while this was going on? What happened to him?"

Danny shook his head. "I don't remember a motorist."

That didn't sound right, so I dropped my shields and listened to his thoughts. Danny remembered the motorist well, because he had taken them all by surprise. Kirk was still alive at that point, and Wade panicked. He pulled out his gun and shot the man five times.

I caught Danny's gaze, trying another tactic to get him to talk. "Is that because you shot him?"

"No... it wasn't me... Wade pulled the gun on him. He shot him." Danny licked his lips. "That's when Kirk started crawling toward the back of the store. Wade could have shot him, but he just kept hitting him instead."

I nodded. "He made you help him, didn't he?"

Danny let out a breath. How did I know that? "Yeah... but... he had a gun, so I didn't have much choice."

"What did Keller tell you to do?" Dimples asked.

Danny closed his eyes. "Wade didn't want the kid taking off again, so he made me tie his hands and feet together." Danny swallowed. "I knew he'd kill me if I didn't do what he said."

Dimples nodded. This was exactly what we needed to put Wade away for good. "Right now, Wade's in prison for something else, but he's getting out in a few days."

Danny rocked back like he'd been hit. "Shit."

"Yeah... we don't want that to happen, so we need you to testify against him. If you do, it will keep him in prison for the rest of his life."

Danny froze, then began shaking his head, not about to agree. Dimples pressed his point. "Look... from what you've told us, you're an accomplice to Kirk's murder, but if you testify, I'm sure we can grant you immunity."

Danny's lips thinned, and he shook his head again. He couldn't face Wade in a trial. He'd never be safe again.

I sat forward. "Danny... we need to keep Wade behind bars. Once he gets out, who knows what he'll do? This is our only chance to keep him where he belongs. We don't want him to kill someone else. We have to act now."

Danny met my gaze. After that night, he'd gotten away from Wade as fast as he could. Wade was bat-shit crazy. That was all there was to it, and he wanted nothing to do with him. "You don't know him like I do. He'll come after me however he can... even from behind bars. I can't do it."

Dimples sat forward, leaning across the table. "You know what that means? Right? It means we'll be prosecuting you for being an accessory to Kirk's murder. Do you really want to end up in jail when you don't have to?"

Danny huffed out a breath. "I don't care. I won't do it."

I picked up that Danny meant every word. He couldn't be swayed, even if it meant he'd end up in jail. He was too afraid of Wade to testify against him, and he didn't care what happened to anyone else if Wade got out.

"You're sure?" Dimples asked. "I can't offer you immunity if you don't cooperate."

"If that's all, I'm done here." He got up and walked out the door, thinking he was done helping the police.

Hawk rushed into the hall, calling after him. "Hey! Where are you going?"

"I'm done, man. I thought this was about your case, and you threw me in there with them."

"I know... I get it, but we can still work something out... unless you want me to arrest you right now?"

Danny ran his hands over his face. "Fine. I'll help you, but I gotta get out of here. I'll come back tomorrow."

"Sure." Hawk watched him go, wondering if he was going to disappear. At least he knew how to track him down if he had to. He shook his head and came into our room. "That was some interview. It's too bad he won't testify. Don't you have anything else you can use?"

Dimples nodded. "Yeah. We matched Keller's blood to one of the bills at the scene, but without Danny's testimony, we need at least one more piece of evidence to bring charges against him."

"Hey... what about the hair they found at the scene?" I asked. "Could that work?"

"That's right," Dimples agreed. "We could see if it's a match to Keller's DNA. We could get a hair sample from him, too. That would do it, even without Danny's testimony. I'll put the call through right now."

While Dimples called, I turned to Hawk. "I hope we didn't mess up your investigation too badly."

He shook his head. "No worries. He'll come around. Besides, it sounds like Harris wants to charge him for this case, so we'll work something out." He scratched his head. "So you really got Harris a room at your uncle's hotel? That's pretty gutsy. I guess that means things are going well with your uncle?"

"Yeah... he's not so bad."

"Well, he sure helped us out. Although Milo Bilotti's untimely death still seems a little suspicious. Tell me... hypothetically speaking... did he have anything to do with it?"

"Absolutely not. He was with me and my family at the time."

Hawk's lips twisted, and he thought there were plenty of ways to kill someone without actually doing it yourself.

I shook my head. "Bilotti died of a heart attack... no one had to do anything. Isn't that right?"

"Yes... of course it is. So... how long will you be here this time?" He was thinking that he wouldn't mind having me take a look at one of his cases if I could stop by his desk for a few minutes. But he didn't want to push it, even though he'd helped me out.

Crap. Why did he have to think that? "Not long. The wedding's tomorrow, and we're heading home the day after that. We have a lot of family stuff going on, so I might not be able to... return the favor this time."

"Oh... I didn't expect that. I'm always happy to help you out." A guilty flush ran over him. It wasn't just what I could do for him... he was interested in my life because we were friends.

That made me feel better. "Glad to hear it... and I would help you out if I had more time... you know that, right?"

"Sure. Don't worry about it. After what happened before, I totally get it."

Dimples joined us with a bright smile on his face. "They're doing the test. I just hope we get the results back before Keller is released."

"Yeah... no kidding. So, are you sticking around here?"

"I think so."

"Good. Well... then I'll see you later. Hawk... it's been great seeing you again." I gave him a quick hug before pulling away. "And don't believe everything Dimples tells you."

"Dimples?" He glanced at Dimples with horror in his eyes. "She calls you Dimples?"

"Yeah." He shrugged. "She called me that before she knew my name, and I guess it stuck." He looked at me sideways. "But don't worry. I have plenty of stories about Shelby to even things out."

Hawk raised his brows. "Oh... I'm looking forward to it."

I rolled my eyes and turned to leave. "See ya."

Chapter 14

I stood outside the New York precinct and checked my phone for messages. Sure enough, Chris had left one telling me that I could find them at a famous pizza place. I hailed a taxi and arrived just in time to grab a piece of pizza and sit down with the whole fam-dam-ly, including Uncle Joey, Jackie, and Miguel.

Miguel explained that he had the next few days off, and commented that it was nice to have all of his family here. Savannah wanted to remind him that we weren't really related, but let it go, realizing how it might sound. Still, she hung on every word he said, and I picked up her feelings of adoration for him.

It alarmed me, but I knew she'd never say anything out loud, so I tried to take it in stride. Besides, I'd picked up enough to know that Miguel's attitude was totally on the friend level.

He knew she was way too young for him, and her huge crush was more than a little awkward, but since he didn't want to get her hopes up, he'd treat her like the cousin she was supposed to be, and hope it all worked out.

I knew it wasn't what Savannah had dreamed of for this trip, but there wasn't much I could do about it. Teenage crushes were the worst, but they also came and went pretty fast. Hopefully, she'd find someone else closer to her age for her next crush. I shook my head. Maybe it was time to put up my shields and try to be normal for a change.

As we left the restaurant, I caught up with Uncle Joey to ask how things were going at home. "Are there any updates on Ricky?"

"Yes. He's doing a lot better, but they're keeping him in intensive care for another night. Hopefully, he'll be well enough to move to a regular room tomorrow."

"That's good. Any news about Gavin or Dagger?"

"Ramos is working on it. Last I heard, he was getting close." He was thinking that Gavin's demise couldn't come fast enough. That went for Dagger, too.

My eyes widened. "He's going to—uh—never-mind, I don't want to know. So I guess that means Ramos isn't coming to the wedding?"

"No. Tracking Gavin is his first priority."

"That makes sense. We don't want him coming after us again."

"Exactly."

"So... are you ready for the big day tomorrow?"

He shook his head. "I guess. I never thought Syd would be my brother-in-law. But I'm happy for him and Maggie. And he knows he has to treat her right or answer to me, so he'll be good to her."

"No doubt."

"So how did your police interview go?"

"It kind of fizzled out, but we have an alternative that looks promising."

He sniffed. "But you're done helping them, right? This trip wasn't supposed to be for working."

"Oh... I know. I'm done with that part, so it's all good."

"Good. So what's going on with your detective?" He didn't want to run into him again, but that didn't mean he wouldn't keep tabs on him. A detective snooping around his business was never a good idea.

"You don't have to worry about that. He's spending the day with Hawk. I might not even see him before he leaves in the morning, so it's all good."

He nodded, still astonished that I'd arranged for the detective to take a room in his hotel. But, maybe it wasn't all bad. If he ever needed a favor, at least he had some leverage on the detective. In fact, maybe he'd let him stay for free... that might do it.

Yikes. That was exactly what Dimples had been afraid of. "Um... you should make him pay. The police are footing the bill, and you know how it looks..." I shrugged and gave him a quick smile.

He narrowed his gaze. "Fine. But I'm still asking for a favor if I need one." He immediately thought of me, and how any favor he asked from Dimples would be for my sake, so I shouldn't get too uppity over it.

My eyes widened, but I decided to act like I hadn't heard that. "So, what's next on the agenda for today?"

He huffed. "That's Jackie's department. I'm just along for the ride."

We spent the rest of the day doing touristy things together and had a wonderful time. After dinner, Maggie invited Jackie, Savannah, and me, over to see her new apartment, while the guys went back to the hotel.

Since Maggie had given up her vows as a sister, she'd decided to reinvent herself, and it showed in subtle ways. She had a new hairstyle, wearing her thick, white curls a little longer, which totally softened her strong jaw. A hint of makeup darkened her eyes and lips, giving her a sophisticated air. She'd spent time shopping with Sylvie and had bought a whole new wardrobe, and it was fun to admire all her new clothes.

An hour later, the four of us caught a taxi back to the hotel for some dessert, meeting the guys in the hotel restaurant. We crowded around a table, and I ordered the delectable chocolate cake, fulfilling my dreams for the trip.

That night, I listened for the ghostly serenade I heard the last time I'd been there, but all was quiet. That probably meant that Uncle Joey's grandfather had moved on. That was good for him, and, since Miguel sounded so much like him, I could hardly complain.

We spent the next morning getting ready for the wedding that afternoon. Maggie had opted for a church ceremony, with only family and a few close friends in attendance. It sounded simple to me until we walked into the church she'd chosen.

It was called The Cathedral Church of St. John the Divine, and it was massive, but I figured ex-nuns could get any place they wanted, so why not? I'd been in a few cathedrals like this before, but it was a first for my kids.

Maggie had encouraged us to enter at the front of the cathedral and walk through the building to get the full effect. After entering, we made sure to turn around and look up at the beautiful, round, stained glass on the western side, admiring the blue hues and intricate design that made up the rose window.

We continued through the building, taking in all the sights, until we came to the altar at the far end where

Maggie's marriage would take place. We took our seats beside the New York Manettos, along with a few nuns, and waited for the ceremony to begin.

Syd came in first and stood beside the priest, looking dapper in his dark suit and tie. I picked up nervous tension from him, but as soon as Maggie came in, holding Uncle Joey's arm, he relaxed. Maggie looked radiant in her beautiful, lavender jacket dress that flowed around her in flirty waves.

As they took their vows, I felt their joy, and my heart swelled. I couldn't help the moisture that gathered in my eyes, knowing how much they looked forward to this new life together.

After the ceremony, everyone gathered around to congratulate the couple, and Maggie introduced us all to the priest who'd officiated. He had kind eyes and a contagious smile. "Everyone, this is Father John. We've been friends for a long time, and I'm grateful he was able to perform the ceremony."

As he shook our hands, he had a kind word for each of us. He'd already seen Miguel in the musical, and he made it a point to tell him how much he'd enjoyed his performance. I also caught that he knew a lot about Maggie's history. He'd heard all about Uncle Joey, but he'd never met him before, and studied him with open curiosity.

On an impulse, Maggie invited him to her celebratory dinner back at the hotel. To my surprise, he accepted, saying he would follow after he'd changed out of his robes. Maggie hesitated, wanting to wait for him, but Uncle Joey stepped up, telling her he'd stay behind and bring the priest with him. He glanced my way, thinking that I should stay behind as well, so I knew he was up to something.

"I'll wait with Uncle Joey." I turned to Chris. "You guys go ahead. We'll be right behind you."

Chris raised a brow, knowing something was up. But since it was Uncle Joey, he wasn't about to argue. "Sure. See you in a bit." He followed after the rest of the family, and soon, we were the only people left.

Father John hadn't missed our exchange and wondered what Uncle Joey wanted. "Thanks for waiting. I'll be right back."

As soon as he was out of sight, I raised a brow. "So, what's up?"

Uncle Joey shook his head. "I'm thinking of making a donation. The church was Maggie's refuge for a long time, and I'd like to show my appreciation." He thought it would also be a nice tax write-off, so why not?

"But why did you want me to stay?"

His lips thinned. "I might have a few questions for Father John, and, since priests have to keep secrets, I'm not sure he'll answer me." He raised a brow. "But you will."

I sucked in a breath. "Really? I'm not sure I'm comfortable with that. I mean... doesn't it break some priestly oath or something?"

"Don't worry, Shelby. You won't get in trouble for it. Besides, it's nothing big, and it might actually help someone."

Before I could answer, Father John came back, wearing his normal priestly attire. "Thanks for waiting." Sensing tension between us, his brows rose. "Is there something I can do for you?"

"Yes," Uncle Joey said. "I'd like to make a donation to the church on Maggie's behalf. And there's another matter I need to address. Is there a place we can talk in private?"

"Of course. We can go to my office. Please, follow me."

Not sure I wanted to be part of this, I lagged behind, following them out of the cathedral and onto the grounds.

Father John slowed until I'd caught up with both of them, sensing that something was bothering me.

"I love these grounds," he began, hoping to put me at ease, and thinking I was in some kind of trouble. "There is great beauty here, even after all the leaves have fallen."

"It is lovely," I agreed, taking in the paths between the buildings, as well as the large garden and walkway in front of the administration building where we headed. Only a few people were out and about, and most of them wore church robes.

Wanting to direct his attention away from me, I asked a question. "Do you officiate at weddings very often?"

"No. In fact, the last wedding I officiated was for my daughter."

My brows rose. He had a daughter? Weren't priests celibate?

Seeing my wide eyes, he chuckled. "I adopted her. She had a difficult start, and I was given the blessing of raising her."

"Oh... right. I guess that makes sense. I'm sorry I thought... uh... anyway...."

"It's fine." He chuckled. "I like to get a rise out of people."

"Oh... gotcha."

He winked, and I instantly liked this kind priest who didn't take himself so seriously.

I listened to Uncle Joey's thoughts, hoping he'd forget about betraying the priest's trust. With nothing like that happening, I asked my own questions. "So I take it that you know Maggie's history? Were you surprised she wanted to leave the sisters and get married?"

He nodded. "She never would have considered it five years ago, but something changed after her brother..." He glanced at Uncle Joey "...came back into her life. It was healing for her... and I think finding out who killed her grandfather and fiancée all those years ago, opened her heart. She's a different person now, and I'm happy for her. Not everyone finds love like that."

"That's true." I glanced at Uncle Joey to pull him into the conversation. "Wasn't Syd a family friend?"

Uncle Joey nodded. "Yes. He knew Maggie when they were younger... before that business with the Bilottis and her becoming a sister."

"I thought so. I'll bet Syd has carried a torch for her for a long time, so I'm glad he finally got his wish. It's saying a lot that she'd give up her vows for him."

"Yes it is," Father John said. "But she gained full permission from the church, so she's still in good standing." He opened the front door to an older, three-story building on the grounds, and ushered us inside. "My office is right through here."

We followed him down a short hallway to a corner office with dark wood paneling, shelves full of books, and a heavy wooden desk in the corner. He motioned to two chairs in front of his desk, and took his seat behind it.

It struck me as a little ironic that Uncle Joey sat in front of the massive desk instead of behind it. Father John opened his top desk drawer, determined to get Uncle Joey's donation before anything else happened, and pulled out a credit card reader and donation receipt. He set everything on his desk and glanced at Uncle Joey with raised brows. "How will you be making your donation? We take cash, check or credit cards."

Uncle Joey's lips twisted at Father John's smooth delivery. "Card."

It only took a few minutes to make the transaction, and, pleased with the amount, Father John smiled and sat back in his chair, knowing there was more. "Now, what else can I do for you?"

"I don't know if you're aware of Shelby's connection to the family?" Uncle Joey began.

John's lips turned down. "I'm well aware that you all lied about it. Has anything changed?"

Uncle Joey paused, surprised that the priest knew. "Not at all. And I regret the lies I told about her being Maggie's long-lost daughter. But now... someone else has approached me, and I don't know what to make of it."

"What do you mean?"

"This person claims that he's Maggie's son. Apparently, he knows that Maggie is a Sister, and his information could ruin her standing with the church. He's willing to go away if I pay him off, otherwise, he'll come forward and make a nuisance of himself. I think he's lying, but he has compelling evidence to support it.

"I was planning to ask Maggie, but I don't want to upset her on her wedding day, so that's why I'm asking you instead. Since you've been close all these years, I thought you might know if it's true. Did she ever have a baby while she was a sister?"

Father John shook his head. "Under the seal of confession, I am not allowed to answer that. But I will say that Maggie has never broken any moral laws or obligations she entered into when becoming a sister."

Uncle Joey knew that was as close as he'd get to an answer, but he had me, so he could be gracious about it. "Thank you Father. I think I get your meaning." He glanced at me, silently asking if I'd gotten the same answer.

Naturally, I had, even though I didn't feel right about sharing it. I gave him a nod, and he turned back to Father John. "Shall we head to the celebration? They should be getting started soon."

"Of course."

Leaving the office building, we strolled through the beautiful grounds onto the large, open walkway around the cathedral toward the street to find a taxi.

Heading my way, I caught sight of a familiar figure with shoulder-length, blond hair, and a heart-shaped face. Was that Ella St. John? She glowed with confidence and purpose, instantly drawing me to her.

A sudden blast of anger hit me with so much force that I stopped in my tracks. Glancing slightly to the right, my heart froze. Just twenty feet in front of us, Gavin stepped out from behind a tall sculpture with his arm raised and a gun in his hand. *Die, bastard.*

At the same time I heard Ramos yelling *Shelby, duck!* I jerked down, but instantly knew Gavin wasn't aiming at me. He fired his gun before I could shove Uncle Joey out of the way. The bullet hit him in the chest, sending him stumbling backward.

Another shot went off, and I cringed, grabbing Uncle Joey's arm. As he slumped to the ground, I held on tight, hoping to keep him from hitting his head. Shielding him with my body, I glanced over my shoulder, but Gavin had disappeared.

Turning back to Uncle Joey, I found a red stain blossoming through his white shirt. "No!"

Ramos rushed to my side, jostling me out of the way. Father John knelt at Uncle Joey's other side and spoke, but my ears seemed blocked with cotton, and I couldn't make out a word either of them said. They took Uncle Joey's pulse and pulled his shirt apart, finding blood oozing from a bullet wound.

"Uncle Joey?" I grabbed his hand and willed him to look at me. He blinked a few times, and tears slid from his eyes into his hair.

"We're here. It's going to be okay."

He closed his eyes, and I picked up his agony. He was thinking that he didn't want to die, not yet, but pain squeezed his chest like a vise, and he couldn't take a breath. *Shelby?* His gaze shifted. *Ramos?*

I gripped his hand. "Uncle Joey!" My voice shook. "Hang on. You're going to be fine. We've got you."

His eyes began to dim. He glanced at me, fear and love waging a war in his mind. He wanted to tell me it was okay, but he couldn't get the words out. As darkness filled his eyes, his gaze shifted to the blue sky, and his consciousness began to slip away.

"No! Don't leave! Please! You can't go!" I choked on my tears, realizing his hand had gone slack in mine. "No!"

A cool presence came to my side, and I found Ella St. John kneeling over Uncle Joey. She was a nurse with a special healing touch. As usual, I couldn't pick up anything from her mind, but her eyes held worry and compassion.

"Ella. Please. Can you help him?" I was afraid this might be beyond her abilities.

"I can try." She glanced at Father John and Ramos. Another man had joined us, and I realized it was her husband, Aiden Creed. "Don't let anyone get close enough to see what I'm doing. I'm going to see if I can heal him."

The other men stepped away to give her space, leaving me to hold Uncle Joey's hand. Licking her lips, she placed her hands over the bullet wound and closed her eyes.

I held my breath, hardly daring to move while she concentrated. Her brows dipped, but her breathing stayed deep and even, like she was in a trance.

Long seconds passed, but Uncle Joey lay still and silent. Strain began to show on Ella's face. Soon she was taking shorter breaths and sweat popped out on her forehead.

I focused on Uncle Joey's face, hoping to see a sign that Ella's healing was working, but he didn't move, and his face remained a blank mask.

Ella's brow furrowed, and she grimaced, like she was in pain. I wanted to encourage her, but I was afraid if I broke her concentration, Uncle Joey would die.

She swayed slightly before pulling her hands away and sitting back on her heels. As she took in great gulps of air, I felt Uncle Joey squeeze my hand. My breath caught, and I grabbed his hand in both of mine. "Uncle Joey? Can you hear me?"

He took a deep breath, and his eyes fluttered open. "Shel..by?"

"I'm right here."

He took a few more breaths until his breathing was even and steady. His eyes regained their focus, and he took in his surroundings. Confusion filled his mind. "What the hell happened?"

"You got shot."

He scoffed. "I remember that." He was thinking that he'd never felt anything so painful in his life.

"But you're okay now. The pain's gone, right?"

He inhaled deeply and met my gaze. "You're right. I don't feel it anymore." Dropping my hand, he sat up, pleasantly surprised that he could. Pulling his shirt apart, he looked at his bare chest. Only a slight pink scar remained. "What the hell?"

On the other side of him, Ella lifted a brow. Her color had returned, and she looked much better. Ramos, Father John, and Creed still stood in a protective circle around us. Ella got to her feet and glanced my way. "Can you help me get him up?"

"Sure."

As I stood, Ella crouched beside Uncle Joey. "Pull your shirt together. We need to make this look like nothing happened. Can you stand?"

"I don't know." Frowning, he pulled his shirt together, thinking that if anyone saw his bloody shirt, they'd know he'd been shot.

"Shelby and I will help you up."

With each of us taking an arm, Uncle Joey managed to get his feet under him.

Ella caught my gaze and raised a brow. "Let's take him to John's office. It's not far."

After managing a couple of steps, Uncle Joey seemed to regain his strength and hardly needed our help. We only passed a couple of people, but with Father John, Ramos, and Creed surrounding us, no one seemed to notice what was going on.

Before we entered the building, Ramos stopped us. "He got away. I'm going after him."

He turned to leave, but Ella caught his arm. "You should stay. He won't make it far."

Ramos narrowed his gaze. "What do you mean?"

"I can't explain it right now, but trust me; he's not going anywhere. We'll help you find him later. For now you should stay here."

Since I couldn't read her mind, I had no idea what she was talking about, but I had a feeling that she didn't want Ramos to kill him.

Ramos's lips flattened, and he glanced at Uncle Joey. "What do you want me to do?"

Uncle Joey's brows dipped. "If she said to stay... then you stay." At this point he wasn't about to cross Ella St. John, not after this. He remembered that I'd told him she had a healing touch, but this seemed much more than that.

Ramos huffed out a breath, unhappy to let Gavin out of his sight. He vowed that he'd go after Gavin as soon as he could, and followed the rest of us inside and down the hall to Father John's office. Ella led Uncle Joey to a high-backed chair, and he plopped down, not quite as energetic as he'd let on.

I patted his arm. "Are you still feeling okay?"

"Yes. I don't understand it, but I feel fine. What happened?" I opened my mouth to explain, but he stopped me. "...after I got shot."

Father John handed Uncle Joey a bottle of water. "Here. This will help."

With a sigh, Uncle Joey twisted off the cap and drank nearly all the water. Wiping his mouth, he caught sight of his bloody shirt and shook his head. Astonishment that he was alive filled his thoughts. How in the world did that happen?

His phone began to ring, and he sighed before taking it out. It was Jackie, and he quickly answered. "Hey... sorry we're not there yet, but something came up." He paused to listen. "Yes, I know... we'll get there as soon as we can, but it might be another fifteen or twenty minutes." He shook his head. "Just go ahead then..." His lips thinned. "I know this is important. I'd be there right now if I could... okay ... sure ... see you soon."

He put his phone away and shook his head. "They're waiting for us, so we'll have to keep it short, but I'm not leaving until someone tells me what happened."

No one spoke, so he glanced at Ramos. "I take it you followed Gavin here?"

"Yes. But I was too late. I took a shot at him after he shot you, but I must have missed, and he got away." He was thinking that he never missed, and if Manetto had died, he'd never forgive himself.

Uncle Joey turned to Ella. "What about you? How did you..." He closed his eyes. "Maybe I don't want to know... but it was pretty bad. Maybe I should have died. Instead, I've got a shirt covered in my own blood and hardly a mark on my skin. What is this?"

Ella met Creed's gaze before turning to Uncle Joey. "I was just stopping by to see my dad." She nodded at John. "Good thing for you I did. You know I have healing hands, right? Well... sometimes it doesn't work, so I guess you're one of the lucky ones."

John chuckled, and shook his head.

Uncle Joey's brow dipped. "What?"

John shrugged. "I guess it's a good thing you just made that large donation to the church. That must be what saved your skin."

Uncle Joey's lips turned down. He didn't like that answer much, but John just shrugged. "If you really want to know, I'd say it was a gift from God. Can you think of a better explanation?"

Heaving out a breath, Uncle Joey's scowl deepened. He didn't like owing anyone, let alone God. Something else was going on here. His wound couldn't have been that bad, or he'd be dead, so the shock of it must have caused him to black out, and her touch brought him out of it.

"Now that you're okay," Ella began, her voice firm. "I think this should make us even... you know... from when you helped us out in Las Vegas?" She met Uncle Joey's gaze. "Especially if you keep it to yourself and don't tell anyone."

It took a few seconds for Uncle Joey to respond, but he couldn't deny her reasoning. "Fine. This makes us even."

Ella's shoulders relaxed, and she gave him a tight nod, but didn't say anything more. In the uncomfortable silence, I caught her gaze. "So Father John's your dad?"

Ella's lips twisted. "Yeah, that's right."

"He told us about you... but I had no idea you were his daughter. It's kind of nuts that we're all here at the same time."

"I know. So what brought you here, anyway?"

"Your dad performed a wedding for Uncle Joey's sister in the church today. They've known each other for a long time. Hey... maybe you know Maggie, too? She was a sister before she got married."

Recognition flooded her face. "Of course. I didn't know her well, but she was always kind to me."

Father John's brow creased. "So Manetto's the one who helped you out in Las Vegas?" He'd heard the story, but Ella had left out the names.

"Yeah. We're lucky he was there with Shelby."

"What a coincidence."

As she nodded, I picked up from Creed that none of this was a coincidence. If Gavin was here, that meant Rathmore and his hitman weren't far behind.

"Wait. You think Rathmore's involved? Why?" He was the sleazy mob boss from Las Vegas that made even Uncle Joey seem reasonable.

Everyone turned my way. Oops. "Uh... it just came to me that he's the thing we all have in common, you know? So what do you think he's got to do with this?"

"Everything." Creed was thinking they'd come to protect Ella's father from Rathmore, but somehow, they'd saved Manetto instead.

My phone began to play the theme song from *Law and Order*. "Uh... that's Chris. I'd better get it." Digging out my phone, I quickly answered. "Hey honey."

"What's going on? Are you guys okay?" I could hear the worry in his voice, and guilt washed over me.

"Yes. We're fine. It's been a little crazy here, but everything's good. We're with Father John right now, but we'll be on our way in a minute. I'll explain everything when we get there." We said our goodbyes, and I glanced at the others. "We'd better get going."

I took in Uncle Joey's bloody clothes. "Father John, do you have an extra shirt that we can borrow? Just until we get back to the hotel?"

"Of course." He twisted his lips, thinking it might be funny to see Manetto in one of his clerical shirts. Shaking his head at the image, he pulled open the bottom drawer of his desk and took out a polo shirt, hoping that Manetto could squeeze into a medium.

Sighing with relief, Uncle Joey shrugged out of his suit coat and pulled his bloody shirt off. Taking John's polo shirt, he slipped it over his head and managed to pull it partway down when it got stuck. I reached out to help him, and, between us, we finally tugged it down. Catching a chuckle from someone's mind, I barely managed not to chuckle myself.

Letting out a breath, I turned to Father John. "Are you still coming with us?"

He caught Ella's gaze. "Is that okay? I don't have to go if you need me here."

She hesitated, glancing at Ramos before replying. "Uh... no... actually, it's fine. Just let me know when you're done, and we'll meet up."

"Sure."

Uncle Joey slipped his jacket over the tight polo shirt and huffed out a breath. "Okay. Let's go."

Ramos stepped beside him. "Now can I look for Gavin?"

"It's fine with me," Uncle Joey said, thinking he wanted the bastard dead. At Ramos's nod, Uncle Joey turned to Ella. "I'm still not clear on everything, but... thanks for... uh..." He couldn't bring himself to say *saving my life*. "Uh... for helping me."

Her eyes widened. "Of course. I'm glad I was here." She glanced at Ramos. "If you insist on going after Gavin, I'd like to help."

"Why?"

"I have an idea about where we can find him."

Ramos shook his head, thinking that Ella was special... kind of like me. If this was all tied up with Rathmore, things were worse than he thought.

My heart sank. Did that mean Rathmore was behind everything that had happened? We all thought it was Gavin, but since they were connected, it made sense that he could be funding Gavin's need for revenge. He certainly had enough money to throw around.

It also changed things. If he was the one behind all this, he probably wanted Uncle Joey dead, and without Ella, it would have happened. Just thinking about the moment his eyes went dim sent chills down my spine. If Ella hadn't shown up... I shook my head. Trying to figure this out was enough to give me a headache, and I wasn't even listening to anyone's thoughts.

I stepped beside Ramos, and gave him a quick squeeze. "Be careful."

He gave me a grim nod, still feeling responsible that Uncle Joey had been shot. "I'll be fine."

I turned to Ella, giving her a quick hug. "I don't know how it happened, but I'm so glad you were here. If you need my help with anything, please let me know."

"Thanks Shelby. I appreciate it."

Uncle Joey stepped beside us, worry tightening his jaw. "I don't want her involved with Rathmore."

Ella's brows dipped and her lips thinned. "Don't worry." Hardening her tone, she met his gaze. "I don't either."

He gave her a short nod. "Good." He turned to Ramos. "Keep me informed."

"I will."

Leaving Ramos, Ella and Creed behind, we caught a taxi to the hotel. Uncle Joey's thoughts were about as messy as mine, trying to make sense of something that just didn't make sense.

Father John was completely at ease, which roused my suspicions, but, being Ella's father, maybe he was used to stuff like this. Nearing the hotel, I began to panic. "What should we tell them when we get there?"

Brought out of his stupor, Uncle Joey shook his head, unable to come up with anything. I turned to Father John. "Do you have an idea? I mean... I know you probably think lying is a sin, but maybe this is an exception?"

"It's best to stick as close to the truth as you can."

I sighed. "Okay. Then why don't we tell them that Gavin took a shot at us, but missed and ran off, and now Ramos is looking for him. How about that?"

Uncle Joey shrugged. "Sounds good to me."

"That might work for your spouses, but I have a better idea," Father John said. "I'll just tell them that something came up and it was my fault. I could even tell them that my daughter arrived unexpectedly. How does that sound?"

"Pretty good," I admitted.

"Just remember..." He turned to look us both in the eyes. "You can't tell anyone about Ella's part in this. Not anyone. That includes your spouses and kids. Okay?"

"Sure." Not telling Chris might be hard, but since it was hard to believe anyway, I could do it.

"Of course." Uncle Joey was happy to leave that secret alone. In fact, he'd rather not think about it at all. Maybe he'd just thought he was dying, and it was only a flesh wound that hurt... a lot. That made the most sense, and relief coursed over him, uncoiling the worry in his stomach.

I tried not to shake my head, but I couldn't fault him. I just hoped that thought process still worked when he tried to sleep at night.

Keeping Ella's secret reminded me that she was in the same boat as me. Only I knew her secret, and she only thought I had premonitions. Still, I could understand why she wouldn't want anyone else to know. Just like me, the fewer people who knew what she could do the better.

Did that mean Rathmore knew her secret? Probably. Chills ran down my spine, and I felt bad for her. At least I had Uncle Joey as a buffer. It bothered me that he'd been so forceful with Ella about not involving me with Rathmore, but I was also relieved.

Thankfully, she'd agreed, but what if she needed my help? What was she doing here anyway? Creed was thinking they'd been here to check on her father. Was he in danger?

I sighed. Maybe I could quiz Ramos about it later. Right now, I had to get ready to face my family and act like nothing out of the ordinary had happened.

In other words, lie.

Chapter 15

We arrived at the hotel, and Uncle Joey went straight to his room to change. Father John accompanied me into the dining room that had been reserved for the celebration dinner, slipping easily into the lie that our tardiness was all his fault.

He was so good that, by the end of his explanation, he'd nearly convinced me it was true. I picked up that everyone else believed him too, mostly because he was a priest. I breathed a sigh of relief, grateful his story had gone over so well.

Uncle Joey had joined us during Father John's explanation with a smile on his face and a rosy glow in his cheeks. It seemed that coming back from the dead agreed with him. After that, I found Chris and stuck by his side for the rest of the night, grateful to be with him and our kids, doing something normal for a change.

As things wound down, Uncle Joey got a phone call and left the room. He came back a few minutes later and motioned to me. I joined him, and we stepped into the hall. "Ramos found Gavin," he began. "But he's in the hospital suffering from a massive heart attack, and it doesn't look good."

"Really? Wow. I wonder how that happened."

Uncle Joey shrugged. "It doesn't matter, but at least he's not a threat anymore. But Dagger is still out there. I wonder if he was one of the Crypto-Knights along with Gavin, and we never knew about him."

"I don't know... when Creed was thinking about Rathmore's involvement, he thought about a hitman as well as Gavin. Maybe Dagger is Rathmore's hitman? That would make sense. Rathmore could have been financing Gavin's plans for revenge and sent some muscle along to help him out."

"Yeah... that could be it." Uncle Joey was tired of all this. "But whatever's going on, I think it's time I talked to Rathmore." He'd been gathering information about Rathmore's organization and thought he might have enough to use as leverage to get him to stop.

Rathmore wasn't as untouchable as he tried to seem, especially when he wanted backers to trust him with their money. It was a good place to start, and, if Rathmore had any sense, he'd back off.

My stomach twisted. As good as that sounded, what if it didn't work? Of course, Uncle Joey was a smooth operator. He knew what he was doing, and I had to trust him.

"If I can help, you'll let me know?"

He glanced at me, affection glinting in his eyes. "Thanks Shelby. I will."

He opened his arms, and I stepped into his embrace, hugging him tight. "I'm sure glad you're not dead."

He chuckled. "Me too."

The next day, it was time to go home. Maggie and Syd were all set to leave for their honeymoon, and Miguel had a performance that night, so we managed to get in a little more time with him before heading to the private airport.

During our stay, Savannah had calmed down around Miguel, which made things a lot more comfortable. Sure she still had a crush on him, but she realized that being his friend was better. She never got that kiss she'd fantasized about, but that special hug was pretty darn good. After a heartfelt goodbye, we boarded the jet and took our seats.

I'd thought going to New York for the wedding would be a nice break. Now, I looked forward to going home. I wasn't sure which was worse, but at least at home I had my own bed to sleep in, and my dog, so I'd call that a win. As for what happened to Uncle Joey, I'd just be grateful he was alive and try not to think too hard about the rest.

Once we got home, Josh needed to pick up Coco from Lance Hobbs, so I went with him. Parking in front of Lance's house, we went around to the back to find Coco and Lance's dog, Scout, doing some search-and-rescue training with Lance.

It amazed me that Coco didn't stop to greet us until Lance gave him the okay, and it hit me that Coco was better trained than I knew. After Lance released him, Coco rushed to us with a happy yip and gave us both a few doggy kisses.

Lance greeted us with a smile. After exchanging pleasantries, he glanced at Josh, thinking that, with his driver's license and now his new jeep, he could come on the next mission. "I'm putting you down for the next call. You up for that?" He glanced my way. "If that's okay?"

"Uh... yes. I think that's great."

"Good." He turned to Josh. "Do you have a minute to go over a couple of things with Coco? I think if you do these exercises every day after school it will keep both of you sharp. Can you do that?"

"Sure."

He motioned Josh and Coco to the center of the yard and put them through a series of drills. As I watched, I could see that Josh and Coco made a great team, and I picked up Josh's motivation to work hard with Coco every day, so he'd be ready when the call came.

My heart swelled just thinking about what Josh and Coco could do to save someone, and I wasn't too worried that they could handle it. They'd found me without hardly any training at all, and I hoped they'd get the chance to do the same for someone else.

The next morning, everyone was dragging a little, and it made me grateful that Josh had his own car so I didn't have to drive him to school. After they'd all left for the day, I got a call from Dimples. "Hey Shelby. How was the wedding?"

"It was really nice. How about you? Did you and Hawk have a good time?"

"Oh yeah. It was real interesting to see how his precinct did things, and it was nice to meet some of the other detectives. He's thinking about coming here sometime to see how we do things."

"Wow. That sounds great."

"Yeah. I just wish Danny would have been willing to testify, but we still have the hair sample. If it matches, I think we can keep Wade locked up until a trial date."

"He's getting out at the end of the week, right?"

He sighed. "Well... I have some bad news about that. I thought it was Friday, but it's actually Wednesday."

"Are you kidding me? That's only the day after tomorrow. Can you get the results back in time?"

"I let the district attorney know, and he used his authority to expedite the test, so let's hope so. Between him and the chief, we have a good chance it will come back soon. Maybe even today. Now we just have to wait."

My stomach tightened. "I hate waiting."

"No kidding."

"Okay... well... keep me updated."

"Will do."

Putting away my phone, I tried not to panic. It troubled me that we were cutting it so close, but there was nothing I could do about it. I just had to trust that Dimples, and the district attorney, would figure it out.

Needing a distraction, I was grateful it was nice enough outside for a walk, so I put on my jacket and took Coco out. Nearly home, my phone chirped with a text from Ramos, asking if I could come in to the office. He didn't say why, but I hoped it meant he'd made progress on finding Dagger.

I arrived an hour later, dressed in my usual outfit of black jeans, boots, and my leather jacket. Jackie waved me toward the conference room, so I hurried inside. Ramos sat at the table with some photos spread out in front of him. But the person at his side surprised me.

"Hey Shelby," Ramos said. He motioned to Savage. "You remember Paxton Savage?"

"Sure. Hey." I gave him a chin lift.

He nodded back, but it wasn't warm or fuzzy, since he was still a little leery of me. It reminded me that I hadn't spoken with Elliot for a few days, and I'd better do that soon.

Ramos continued. "Savage was there the night Dagger stabbed Ricky, and he managed to follow him for a while." He turned to Savage. "You got pretty close, right?"

"Yeah. But I lost him after he slipped around to the back of an apartment building not far from Cal's place. I don't know if he went inside or kept going, so while you guys were gone, I kept an eye out, but I didn't see him again. He may be miles away or staying in the apartment building, but so far, I haven't seen him."

Ramos met my gaze. "I told Savage that you gave the police a description, so we went through the surveillance videos and managed to print the best views of him. Do you want to take them to Harris and see if it helps?"

"Sure."

Ramos picked up my lack of enthusiasm and raised a brow.

"I'm just not sure how to explain them... you know?"

"Oh... right." He thought it was easy. I could tell him I'd found them on my own. I was a PI after all. I opened my mouth to answer, and he tilted his head at Savage.

I let out a breath, and followed his lead. "But... I'll see what I can do." I stepped to the table and studied the photos. Dagger was a little blurry in most of them, so it was hard to tell him apart from everyone else. "Sure... I'll take them. Who knows, they might help."

Ramos nodded. "In the meantime, we'll just have to keep watching the apartment building and surrounding area." He glanced at Savage. "That's your job."

"You got it." Savage glanced my way, wishing there was a way to talk to me alone. He wanted to know more about the guy who'd attacked him at the precinct. I'd called the man Elliot, so I knew him, but he'd never seen him before. So what did I know about the guy, and why did Elliot want to kill him?

Those were good questions, but that didn't mean I had to answer them. I figured Savage was better off not knowing. "I need to talk to Uncle Joey. Thanks for the photos." I picked them up and started for the door.

"I need to go too," Savage said, following me out. He glanced over his shoulder at Ramos. "I'll head back to the building and keep an eye out for Dagger."

"Sure," Ramos said, his gaze narrowing, and picking up that Savage had left so fast that he must want to talk to me. "Call if you see anything."

Savage nodded and followed me out the door. Since I kept going down the hall, he rushed to catch up. "Shelby, wait. Do you have a minute?"

Dang! "Uh... I guess. What do you need?"

Savage glanced behind us, noticing that Ramos had come out of the room and was speaking to Jackie. "It's private. Can we go someplace else?"

Pursing my lips, I continued toward my office and opened the door. "How about my office?"

Letting out a breath, he nodded and stepped inside. I glanced down the hall to find Ramos watching me. He wondered if I was okay alone with Savage. I gave him a thumbs up and let the door shut behind me.

Savage stood inside, studying the beautiful painting on my wall. He didn't know anything about abstract art, but something about that painting drew him in. Finding me behind him, he hurried to sit down in the chair in front of my desk.

Since he liked the painting, I wasn't quite so irritated with him. Sitting down, I slipped my purse into the bottom desk drawer and sat up straight, trying to channel Uncle Joey. "What can I do for you?"

Wanting to get to the point, he met my gaze. "I need to know who Elliot is and why he tried to kill me."

"Right... I'll be straight with you. He's a client of mine." I figured I might as well tell him some of the truth, and lie about the rest, just how I'd learned from Father John.

"A client?"

"Yeah. I'm a private investigator, and I'm helping him solve his sister's murder. We were supposed to meet up after I got done at the precinct the other day, but I didn't realize he'd followed me there. So, when you accosted me in the parking lot, he thought the worst of you and attacked you to keep me safe."

Savage shook his head. That's not how it went down, so why was I lying? "Really? That's not how I remember it."

I huffed out a breath and sat back in my seat. "Okay... maybe you're right, but I'm not sure I can tell you since he's my client... you know?"

His lips turned down. "No, I don't know." He thought that, since we both worked for Manetto, I'd be on his side instead of some random client. "Can you at least tell me if I'm going to see him again? I'd like to be prepared."

My lips turned down. This was not going well. "Okay... look... I don't think you have to worry about him. At least that's my plan." I hoped that was true, but since I hadn't spoken with Elliot for a few days, I didn't know for sure. "If anything changes, I'll be sure to let you know."

Savage raised a brow. That made no sense at all. Why would I say that, unless Elliot was really after him in the first place? He knew there were a few people who probably wanted him dead. Was Elliot one of them? "You're being straight with me... right?"

I sighed. I was a terrible liar. "Look... he may have wanted you dead, but he doesn't anymore."

His brow cleared. "What changed his mind?"

"Me. I talked him out of it."

"You did? Why would you do that?"

I let out an exasperated sigh. "Because killing people is wrong." I couldn't believe I had to explain that.

"Oh... right... and you'll let me know if he changes his mind?"

"Yes." I stood, ready to send him off to find Dagger... another killer that we'd be better off without.

He got to his feet, still puzzled about the whole thing. "Uh... okay... thanks."

"No problem. Good luck finding Dagger. Don't kill him if you can help it. I'm sure Uncle Joey will want to question him first."

"Right." He thought I was a little weird, but if it kept him alive, he couldn't complain.

After he left, I hurried to Uncle Joey's office. His door was closed, so I knocked before poking my head inside. "Can I come in?"

The worry cleared from his face, and he sent me a smile. "Sure."

I took the chair in front of his desk and smiled up at him. "How's it going? You feeling okay? Any residual effects?"

He shrugged. "No. I'm good." He wasn't just good, he felt better than he had in a long time, and it was a little disconcerting. "So did Ramos show you the photos of Dagger?"

"Yeah. I'll take them to Dimples and see if it helps. Between us and the police, let's hope we can find him."

He nodded. "Don't worry... with any luck we'll track him down."

I took a breath. "So... did you call Rathmore?"

His brows rose. Is that why I was there?

I sighed. "Of course it is. I'm a little worried about that."

"Shelby..." His lips twisted, and he shook his head. "I'm not an amateur. I know how to deal with people like him. It's what I do... trust me."

"I'm sure you do. But can you at least tell me what he said?"

He frowned, but since I was involved, he might as well lay it out. "I spoke with him this morning. It didn't go as well as I'd hoped, but he's backing down for now."

My brows rose. "He wanted something from you, right? What was it? If it's about me, I'll do whatever it takes to keep the family safe."

He raised his hands. "No. No. There's always another way."

"So he did want something from you. What was it?"

Uncle Joey sighed. "First of all, he denied sending Gavin my way. Said he had no idea Gavin had gone so far, but then he shut up pretty quick when I told him that Gavin was in the hospital with a heart attack. I didn't tell him about Ella, but he asked me if anyone got hurt during the confrontation, which seemed suspicious. Of course I denied it.

"That's when he made me an offer. He said if I invested the hundred million I'd earned in that cryptocurrency scheme into his smart city, he'd make sure nothing like that ever happened to me again. Since it was so personal, it sounded like he knew I'd been shot."

He shook his head. "I told him that was way too much, and we bartered down to fifty million. I told him I'd think about it and left it at that."

"Holy hell. That's a lot of money."

Uncle Joey shrugged. "It might be worth it, even though it galls me to have to pay him off."

"That's just wrong. You shouldn't have to do that."

"There might be another way... but my time is limited."

My heart sank. "What do you mean?"

"He gave me until Friday."

"Damn! I just want to punch him in the face."

He snorted. "Yeah? Get in line."

"I wish there was something I could do." I caught his gaze. "You sure he didn't want something from me?"

He shrugged. "I'm sure he would eventually. That's why I'm thinking of paying him off. But I don't know if it would stop there." He rubbed his face. "But don't worry, I'll think of something. I just need a little more time to come up with a plan."

"Right. Well... if there's anything I can do to help, let me know."

His brows rose. "You can post a review of Jackie's book. I'm sure she'd appreciate it."

I grinned. "Oh... I already have, but I'll get my best friend to post one. I let her borrow my copy, and she loved it."

Ramos came through the door, looking dangerous and sexy at the same time. Since we were discussing Jackie's book, he reminded me of her hitman with his 'smoldering eyes and sexy lips.'

"We were just talking about Jackie's book. Have you had a chance to read it?"

"Uh... not yet."

"That's okay. You can start tonight."

He was thinking that he had plans for tonight, but he might be able to squeeze in a few pages before he went to bed.

I nodded. "Good idea. I usually read in bed, too... it's about the only spare time I have. Just remember that once you get started, you'll probably stay up half the night. It's a real page-turner."

Ramos lifted a brow. If I was trying to convince him to read it, I wasn't doing a very good job. He had no interest in staying up half the night reading when he could be doing other things.

I rolled my eyes, but didn't argue, mostly because I didn't want to pick up what those other things were. My phone began playing the *Scooby Doo* theme song, and both Ramos and Uncle Joey frowned, knowing it was Dimples.

"Uh... I'd better take this." Not wanting them to hear my side of the conversation, I slipped out the door and down the hall to my office. Pushing the door open, I quickly answered. "Hey there. What's up?"

"You're not going to believe this, but I just got a call from the prison. Keller wants to talk to us."

"Did they say why?"

"Just that it has to do with the case, and he'll only talk to us."

A chill ran down my spine. "Hmm. I wonder what he wants."

"Yeah, me too. I thought we could go now if you're available."

I let out a sigh. Seeing Keller again was the last thing I wanted to do. "Sure. I can be there in a few minutes."

"Great. See you soon."

Ugh. I'd been looking forward to a motorcycle ride on this beautiful day, and now I had to head to the prison and see a cold-hearted killer. Damn. I grabbed my purse and stepped into the hall, my shoulders drooping with disappointment.

Ramos stood in Uncle Joey's doorway and raised his brow as I stepped out. "Going somewhere?"

"Yeah. I have to go visit someone in prison. Remember the rose on the grave guy?" At his nod, I continued. "Well, it looks like his killer wants to talk."

"Sounds fun."

"It's going to be awful." I heaved a dramatic sigh. I may have even raised my hand to my forehead.

His lips twisted. "Well... I have some errands to run. I suppose I could wait until you get back if you're not gone too long."

"Really?" Hope filled my heart. "That would be amazing."

He chuckled. "Okay... go on. I'll be here when you get back."

"Thanks. You're the best."

He rolled his eyes, knowing I was buttering him up, but deep-down, he knew that it meant that I loved him, so he was okay with that.

I huffed out a breath and shook my head, but sent him a big grin before hurrying out of the office. Before I knew it, I was pulling into the precinct parking lot and getting out of my car. I sent Dimples a text that I was there, and he came right out. "That was fast."

"That's because I want to get this over with." We walked to his car and got in. "I was hoping I'd never have to see Keller again."

"I don't blame you. Didn't you puke last time?"

"No! It was close but... jeez... thanks for reminding me."

He snickered. "Anytime."

The ride to the prison hardly took much time at all, but that was because Dimples told me more stories about his visit to New York and his time with Hawk.

"So he's really going to come out here?" I asked.

"That's what he said."

"Nice. When he does, you have to tell me."

"Absolutely."

After parking, we went through all the procedures to get inside the prison. We were led to the same room as before, and I tried not to think too hard about what I'd picked up from Keller's mind last time.

A guard brought Keller in, and he sat in the chair across from us. He was thinking that he had to play this right, and he did his best to look contrite.

"We're here." Dimples sat back in his chair, trying to look bored. "What can we do for you?"

Keller sat forward. "I've been thinking." He licked his lips. "I might know who killed those people. Maybe we can make a deal, and I can tell you everything I know."

Dimples's brows rose. "A deal?"

"Yeah. I'll tell you who the killer is in exchange for immunity... or time served... whatever works best."

Dimples turned to me. "What do you think, Shelby?"

"I say let's hear him out. If he knows who the killer is, then I'm all ears."

"All right." He turned to Keller. "We'll bite. What can you tell us?"

"I was there that night with my friend Danny. He's the one who killed those people." He lowered his head. "I tied that kid... the attendant... up, but Danny's the one who beat him to death. He's also the one who shot that motorist because he interrupted him."

"What made you change your mind about telling us?" I asked.

He was thinking it was because of the hair sample they took. "I'm getting released soon, and I don't want this coming back to haunt me. I want a clean slate, you know?" But he was thinking about the money he'd hidden away. With that, he could go anywhere he wanted and disappear. Chelsea had told him she couldn't find it, but since he didn't exactly trust her, he'd dig it up himself. Once he got rid of her, he'd be home free.

"We visited your mom the other day, and Chelsea stopped by for your things."

He straightened. "So?"

I shrugged. "She spent a lot of time in your old room and came out with a box of your stuff. I guess you asked her to do that?"

"Yeah. She's excited for my release so we can finally be together." He shook his head, not sure what that had to do with anything. "Do we have a deal? I gave you what you wanted. Danny Fowler's the killer, and I'll be happy to testify... or do whatever you want."

Dimples sighed. "Yeah... well, that would work, only it's not true. We know he was your accomplice. You're the one who killed Kirk Wahlen and Rodney Shepard."

"No... you've got it wrong. It was Danny, not me."

I shook my head. "Cut the crap, Keller. Danny said it was you. With your blood on the money, and the matching hair sample, it's over. You won't be getting out of here for a long time."

Keller jerked on his cuffs. "That son of a bitch." He'd kill him. Once he got out, the guy was dead. "He's lying. He twisted it all around so he wouldn't get the blame. I didn't do it, I swear."

I shook my head. "Your plan wouldn't have worked anyway. Your mom spent most of the money, so you wouldn't have gotten far."

Keller slammed his fists on the desk, his eyes turning black with rage. "You can't do this to me. I'm getting out."

He jerked to his feet and would have attacked us if not for the cuffs attaching him to the table. Dimples and I jumped to our feet and backed toward the door while the guard rushed to Keller's side, taking an arm to restrain him.

Keller jerked against the guard's hold, and the guard who'd been posted in the hall ran inside the room and grabbed his other arm. Keller yelled and swore as they dragged him out of the room.

Once the door shut, the silence was almost deafening. Dimples turned to me and shook his head. "You couldn't resist could you?"

"I know... it's a terrible weakness, but you didn't hear him thinking about the money and how he was going to disappear." I knew I shouldn't have said that, but it sure felt good. He was a slime-ball.

Dimples closed his eyes. "Let's get out of here."

We were both subdued on the drive back. What if the test results didn't come in? Worse, what if they didn't match? Then what? Why did I taunt him like that?

"They'll match, right?"

Dimples glanced my way, taking in my worry. "I'm sure they will." Facing the road, he continued. "But I'm not going to lie... I can't wait to turn this thing over to the prosecuting attorney and be done with it."

"No kidding. At least the chief will be happy we solved the case. How did he take the news anyway? You didn't tell me."

"He was good with our progress, but he's not telling his daughter until we have a positive match. He's playing it safe, you know?"

"You mean like I should have?"

He hadn't said that... but he was sure thinking it. "Shelby... it's fine. We all mess up. Don't worry. We'll get the results back today, and it will all work out. You'll see."

"I sure hope so."

We pulled into the parking lot, and I jumped out of his car, needing to forget all about the case and my epic screw-up. "If you don't need me for anything, I'll be going. I've got... errands to run." At his nod, I continued, "Let me know the minute the results come in."

"Will do."

I jumped into my car and made the drive to Thrasher in record time. On my way to the elevator, I checked to make sure the motorcycle was still there. Finding it, relief and anticipation filled my chest. Working hard to keep my cool, I hurried to the elevator to catch a ride to the twenty-sixth floor.

Jackie's desk sat empty, so I wandered down the hall to Uncle Joey's office. After a quick knock, I opened the door to find Ramos sitting in Uncle Joey's chair with his feet resting on top of the desk. He sat back in the chair with an open book in his hands.

"Whoa... you're lucky I'm not Uncle Joey or you'd be in trouble. Hey... are you reading Jackie's book?"

His gaze rose to meet mine before quickly returning to the book. "Yeah. You know you're right... this is a page-turner. I guess those errands will have to wait... maybe we can go tomorrow."

He returned to the book, and I could hardly believe it. From his mind, I could even pick up what part he was reading. "Are you freaking kidding me?"

His lips quirked up. Then he shut the book on his finger and raised a brow. "I guess it can wait." He pulled his feet off the desk and stood up to stretch.

I tried not to admire the sight of all those bulging muscles, but how could I resist? "Uh... where did Uncle Joey and Jackie go?"

"They went to lunch." His brows lifted, and he leaned over the desk, naturally showing his toned arms to perfection. "It looks like we're here alone." He thought about the scene he'd just read in the book where the hitman and the damsel in distress had a 'moment' together.

"Oh no." I backed up. "Don't you dare go there."

"Spoilsport."

I rolled my eyes. "Are we going, or not?"

"Sure." He tucked the paperback under his arm and followed me to the elevator. "I like the book more than I thought... I mean... for a romance novel there's a lot of action."

"Yeah. It's great. So... I never got the chance to ask you about Gavin. It seems strange that he had a heart attack. How did you find him anyway?"

Ramos shook his head. "It was Ella who found him. We started out in the direction he'd gone, and found him about a block away. He was lying unconscious in an alley. She reached out to touch him, but pulled back and called nine-one-one instead.

"Before the paramedics came, I asked her what was going on. I mean... I was glad she didn't try to heal him, but it seemed like she knew more than she was saying."

He let out a breath. "She said that Gavin had suffered a massive heart attack. Then she looked me in the eye and told me never to hurt anyone while she was around, because if she helped them, I would pay the consequences." He swallowed. "Creed said 'karma's a bitch,' so I got the message loud and clear."

"Wow... that's..." I didn't have a word to explain it. "What the freak?"

"I know. I don't know if I should admire her, or be afraid of her."

I shrugged. "Well... since she saved Uncle Joey, let's just be grateful, and leave it at that."

We reached his motorcycle, and Ramos popped his car trunk open, revealing my new motorcycle jacket, helmet, and gloves. He handed them over. "You'll want these. It's not too cold out, but you'll stay warmer with them on. Plus, we have a longer ride today."

"Really? Where are we going?"

"I'm picking up a package from Manetto's private airstrip... and I'm taking the back roads."

"Sweet!" I donned my riding gear and climbed on the bike behind Ramos. As we took off up the ramp, I wrapped my arms tightly around him, letting all the darkness from meeting with Wade Keller, and the mystery that was Ella St. John, fly right out of my mind.

Chapter 16

The next morning was gray and overcast and I hoped it wasn't a precursor for what was to come. Last night, I'd told Chris all about my visit to Wade Keller in prison, and how I'd let it slip that his money was gone, along with all his hopes and dreams.

Chris hadn't been too happy that I'd done that, but since it looked like he wasn't getting out of prison, he let it go. Not me. I'd stewed about it all night, worried that I'd been a dummy to throw that in his face. What was I thinking?

That's why I called Dimples as soon as I got the kids off to school.

"Hey Shelby. What's up?"

"Oh, not much. I'm just anxious to know if you got the results on Keller's hair sample yet."

"Right. I checked first thing this morning, but it's not in yet. Try not to worry, we've still got the rest of the day. With the rush we put on it, we should be fine."

"Okay... good. I guess I'm just nervous after meeting with him yesterday, you know?"

"Yeah. He wasn't too happy with us, but I understand why you let him have it. Sometimes it just feels good to put someone who deserves it in their place."

I nodded. "You're right. I guess that's why I couldn't resist. But now I'm worried. Anyways... let me know when it comes in."

"I will."

"Thanks. Hey... any progress on that other case I'm helping you with? That apartment homicide?" I almost said Cal's name, but I couldn't remember how much I was supposed to know about that.

"Yeah. I think Bates has a good lead he's working on. He hasn't really told me what it is yet, so I'll have to talk to him about it."

"That's good news. It would be nice to have that one work out, you know?"

"Yeah. For sure."

I sighed. "Okay... well, I gotta go. Be sure to let me know if you hear anything."

"Will do."

We disconnected, and I felt somewhat better. The results would come through. I didn't need to worry, and I wasn't that stupid for saying what I did to Keller. Things would work out just fine.

Needing a break from all I had going on, I put on a warm jacket and braved the cool temperatures to take Coco on a walk. The wind blew what remained of the leaves, and they crunched under my feet.

I tried to enjoy the brisk breeze, but even that couldn't stop me from thinking about my troubles. There wasn't a lot I could do about most of it, but I could give Elliot a call. Maybe he'd meet with me, and I could convince him not to kill Savage for real this time.

Back home, I put the call through. He didn't pick up, so I left a message that I wanted to meet and took a nice long shower. As I got dressed, my phone dinged with a text notification. Picking it up, I found a short message from Uncle Joey asking me to come in. He didn't say why, so I quickly finished up and drove to Thrasher.

Finding Ramos's motorcycle parked in the usual spot lightened my heart. I was glad we'd gone on a nice, long ride yesterday, since it looked too stormy to ride it anywhere today.

Stepping into Thrasher, I stopped to say hello to Jackie. "Hey Jackie. Did Ramos talk to you?"

"About what?"

"To tell you he's reading your book." Her brows rose, and I smiled. "He told me he was really enjoying it, and he hadn't thought a romance novel could have so much action."

A big grin brightened her whole face. "That's so cool."

"You know it. I thought about calling him Stone yesterday, just to tease him." That was the hitman's name in Jackie's book.

"Ha! That might be funny, but you probably shouldn't." Jackie didn't want him to draw too many parallels to the hitman in her book since he was totally based on Ramos.

"Yeah... probably not." I glanced down the hall. "So, what's going on around here?"

She shrugged. "Just the usual. Joe and Ramos are in Joe's office cooking up ways to keep Rathmore out of our lives."

"Oh... I'd better go see if I can help with that."

I hurried down the hall, stopping at my office to put my purse into my desk drawer. Continuing to Uncle Joey's office, I knocked and opened the door. "Hey guys. How's it going?"

Uncle Joey waved me in. "Come on in. We're just looking into Rathmore Enterprises for more information on that smart city investment he wants me to make. It looks like the idea was started by a man named Derrek Vaughn. Does that name sound familiar to you?"

"Oh yeah... I remember him. He was in the meeting that Ramos and I went to in Las Vegas. I picked up that Derrek Vaughn was dying from cancer, and I had to tell Rathmore."

Uncle Joey nodded. "Then that explains the recent merger. It looks like Rathmore joined forces with Vaughn's tech company to build a smart city. He must have promised Vaughn something to get him to agree to the merger."

I shook my head, more convinced than ever that we shouldn't get involved with Rathmore in any way, shape, or form. "You can't give in to his demands."

"Believe me, I don't want to. There has to be something we can do, I just don't know what it is yet. At least we have until Friday."

"Maybe Forrest can hack into his computer files? Have you thought of that?"

"No... but that's a possibility. If we found something that I could use as leverage, it might hold him off for a while. Thanks Shelby, I'll see what he can do."

I smiled, glad I could help. "So how's Ricky doing?"

"They're sending him home today, but he'll be out of commission for a few weeks. That means I need to find a new driver."

"I'll drive you until he gets back," Ramos said. He glanced my way. "In the meantime, I have a couple of errands I need to run."

My hopes rose. "You taking the bike?"

"I don't know. It looks a little stormy out there."

"True... but I have a really nice weatherproof jacket. It should okay, right?"

His lips twisted. "I suppose."

I jumped up. "Good. Let's go." I ignored Uncle Joey's head shake and hurried to the door. "I have to get my purse, so don't leave without me."

Inside my office, I sat down to pull the drawer open and grabbed my purse. After slinging it over my head, I stepped to the door. The sound of raised voices came from the hallway. Alarm ran down my spine, and I pulled the door open to see what was going on.

My breath caught. Detective Bates stood beside Jackie's desk with two uniformed officers. Ramos stood next to them, his posture deadly and ready for anything. As I pulled the door wider to step out, Uncle Joey barred my way, blocking me from sight. He spared me a glance, thinking that I should stay put for the time being, and continued to Ramos's side.

Swallowing, I let the door close, leaving it open a crack so I could hear what they were saying.

Uncle Joey stepped beside Ramos. "What's the problem?"

Bates frowned and motioned toward Ramos. "We'd like to ask Mr. Ramos to come to the station with us. We have a few questions for him."

"About what?"

"The murder of Cal Schaefer."

Uncle Joey's lips thinned. "Are you arresting him?"

"It would be better if he came in without that, but if that's the only way—"

"There's no need to do that. Just ask your questions here. You can use my conference room."

Bates swallowed, but stood straighter. "I'm afraid that won't work."

Uncle Joey studied him before turning to Ramos. "It doesn't look like you have a choice, so go ahead, but don't say a word until my lawyer gets there."

He was thinking that the detective must have a damn good reason for barging in like this, especially knowing that Ramos would lawyer up. On the downside, he knew they usually didn't make an arrest until they were in the station. Did that mean they had evidence to pin on Ramos for Cal's murder?

My eyes widened, and my heart rate spiked. This was bad. I zeroed in on Bates and picked up that he'd known Ramos would lawyer up, but once he was in the station, they could arrest him and do everything by the book so he couldn't slip through their fingers.

As they left the office, Ramos kept his cool, flinty-eyed stare, but inside, he was seething. He thought they had to have something on him, or they'd never bring him in like this. Someone must have seen him and come forward... ignoring Manetto's threats. He—

I lost his thoughts as they stepped into the elevator and the doors shut behind them. Uncle Joey held his phone to his ear, already calling Chris. As he began to explain, I hurried to his side. I needed to do something to save Ramos, but what?

The *Scooby Doo* ringtone sounded on my phone, and I quickly answered. "Dimples? What's going on? Bates just took Ramos to the station."

"I know... that's why I'm calling. Look... I shouldn't be talking to you at all, but I thought I should give you a heads-up. Ramos is going to need a good lawyer, because they're planning to charge him with Cal Schaefer's murder."

"But he didn't do it." I hesitated, knowing Dimples wouldn't like hearing my confession. "I know, because I was there."

Dimples took a sharp breath. "What the hell?" He sputtered a few more choice curses. "Why didn't you tell me? Wait. Don't say another word. Just... stay out of it, okay? And don't come in. I'm trying to protect you, so stay away."

"But—"

"Listen to me! There's no mention of you right now. So stay the hell away." Dimples hung up.

"Dammit!" I wanted to hurl my phone at the wall, but took a deep breath instead. Uncle Joey was still talking to Chris, so I tugged on his arm. "I need to tell him something before you hang up."

He gave me a nod and cut in. "Shelby's right here, and she wants to talk to you."

I took the phone from him. "Chris... Dimples just called me. I'm sure he wasn't supposed to, but he wanted to tell me that they're planning to arrest Ramos at the station."

"Did he say why?"

"Yes... for Cal Schaefer's murder."

Chris sighed. "Okay. Got it."

"Should I come? I know he didn't do it."

"No!" Chris exclaimed. "You were with him that day, so I don't want you anywhere near the station. They could charge you as an accessory."

I huffed out a breath. "That's what Dimples just said."

"Then you should listen to both of us."

"But I need to be there. I know he didn't do it, and I know who did, so, if there's any way I can help him, I have to go."

"I get that, but showing up will look bad, especially if I'm there too. It's too much of a risk."

"But don't you see? I'll know exactly what's going on. I'll know their strategy, and what kind of evidence they have... like fingerprints, or a witness. I need to be there. Besides, Dimples said that there's no mention of me... none. Doesn't that mean something?"

"Yeah. It means you shouldn't push your luck."

"No it doesn't. It means that there's nothing for me to worry about. Besides, I was at the crime scene helping the police investigate. It would be natural for me to show up, and I bet you anything that Bates would love my help. He believes in my psychic powers, so he'd want me there." Chris didn't say anything, so I knew I was wearing him down. "And don't forget that I'll know what's going on before anyone says a word. I can leave if I need to."

"I know... I get it... you have a point, but the fact that Dimples doesn't want you there worries me."

"Yeah, but it's only because he knows all about my connection with Ramos and Uncle Joey. The others aren't so informed... at least... I don't think they are. Look... I'm going. If you see me, try to act surprised, okay?"

"Shelby—"

"Bye!" I disconnected and handed the phone back to Uncle Joey. He shook his head, thinking it would be hard to be married to me, but... he liked that I was standing up for myself.

I narrowed my eyes, knowing he'd thought that last part for my benefit. "So you're okay with it?"

He shrugged, thinking it was useless to try to stop me. "If I'm not, would you go anyway?"

"You know I would."

"Then I'm okay with it. I think you made a good point. And if anything happens, you'll already have a lawyer there to stick up for you. What have you got to lose?"

My brows dipped. "Well... I guess that's one way to look at it."

—◦►‹❊❊❊❊›◄◦—

I arrived at the precinct with nervous tension rolling through my stomach. I may have sounded sure of myself when I spoke with Chris and Uncle Joey, but, now that I was here, I had second thoughts.

Still, it was Ramos, so I had to do something to help him out.

I pulled my phone from my purse and sent Dimples a text, telling him that, since I was involved with Cal's case, I was coming in to help. I waited for several seconds to see how he responded, but nothing came through.

As I opened my car door, my phone chimed with a notification. I whipped it out to find a head-exploding emoji. Oops. Oh well... he may not like it, but at least he knew I was here, so he wouldn't be surprised to see me.

I slipped my lanyard over my head and stepped inside the precinct, going straight to the detectives' offices. Dimples waited for me, his arms crossed and his lips forming a thin line. He was thinking *you couldn't stay away, could you?*

"Nope."

Wanting to throw up his hands, he just shook his head and turned toward the interrogation rooms. "Bates is questioning Ramos right now, but you're not getting in there. The best I can do is to let you watch through the observation window."

"That's fine. You can come with me and fill me in on the case."

He opened the observation door, and we stepped inside. Ramos sat at the desk with no expression on his face and his mouth shut tight. Bates kept throwing out questions that kept going unanswered.

Getting nowhere, Bates started fidgeting with the crime-scene photos spread out in front of him, and I could tell his frustration was mounting. His questions turned from the bloody photos to more personal things, like how they were going to nail Ramos to the wall, and that he wasn't going to get away with it.

Ramos hardly blinked an eye, further annoying Bates. Before he could ask another question, the door opened, and an officer ushered Chris inside. He gave Ramos a nod and set his briefcase down on the table. "Are you bringing charges against my client? Because, if you're not, we'll be leaving."

"Fine. I didn't want to do this, but you leave me no choice. Alejandro Ramos, I'm arresting you for the murder of Cal Schaefer." He made Ramos turn around and cuffed him. Then he pulled out a card and began reading Ramos his rights. After he was done, he told the waiting officer to book him, and after that, to bring him straight back for a lineup, so the witness could identify him.

"You staying?" he asked Chris.

"Yes."

"Fine. Wait here."

I turned to Dimples. "Does Bates know that Chris is my husband?"

"Of course."

"Oh... dang. So what's going on? You have a witness?"

Dimples let out a long breath, and I picked up a thread of anger directed my way. "Yes. He came forward just this morning. He gave us a description of Ramos, along with the license plate number for his motorcycle. When Bates asked if he thought he could identify him in a line-up, the guy said he'd be happy to try. That's what Bates is arranging right now."

"So the witness is here? Now?"

"Yes."

"Then I need to talk to him. Because I know he's lying. I gave you the description of Cal's killer, and he looks nothing like Ramos. You've got to know this is fishy, right?"

Dimples's lips turned down, and his disappointment washed over me. "Shelby... don't you know you lied to me about this case? Why didn't you tell me you were there?" It stung that I hadn't trusted him with the truth. Now, here I was, acting like I hadn't done anything wrong. He'd even stuck his neck out to warn me about Ramos's arrest. Was I just using him now?

"Oh hell." My heart sank. He was right. Why hadn't I told him the truth? He deserved that and more, and I was a terrible person. "You're right. I should have told you. There just wasn't a good time."

"You mean like when I called and asked you to come help me? That wasn't a good time?"

Ouch. He had a point. That would have been the time to do it, but I'd just played along instead. "Yeah... I see what you mean. I should have told you then."

"So why didn't you?"

"Probably because I was with Uncle Joey and Ramos when you called. At least... that's most of it... but there was also the fact that I'd left the scene of the crime. Chris said it was a felony, and I could be in a lot of trouble for it."

I let out a long breath. "But I should have trusted that you wouldn't arrest me, and we could have worked it out. I'm sorry. I know I've let you down, and I feel terrible about it. Can you ever forgive me?"

Dimples rubbed his face, totally exasperated with the whole situation. "Probably. But not right now." He shook his head. "So you think the witness is lying?"

"I know he is."

"All right. Let's go with that angle, and I'll see if I can get him in the room with you after the line-up is over. You'll have to give me a few minutes to work it all out."

He left, still unhappy with me, but at least he hadn't given up on me yet. Blowing out a breath, I glanced through the window and found Chris looking at the file that Bates had left on the table. I wasn't sure that was ethical, but it seemed like a good idea to me. After a quick perusal, he went back to his seat. A few seconds later, Bates opened the door and asked Chris to follow him out.

I waited for Dimples to come and get me, but nothing happened. Not wanting to miss my chance, I pulled the door open and peeked out. Chris and Bates were gone, and I caught a glimpse of Dimples coming toward me. I stepped out to meet him. "Are they doing the line-up now?"

His brows rose, but he nodded. "Yes. They're almost ready. As soon as they're done, I'll bring the witness here, and you can talk to him then."

"Oh... okay. Are you sure I can't watch him during the line-up?"

"Huh. Let me think about it. No."

I blinked. Was he being sarcastic?

He huffed. "Shelby... your husband is witnessing the procedure. I don't think it's a good look for you to be there too."

"Oh. I didn't know that. Okay... I'll wait."

Dimples opened the interrogation room door and motioned me inside. "I'll be back."

Ten long minutes later, Dimples ushered a man into the room. He looked about thirty-five, was clean-shaven, with short, dark hair, and wearing glasses. He hunched his shoulders, making him seem small and insignificant, and walked with unsure steps, like the mere thought of being in the police station frightened him. "You want me in here?"

"Yes. Please take a seat."

The man noticed me and stopped in his tracks. Wanting to put him at ease, Dimples motioned toward me. "Dorian, this is Shelby Nichols. She's a consultant for the police and is helping with this case. She just has a few questions for you."

Dorian's gaze widened for just a second. He'd never expected to see me here. Using his surprise to build on his nervous tension, he acted even more discombobulated. "Hi. Uh... I need to get back to work. This won't take long, will it?"

"Just a few minutes, right Shelby?"

"Right."

As he slipped into the chair across from me, he pushed his glasses back on his nose and gave me a tentative smile. His fingers shook slightly, and he sat on the chair like it was about to bite him.

He wondered how it was possible that I worked for both Manetto and the police. Good thing he'd changed his persona, or he might have been worried that I'd recognize him. Still, he decided to exhibit even more nervous tension to keep up his act.

If not for my ability, he would have totally fooled me. Still, Dagger was the last person I expected to see sitting across from me.

I took a breath, trying to figure out how to proceed. I couldn't exactly tell Dimples that Cal's killer was right in front of us, especially the way he looked now. "Thanks for staying a little longer... I appreciate it."

He nodded, and I chewed on my thumbnail, trying to come up with some kind of a question. "I guess I'm a little behind on your part in the case. Could you explain to me how you saw Cal's alleged killer?"

His brows dipped. "I already told the detectives everything."

"I know... just a quick summary would be great."

He let out a sigh and shoved a hand through his hair. "Fine. I was visiting my mom. She lives on the same floor as the guy who died. I was taking out the garbage for her when I saw a man standing in front of Cal's apartment. He had a gun in his hand, and he forced the door open. I ducked back into my mom's apartment, so he wouldn't see me. I wasn't sure what to do, but then I heard the gunshot. I glanced into the hall and spotted him running down the hall to the stairwell."

"So you got a good look at him?"

"Yeah." His eyes darted between me and Dimples before he rubbed his hands on his pants and swallowed. "I picked the right guy, didn't I?"

Whoa. Was he ever playing it up.

Dimples seemed to believe him and nodded. "It looks like it. We've taken him into custody for the murder."

"Good. That's a relief. I don't forget faces, and his is hard to miss..." Dorian directed a knowing gaze my way, thinking a handsome man like Ramos would catch any woman's eye. In fact, maybe I had something going on with him? From what he'd seen, we were definitely chummy, and Ramos had certainly come to my rescue that day with his guns blazing.

He frowned, thinking it was probably a good thing, since he wasn't supposed to kill me. That would have been a disaster. How had I sneaked up on him, anyway? After Cal's feeble attempt to get his money early, he'd thought he had plenty of time to kill him.

"Did you check on Cal after the guy left?" I asked.

"Uh... no. I didn't want to get involved, so I went back to my mom's apartment. I wouldn't have said anything to her, but she heard the pop, and I had to tell her what I'd seen."

My brows rose. "Then why didn't you tell the police when they came around asking for witnesses?"

"Like I said... I didn't want to get involved, so I went home before they showed up. Later, my mom called and begged me to talk to the police. She... she's worried about living there, and she thought if the killer was caught, it would send a message. She's even talked to the landlord about getting a security system. Maybe now he will."

He glanced at me before turning to Dimples. "So that guy needs to stay behind bars. I don't want him coming after me. If you think he will, I won't testify."

Dimples raised both his hands. "Don't worry. He has no idea who you are. We'll make sure you're safe."

"Good. Can I go now? I really need to get back to work."

Dimples nodded. "Sure. Thanks for your time. I'll show you out."

Dagger nodded and stood, making a point to stay a little hunched over, and hurried to the door. He glanced back at me with a slight twist to his lips, but he was thinking *see ya later sucker*, and continued out the door.

Dimples ushered him into the hall where an officer escorted him out. He came back into the room and sat down, thinking that Bates was watching through the two-way mirror, so I needed to be careful.

His warning warmed my heart, since it meant that he still cared, even if he hadn't forgiven me. I sent him a grateful smile.

His lips twisted. "Did you get anything useful?"

"Uh... maybe. It seemed a little strange that he had a sudden change of heart and came forward after all this time. It makes me wonder if someone paid him off, you know?"

His brows rose, and he was thinking that I needed to be careful or Bates might come storming in here. "Yeah... I can see how it looks, but I'm sure Bates checked him out. He's a credible witness, or Bates wouldn't have arrested Ramos."

"Really? Hmm... so you're sure it's his mother who really lives in that apartment?"

"Uh... I would think so. I mean... Bates should have made sure—"

The door crashed open, and Bates stepped through, his mouth a flat line. "What are you saying? That I didn't do my job?"

"No... no. Not at all. I'm just getting something fishy about the guy, that's all. That's why I'm throwing out a few questions to help me get to the bottom of this feeling I have."

Bates huffed out a breath, his nostrils flaring. "Fine. So what's fishy about him?"

I shrugged. "Uh... I don't know. I might want to talk to his mom. Maybe if I do that, I'll figure it out."

"It's a waste of time. I already talked to her." He was thinking that she hadn't said much. In fact, she mostly just nodded when he'd asked if her son had been there that day and seen the shooter. But Dorian was obviously telling the truth... anyone could see that. He was too scared to be lying, and he didn't want me to come on too strong and scare him off, especially since he was their only lead at the moment.

"Oh... right. Well... I don't mind talking to her, and it's not a waste of time if it helps the case, right?"

He let out a strangled huff. "You're something else to think you can pull this crap on me. I know your husband is Ramos's lawyer. So, from now on, you're not coming anywhere near this case." He sent Dimples a frosty stare. "And you should have known better than to let her talk to our witness. If this happens again, I'll file a complaint with Internal Affairs."

Before Dimples could utter a word, Bates stalked out of the room, slamming the door behind him.

I jumped a little. Did I just get Dimples in trouble? "Oops. Sorry."

Dimples sighed and shook his head. "I think that's your cue to leave."

"Right... okay." I got up and Dimples followed me out. As we turned down the hall, I spoke in a low tone. "We need to talk."

"Ya think?" His lips twisted, but he figured there had to be some kind of an explanation. He just hoped it was reasonable enough to make getting on Bates' bad side worth it. "I can take an early lunch. Let's go."

Chapter 17

W e passed through the office and continued down the hall and out the doors.

Stepping outside the precinct helped relieve some of the tension in my shoulders. Too bad Ramos was still in there, but at least Chris was taking care of him. Hopefully, Chris could get Ramos a quick arraignment so he could get out on bail and not have to stay overnight. With Uncle Joey's influence, I hoped it could happen.

Dimples let out a sigh and glanced my way, shaking his head. He wanted me to know that he still hadn't forgiven me, but he'd hear what I had to say. He was concerned that Bates had put me on the enemy side of the list, but he couldn't worry about that right now.

So I was the enemy? This whole thing was so messed up. Now I wasn't sure Dimples would believe me when I told him the truth.

"The food trucks are at the Galvan Center, so we can walk over there, and it will give you plenty of time to explain everything."

"Right. It's just hard to know where to start."

"Start with the witness."

I nodded. "Sure... but..." I caught his gaze. "Don't freak out, but he's the killer."

Dimples stopped in his tracks. "What? You said the guy had a beard and long hair."

"I know. But, believe me... it's him." At his scoff, I continued. "It's a long story, but I'll tell you the whole thing, as long as you promise not to arrest me when I'm done."

He rolled his eyes. "As if. But it better be the whole truth, or I won't promise a thing."

"It will be... jeez." I began with the data breach of Uncle Joey's files at the Berardini's offices. Then I continued with the incident at Jimmy's restaurant, and how someone had paid off the health inspector to shut it down. After that, I told him about the goons who were hired to stop Uncle Joey's construction project.

By then, we'd reached the food trucks, and I took a break until we got our food. There was an empty table on the square, and we sat down. All the stress had messed with my stomach, so I wasn't hungry and just got a soda and some chips. Not too healthy, but it was the best I could do at the moment.

Dimples took a bite of his sandwich and motioned with his hand, thinking *you can talk while I eat.* He wasn't too sympathetic about the whole thing, but I could tell he was trying his best to withhold judgment until I got done.

"Okay. Where was I? I told you about the data breach, the restaurant, and the construction site. Oh yeah... next came the jewelry store... you know... the place where you got Billie's wedding ring."

His eyes widened. "Right... so what happened to them?"

"There was a break-in. Or maybe it was more like vandalism since only a couple of things were stolen, but that's because of the cat."

"A cat?"

"Yeah... it's like an attack cat. When the perp reached through the broken glass to take the jewels, the cat scratched him up pretty bad. It's in the police report, if you don't believe me."

He nodded. "Oh, I believe you. Cats can be unpredictable." It brought to mind the cat that ran up his leg a few months ago, and a shiver ran down his spine.

I chuckled. "Yeah... that was pretty funny... I mean... awful, just awful."

Dimples grimaced and swallowed down the rest of his sandwich. After taking a big swig of his soda, he shook his head. "So how is that related to what happened today?"

"Oh... there's lots more."

His brows rose, and he wiped his hands on his napkin. "Of course there is. Go on."

"Well, after that, there was another data breach on Uncle Joey's files, but Nick had replaced them with dummy files, so that was good because they didn't get anything."

Dimples groaned, thinking that his lunch hour would be long gone before I ever got to the point. "Go on."

"Right. Um... so, by then, we figured someone was targeting Uncle Joey, and we had a brainstorming session about what they might target next, but come to find out, they'd already tried something at Uncle Joey's club... you know, The Comet Club?"

Dimples closed his eyes. "Sure. Go on."

I leaned forward. "But get this. It had already been stopped by an employee. In fact, that employee was Paxton Savage... the guy you interviewed about Cal's death?"

Dimples straightened. "Finally we're getting somewhere. So what about him?"

"Savage beat up Cal that night because Cal was stealing from Uncle Joey, but it turned out that he was there to burn the place down... or at least set it in motion."

"Who was? Cal or Savage?"

"Cal. That's why Ramos and I went to his apartment to talk to him. We wanted to find out what Cal had planned to do, and who had hired him to do it."

Dimples nodded. "Right. So he was alive then?"

"Yes. That's how we found out about the fire. It was supposed to happen the next night, so we talked Cal into setting a trap for the guy who'd hired him. He goes by Dagger... and he's the one who killed Cal."

"Wait... did this happen before the trap or after?"

My brows dipped. "We never got to the trap. I guess, in retrospect, we should have figured that getting Cal to set up the trap was the real trap, instead of the trap we'd planned."

Dimples rubbed his face. "So what are you saying?"

"Well, we had Cal call Dagger and ask for half the money up front. He told Dagger that he wouldn't go through with the plan to burn down the club without it. We set the meeting up for that night at a used car dealership, but after we went back to Thrasher and told Uncle Joey the plan, he thought Cal might be in danger. That's when we went back to his apartment. We were going to get him to leave so we could protect him. But, by the time we got back, he was already dead."

"And Dagger had killed him? How do you know that?"

"Because I went up to the apartment and found Dagger pointing a gun at Cal. I yelled at him to stop, and he took a shot at me. I ducked out of the way and heard another shot. That's when I ran like hell down the stairs. He followed me out and took a couple more shots in the stairwell.

"As I got to the bottom floor, Ramos crashed through the door and took a couple of shots at Dagger, giving me the cover I needed to get away from him. Then Ramos started up the stairs after Dagger and he took off. I think Ramos followed him all the way to the top, but I'm not sure. At some point, he lost him. While he did that, I went back to check on Cal, but he was dead. Ramos found me and... encouraged me to leave."

I caught Dimples's gaze and licked my lips. "I didn't want to, but I had to, you know?"

Dimples huffed out a breath. "Right. So you're the one with the description of Dagger." It irked him that I'd used the neighbor and my mind-reading skills to lie to him.

"Wait... no I didn't. The neighbor really did see him. I didn't make that up."

"Oh... okay. But didn't she see you too? And Ramos?"

"Well, yeah, but when I came to her door and told her I was with the police, she accepted that as the reason I'd been there earlier."

"Right." Dimples rubbed his face again. He still didn't understand any of this. "So why would Dagger decide to frame Ramos?"

I chewed on my thumbnail, realizing I had no idea. "I'm not real clear on that. Maybe to get back at Uncle Joey?"

"So what did Manetto do to him?" He was thinking that Uncle Joey must have killed the guy's father or ruined his business and left him destitute. It had to be something huge to go to all this trouble.

"Well... I'm afraid there's more."

Dimples's brows rose. "More than that? What the hell?" I kept my mouth shut while Dimples cursed in his mind. Finished, he caught my gaze. "Do I want to know?"

"Actually... I'm not sure it will help with this case, but it involves a matter of revenge over that business with the stolen cryptocurrency. You remember that, right?"

At his nod, I continued. "You probably know that Uncle Joey got it back, but one of the guys with the Crypto-Knights, who wasn't murdered or arrested, got upset. Anyway... last I heard that guy's in a hospital in New York."

Dimples raised his brows, thinking that Ramos probably had something to do with that.

I shook my head. "No... he didn't. The guy had a massive heart attack. At any rate, we don't have to worry about him anymore, but he was working with Dagger, and I guess Dagger is still trying to cause trouble." I didn't want to mention Rathmore, because that was one more layer to this whole thing that might confuse Dimples even more.

Dimples's mouth dropped open. Was I being serious? A huff of breath escaped his lips, then another. Soon, little bursts of laughter popped out. He tried to hold them in, but the more he tried to hold them back, the worse it got. Pretty soon, he was laughing his head off.

Naturally, I began to laugh along with him. Not because I thought it was funny, but because laughter like that is contagious, especially after a lot of stress. And maybe it was a little bit funny, in a twisted way. I mean... putting it all out there like that made it seem a little unbelievable, and I hadn't even explained what had happened in New York.

It took several minutes before we'd calmed down enough to talk normally. Wiping his eyes, Dimples stood from the table to throw away his garbage. "I've got to get back."

I got to my feet, and we began the trek back to the precinct. "So what do we do now?"

He shook his head. "Hell if I know." That sparked another round of laughter, but we calmed down a lot faster this time.

"I'm sorry I didn't tell you what was going on before."

He waved me off. "Don't worry about it." He was thinking that sometimes real life was crazier than fiction. Who could make up stuff like that? "At least I know that the witness is the killer." He started to chuckle again. "As crazy as it sounds."

"I know, right?"

Stopping in front of the precinct, he took a deep breath. "I don't think you should come in. In fact, you should probably stay away until this whole thing is resolved."

I sighed. "Yeah... I guess that makes sense. But what about the cold case we're working on? What if I have to come in for that?"

Dimples shook his head, shifting his thoughts to Wade Keller. "We probably won't know anything until late tonight or early tomorrow... and I don't think you'll need to come in for that." He shook his head. "I think it's best if you stay away for now."

"Okay... at least keep me posted."

"I will." He thought that, between Keller and Dagger, my life was a mess, and that was probably just the tip of the iceberg. It made him grateful that his life wasn't so bad compared to mine. In fact, the only thing abnormal about his life was me, so it only made sense that these kinds of things happened when I was involved.

He met my gaze. "I mean that in the nicest way possible."

My eyes narrowed. "Sure you do."

He grinned, giving me a glimpse of his glorious dimples. Naturally, I grinned back. He clapped me on the shoulder. "If you figure out what's going on, let me know. Okay?"

My brows rose. "I'll do my best."

He nodded before heading into the building. Letting out a sigh, I hurried to my car. At least he wasn't angry with me anymore, but I wasn't sure telling him the whole story had helped. Of course, we'd both gotten a good laugh out of it, so how could I complain?

I pulled into the parking garage a few minutes later and took the elevator up to Thrasher. Stepping into the office, I found Jackie busily typing away on her computer. She was on the third chapter of her next book, and the hitman had just been arrested for murder.

Hmm... I wonder where that idea had come from?

She spotted me and motioned toward Uncle Joey's office. "Oh good. Joe's in his office. I hope you have some good news."

"Uh... I found out a few things."

"Good." She was itching to know what they were so she could add it to her story, but I hurried down the hall instead of telling her anything. She'd find out from Uncle Joey soon enough.

In a way, I could hardly wait to tell Uncle Joey what was going on so he could take care of it. I was so overwhelmed with everything that all I wanted to do was go home and take a hot bath.

I pushed his door open and stepped inside, finding him talking on the phone. But he wasn't alone. Savage sat in Ramos's usual spot. What was he doing here? He met my gaze and gave me a chin nod.

"Hey," I answered. "So I guess you heard about Ramos?"

"Yeah. That's messed up."

I nodded. "Did Uncle Joey ask you to come in?"

"Sure did." He didn't elaborate, but I picked up that Uncle Joey wanted him in the loop since Ramos had been arrested. Savage thought that, with both Ramos and Ricky out of commission, Manetto needed him to fill in, and he was more than happy to do it.

Uncle Joey waved to a chair, and I sat down.

"Yes. My lawyer is on his way. I appreciate your help." He paused. "I understand if that's the best you can do...."

Sure. You know I'm good for it... yes... thanks... see you then."

He disconnected, and I lifted a brow. "Who was that?"

"Jack."

"Jack-the-judge?" He was one of Uncle Joey's poker friends, and still involved with Uncle Joey's ex-wife, Carlotta.

"Yes. He's trying to squeeze Chris in on his docket so he can get Ramos's arraignment scheduled for later this afternoon. If not, he'll make sure it's first thing in the morning. Then we can get him out on bail."

"Oh, good. I was hoping you'd work something out."

"So, how did it go at the station?"

"Pretty good." I opened my mouth to tell him what I knew, but with Savage there, I had to be careful about giving my secret away. I motioned toward Savage with my head, and Uncle Joey got the message.

"Savage, could you give us a moment?"

His lips turned down. "Uh... sure. Where do you want me?"

"Just wait by the front desk. I'll be done in a minute."

"Sure, boss."

After he left, Uncle Joey turned to me. "Sorry about that. I asked him to come in because I might need someone to run some errands for me."

"That's fine."

"So what happened at the station?"

"Dimples managed to get me an interview with the witness."

"He did? Nice." He was thinking that Dimples was a great resource for us to have. He knew giving him a good deal on the hotel room would pay off. "What did you find out?"

I wanted to tell him that Dimples was more than just a resource to me, but it wasn't something Uncle Joey wanted to hear, so why bother? "The witness is someone we know."

Uncle Joey's brows rose. "Who?"

"Dagger."

"Dagger? Holy hell."

"I know. He changed his hair, his clothes, and even his mannerisms, but he couldn't fool me. He told the police that he was at his mother's apartment down the hall and saw Ramos break into Cal's room. After he heard a gunshot, he claims he saw Ramos come out and run into the stairwell."

Uncle Joey shook his head. "And they believe him?"

"They must. The police vet their witnesses, so his backstory has to be convincing. That means he's gone to a lot of trouble to frame Ramos. I mean... somehow he must have paid off that lady to say she was his mother, right?"

"Yes." Uncle Joey's lips turned down.

"There's something else. He was thinking that it was a good thing Ramos took a couple of shots at him, or he might have killed me, and he wasn't supposed to do that."

Uncle Joey's eyes narrowed. "I wondered why there was no mention of you in his narrative. Since we know he's working for Rathmore, it makes sense that Rathmore wouldn't want you harmed. He's probably planning on using your skills in the future."

My stomach twisted, knowing the only thing between me and Rathmore was Ramos and Uncle Joey. They'd nearly killed Uncle Joey, and now they were targeting Ramos.

"What's Rathmore up to? Did you pick up anything from Dagger about that?"

I shrugged. "No. But at least he doesn't know that I know who he really is."

"Yes. That gives us a big advantage."

"So why would he frame Ramos? What does he have to gain?"

Uncle Joey's eyes narrowed, and his face cleared. "I think I know. Rathmore must have put him up to it to push me into *investing* my money into Rathmore's pet project. I hand over the fifty million, and Dagger disappears." He shook his head. "I'll have to see what Chris thinks about Ramos's chances of beating the charges."

My brows rose. "That's risky isn't it?"

"Yeah... but I'm not ready to give in yet." He thought fifty million was a lot of money to make Dagger's testimony go away. But maybe there was another way to get rid of him. Savage had offered. That might work.

I sighed. How did I get involved in this again? Oh yeah. Because I got shot in the head at the grocery store. I used to think I'd hate it if I ever lost my ability. But now? Not so much.

The ringtone from *Law and Order* played on my phone, and I dug it out of my purse. "Hey Chris. How's it going?"

"Are you still at the station?"

"Not anymore. I'm at Thrasher with Uncle Joey."

"Okay, good. Tell Manetto that Ramos's arraignment is scheduled for first thing in the morning, so it looks like he'll be here overnight."

Uncle Joey held out his hand, wanting the phone. "I think he wants to talk to you. Here he is."

I handed my phone over, and they spoke about the arraignment and bail before he handed it back. "Put it on speaker."

"Okay. Chris, I'm putting you on speaker. So tell us what's going on."

"The witness identified Ramos as the shooter, but that's about all they have. I don't think it's enough to convict him, so Ramos has a pretty good chance of beating it. How about you? Did you find out anything that could help?"

"Yeah... I talked to the witness and found out he's lying, but now I've been banned from the case. Bates was pretty upset that I got in to see him. Bates might even file a complaint against Dimples."

"That's not good. Listen... I've got to go. I might be a little late tonight, but I'll see you at home."

"Okay. Bye." We disconnected, and I met Uncle Joey's gaze, catching his thoughts of silencing Dagger. But that would only happen if Savage found him first. It made me realize that, without Ramos to protect him, Uncle Joey could still be a target. Gavin had failed, but Dagger probably wouldn't.

I swallowed. "Before you go too far down that path, I think you should consider your own safety. With Ramos out of the way, what's to stop Dagger from coming after you? If you're going to... end... Dagger, you should wait until Ramos is around. Right?"

Uncle Joey nodded. "You're probably right. I hadn't thought of that."

He absently rubbed his chest where he'd been shot. There was no reason it should hurt, but phantom pain made it hard to breathe. "You didn't happen to get an address for Dagger, did you? I mean... shouldn't it be in the police database? If we find him first, we'd have a better chance of stopping him"

"Yeah... an address should be in the case files, but I can't go back there."

"Maybe not now, but don't you have another case you're working on?"

"Well... yeah. I do. Dimples is supposed to call me about it, but probably not until later tonight or tomorrow morning."

Uncle Joey's lips twisted. "Then maybe when you go in for that... you can look up the address."

"Yeah... that should work, but I have no idea when it'll happen."

"That's fine. In the meantime, I'll have Savage watch my back. He's been looking for Dagger anyway, so we'll see if he's found out anything useful."

I wrinkled my nose. I didn't like Savage much, and it bothered me that Uncle Joey was so willing to use him. But... since he was a lot like Dagger, and Dagger might want to kill Uncle Joey, it was probably okay.

I rubbed my temples and stood. "Uh... I think I'm going to go home... I have a headache. Will you be okay for a while without me?"

Uncle Joey came to my side and put his arm around my shoulders. "Of course. I'm sure this has been hard on you. I'll take care of everything. Try not to worry."

I let out a sigh. "Thanks. It has been a little rough."

"We'll get Ramos back; you'll see." Uncle Joey opened his office door, and I stepped out.

"Thanks, Uncle Joey. I'll talk to you later." I stepped down the hall. Behind me, Uncle Joey called for Savage to come back into his office, and Savage gave me a nod as he passed by, thinking how great everything was turning out.

Shaking my head, I said a quick goodbye to Jackie, and hurried out of the office.

In the parking garage, I took a detour past Ramos's motorcycle. I ran my fingers over the leather seat, sorry that that he was in jail. It had all happened so fast that it was still hard to believe.

At least Chris was helping him, and he'd be out in the morning. Still, it chilled me to my bones that he was in trouble. At least I didn't need to worry about Uncle Joey, since he had Savage to watch his back.

It reminded me that I hadn't spoken with Elliot since that day at the coffee shop. What if Elliot went after Savage while he was protecting Uncle Joey? My headache pounded extra hard, so I pushed that thought away and continued across the parking garage to my space.

Between one step and the next, I caught a shadow of movement out of the corner of my eye. I jerked to a stop and glanced in that direction, but couldn't see anything. Still, I opened my mind and caught Elliot's anger, along with his need to confront me.

"Elliot? Is that you?"

As if conjuring him from thin air, he stepped from behind a pillar, his hands in his pockets, and his mouth twisted. "Sorry. I didn't mean to scare you."

"What's going on?"

He huffed. "I don't get it. I followed Savage here. Then you showed up. I can only guess what you were doing here with him, but I figured I'd better find out before I made my move. So what's going on?"

I tried not to roll my eyes, but what the hell? "Actually, I work for Mr. Manetto, and his offices are in the building. He's the one who wanted me to talk to your boss, Howard Hoffman, remember?"

"Oh yeah... right. So what was Savage doing here?"

"Elliot... why are you still following Savage? I thought you'd given up on that."

He bristled. "No, I haven't. You didn't answer my question. Do you know why Savage is here?"

"Yes. I do." I decided to keep it short and summarize. "He's meeting with Mr. Manetto about a stabbing incident that happened at Manetto's club."

His eyes brightened. "Did Savage do it?"

"No. In fact, Savage is trying to find the guy who did."

"So... does that mean Savage works for Manetto?"

"He does now."

Elliot threw his head back and thought, *why me?* He was hoping that I'd figured out a plan to help him like I'd offered. But, apparently, I was siding with Savage now, and it was probably because we both worked for Manetto. Why did nothing ever go his way?

I rolled my eyes and took a calming breath. It didn't work and my head pounded even harder. "Elliot. We need to talk. Let's go get a coffee. My treat." He hesitated, so I motioned to the stairwell. "Come on. Let's figure this out."

He huffed out a breath before joining me. I picked up that he wanted to kill Savage so bad it hurt, but he couldn't bring himself to do it. What was wrong with him? Savage deserved death.

We exited onto the street and walked past Uncle Joey's building to the coffee shop on the corner. I'd only been there a few times to get coffee for everyone, but luckily it wasn't as crowded as I'd remembered. Soon we had our orders in hand, and we found an empty table in the back corner.

I smiled to put him at ease. "I'm glad we bumped into each other. I called you this morning, but you didn't answer."

He shrugged, thinking he already knew what I wanted to say, so why bother? "Do you have something new to tell me? You said there might be an alternative... like putting him in jail."

Since I hadn't thought of a way to do that, I had nothing to offer. "Uh... yeah, I'm still working on that."

His eyes narrowed. "You haven't even thought about it."

"No... the thought's crossed my mind several times, but I've been a little busy. Plus, he's working for Unc... uh... Manetto. It makes things a little more complicated."

"So keeping Manetto happy is more important. I get it."

"No, of course it's not." With my head pounding, I was making a mess of things. He was so combative that he wouldn't listen to me. I knew it was his pain talking, but I only had so much patience.

Elliot sipped his coffee, nursing his anger. It was better than the grief and remorse that filled his heart. He should have done more to protect Zoe. If Savage were dead, he knew he'd feel better. "I'm sorry... but you're no help at all. If you ask me, it looks like you're helping Savage. I mean... he just got out of jail, and he already has a good job with your boss."

"Hold on. That's not my fault. He was working for him before you hired me."

"Well... I'm done with you. I want a refund."

Something inside me snapped, and I slapped the table with both hands. "Oh my gosh! Fine. You can have your stupid money and do whatever the hell you want. I quit."

As I stood to leave, the scent of juniper and sage rushed over me, freezing me in place. *Please, help him.*

I squeezed my eyes shut. Not this again. "What do you want me to say?"

Elliot's eyes widened. "You talking to me?"

"No. Zoe." I sat down. "For some reason, she wants me to help you."

"Right, and how are you supposed to do that?"

"By telling you that she doesn't want you to kill Savage."

He snorted. "Yeah... right. You already used that on me. You're just saying that to convince me not to go through with it and you're using her to make me listen."

Tell him that he's wrong and you'll prove it.

Damn! I hated her voice in my head. *If I tell him he's wrong, will you promise to get out of my head?* She didn't answer me, so I took a breath and met Elliot's gaze. "She thinks you're wrong... and she'll prove it."

His eyes narrowed. "How?" He let out a mirthless laugh. "Fine. I'll call your bluff. Go ahead. Prove she's talking to you right now."

I closed my eyes and listened to her commentary. She had a lot to share, and some of it was pretty funny. At least I managed to keep from laughing, but it was close. "Okay... I'll tell you... but just remember that you asked for it."

"Whatever... just tell me, already."

"Fine. Remember that time at your cousin Jenny's birthday party when you peed your pants and Zoe helped hide you before anyone found out? She said she put you in Jenny's closet until your mom came."

His mouth dropped open, but I kept going. "And what about your company party? Your plus one ditched you, and Zoe dropped everything to take her place. Does any of that ring a bell?"

His face paled. "Zoe?" He glanced up at the ceiling. "Is she here right now?"

My heart softened. "Yes... she's here. And she wants me to tell you that the best way you can honor her is by remembering her for who she was and to quit focusing on how she died. Killing Savage won't bring her back, and she doesn't want you to carry that burden anymore. She wants you to live your life and be happy."

I hesitated. "She wants me to ask you a question." I waited for him to nod before continuing. "If your roles were reversed, and you'd been murdered, would you want her to kill the person who killed you?"

He glanced away. "Of course not."

"She says that's your answer... and if you don't follow her advice, she'll haunt you for the rest of your life."

His lips twisted. He swallowed, and regret filled his eyes. The last time he'd spoken to her, he was a total jerk. "Please... tell Zoe that I love her... and I'm sorry for being such a jerk. I won't kill Savage. She doesn't need to worry about me anymore."

The scent of juniper and sage wafted over us, then she was gone.

Elliot's face filled with wonder. "Did you smell that? It was her perfume... that was her, right?"

"Yeah. It was. I think she's finally at rest now."

Tears filled Elliot's eyes, and he blinked them away. "Thanks Shelby. I guess I'll leave Savage alone."

Relief washed over me. "Good. I'm glad to hear it."

He nodded, suddenly realizing that a weight had lifted from his shoulders. He felt lighter than he had since the day Zoe died. He smiled at me. "If she ever talks to you again, will you let me know?"

"Uh... sure... but I think she's moved on." A sense of sadness washed over him. I reached over and patted his arm. "Remember the good, okay? And that she'll always love you."

"Sure. Thanks Shelby."

Chapter 18

The drive home passed by in a blur, and I pulled into my driveway, relieved to be away from it all. It was early enough that the kids weren't here yet, and I relished the time alone.

Coco was elated to see me, and, after taking a couple of pain relievers, I took him into the back yard and sank down on the patio swing. The sun had come out from behind the clouds, but the autumn air was brisk. Still, I loved the feel of it on my face. Relaxing, I laid my head down on the cushions and promptly fell asleep.

"Mom! Are you okay?"

I jerked my eyes open to find Savannah looming over me. I'd been so still that she'd thought I was dead.

"I'm fine. Just tired. It's been a long day." I sat up and moved over, patting the seat beside me. "Come and sit down. It's so nice out here."

She sat beside me with a sigh, relieved to just be herself for a change. "We haven't gone to Aikido for a while. Can we go tonight?"

"That's a great idea. Let's get ready and go now."

"Really? Okay."

She jumped up and hurried inside, passing Josh, who was coming out onto the patio. He had a bag of treats and planned to do some training exercises with Coco.

"Hey... is it okay if Savannah and I go to Aikido for about an hour?"

"Sure. Just as long as you stop and get some pizza on the way home."

"Sounds good to me."

Much later, Chris came home. He'd stayed late to finish up a few things, as well as get everything together for Ramos's arraignment the next morning. I greeted him with a long hug. "I hope you're not mad at me."

"For what?"

"Going to the precinct. I actually saw you through the mirror when you came into the interrogation room."

"I'm surprised Bates let you in."

I huffed. "Oh... he didn't know I was there. It was Dimples who arranged it. But Dimples was sure mad at me. I had to explain everything that was going on with Uncle Joey and why Ramos and I had been at Cal's apartment."

He shook his head. "I was afraid something like that would happen. At least he didn't arrest you for leaving the scene of the crime." Chris thought that Harris had every right to be upset. By not being honest with him, I'd broken his trust.

"I know... I know. But after I explained everything, he mostly understood. At least... I think he's forgiven me. Anyway... there's something huge I found out, so it's a good thing I went."

"What's that?"

I took a deep breath. "Like I told you, I spoke to the witness... and I know who he is." Chris raised his brows, so I quickly continued. "He's the killer. It's Dagger, only without the long hair and beard."

"Holy hell."

"Yeah."

"So... wait a minute. Why would he accuse Ramos?"

"It's a long story, but Uncle Joey and I think Rathmore's behind it." I explained all about the pressure on Uncle Joey to sink fifty million into Rathmore's smart city project.

Chris's eyes narrowed. "So it's blackmail. Manetto gives him the investment money, and Ramos's accuser goes away?"

"Yeah. But Uncle Joey still doesn't want to pay. He wondered if you thought Ramos could beat the charges. If you do... he'll take a chance and not give in to Rathmore."

Chris nodded, and his lips twisted. "That's what I'm trying to figure out. They only needed the witness's testimony to arrest Ramos, but they'll need more for a conviction. I think they must have something else, but I don't know what it is yet."

"Don't they have to tell you?"

"Yes, but that comes after the arraignment. Luckily, it's on the docket for first thing in the morning."

"That's too bad Ramos has to stay in jail overnight."

Chris shrugged. "He'll live." He thought if anyone could take care of themselves in jail, it was Ramos.

"That's true. So... Bates kicked me off the case and threatened to file a complaint against Dimples with internal affairs, so I'm sort of banned from the station until this is over."

"Good."

I frowned. He didn't have to be so happy about that. "So... I was thinking that I could help you with the case instead. You know... be your investigator. So what kind of snooping do you need?"

"Wait... so does Manetto know about Dagger being the witness?"

"Yeah. I think he wants to find him and... uh... get rid of him."

Chris closed his eyes. "I'd better call him. That should be our last resort." He pulled his phone from his pocket and called Uncle Joey. While they spoke, he walked into his study and shut the door.

Since he knew I couldn't hear his thoughts on the other side of the door, it kind of hurt my feelings. What did he need to hide from me anyway? Of course, maybe it was okay not to know everything right now. I'd find out soon enough, and I might sleep better tonight if they kept me in the dark.

Letting out a breath, I went upstairs to my room and started a bath. I was exhausted, and all this stress was getting to me. Half an hour later, I dried off and got ready for bed. Chris came in and offered to rub lotion on my back.

Not about to pass that up, I handed it over and closed my eyes. His touch soothed me as much as the bath had. After a moment, I turned in his arms, needing to feel his body against mine. Kissing him soundly, it wasn't long before I heard some of my favorite words.

"Oh baby, oh baby."

The next morning, I sat in the back of the courtroom waiting for the cops to bring Ramos in for his arraignment. Chris hadn't wanted me to come, but I'd insisted that I needed to be there. I mean... how else were we supposed to know what the prosecuting attorney had on Ramos without me and my mind-reading skills?

The judge sat on his bench, doling out judgments on bail and the consequences of guilty pleas. Ramos's turn finally came, and a couple of guards brought him out. He wore an orange jumpsuit with chains around his ankles and wrists.

All the other prisoners had worn handcuffs, and it made me mad that they'd treated him like a dangerous criminal. But... in a way I couldn't blame them since his size alone made him look the part... only in a totally hot way.

As he shuffled to his seat, I picked up his annoyance, along with his eagerness to get this over with. After his night in jail, all he wanted to do was go home and take a shower. He caught sight of me and raised a brow, thinking *thanks for coming.* And he hoped I wasn't in too much trouble with my police buddies.

After the verdict of manslaughter in the first degree was read, they asked him how he pleaded, and Chris said, "Not guilty."

When they got to setting bail, it was clear the prosecuting attorney didn't want Ramos out of jail. "He has an arrest record, and I believe he is a flight risk. Because of the serious nature of the charges, he should remain in jail until his trial."

Chris countered that Ramos was an upstanding citizen with no convictions. "Your honor, my client has no intention of going anywhere. He has been wrongly accused, and it would be an undue hardship for him and his family if he had to remain in jail."

The judge waved dismissively and set bail at two million dollars. He hit his gavel on the sounding block and motioned for the next case to come forward. The guards ushered Ramos out, and Chris came back to join me.

"Why don't you head back to Thrasher? I'll bring Ramos as soon as I post bail and he's released."

"Sure. Do you know when that will be?"

"Um... a couple hours."

"Okay. See you then."

I stepped into Thrasher, and Jackie greeted me with wide-eyed enthusiasm. "How did it go?"

"Pretty good, I guess. He's getting out on bail."

She asked a lot of detailed questions, and I answered them all, mostly because I knew they were for the scene in her book, and she wanted to make sure she got it right. After I gave her all of the details about the judge, she asked me how the courtroom smelled, and I knew it was time to go.

"Uh... a little stuffy... you know... like an old building. Hey... I'd better give Uncle Joey an update."

"Oh... right. Thanks Shelby."

"Sure."

I knocked before pushing the door open. Uncle Joey was in his chair behind his desk, but Savage sat in Ramos's usual spot. It surprised me how quickly he'd taken Ramos's place, and I couldn't help the resentment that rose in my chest.

"Shelby... come in, come in. How did it go?"

I took my seat beside Savage. "It went well. Chris will bring Ramos back here as soon as he's posted bail and Ramos is released."

"Good. I was just going over a lead with Savage. He might know where to find Dagger."

"Oh?" I met Savage's gaze. "That's great."

Savage nodded, but all he had were a few guesses. Still, what Manetto wanted, Manetto got, even if he had to make it up. He wanted to keep the mob boss happy until he came up with a real lead, which so far, was absolutely nothing. Dammit to hell. He was good at killing people, not finding them.

I studied him, realizing he had that deer in the headlights look in his eyes, and my annoyance faded. Uncle Joey expected him to fill Ramos's shoes, but who could ever do that?

"Why don't I help you find Dagger? In fact, I can call my source with the police and see if he'll give me some information on him."

Uncle Joey frowned. "I thought you were banned."

"I'm banned from being there, but Dimples might be willing to talk to me about what they know."

"Does he know that Dagger and the witness is the same person?"

"Yes. That's why he might help me. But only if I promise him that you won't kill him... Dagger, not Dimples."

Uncle Joey sighed. "Sure. Chris already talked me out of that." He didn't say *for now*, like he was thinking.

"Okay... good. I'm going to my office. I'll let you know what he says."

Uncle Joey frowned, not happy that I was leaving to make the call. But he realized I couldn't be as open with him as usual because Savage was in the room and didn't know my secret.

With pursed lips, I gave him a nod to let him know he was right, and hurried to my office. Sitting behind my desk, I took a minute to unwind before putting the call through. Dimples answered right away. "Detective Harris."

"Hey, it's me."

"Yes... how can I help you?"

"Is Bates standing right there?"

"That's right."

"Can you call me back?"

"Of course, I'll look into it and let you know."

"Thanks." I disconnected and sat back in my chair. It bothered me that Dimples was being so formal, but what did I expect? I was the enemy. He might not even call me back. Then what would I do?

The *Scooby Doo* ringtone sounded, and I grabbed my phone. "Hello?"

"Hey. Sorry about that, but Bates is on the warpath, so I have to be careful."

"Oh... I totally get it. Thanks for calling me back. I'm mostly calling about Dagger. Would you happen to know if he's coming to the precinct as Dorian today?"

"Why? So you can follow him?"

"That would be helpful, but not something you need to know."

"If he ends up dead, Ramos will be in more trouble than he already is."

"I know. That's not going to happen."

"Good." He sighed. "You might want to check the apartment where his 'mom' lives. It's number two-twenty. Maybe she's seen him."

"Oh... okay. Thanks."

"Umm... there's something else you need to know."

My stomach twisted. From his tone, I knew it was bad.

"The results for Keller's hair sample haven't come back. The chief thinks the report must have gotten lost, so they're doing it again."

My chest froze. Holy hell! In all the drama over Ramos's arrest, I'd totally spaced that Keller was getting out today. "But today's Wednesday. Is he still getting out?"

"We still have time. They usually process them out in the afternoon, so we have until about four. The chief is working with the prosecuting attorney to keep him in jail another day. The attorney's request will be in front of the judge in the next hour. With the matching blood on the money, and the fact that we have a hair sample, I'm pretty sure the judge will allow it."

"But what if they don't?"

"If they don't, you're the first person I'll call. In the meantime, try not to worry. They could still find the results, so it could still work out."

I closed my eyes and heaved a sigh. This was terrible news. "If I don't hear from you by four o'clock, I'm never speaking to you again."

"You will. I promise."

"Okay."

"Don't worry. I'll call you soon."

We said our goodbyes, and I slipped my phone back into my purse. Taking deep breaths, I tried to still the fear that had me shaking all over. How could something like this happen? If he got out today, who knew if we'd ever find him again? I just knew that someday he'd come after me, and I'd go crazy looking over my shoulder waiting for him to strike.

I closed my eyes and tried to be reasonable. He wasn't out yet. Dimples and the chief would do everything in their power to keep him behind bars. It could still work. But if the worst happened and he got out? Well... I could make some plans of my own. I wasn't totally helpless, and I had friends who were scarier than him.

I was sure once Ramos got back, he would be happy to be at the prison when Keller got out. He'd keep track of him, and, when the results finally came in, we'd know where he was, and Dimples could arrest him. It could all work out. I didn't need to be afraid.

Swallowing my fear, I checked the time. It was nine-thirty, plenty of time before four o'clock. Ramos should be out on bail by then, and, even if he wasn't, I was sure Uncle Joey had someone else who could help me... even Savage could do it.

In the meantime, I needed to keep busy or I'd go crazy. With a couple of hours before Ramos got out, I could follow up on that lead and talk to Dagger's 'mom.' Who knew? Maybe by the end of the day, both Dagger and Keller would be behind bars... or maybe dead... and all my worries would be over.

Feeling more positive, I stepped into Uncle Joey's office. "I have a lead on Dagger, but before I explain, I might have a problem."

"What's that?"

"There's a cold case I've been helping Dimples with, and we've run into a snag." I explained that Keller might get out on parole before the results came back, and, since he'd threatened me, I needed some protection.

Uncle Joey's eyes narrowed. He was thinking that helping the police sure got me into a lot of trouble. Good thing I had him to help me out. At this rate, he should start billing the city. "Don't worry about it. Ramos will be here soon. Once he knows the problem, I'm sure he'll be happy to take care of it."

I let out a breath. "Yeah... but he's not going to kill him, right?"

Uncle Joey raised a brow, thinking *why the hell not,* but pursed his lips. "If it can be avoided... no... but if he comes after you... then hell yes."

"I'm hoping the results will come in long before that happens. Then Dimples can arrest him."

"Of course. We'll discuss it more after Ramos and Chris get here. In the meantime, tell me what you know about Dagger." He'd taken in my pale face and knew I was barely holding it together, so focusing on Dagger would take my mind off it and keep me from falling apart.

My brows dipped. He thought I was going to fall apart? I'd show him. "I want to head to Cal's apartment building to talk to the lady who's posing as his mom. I..." I glanced at Savage and changed my wording. "...have a feeling that she might know more than she's saying."

"Good idea." He pulled his bottom drawer open and took out a cash box. After tapping in a code, he lifted the lid and took out five one-hundred-dollar bills. "This might help loosen her tongue." He handed them to me before turning to Savage. "Go with her. I want to make sure she's safe."

I wanted to tell Uncle Joey that Savage was planning to kill Dagger if he got the chance, but I couldn't say that out loud. I turned to Savage. "But no killing... we need him alive, right Uncle Joey?"

Uncle Joey turned his flinty gaze on Savage. "That's right."

Savage jerked his head up and down. "Sure... sure. I got it."

"And make sure you do whatever Shelby says. She is your first priority. Got that?"

"Sure, boss."

"Okay. You can go." Uncle Joey glanced at me, thinking that he'd handle things, and I shouldn't worry about the ex-con. Nothing was going to happen to me. Ever. He wouldn't allow it.

With my throat tight, I stepped into his arms, grateful to have him on my side. His warm embrace bolstered my courage. After a tight squeeze, he pulled away. "Now get going."

I nodded, wiping a tear from my eyes. He shook his head, thinking that it was a good thing Savage was going with me, especially if we found Dagger. Somebody had to help me put him in the trunk, right?

I chuckled and gave Uncle Joey a watery smile. Savage dutifully followed me to the elevator and into the parking garage. He kept his mouth shut, totally intimidated by me. Plus... he'd seen how much Uncle Joey loved me, so he knew he had to be on his best behavior.

I led the way to my car, and we drove to the apartment building in silence. After parking, I figured we should have a game plan. "I don't want her to see you and get spooked, so I need you to stay out of sight. Maybe you can wait in the hall."

"Sure." He didn't like that idea, but I was the boss.

I strode to room two-twenty and knocked. I could hear the TV blaring inside, so I knew someone was there. After a few seconds, the door opened, and a nice little old lady looked up at me. She had silver hair, large glasses that made her eyes look huge, and wore a flowered house dress. "Can I help you?"

"Hi. I'm Shelby Nichols. I'm a private investigator. I'm looking for your son, Dorian. Is he home? I just have a few questions for him."

"My... oh... him. No, he's not here."

"That's too bad." I took a hundred-dollar-bill from my purse. "Maybe you could help me? Could I come in and chat for a minute?"

Glancing at the money, she licked her lips. Her eyes narrowed, and she looked me over before snatching the money from my hand and pulling the door wide. "Of course. Come in."

I stepped through the doorway, motioning to Savage to stay put. Inside, the room was filled with old, worn-out furniture and covered with doilies in all different shades of pink.

"Please sit down. Would you like some iced-tea?"

"Uh... sure. Thank you."

She left, hoping that I had more money she could milk me for. Dorian had given her two thousand dollars. How much did I have? She came back carrying two glasses of iced tea and handed one to me.

"Thanks so much." I took a sip and tried not to grimace. It was so sweet that it made my teeth hurt. I set it on the coffee table and turned to face her. "So... I'm looking for more information about Dorian. Do you have an address for him?"

She smiled. "I do." She waited, thinking that I needed to cough up another bill or two before she'd give me the address.

Twisting my lips, I reached into my purse and pulled out another hundred. I held it up, and she tried to grab it, but I pulled it away and kept it just out of reach. "The address?"

She huffed out a breath. "It's in the kitchen. I'll get it." With a sigh, she hurried into the kitchen and grabbed the paper under the magnet on the refrigerator door. "This is my only copy, so you'll have to write it down."

I pulled out my phone and opened the notes app. "Go ahead."

She rattled off the address and waited while I put it in. Then she held out her hand, thinking the address was totally bogus, since he'd only given her a phone number, but what did I know?

I narrowed my eyes and slipped the money back into my purse. "Shall we try this again? Only this time I'll take the phone number he gave you."

"But... what about this?" She held up the paper, her brows dipping with confusion.

I lifted a brow. "I don't know whose address that is, but it's not Dorian's."

Her shoulders slumped, and her lips parted. How did I know? She turned the paper over and let out a breath. "Fine. Here's the number he gave me. I've never used it, but he told me to call him if the police came back asking for him."

This time, she was telling the truth. "Great. Go ahead." As she read it off, I added the phone number to my notes app, knowing I'd have to erase the address later.

"Thanks." I took out the other hundred-dollar bill and held it out. "Please don't mention my name to the police... if they come by."

She snatched the money. "I wouldn't dream of it."

"Thanks. I'll show myself out." I popped off the couch and hurried to the door. Relieved to be done, I stepped into the hallway, and closed the door behind me.

Savage waited just outside the door, and we hurried to the elevator.

"I got something. Let's go."

"What is it?"

"A phone number. It's not much, but I think Uncle Joey will be pleased."

"Sure." He thought a phone number wasn't much to get excited about. Weren't we supposed find Dagger and bring him in? "Why don't we just call it and see if we can find him?"

I shook my head. "Let's tell Uncle Joey first. Besides, Ramos might want to be involved, you know, since Dagger's the one setting him up?"

Savage shrugged. "Sure." His lips twisted, and disappointment washed over him. Catching Dagger would have impressed Manetto. Now he'd have to find another way to do it. Still, he was with me, and basically taking Ramos's place, so that said something about Manetto's trust in him. For now, he'd just keep his head down and do what he was told.

"Good. Let's go." Wow. Savage was making a real effort here. Maybe he was serious about making some changes in his life and having him on the team wasn't so bad after all.

Back in the car, my phone rang. It wasn't a number I knew, and it didn't have a name to go with it, but I figured I'd better answer. "Hello?"

"Is this Shelby Nichols?" The woman's voice shook, setting off alarms in my head.

"Yes."

"Thank God." She sniffed, holding back a sob. "This is Chelsea. I'm Wade Keller's girlfriend... we met at his mom's." She took short, panting breaths. "Wade got out this morning. We're at his mom's... I think... I think she's dead. He just k..killed her." She started crying in earnest. "You need to come... or he'll kill me too. Please... I don't want to die."

The phone dropped, and I heard a muffled scream followed by a wail of pain. My mouth went dry. Someone picked up the phone. "Is that you, Shelby?" His low, raspy tone sent shivers down my spine.

"What did you do to her?"

"Don't worry. She's still alive... but for every minute it takes you to get here, I'm going to cut her...nice and deep. I'll try to stay away from the main arteries, but deep cuts bleed a lot, and they're quite painful, so I'd suggest you hurry."

Moaning sounded in the background, then came more pleading from Chelsea. "No please... please don't do this... please. I didn't take it... you have to believe me... no!" Another shriek was followed by cries of pain.

Keller came back on the phone. "Oh... and come alone. Anyone else shows up, and she's dead."

The call ended, and dread tightened my throat, making it hard to speak. "That... that was Keller. The killer I told Uncle Joey about. He's out."

Savage began to swear. For some reason, his outburst helped calm me down. "We need to switch places. You need to drive." His brows dipped, so I raised my voice. "Now!" I crawled over the seat while he hurried around the car.

Jumping in, he started the car up. "Okay. Where am I going?"

I shook my head. I didn't have an address, but I pointed him in the general direction. "Just start going southwest." I pushed Dimples's number and prayed he'd pick up.

"Detective Harris."

"Keller's out! They let him out already." Dimples swore, but I spoke over his outburst. "He just called me. I need his mom's address. Hurry, every minute it takes me to get there, he's cutting up Chelsea."

"You can't go. He'll kill you."

"Then what should I do? If he sees the police, he'll kill her."

"Hang on..." Holding the phone away from his ear, he yelled, saying that he had a hostage situation and an officer in trouble. Then he started running, and I heard footsteps and other shouts. He came back on a second later. "Here's the address." He rattled it off, and I put it in my phone notes.

I glanced at Savage, repeating the address. "Did you get that?"

He nodded and made a couple of turns to head in the right direction.

"Who are you talking to?" Dimples asked.

"I'm with Savage... he's driving. We're probably about ten or fifteen minutes away. What should I do when we get there?"

"Stop a couple houses away and wait for me. I'll be there soon." I heard him yelling more instructions before the phone disconnected.

Savage glanced at me sideways. "So the guy got out, and he's after you?" He could hardly believe the mess I was in. Wasn't this supposed to go down this afternoon?

"Yes, and now he's hurting Chelsea to get to me. We've got to get there before he kills her."

"Okay... but the police are coming too, right?"

"Right. But we'll probably get there first."

"Sure... but we're waiting for them, right?"

"Yes." I closed my eyes and shook my head. "How did he get out early? He was supposed to be released at four, not this morning. Dammit!"

It seemed to take forever before Savage turned down a street that I recognized. Today, it seemed even more run-down than the last time I'd been there. "It's that house there... the brick one." Savage stopped a few houses away, and I licked my lips. "Did you bring a gun?"

His brows rose, but he nodded. It went against his parole to have it, so if the police got involved, he could get sent back to prison.

"Don't worry. I'll tell them it's mine. Dimples will understand."

"Dimples? Who's that?"

I shook my head. "Detective Harris... I call him Dimples."

"Oh... the one who interviewed me?"

"Yeah."

He thought that was weird, and he was glad I called him Savage. Of course, it was the perfect name for a hitman. He just hoped I didn't do anything stupid, and he'd have to kill the guy. They'd probably send him back to prison for that.

I wanted to tell him that Uncle Joey would take care of it, but I just pursed my lips together instead. There wasn't any movement at the house, but a car that had to belong to Chelsea sat in the driveway.

"What's taking so long?" I checked my watch. "It's been almost twenty minutes." I opened my door, but Savage grabbed my arm.

"What are you doing? We can't go down there."

"How about I walk to the house? You follow, but stay out of sight. When he comes to the door, you can jump out and shoot him."

"You want me to kill him? Maybe you should take the gun and shoot him."

I shook my head. "No. He'll see me holding it. Besides, I thought you wanted to be a hitman. Now's your chance."

"Well sure, but not like that. It needs to be planned so I don't get caught."

"Fine. Give me the gun."

"No. Manetto..." His gaze shifted to the house. "Wait... is that smoke?"

A plume of smoke rose from the house. "Oh no." I jumped out of the car, and Savage followed. We crept closer, trying to stay out of sight.

Nearly to the house, I heard a wailing scream coming from inside. The hairs on the back of my neck rose, and I held a hand out to Savage. "Give me the gun."

"No... I've got this." He pulled the gun from his belt and flipped off the safety. "I'm ready." If he had to go back to prison, so be it. This was his job, and he wasn't going to let Manetto down.

We rushed to the front door. I crouched low and pulled it open. Smoke billowed out, and we could barely see inside. I darted in and found Chelsea on the living room floor, covered in blood. Her wrists were bound together, and blood covered her arms and legs. As smoke began to engulf us, Savage slipped his gun into his waistband and hefted her under the arms. I lifted her legs, and we carried her out the door.

Out on the lawn, we lowered her to the ground, and both of us began to cough from the smoke. Finally catching my breath, I crawled beside Chelsea and checked her pulse. She was unconscious, but still breathing. Where was Keller?

From behind me, I heard a click and whirled to find Keller, holding a gun pointed at my face. "Get in the car." He motioned toward Chelsea's car. "Now!"

My heart raced. I zeroed in on his thoughts, picking up that he could hardly wait to carve me into little pieces... just like Chelsea. Hearing me scream would make him feel better, since I'd ruined his plans.

Shit! I'd rather die here than get into that car with him. "No."

His brows rose. "Get in the car!" His gaze darted between me and Savage, and I picked up that he had only one bullet in the chamber, and he'd use it on me if he had to.

Knowing there was just one bullet evened the odds, giving me a chance to get out of this. I just needed a distraction so Savage could shoot him.

Sirens sounded in the distance. Keller's heart raced, and he panicked. With a quick lunge, he grabbed my arm, giving Savage time to draw his gun. Seeing the threat, Keller pointed his gun at Savage. I threw my weight against his hold, hoping it would throw off his aim.

Keller fired his gun, and another shot sounded at the same time, this one coming from Savage. Keller let go of me and reeled back from a round to his shoulder, but managed to stay on his feet.

Growling with rage, Keller advanced on Savage, still firing his empty gun. Savage returned fire, hitting Keller in the chest. Keller jerked each time a bullet hit him but kept going. With his arms reaching toward Savage, Keller's body finally gave out, and he collapsed onto the ground, twitching a few times before going still.

Savage heaved a heavy breath before falling to his knees. My eyes widened to see a dark, red stain spreading down his chest. I rushed to his side and caught him as he slumped to the ground.

Shaking with panic, I took his hand, not sure what to do. "Savage... I've got you. Hang on. Help is on the way."

His gaze met mine. "Tell Manetto... I kept... my word... I... kept you... safe."

Tears filled my eyes. "You can tell him yourself. Hang on... you're going to be fine."

He tried to shake his head, but his strength was gone. "It's okay ... I did something ... good..." I found no remorse in his thoughts, and he kept his gaze steady on mine, waiting for a response.

I swallowed. He wasn't going to make it... and it was because of me. Pushing back my remorse, I nodded. "You did, Savage. You did... you saved me. Thank you... thank you for doing that."

A faint smile twisted his lips. Still holding his gaze, I felt peace envelop him. Then his eyes began to glaze over, his hand went limp in mine, and death took him away.

"Shelby! Are you okay?"

Dimples fell to his knees beside me, and I turned my face into his chest, tears streaming down my cheeks. "I'm... I'm okay." I pulled back. "You need to check on Chelsea."

He kept his arms around me. "We are... and the paramedics are coming. You sure you're good?" He looked me over, worried about the blood on my hands.

"It's not mine. It's... Savage's... I think he's dead."

Dimples had already come to that conclusion.

"What about Chelsea?" I asked.

"I brought Clue. She's helping Chelsea." As he spoke, more police cars pulled up to surround us, and several officers jumped out to secure the area.

Not ready to let me go, Dimples glanced at Chelsea, thinking she didn't look so good. Clue found a pulse and was yelling for a first aid kit. Someone brought it over, and they began to staunch the bleeding.

Another officer checked Savage, taking in his sightless eyes. When I'd told Dimples I was with Savage, he could hardly believe it was the same person we'd interviewed for Cal's murder. He shook his head. What the hell was going on? What was I doing with him?

"He saved my life."

"Yeah... I can see that." He turned his attention to Keller's inert form, noting all the bullet wounds in his torso, along with the gun he still held in his hand. "Come on... let's get you out of here. You can sit in my car while we get this all straightened out. Then you can explain what happened."

His car had been the first to arrive, and the front tires were resting on the lawn. As he helped me inside, a fire truck pulled in front of the driveway. "Are you okay for a minute?"

"Yes."

Closing the door, he hurried to help set a perimeter around the bodies, directing the firemen around them to run inside the house. A few minutes later, the fire fighters reappeared, carrying a smoking trash bin that had been the source of all the smoke. Once they'd taken care of that, the police could secure the scene.

In the meantime, the paramedics arrived. As they left with Chelsea, I caught their optimism that she'd recover. The forensics van pulled up next. Two of the team members jumped out and began photographing the bodies. Dimples disappeared inside the house, coming out to tell them there was another body inside.

I shook my head. It had to be Keller's mom. How could he kill his own mother?

Dimples came back to the car and slipped into the driver's seat. "Dammit. He killed her. I should have warned her, but I thought I had more time."

"I know... how were we supposed to know he'd get out early? How did that happen anyway? Do you know?"

"No... not yet. But I'll find out who screwed up and give them a piece of my mind." He took in my pale face and red eyes. "Are you okay to tell me what happened?" From what he'd seen, he had a pretty good idea, but he needed to hear all the details from me.

"Sure, but before you get mad, I want you to know that we were waiting for you guys, but when we saw all the smoke... and heard Chelsea screaming..." I swallowed. "I didn't even think... I just got out of the car. Savage backed me up. That's why he's dead, and not me."

"It's okay... I get it. I'm not mad. So what happened after that?"

I heaved out a breath and told him the rest, grateful that it didn't take as long as I thought to fill him in. As I finished up, my phone rang with the theme from *Law and Order*.

"Is that Chris?" Dimples's lips quirked up. "Makes sense."

As I answered, he wondered what his ring tone was, and I figured I'd better change it before he ever found out. "Hey, Chris."

"Shelby... good, you're there. Sorry it's taken so long. We've had to jump through a few hoops, but we're finally done here. Ramos and I are heading to Thrasher, so we'll be there soon."

"Sounds good. Uh... I'm not there right now, but I shouldn't be long."

"Oh? Where've you been?"

I took a deep breath to hold back my tears, but it was hard. Hearing his voice made me want to start bawling. "Uh... following up on a lead. I'll tell you all about it when I get there."

"Okay. See you soon." He disconnected, and I slipped my phone back into my purse, only to have it ring again. This time it was the theme from *Scooby Doo*, and my heart sank.

I glanced at Dimples to see his eyes widen. "*Scooby Doo?* Are you freakin' kidding me?"

I shrugged, hoping he wasn't upset. Then he burst out laughing. Shaking his head, he disconnected the call. "I guess it's okay... but now I'll have to come up with one for you to get you back." He was thinking of the song "Don't Speak."

"Ah... that's a good one."

"I know... right?" He huffed out a sigh. "I need to finish up here. Are you all right if I head back out there?"

"Sure, as long as it's okay if I leave."

"You sure you're okay to drive? I mean... it probably shook you up a bit. I could have someone take you..."

I shook my head. "I'm okay. It did shake me up, but I'm doing well enough now."

"Okay. We'll wrap things up later at the station."

"Sounds good."

Dimples escorted me to my car, and I tried not to look at the covered bodies on the lawn. At my car, Dimples thought about giving me a hug, but he wasn't sure if it would turn me into a blubbering idiot.

I shook my head and gave him a quick hug before sliding into the driver's seat. Luckily, the keys were still dangling from the ignition, so I was able to start it up. Dimples gave me a wave and watched me until I turned the corner.

Letting out a breath, I held my emotions in check. I turned on the radio and concentrated on the news to keep me distracted. After pulling into the parking garage and turning off the ignition, it hit me that, just a couple of hours ago I'd left with Savage, but now I was coming back without him.

Chapter 19

I walked into Thrasher and found Jackie's desk empty. Uncle Joey's office door stood open, and I could hear voices, so I headed in that direction. Barely holding back my tears, I paused before stepping through the doorway. Uncle Joey sat behind his desk, with Chris and Ramos sitting in front.

Seeing me, Uncle Joey's eyes lit up. "Shelby... I was just telling Chris and Ramos that you were checking out a lead. Did you find anything?" He glanced behind me. "Where's Savage?"

My throat got tight, and I couldn't speak. Taking in my disheveled appearance and pale face, Uncle Joey jumped from his chair and rushed to my side. "What's wrong?" He pulled me into his arms, and I leaned against his chest, blinking back my tears. "Let's sit down."

Keeping me in a firm grip, he led me to the couch at the side of his office. He sat down and pulled me with him. By now, tears were streaming down my cheeks. "Ramos... grab a tissue will you?"

Ramos held out the tissue, and Uncle Joey put it in my hands. I took a couple of breaths and calmed down enough to wipe my eyes and nose. "Thanks. Sorry about that."

"No, no. It's fine. Take your time. We can wait."

Chris sat down beside me, and Ramos pulled up a chair. I picked up worry, confusion, and a lot of speculation. Had I found Dagger? Had he managed to get away? They all knew something bad had happened, and, to varying degrees, none of them wanted to wait a moment longer to find out what it was.

I finished wiping my nose and took a calming breath. "I did find a lead on Dagger. I got a phone number from the woman he paid off to be his mother. She said it was a way to contact him, so it might help."

Fresh tears sprang from my eyes. They were all totally bewildered, and I knew I had to get under control. I shook my head. "Okay... sorry. You're right. Something else happened... and it was awful."

I swallowed and wiped my nose again. "While Savage and I were on our way back here, I got a phone call. The cold-case killer somehow got out of prison early, and I had to go help save his girlfriend... from him. He'd already killed his mom, and he was hurting Chelsea.

"He told me that, for every minute it took me to get there, he'd cut her up more. I called Dimples, and he came, but Savage and I got there first. We were going to wait, but smoke started pouring from the house. We heard screaming, so we ran inside.

"We got Chelsea out alive, but Keller ambushed us. He wanted me to get in his car, but I refused. Then Savage pulled his gun, and Keller shot him. Keller only had one bullet, but he kept coming at Savage, so Savage kept shooting at Keller. He must have shot him about six times. Keller finally collapsed and died, but then Savage... he'd been shot, and he collapsed too. I tried to help him... but he... he died."

I blinked back my tears and turned to Uncle Joey. "He wanted me to tell you that he did his job." Grief tightened my throat, making it hard to speak. "He did what you told him and kept me safe... just like you asked. He wanted you to know."

Sorrow filled Uncle Joey's eyes, and he pulled me close. A long sigh escaped him. How had this happened? I'd come so close to death, and he hadn't been able to protect me.

"Yes you did... you sent Savage. He protected me because you asked him to."

Uncle Joey nodded. "Then for that, he deserves our respect. I'll see that he gets a proper burial."

"Good. He deserves it." I knew it wasn't much, but it sure helped me feel better.

"Chris, take Shelby home. I think we're good for now." He gave me a tight squeeze before helping me stand. "Before you go... I think Ramos would like that phone number."

I pulled out my phone and turned to Ramos. "Sure... but don't kill him. I mean... I'll help with the questioning... okay?"

Ramos nodded, his eyes full of concern. "Whatever you say." He didn't want me to worry, but he was thinking that if he found Dagger, he couldn't promise me anything.

I held back a sigh before meeting his gaze, and caught how relieved he was that I was alive. It angered him that I'd come so close to death... and maybe I should stop helping Dimples for a while... or maybe forever.

Since I agreed with him, I gave him a quick nod, realizing that it sounded a lot like something Dimples would say, only in reverse.

Was my life crazy, or what?

Chris ushered me down the hall to the elevator, his arm around me, and his thoughts in turmoil. Since he knew I was probably listening, he tried not to be too upset, but what the hell?

"I know... I'm sorry."

"Shelby... sweetheart... you don't have to apologize. None of this was your fault. I'm upset, sure, but I'm glad you're okay. I may not have liked Savage, but I'll never forget what he did for you."

Chris worried that I would blame myself for his death, even though it was Keller who'd pulled the trigger.

I shook my head. "I might, only... right at the end, Savage seemed at peace that he'd done something good." I sniffed back my tears. "I'll never forget him for that."

He nodded. "I won't either. I guess your special skills come with a price. But don't forget that it goes both ways."

"In that case, I'd better look on the bright side as much as possible."

He grinned. "That's right. But if that gets hard, don't forget that you can lean on me."

My throat got tight, and I wrapped both my arms around him and held him for a long minute.

Stepping back, he took my hand. "Come on... let's go home." He planned to pamper me, hold me, feed me, and do whatever it took to help me feel better.

Not about to argue with that, I let him tug me away.

A few days later, Uncle Joey's limo pulled up in front of my house, and I hurried out. As I slid inside, Ramos made room for me between him and Uncle Joey. To my surprise, Ricky sat in the driver's seat.

"Ricky! How are you doing?"

"Well enough to drive."

Uncle Joey shook his head. "He insisted. But that's all he's doing for the day. Then he's going home to rest up, right?"

Ricky gave him a two-fingered salute. "Yes sir."

I glanced at Ramos. "So how does it feel to be a free man?"

In the days since Ramos had been charged, Dagger had disappeared. I knew Ramos probably had something to do with it, but he wasn't sharing. Since I wasn't sure I wanted to know the details, I didn't mind.

Just this morning, Chris had appealed the case to the judge and the charges had been dropped. With no witness and no other evidence to prosecute Ramos for Cal's murder, the prosecution had no case.

He grinned. "I'm glad it turned out."

"Yeah. And Uncle Joey didn't lose his fifty million to Rathmore."

"That's right, but I'm not convinced this is over."

Uncle Joey shook his head. "I'm not so sure. I think a lot more has been going on that we don't know about."

My brows rose. "What does that mean?"

Uncle Joey shrugged. "Let's just say I heard it through the grapevine that Rathmore's had a major setback."

My eyes widened. "By you?"

"No... I had nothing to do with it."

He was telling the truth, so what had happened? Was Ella involved?

He went on, not wanting to share more than that. "In the meantime, let's enjoy the fact that he's out of our lives... hopefully for good."

I let out a breath. If he was out of our lives, then this was definitely a good day. Too bad we had a graveside service to attend.

The limo pulled to the curb inside the cemetery, and the three of us got out. Walking between Ramos and Uncle Joey, we made our way to the casket that held the remains of Paxton Savage.

The graveside gathering consisted of a few friends and family members, along with the three of us, and a pastor from a local congregation giving a short eulogy. It didn't take long before the service was over, and people began to leave.

It was hard to hear some of the thoughts from his family, mostly because they were full of disappointment in the type of life he'd led. Being in and out of prison, and part of a ruthless gang, hadn't been the best life choices, so it made sense. Still, he'd made a difference in my life, and I'd never forget him for that.

I caught sight of someone who stood apart from the rest of us, and surprise washed over me. I told Uncle Joey and Ramos that I'd be right back and hurried to his side.

"Hey Elliot. I'm surprised to see you here."

He rocked back on his heels. "Not as surprised as I was to hear about Savage's death." He lowered his voice. "Did you have something to do with that?"

I took a deep breath. "I guess I did, but it's not what you think. He was actually protecting me from a really bad person. In fact, he saved my life."

His brows rose. "What? Are you serious?"

"Yup. If he hadn't been there, I'd be dead." I glanced at the casket and sighed. "So I'm really glad you didn't go through with your plans to put him in an early grave."

Stuffing his hands in his pockets, he lowered his gaze, thinking he'd been so caught up in his grief that he hadn't been thinking straight. "Me too. I guess you never know about people."

I nodded. "That's the truth."

"Well... I'm glad you're okay. I'd like to hear the story sometime." He smiled, and his brows lifted. "We could get coffee. How about Friday?"

I grinned. "Sounds good."

"Great... see you then."

I turned back toward the limo and caught up with Ramos and Uncle Joey. I tugged on Ramos's arm and smiled up at him. "Hey... I was wondering... if the weather holds, would you mind taking me on an errand?"

His lips twisted. "You mean on the bike?"

"Well... yeah. There's someone I need to see this afternoon."

He raised a brow. "I guess... as long as it's okay with the big boss."

Uncle Joey shook his head. "Oh, go on. As long as it doesn't include recently released criminals, then it's okay with me."

Seeing the irony, we all laughed.

An hour later, Ramos pulled the bike into another cemetery. This one held the remains of Kirk Wahlen. As I made my way to his grave, I found two women already there, standing beside his headstone. A red rose rested on top.

I waved and joined them. "Thanks for meeting me."

"Sure." Heather introduced me to her daughter Fern, a beautiful young woman with long dark hair and freckles across her nose.

"Hi Fern. It's nice to meet you."

"You too." She pinned me with a curious gaze, thinking that she'd never met a real live private eye before. From the story I'd told her mom, it was amazing that I'd survived the encounter with her dad's killer.

Heather motioned to the grave. "I thought I'd bring another rose after hearing that you solved the case. I'm glad to know that Kirk's killer didn't get away with it."

"Yeah... it was close, but the DNA from a hair sample and the blood on the dollar bill confirmed it was him. I'm sure he would have been convicted if we could have put him on trial."

"Well... he's dead now, right? So I guess he got what he deserved."

I couldn't argue with that. He was awful. But not all bad people were like him. I mean... Savage was bad too... but he'd saved my life, so who was I to judge?

"I visited Kirk's mom yesterday. She was grateful to know what happened. She still misses him... every day. I know you might not want to hear it... but I think she would be delighted to know that Kirk has a daughter."

I glanced at Fern. "She seems like a great person, and I'm sure she's got a lot of stories she could tell you about your dad if you want to meet her."

Heather opened her mouth to object, but Fern held up a hand. "I think that's a great idea." She turned to her mom. "You don't have to come, but I'd like to meet her." She thought it was about time her mom let go of her grudge, but if she wouldn't, she'd meet her grandmother on her own.

Heather swallowed. "Maybe you're right. You remind me so much of him right now. I think he'd be proud." She glanced my way. "Thanks Shelby... for everything."

"You're welcome."

A sense of peace came over me, along with the scent of musky vanilla. After a quick goodbye, I left them to work out the details of visiting Kirk's mom, and started back to Ramos and the bike.

The song "Kissed by a Rose" began playing in my mind, and a smile curved my lips.

"What are you smiling about?"

I grinned up at him and shrugged. "Oh... I don't know... maybe that I'm glad everything worked out."

His left brow rose. "And?"

"And what?"

He handed me my helmet, a knowing smile on his lips, thinking that wasn't being with him the best part of everything working out?

I snatched my helmet from him. "Well yeah. That... *and* the bike."

His lips twisted, but he straddled the bike and held out a hand. "Then you'd better climb on, because I'm taking you somewhere you've never been."

A thrill shot through me, and I quickly fastened my helmet. "Oh yeah? Where's that?"

"Get on, and you'll see."

With joy in my heart, and a smile on my face, I took his hand.

Thank you for reading **Grave Duty: A Shelby Nichols Adventure.** I am currently hard at work on Shelby's next adventure and promise to do my best for another thrilling ride!

If you enjoyed this book, please consider leaving a review on Amazon. It's a great way to thank an author and keep her writing! **Grave Duty** is also available on Kindle and Audible!

Want to know more about Ella St. John? Get **Angel Falls: Sand and Shadows Book 1** and find out how Ella, the nurse Shelby meets in Ghostly Serenade, ended up in Las Vegas with Aiden Creed. It is available in ebook, paperback, hardback, and audible. Don't miss this exciting adventure and the sequel, **Desert Devil: Sand and Shadows Book 2!**

Ramos has his own book! **Devil in a Black Suit** is about Ramos and his mysterious past from his point of view. It's available in paperback, ebook, and audible formats. Get your copy today!

NEWSLETTER SIGNUP For news, updates, and special offers, please sign up for my newsletter on my website: www.colleenhelme.com. To thank you for subscribing you will receive a FREE ebook.

SHELBY NICHOLS CONSULTING Don't miss Shelby's blog posts about her everyday life! Be sure to visit shelbynicholsconsulting.com.

ABOUT THE AUTHOR

USA TODAY AND WALL STREET JOURNAL
BESTSLLING AUTHOR

Colleen Helme is the author of the bestselling Shelby Nichols Adventure Series, a wildly entertaining and highly humorous series about Shelby Nichols, a woman with the ability to read minds.

She is also the author of the Sand and Shadow Series, a spin-off from the Shelby Nichols Series featuring Ella St. John, a woman with a special 'healing' touch. Between writing about these two friends, Colleen has her hands full, but is enjoying every minute of it, especially when they appear in books together.

When not writing, Colleen spends most of her time thinking about new ways to get her characters in and out of trouble. She loves to connect with readers and admits that fans of her books keep her writing.

Connect with Colleen at www.colleenhelme.com

Follow her on Social Media here:
Colleen Helme Author | Shelby Nichols Consulting | Facebook | Twitter (X)| BookBub | Amazon Author Page | You Tube | Amazon Series Page

Printed in Great Britain
by Amazon

31240090R00212